EAST OF OUTBACK

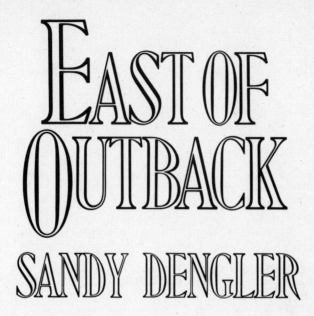

EAST OF OUTBACK

SANDY DENGLER

BETHANY HOUSE PUBLISHERS
MINNEAPOLIS, MINNESOTA 55438

Cover illustration by Dan Thornberg,
Bethany House Publishers staff artist.

Published by Bethany House Publishers
A Ministry of Bethany Fellowship, Inc.
6820 Auto Club Road, Minneapolis, Minnesota 55438

Printed in the United States of America

Library of Congress Cataloging-in-Publication Data

Dengler, Sandy.
     East of outback / Sandy Dengler.
          p.   cm. — (Australian destiny ; 4)

     I. Title.   II. Series: Dengler, Sandy. Australian destiny ; 4.
PS3554.E524E27   1990
813'.54—dc2   90–472
ISBN 1–55661–117–X   CIP

AUSTRALIAN DESTINY SERIES

SANDY DENGLER is a freelance writer whose wide range of books has a strong record in the Christian bookselling market. Twenty-six published books over the last nine years include juvenile historical novels, biographies, and adult historical romances. She has a master's degree in natural sciences and her husband is a national park ranger. They make their home in Ashford, Washington, and their family includes two grown daughters.

CONTENTS

CHAPTER ONE

LEVIATHAN PLAYING
1925

Laughing, splashing, dancing ripples of light pierced the ocean surface and splintered across the shallow world below. They burned away a bit of the blue-green and let hints of color flash here and there among the endless coral, the outcrops of dark, stolid rock, the shifting sand. Then they fell upon a gray form ranging, and the laughter ceased.

With the chill arrogance of a hunter born at the top of the food chain, the shark cruised sinuously, its seventeen feet of power undulating. Two fathoms above, the water's restless surface broke up the light, creating unusual shadows and patterns. Such patterns might confuse an untuned eye, but this one did not hunt by eye. It read its waters by taste and smell, and hearing. Not even the tiniest waterborne vibration, the faintest aquatic odor, escaped detection.

It caught a vague essence of sea turtle drifting up from near the ocean floor three fathoms below. Vibrations. There. Ahead. A sea turtle struggled in the grasp of an unfamiliar predator. The predator stood erect, vertical against the sea floor, less than a fathom tall. Its head was encased in a huge shell, its torso and appendages in soft skin. A cascade of bubbles followed two endless antennae toward the surface.

The shark circled warily. Although half the shark's size, the predator was dangerous. This very shark had once been struck on the snout by such a predator—an experience not to be repeated.

And yet, the turtle—that rich, meaty turtle. . . .

The predator's head moved inside its shell, watching the shark. A sudden burst of bubbles roared out of its appendages. Startled, the shark veered away.

It turned. Again it came arcing in. Turtle blood! The scent called; it tantalized; it commanded. Nothing else mattered now. The shark rolled onto its side, its maw wide open, and rushed past predator and prey. Its ten-score teeth sheared meat and bone. Blood! It came whipping around into another pass.

Amid a howling, vibrating cloud of bubbles the predator ascended through the crystal green. The bubbles shook the shark, confused its senses. It tilted away and swung around again. Another smaller shark approached, drawn by the blood. They spiraled upward together in a deadly helix toward predator and prey.

"Fahster, lahds!"

Colin gave up trying to roll the air hose onto its reel. He hand-over-handed it up over the side, blindly letting it fall on the deck behind him. Beside him Dizzy cranked mightily at the winch as Captain Foulard dragged in the lifeline.

A brass dome exploded out of the churning froth of the sea surface. Colin and the captain together lunged over the side, grasping. Colin gripped a random handful of the canvas diving suit and pulled. He hooked his other hand under the diver's arm and leaned back, lest the weight pull him over the side.

Dizzy grunted, the line on his winch as taut as a guitar string. With clangs and clunks, Sake the diver came up over the *Gracie's* gunwale helmet first. Colin reached for a leg, for the final tip up and over, and froze. A pink maw, followed by a white belly, broke the surface and slid by, missing Sake's diving boots by inches.

Colin stared numbly. "That thing's half the length of the boat!"

Dizzy hit the rail beside him for a fleeting glance as the shark melted into the green. Rapidly he crossed himself. He looked wide-eyed at Colin and shook his head slowly. "This place ain' no place for me, Col. Goin' home. I swear to you I'm goin' home."

"Yair." Colin couldn't always sift out Dizzy's tortured Spanish accent, but he understood that speech. He clapped his chum on the shoulder and turned to the more pressing problem at hand—Sake.

Captain Foulard and Ariel, the Koepanger cook, had propped the slight, stocky little pearl diver in a half-sitting position against the hatch cowling. They wrenched the spherical diving helmet loose and lifted it away.

For a few moments, Sake Tamemoto studied infinity with vacant eyes. His skin, normally the warm yellow ochre of the sun-tanned Japanese, had paled to dirty ashes.

"Sake!" Captain Foulard shook him. "The beast bite you?"

The man suddenly returned. His eyes changed focus from infinity to the rail before him. "No. No, he did not. The turtle, though—he bit the turtle."

"Turtle!" The captain exploded. "How many times I tell you, leave dem turtles alone! Cause nutting but trouble, like now. You cahn't be daht sick of salt pork, you gotta risk your neck for turtle!"

The crackling eyes twinkled. Sake was back again. He smiled. "Oh, yes I can." He looked at Ariel. "A cup of tea, please, to soothe the nerves. Then I go back down. Thank you."

Ariel left, shaking his head.

Colin glanced at Dizzy. "Sake, you're really going back down? When you know what's down there?"

"There are two sharks there, lad. They will tear apart the turtle. Then they will go on. Good shell remains. We must not leave this place yet." His color was starting to return; Colin watched it seep back by degrees.

"Yes, but—"

Sake raised a slim, almost feminine finger. "Captain Foulard is correct. Except for the turtle I would be in small danger. A shark comes, you release some air from the cuff of your diving suit. The bubbles repel him. Boot him on the nose if he passes by. But sharks love turtle meat even better than I. They will not so mildly go away if you have a turtle. Still, sharks are not the danger; whales are."

"Whales?" Dizzy shook his head. "Sharks, they eat people, eh? *Muy peligroso*. Whales they don' eat people, dangerous alla same." Dizzy was as small and slight as Sake, and quite a bit thinner. Yet, he could lift any weight, perform any feat of strength. Immense power. When he rested he went completely flaccid; when active, he bounded about, swift and smooth, ever moving.

If mankind could somehow harness the energy in Desiderio Romales, Colin thought, *we could get along without the sun.*

"Why are whales dangerous?" Colin settled onto the deck beside Sake. Ariel delivered the tea.

Sake sipped a few moments. "So big. Just so big. When they panic, nothing you can do. One time, a time I will not forget: we were diving off Adele Island when a pod of humpbacks came among us. Playful. They were playful. I was young then, like you, Colin. Young enough to know everything. You are how old?"

"I'll be seventeen in July." Colin felt his cheeks grow warm.

Sake nodded, sipped. "You are very strong for one who is young. I was not strong, but clever. Ah, so clever. Other divers in the area rose, went aboard to wait until the whales left. Not I. I was winning much good shell, and as you know, Dizzy, whales are harmless. I would complete my task."

The wind was picking up. Colin jammed his fingers into his brown hair and shoved it up off his face. The breeze tossed it right back again. If Mum knew how badly he needed a haircut. . . .

"A big bull came along, a humpback bigger than our boat. As he passed overhead it was like night descending, to be in his shadow. I stood in awe, my whole body arched back that I might watch the monster glide by. Those flukes! Each bigger than a dinghy."

Colin glanced at Dizzy. The little man was probably pushing thirty, yet he sat rapt as a child of six.

Sake drained his cup. "A crosscurrent caught my line just then, and drew it out wide. It hooked on the passing flukes. Instantly, the whale panicked. He shot forward. He broached. And with each great flap of his flukes I was yanked thus! And so! I was jerked from the water. I was dragged through the water."

"Your air line couldn't have stayed together with all that."

"True, Colin. Yes. One moment I can hear the *click-clack, click-clack* of the pump. Then, silence. Of great fortune, I thought to close my air valve just as the fluke caught. Air came into my suit, but air did not leave it, you see."

"Sort of like blowing up a balloon?"

"Just so! And when the line broke, I closed the other valve to keep out the water. Like a fool the whale began to run, perhaps three fathoms deep. I am dragged along behind, turning rapidly like a propeller. I managed to free my knife. I cut the lines and came up on my own air. The lugger had given chase. It rescued me, and just in time before my air was gone."

"And now you come up as soon as there're whales around."

"Too right." Sake lurched to his feet. "Too right. You will be wise to learn from your mistakes, young Colin. And much wiser if you learn without making them!"

It took Colin a while to sort the air line and reel it up properly. Then Sake's lead-weighted boots clunked their way down the outboard ladder; his great round diving helmet disappeared below the gunwale.

Dizzy manned his station. His was an exacting task, nearly as glamorous and specialized as Sake's, for Dizzy was the diver's tender, and Sake's life lay in his hands. Dizzy minded the diver's air line and kept the air pump working. Much more intricate was the task of handling the lifeline properly. If the diver traversed areas of the sea bed devoid of pearl shell, he kept his boots off the ground and let the lugger's gentle drift carry him along. Should he spot shell or cross a promising area, he would signal, and Dizzy must correctly interpret the signal. Urgent signals such as "up quickly," "shark," and "stage," in which the diver, working deep, wished to rise by stages, required that he give the diver the proper amount of slack when working, yet not so much that the line might become tangled in coral.

Amidships on the little boat, Colin returned to his own task—that of shell opener. With a flick of his knife he opened each oyster, casting the valuable shell onto a pile, groping through the slimy-soft body for the one-in-a-thousand chance of a pearl, then throwing the meat overboard. Over and over again. His fingers were stained greenish and crisscrossed with dirty, dry cracks, like weathered wood. There were worse ways to earn a quid, but Colin couldn't think of any.

Up from the galley drifted the aroma of sliced onions. Ariel was hard at work on supper. Salt pork, no doubt.

Blister. A hemispherical bump interrupted the glistening hard inner surface of this shell. Colin laid it aside and picked up the next oyster. Blister and baroque—oddly shaped mother-of-pearl—were to be kept separate.

The captain came topside presently, and stood a moment watching Colin at work. Wherever he stood, Captain Foulard towered, huge and boisterous, with warm brown skin and black, wavy hair. His polyglot French/Islander accent challenged Colin's ear almost as much as Dizzy's Spanish, Sake's Japanese inflections, and Ariel's Koepanger gibberish.

The captain smiled. "You, Colin Sloan, you not like most fellers work de pearl fishery. Different. More school, mebbe. What you think about, you sit here all dese hours doing dis?"

Colin shrugged, mildly embarrassed. "Lots of things."

"Like?"

"Like, uh, how different Broome is from Sydney, where I grew up. And how the people here are different, too. The way of life—everything. And working. I like working, doing something with my hands." He grinned and raised a hand. "Even when the work does things like this to them."

The skipper chuckled and flopped down on the deck beside the shell pile. "Live in Sydney, huh? Papa got lotsa money, hey?"

"Yeah, might say that. He's a commodities broker. He and Mum never went in much for flash—no fancy parties and touring cars and such—but they got enough money, and then some."

"And you don' like Papa's money." There was a twinkle in the captain's voice. He was teasing, but just how much?

"There's money and there's money. I 'bout starved when I first got to Broome, but I'm making enough now."

"When you come to Broome?"

"Coupla months ago. Five months now, I guess. November last year, 1924. Just as the boats were coming in for the lay-up season. I thought I missed the action, but there was plenty of work building boats, and refitting and rousting on the pier."

"Why you come up here to Broome? Why not someplace else?"

Colin had to think about that a moment. " 'Bout as far as you can get from Sydney, I guess," he chuckled.

The captain slapped Colin's shoulder. "Mebbe your Mama ain' flahsh, but she raise a good kid. Good worker. Glahd you aboard, lahd." He rose quickly and headed for the galley.

"Thank you, sir." Now what was that all about? In the month Colin had worked aboard this pearling lugger, this was the first time the captain had singled him out for conversation.

He froze. His probing fingers had felt what they always looked for. Pearl! Only twice before had he discovered the hard little knot in the slimy oyster meat. This was by far the biggest of the three. He pinched and squeezed, separating the pearl from its gooey matrix. He dropped it in his shirt pocket, cleared the shell, and tossed the meat into the water.

Ever since his arrival in Broome, Colin had been hearing whispered tales of the fortunes in undeclared pearls that changed hands in the booming, open town. Snide pearls, they were called, pearls pocketed by the shell openers and never reported to the lawful owners. It was said that thousands of pounds changed hands in the illicit snide trade.

True, Colin would earn a share of the proceeds of this vessel, come lay-up season. But it would be a small share, a minuscule share, for he was no more than a casual hand, a laborer at the very bottom of the complex pyramid of the shell fishery. This pearl, this one pearl, could keep him nicely through the four months' lay-up and beyond.

It isn't yours! his mind screamed. *It is now*, boasted his heart. *Isn't! Is! Isn't. Is!* The frenetic argument within him roared away all afternoon and into the evening. The pearl, nestled snug in his pocket, seemed to burn there. He ended up with a basher of a headache.

An hour before sundown, Sake surfaced on his own air and came aboard. Colin helped Dizzy remove the helmet and assist him out of his diving suit.

Sake's bronzed face beamed, as it so often did after a good day. "How did we do?" he asked, looking right at Colin.

"Lots of good shell won today," he replied, his conscience gouging at his aching forehead. Not only Captain Foulard would lose if he did not declare the pearl; Sake worked on shares, too.

"See more sharks?" Dizzy hung the limp suit to dry.

"One. But, I do not think it was the same that stopped by earlier. It sniffed about and went away."

Colin shuddered. He spent the few minutes left before dinner opening the last of the shell Sake had won. Won at what price? The little diver could be dead or mutilated by now. It happened, and not infrequently. And what price the pearl?

He bagged the new shell. With part of it he topped off the three-hundred-pound hessian sack they had commenced filling two days ago. He sewed it shut with huge clumsy stitches. Monk's cloth, sackcloth, burlap, hessian—whatever you called it, the stuff was scratchy and hard. He could imagine a penitent wearing it as punishment.

Punishment.

With the small amount of shell still left he started another sack.

Captain Foulard cried out. From the galley, from below, everyone ran to join him on the stern. A thick, black cloudbank squatted against the flat line of the sea to the northwest.

Dizzy crossed himself. "We far 'nuff from shore we gunner ride it out, you think?"

"Gunner hafter be. You and Ariel strip dis boom, get de spare out. We build a sea anchor, slow us down mebbe."

The two seemed to require no further orders. They hurried off.

Colin could not take his eyes off the burgeoning, black storm cloud. "Last month, sir, when that cyclone ripped up Port Hedland, they were saying then it was the last storm of the season. That's why all the luggers lay up over summer, isn't it? To avoid the storms?"

"*Mais oui*. But who gunner tell daht willy-willy it's a month late? Dis is why no insurance house touch de luggers. Storms don't know how to read cahlendars. You go below now, make sure nutting gunner move around down dere. Don' want no cargo shifting."

"Yes, sir." And he hurried below, thankful for something to do.

Colin started sweating instantly in the hot, dank, stinking hold as he dragged sacks of shell about, laying them down flat. He thought about the monument he'd seen in Broome's cemetery, erected by Japanese mourners to commemorate their brethren lost in the cyclone of 1908—just three months before Colin was born. Seventeen years ago this very month. A chill ran down his spine despite the heat.

Sake appeared in the gloom beside him. He stuffed his diving gear and helmet into a little locker in the stern. "I give you help with these things." His smooth, slim hands, as strong as any other man's, gripped a filled sack and dragged it down among the others.

"Sake, were you out during that storm in aught eight?"

The Japanese diver paused, studying infinity again. "Three schooners lost. Three other ships. Thirty-nine luggers. Over a hundred men, forty of them Japanese."

"So you *were* there."

"No. I was but a lad, working in the sorting sheds. My father, though—he was one of the forty."

"I'm sorry."

"It is the price paid for shell. For beauty." The bronzed man straightened and smiled suddenly, his teeth bright in the darkness. "Diamonds, sapphires—so cold, lad. Brittle. But a pearl is living, soft, like a woman. Diamonds are stones, flashing like a wanton woman. But the pearl, it glows gently, like a woman of virtue. Men lose their lives every day, some way or other. Serving pearls—like virtue—is good a way as any, right?"

"Yes, sir." Colin hesitated. "You think we'll die tonight?" He was surprised at his own casualness at discussing the subject.

"Perhaps," he sighed. "Perhaps."

CHAPTER TWO

PEARL OF GREAT PRICE

There is one thing worse than impending doom—a feeling of utter helplessness to prevent it.

Inexorably the storm bore down upon them. Its squall line hit *Gracie* two hours past sunset.

The little lugger lurched. She heaved. Caught in the screaming wind she lunged forward, breasting unimaginable waves. They battened down as best they could. They threw out their jury sea anchor, a huge canvas cup kept in shape by spars. They cast all her anchors with as much chain and hawse as she had aboard. The anchors and her dragging sea anchor kept her tail to the wind. But for the lightning that occasionally ripped between heaven and hell, all was blackness.

"To the pumps, lahds!"

Colin groped his way through the darkness, hands on the cabin, hands on the lifeline stretched amidship. He and Dizzy took one side of the bilge pump bar, Sake and Ariel the other. In total darkness, in wind that could push a man over, in slinging, drenching rain Colin worked the bilge pump, up and down and up and down.

The little boat jerked, a motion somehow apart from her pounding leaps. Colin barely heard a *pung*.

"What's that?" he gasped, choking a scream.

"One of the anchors snagged. The chain's parted!" Sake yelled.

The chain's parted? Colin thought. *Welded links over an inch long parted, and the storm is just beginning!*

Despite the backs of four strong men, the pump worked heavily, sluggishly. A massive presence stepped into the blackness beside Colin. Captain Foulard put a hand to the pump. "Hull must've sprung; we're pumping green water!"

Green water? Colin could see nothing, not even Dizzy working hard beside him. No doubt *green* referred to more than color, something ominous.

Under normal circumstances on the flat sapphire ocean, the captain's voice rang loud enough to call in distant buoys. In this storm his voice carried three feet at most. "You lahds know what to do if she breaks up. Grahb yourselves anything daht floats, aye?"

Colin's arms were ready to fall off, but not in a million years would he dream of letting up! Somewhere above him a loud *crack* snapped above the howling.

"Down, lahds! De mahst!"

The boat shuddered, throwing Colin to his knees. Behind them a horrendous crash hit the deck and cabin. He heard the port gunwale give way with a crushing sound. Suddenly *Gracie* lurched alist to port, her deck so steep Colin slid into the bilge pump.

The boat lurched again. Scraping, thudding—the ragged mast end whipped close past Colin, tearing his sleeve. In the darkness Dizzy screamed.

"We're broaching! Every mahn for himself!"

The lugger had cast herself broadside against the sweeping wind and waves. She rolled. Colin felt himself lifting off the deck.

The captain's long arm wrapped around his waist. Desperately Colin clung to that arm. They flew through the searing, rain-thick air together.

Colin choked. He gagged. He was bobbing in the wild water and that robust arm still held him.

"Grahb on here, lahd! Y're not done yet."

He grasped at nothing, at a straw. His arms hit a spar and he latched on to it. His nose and lungs burned with salt water.

The captain's arm disappeared. "I'm gunner cut the cahnvas free; hang on!"

Colin hung on. His arms, already weakened by that stint at the bilge pump, threatened every second to let go. He wrapped around the spar, crossed his wrists and gripped his forearms. It gave his arms a rest, but the bounding waves kept smashing his face against the boom.

A voice called out in the blackness, but Colin could not identify it. He heard rushing and gurgling. Something struck his spar heavily and nearly shook him loose from it. The very waters sucked him under, spar and all. He swirled in the black ocean, clinging. He was on the surface again, his ears so full of water that even the shrieking wind sounded distant.

How did he manage to stay afloat? He had no idea. How many hours passed? He had no idea. What had become of the others? He had no idea, not even of Captain Foulard's fate.

The storm lightened. Although the rain beat harder, the wind seemed to relax a bit. And the sky grew lighter.

———————

Just past dawn, Colin saw a man in a snappy little sulky driving across the waves. His pony's white mane billowed. "Come, lad," he called. "Get in with me and I'll take you ashore."

"I must bring my spar. Do you think it'll fit?"

"No, lad, you must leave that."

"No. I think not. G'day."

The cart whipped silently away over the leaping water.

Captain Foulard's voice behind him called, "Here, lahd! Leave daht boom and take an end of my gahff here. 'Tis easier to hold on to."

"No. I think not. G'day."

Time passed unmeasured. Rain. Torrents of rain. Wind. Heaving, cresting, pitching seas. The sky grew dark. Colin bobbed again in a black and formless world.

"Listen, lahd! Breakers! Y' hear 'em?"

He could hear something in the distance, though his sodden ears refused to tell him what.

"Let loose, lahd! We can swim for it; I'll help."

"No. I think not. G'day."

Bobbing. Blackness. Timelessness.

Something brushed his foot. Colin groped with a toe. Sand! A wave lifted him high, crashing him down—onto sand! Struggling, kicking, he got his feet under him and pulled at his spar, dragged it forward. He must not let loose this boom. Surging surf yanked him about and tossed him up and down, but he would not let go of the float.

He stumbled, flailing his free arm, and then was upright. He might be on land, wonderful land, or he might be out on a spit at low tide, to be washed away when the tide returned. He must not forsake the spar. He dragged it as far up the sand as he could and collapsed across it.

The world seemed to laugh at him. A sea gull was surely laughing. The distant surf was spewing and spitting its mockery. And Captain Foulard was laughing.

Colin took a deep breath and coughed viciously. But no matter how hard he coughed, his chest rattled and wheezed, waterlogged. A huge hand pounded his back.

At last Colin opened his eyes. A pink crack at the base of the leaden sky told him dawn had come, and between Colin and that pink crack stretched a continent of solid land.

He wrenched himself to a sitting position. Wet sand stuck to his face, his hands, his clothes. Rain drummed all around him, quiet and steady.

Captain Foulard plopped to the sand beside him, still laughing. "Y're a tiger, lahd. Couldn't convince y' to let go daht boom for nutting. Hahf 'spect you to drahg it clear bahk to Broome."

"Wha—What about the others? Surely we're not the only ones. . . . " Colin couldn't get his chest and throat to clear, and he still coughed violently.

The captain sobered. "Cahn't say, lahd. When you feel more like it, we'll start de long walk home. No doubt we'll pick up a clue here and dere 'long de way."

"I'm up to it now," Colin lied. He managed to gain his feet on the second try. He felt a deep urge to take the boom along. "This is part of your sea anchor, isn't it?"

"Aye, lahd. She tore loose ahnd we broached." The captain led the way, the distant ocean on their left, the endless beach before and behind them.

A dark spot on the horizon became a beached boat as they approached. *Hardin Belle* could be distinguished on her trailboards. Colin didn't recognize that one.

He turned to gaze out over the water, and stopped suddenly. "Captain Foulard! Look out there—on the surf."

"Aye, lahd. Let's take a look."

They left the high water line and walked through spongy sand to the sloshing surf. The limp form of a man's body washed in and out, in and out, face down. The two reverently dragged it above the high tide line and left it, neither having the strength to bury it. It was unmistakenly the body of Sake Tamemoto.

As the sun rose higher, the rain ended, and the leaden overcast began to break up. "Rest," said the captain, and with that Colin flopped prostrate, gratefully, on the sand.

"Captain?" he mused, "Where you from?"

"Lotsa places. Born in Hawaii, raised in Tahiti."

"Kanaka?" He was almost incredulous.

"Aye. Now, why you giggling?"

Colin watched the clearing sky overhead as it changed from gray to patchy blue. "My father and grandfather both came to a lot of grief for using Kanakas in the sugar cane fields at the beginning of the century. Labor troubles."

"Slavers."

"So they say, but my father wasn't. If you met him you'd know. He's so—so pious. Righteous. He hired many, not just Kanakas. In fact, he hired Mum out of Ireland."

"And mahrried her. A romahntic tale."

"Yair, guess so. Mum says 'twas a handsome planta- tion. Sugarlea."

"Ahnd daht's why you were giggling?"

"No. Just thinking. My father had all that trouble about Kanakas, and didn't like them a bit, and now here's one who saved his son's life. There's a twist, you see?"

"You saved y'r own life, lahd. Nivver seen a mahn cling to nutting like you clung to daht boom."

"But you attached me to it." Colin sat up, cupping his ear. "Listen! Is that a motor car?"

"Or a truck. 'Twill be ahead of us, coming south from Broome. Rescuers come to clean up de beach, I vow."

"Captain? You think maybe the *Gracie* made it?"

"I know she didn't." Deep, deep sorrow rumbled in his muted voice. "Heard her go down in de dark, gurgling. Al- most sucked us under with her as she went."

Colin watched the cloud of sand and dirt the vehicle kicked up, and then the truck came into full view.

As the open, stake-sided truck came rumbling down the beach, a familiar voice called to them from the truck bed. Colin scrambled to his feet, and it ground to a trium- phant halt beside them.

"Is you! Hey, is you!" Dizzy came leaping joyfully over the side. He hugged Colin. He shook the captain's massive paw. He bubbled over between his Spanish and fractured English.

Colin grabbed both his arms and shook him. "Sake's drowned. What about Ariel?"

"Sake?" Dizzy's face melted instantly from joy to sad- ness. "Don' know 'bout Ariel. That mast, Col, it wipe me right off the boat. I thought I was gone, but that mast, Col,

it saved me. I tied myself onto it and it saved me. Don'
know 'bout Ariel." He shook his head. "Sake!"

The truck driver and his two companions were urging
Colin into the back of the truck. He clambered up into the
bed and leaned against the stakeside; the captain followed
and sat beside him. They lurched on down the beach, as
fast as could be managed on the wet sand.

"Captain Foulard," Colin asked after he'd collected his
thoughts, "what're you going to do now?"

"Sign on with some other lugger, and start saving up."

"You really don't have any insurance?"

"Naw! De insurance men, dey never risk deir money on
no lugger. She sail good for twenny years, den some cock-
eye bob come 'long like dis one, she go down. You lose her,
you lose her. Got nutting now, same ahs when I was born."

Colin felt his breast pocket. *Could it be there yet?* Yes!
It had not been lost in all that wild, terrible storm.

"That's not exactly true, sir." His fingers groped in the
sandy, wet pocket, still sticky from the oyster flesh. He
fished out the pearl and laid it in the captain's hand, and
in the same instant an immense weight lifted from his
heart and soul. Who would guess a pearl could weigh so
heavily? "This should make a down payment on a new lugger, don't you think? It was won from that last day's shell."

Everyone in the back of the truck—the two strangers
with shovels, the captain, and Dizzy—froze, arrested by
the cleanest and loveliest of all gems. They crowded
around, slamming into each other as the truck lurched
forward.

The captain studied Colin with a gaze of unmistakable
awe. "Y're a dinkum lahd, a thousand times over! Ahbso-
bloody-lutely!" He turned it around and around in the
palm of his hand. "Looka daht! Best pearl come outta
Broome in years. Seventy, seventy-five grains, aht least."

The sun emerged full strength and set the pearl to
glowing.

"Down payment? The whole lugger, lahd, and den some. But money be de least of it. Ah, lahd, think of the price paid for dis pearl. Think of de price."

CHAPTER THREE

MADMAN'S TRACK

Amid salmon-pink sand dunes and endless flats, just north of the dense, green mangrove thickets of Dampier Creek, Broome marched to her own secret drummer. Mostly her ear bent to the endless tides, quite deep on this northwestern Australian coast. At high tide large ships tied up at the long white jetty. Come low tide, they lay atilt like stranded whales, a quarter of a mile from water.

She listened, too, to the seasons of storms, the gentle sun of winter and the raging destruction of the occasional willy-willy come down off the Timor Sea. Sydney throbbed to its own bustling beat; Broome adopted the gentle pulse of the world God made.

Colin Sloan stood at the crest of a pink dune on Broome's foreshore, contemplating lines. The ragged green line to the south marked the mangroves of Dampier Creek. The fluffy green line behind him marked the trees shading Broome's streets and bungalows. The hazy ruler-level line before him divided emerald sea from azure sky.

Quiet sea. Serene sea. Cloudless blue heavens. Why could Colin not feel any of this peace?

He turned, in no particular hurry, and skidded down the dune. Near the tin sorting shed where the street ended above the sloping beach, he sat down to empty the sand from his shoes. From within the shed came the gentle clack of shell on shell. Colin wandered over and looked inside.

In the gloom lay mounds of shell, mountains of shell. So this was where all the three-hundred-pound sacks of the stuff ended up. In the midst of the mountains came that clacking. Colin waited until his eyes adjusted, then went exploring.

An Aboriginal half-caste sat on a stool tossing shell. Nearly as broad as he was tall, he filled the little stool and then some. He glanced at Colin and grinned, his huge teeth as bright as any pearl.

He flicked two small, thin shells into a bin reserved for the smaller variety. "I know him. Him be Sloan feller survive *Gracie*."

Colin felt his cheeks warming. "I'm that famous?"

"Pearl you save, famous. Gus feller, already get bid—new boat."

"That was just this morning. You must hear all the news. Do you know if they found the Koepanger yet? The one called Ariel?"

"Him bad gone, no find. Shark maybe."

What price, pearls. Colin thought, but he didn't speak it out.

A small brown shadow, a merest motion, caught the corner of Colin's eye. "You have rats in here. I just saw one."

"Too right. Rat heaven; him lotsa place hide, lotsa dry bits oyster him eat."

Clyde Armbruster used to tell Colin that if you see a rat out in broad daylight, you can count on a hundred lurking undetected. In fact, just after the great war Clyde bought two big tomcats for the stables, simply because he saw one rat at noon. Were there hundreds right here in the shed? Colin shuddered at the thought.

"I never knew what happened to the shell after you unload it at the jetty. You sort it out by size?"

"Too right. Here. Him grade Extra Heavy, see?" The man held up a thick shell, seven inches across at least. He threw it over into a bin of similarly sized shells. "Big shell, little shell, no worries. Easy sort. Middle shell—no big, no small—him make puzzle; need good eye."

Colin spent another twenty minutes with the lively man, trying to tune his ear to this Aboriginal brand of semi-English, talking about shells, and learning more than he really wanted to know about boats lost in past storms. Finally, he took an opportunity to leave, and walked out into the dusty street.

Not much sign of the killer willy-willy remained here in town. *I wonder what it looks like down in Port Hedland?* News reports claimed a killer storm a month ago had wrecked that port. No serious wreckage marred the tranquility here on the rim of nowhere. The solid wooden storm shutters on the white bungalows, lowered during high wind to protect windows, were all raised again. A few trees were down, a lot of branches and fronds, a couple of fences. That was all. Colin had noticed earlier that some buildings were literally tied to the ground with cables and guy lines. Now he understood why.

Captain Auguste Foulard stood under a tree near Sheba Lane, in a cluster of half a dozen men. Out of sheer curiosity, Colin crossed the wide street and joined them.

They were gathered around a rickety little table under a poinciana tree, and at the table sat a wizened fellow of undecipherable ancestry, probably Malay or similar descent. He had planted both elbows on the table, and with a three-corner needle file he was working away at a pearl, inches from his face.

A powerful hand slapped Colin's back. "Here's de lahd!"

Colin smiled and caught his breath. Quickly regaining his composure, he asked, "Is this your pearl he's working on, sir?"

"Aye, lahd."

"Thought you were going to sell it."

"Feel risky today." The captain smiled. "You see, lahd, a pearl must be cleaned, like dis mahn is doing. Remove one skin or more until all de blemishes be taken away. Wit every skin, another grain is gone. De pearl trader, he pay me good money for de pearl, den he take a risk, see how small de pearl become. But mebbe I cahn get better money—if I clean it first ahnd it stays big, I win. If it grows small, I lose."

"I see. And you think it's worth the risk."

"Too much hahppen to daht pearl, lahd. Charmed, daht pearl. I'll win."

Colin dropped to a squat, bringing his eyes closer to the level of the pearl. Rapt, he watched the skill and precision of this nameless pearl cleaner. For a long time the fellow worked, and no one moved. There was nothing hurried about the beat of Broome's drummer. The man dipped the pearl in a little dish of powder, rubbed it, swished it in a cup of scummy water, then laid the pearl on the pan of a tiny scale.

The onlookers craned their necks to get a reading. Those who could see nodded knowingly and smiled.

The captain beamed. "Knew I'd win! Less'n three grains lost in the cleaning! And is perfect!" His voice dropped. "Perfect."

For the first time the pearl cleaner raised his head. His eyes glowed with pride and triumph. He dropped the pearl into Auguste Foulard's waiting palm. The captain held it out on display.

Colin caught his breath. A murmur of approval and awe rose from the onlookers. Even before cleaning, this pearl delighted the eye. Now, with its soft rose glow, it absolutely dazzled the mind and heart. *Like a virtuous woman.*

Colin could not refrain from asking the question everyone else either knew already or wanted to ask: "What is it worth, Captain? Do you know?"

"My new lugger ahnd den some, lahd. Ahnd den some! Now I go to de buyer. Dis is so perfect, it likely bring seven thousand aht least."

The show over, most of the group dispersed. Colin followed Captain Foulard out into the street.

The captain was nodding, with a spring to his step Colin had not noticed before. "Five hundred pounds to Sake's widow and his kids. Commission to Ben dere, de cleaner. Couple hunnert pounds to you, lahd, for saving it, and I still got my next lugger!"

A couple hundred pounds! That was certainly more than Colin had expected to have in his pocket. When your boat goes down you use up all your luck surviving. There's nothing left, including your job. All the luggers out working were fully manned, and there was scant employment ashore here until next lay-up.

Colin saw a familiar face across the street. "Excuse me, please, sir. G'day."

"G'day, lahd!" The captain whanged him another clap on the back. Captain Foulard went his way toward the pearl buyers, and Colin crossed the street to Dizzy.

The little man sat dejected on the bench in front of the post office, staring at the pink dust.

Colin flopped down beside him. "G'day, mate."

"*Buenos días.*" No smile. Not an acknowledging nod. Abject gloom.

"Let me guess. You didn't get that job you wanted out at the livery stable."

"Good bet. You win." Dizzy lurched suddenly, rearranging his wiry body. "He said he don' need more ringers, he need less horses. Ain' nobody use horses no more; he got too many, no work. Gonna slaughter a couple if he don' sell 'em."

"Mmm." Colin sprawled on his spine awhile, in no hurry to either move or think. The ubiquitous flies buzzed all about, pesky armies of them. "So whatya gunner do, mate?"

Dizzy jerked his shoulders, a spastic excuse for a shrug. "Dunno. Wisht I could go home, eh?"

"Maybe you could get a job when Captain Foulard starts building his new boat. Shouldn't take too much money to get to the Philippines."

"Philippines? Ain' going to no Philippines. Tha's the wrong d'rection, Col."

"Everybody in Australia who speaks Spanish comes from the Philippines, I thought."

"Sí, only I didn'. Guess I'm the only Tejano in Australia, eh?"

"What's a Tay-hahno?"

"Texas. 'Murrica. Gonzales, Texas, is where I'm from."

Colin gaped. "You mean like cowboys and that?"

"You bet!" And for the first time in weeks, Dizzy's face lit up a little. "Ain' nobody better with a herd or a gun. Tejanos—we're the best shooters, best riders, fastest, smartest cattle drovers in the world. Hafta be. We got the fastest, smartest cattle in the world. Half-devil, them Texas range cattle."

"So why are you over here?"

And the light faded. "Ain' the same no more, Col. Lotsa Anglos coming in, messing up the place and claim they're civilizing it. Hardly no longhorns left—just them whiteface cows. Stupid beasts, comparing 'em to longhorns. Lotsa rules and laws, didn' use to be. So I come over here, to get rich punching cattle, or maybe mining."

"Punching cattle?"

"Sí. Cowpuncher. Cowhand. Never knew you people don' even talk English. Ringer. Drover. Tailer, if it's horses."

"And you ended up tending divers."

"Big money, they said. *Mucho dinero.* Said I got a gift for it. Did pretty good, too, first coupla years. Miss the horses, though, Col, and the cattle. Tejano, y'know? Ain' no sailor."

"Me either."

"Ride much?"

"Used to when I was growing up. My father owns some racehorses. He got started in it with an old trainer named Clyde Armbruster, 'bout the time he and Mum married, and they got lucky. I used to pony racehorses at the track for Clyde. Great fun for a lad growing up."

"Come along a minute, eh?" Dizzy lurched to his feet.

Colin followed, with nothing else pressing to occupy his time. Dizzy led the way down through the broad avenues to the north end. They were nearly there before Colin realized they were headed for the stable.

Did he think the flies were thick downtown? Colin thought that if this livery were somehow put on a huge balance and weighed, the flies would weigh more than the horses.

Besides the flies, horses, and Dizzy, Colin saw only one other living thing in the place, and he took an instant dislike for it. A blue-gray brindled dog lay beneath the paddock rails. Here was perhaps the ugliest old dog Colin had ever seen—scrawny, ragged, with a salt-and-pepper muzzle. It bared its teeth and growled.

Dizzy wagged his head. "Owner here calls him Max."

"Doesn't seem very friendly."

"He jumped me once, the last time I came. I ask the owner why he keep a vicious dog around, eh? He says Max ain' his. It jus' hangs around here."

"Can't be doing much to improve business."

"Tha's what I told him, after I didn' get the job." Dizzy crossed briskly to the paddock, the corner farthest from the surly dog. In one smooth, flowing motion he hopped onto the top rail and hooked a leg over.

Max lurched to his feet and stepped out into the sun, his back bristling. He must have decided the effort was too great in this heat. He flopped down in the shade again, regarding the two with suspicious, steely eyes.

Colin climbed up beside Dizzy. The paddock held perhaps a score of horses. None looked fit to butcher, let alone ride. Their spines, ribs, and hipbones protruded, covered with dull and ragged hides. "Hatracks, Diz, the whole lot of them."

Dizzy pointed. "Tha' 'un there, see 'm? Tha's one nice horse; put a little meat on him, y'know? Probably knock him down to two pounds, eh? Maybe one-ten."

"What? Buy him? Then what?"

"Get 'im out onna track, take it easy; let the horse fatten up. Ride down maybe to Kalgoorlie, maybe stop in between, find a job. Ain' no good work here, and I ain' sailing the sea no more, y'know? Done with that, Col. Rather die inna desert than drown inna ocean."

"And you will, too. Know what they call the track between here and Kalgoorlie? Madman's Track. Guess why."

Dizzy twisted a bit to face him squarely. "You gotta remember where you are, Col. You in with seafaring people, and they the ones named that road. They think anybody who don' sail in boats is crazy. Me, I think anybody's crazy who *does*. Now who's the madman, eh?"

Colin laughed. "What're you gunner buy it with?"

"Tha's a problem. Thought maybe a loan, y'know?"

"Mmm. I'll think about it. If I get a couple quid I'll think about it."

"Me, too. Maybe I get lucky, earn enough to buy a horse and do some real traveling, eh? Been too long floating on that miser'ble ocean."

Colin couldn't have said it better himself.

They wandered back into town, and long before they reached Sheba Lane and parted, Colin knew what he would do. Should Captain Foulard come through with his promised gift, Colin would buy two or three horses and join Dizzy on an odyssey to adventure.

Curious, that Dizzy should mention Kalgoorlie. True, it was an important gold mining area, and thus a good place to seek work. What Dizzy did not know was that Colin's two uncles owned a mine there. Surely his father's brothers would hire on a couple of swagmen, especially if one of those swagmen were a nephew.

The news swept through the town end to end—instantly—Captain Foulard had his seven thousand pounds, the price of the finest pearl to come out of Broome in years. That night at his favorite pub in the Port Cuvier Hotel, the captain laid a twenty-pound note on the bar and instructed his chums to drink it up. Colin watched the festivities from afar, from the rail of the veranda on his little room across the street, afraid to become a part of that happy mob, but wishing desperately that he were.

The next afternoon when he woke up, the captain made good on his promise, both to Colin and to Sake's widow. Colin didn't tell Dizzy how much the captain gave him. He simply said he had enough now to buy a couple of horses, if the price was right. He let Dizzy, the Tejano with the penchant for horses, choose their two mounts. Max the mangy dog threatened mayhem, but the owner drove him off with a pitchfork.

Just one week after the petulant sea decided not to kill him after all, deigning instead to toss him onto Eighty Mile Beach, Colin Sloan loaded everything he owned on a horse worth less than his boots and rode off seeking adventure down the Madman's Track.

CHAPTER FOUR

THE MOUTHS OF BABES

Through the darkness of the manse shed crept a small form. Above that form loomed black iron and the smell of oil. Tiny hands threw an end of clothesline rope over a back axle and swiftly, deftly, knotted it. The silent form withdrew.

With a heady thrill of anticipation the bishop threw open the shed doors. White light burst into the dank darkness. For a moment he mentally reviewed the steps; magneto, choke, throttle, crank. He arranged the controls. He inserted the crank, gripping it with his thumb behind the bar lest it kick back and break his arm. The automobile dealer had warned about that.

Kishugga. Kishuhuhuhgga. Kishugugugugga. Kuhchuchuchuchu. . . .

Ebullient, the gentle man leaped into the leather-upholstered driver's seat as rapidly as his cassock would allow. He adjusted things until the marvelous internal combustion engine dropped from a ringing, howling thunder to a more stately, pulsing roar. He pressed the appropriate foot pedals, and the bishop's magnificent new Ford touring car, the finest the world had to offer, lurched forward and out into the brick street.

He drove into Bathurst Street first, careful to maintain the appropriate demeanor, avoiding any suggestion that he had slipped into the sin of pride. He was God's servant driving one of God's tools. That was all.

People smiled and waved. They laughed. A few of the less well-bred pointed in an unmannerly fashion. The bishop turned into busy George Street.

Automobiles were becoming plentiful in 1925. Ten years ago the bishop would have expected a lot of attention. Today he fully anticipated being noticed, of course, for he had once preached against the horseless carriage as being a vehicle of vanity and folly. However, it puzzled him somewhat that he was garnering *so much* attention. Ah, well, it's not every day you see a prelate rolling about in such high fashion.

He had no business to attend today, so he made no stops. He simply wanted to ascertain, before the church made the final payment, that the vehicle performed as promised. He tested the motor car out on Market Street and Elizabeth Street. Then he drove through Hyde Park simply to enjoy the shade of the huge arching gum trees. The noise was a bother—that constant chug-chug-chug drowned out everything else. But that was a small price to pay for its obvious convenience and maneuverability. Yes, this touring car was certainly far superior to the horse-drawn carriage. Just look at the stares of all these happy people! He was certainly making an impression.

As he turned eventually into Bathurst Street and home, the two youngest Sloan children waved at him from the corner. What a cherub that little Hannah was! Her dark, glossy hair cascaded in ringlets down her shoulders. No doubt she'd start wearing it up soon; if she had not yet entered her teens, she would shortly. She looked so sweet and innocent, it seemed a shame she had to grow up, particularly in this vile and evil age. She giggled, bright-eyed, as he passed.

Her brother (was Edan his name? The bishop could not quite remember) stood beside her, gaping in what looked like disbelief. Strange lad, that. Like the girl, he had his father's looks, but he was quiet, even ordinary. He was either a deep thinker or a bit dull. He certainly lacked his sister's sparkle.

Backing up was going to be tricky. Fortunately, the bishop didn't have to. He would simply park here beside the shed and have a few of the vicars push the vehicle inside by hand. He began turning things off. Sudden silence thrummed in his ears. Cautiously he climbed down out of the seat. A satisfactory jaunt, completely satisfactory. He was smiling broadly.

Then the smile evaporated as quickly as it came.

Realization splashed chilling shame upon the hot fires of the bishop's pride. He knew now why so many people smiled and pointed as he passed. Someone had wired together a very old, very dead sheep skeleton. Those bones had rattled along, six feet behind the touring car, the whole length and breadth of Sydney. Without the bishop's knowledge, someone had attached them by a length of clothesline rope to the car's back axle.

———

Hannah Sloan shooed a fly away from her face as she perched on the front stoop waiting. He'd be home any time now, unless he had some sort of business meeting downtown. She sat up straighter, listening. Here came the Austin! She could pick its motor sounds out from all the other sounds of the busy street.

Papa pulled the black Austin deftly to the curb. The motor died with a choke, and he came bouncing out of the car with a lad's vigor, his newspaper tucked under his arm. His dark, dark hair, his slim waist and broad shoulders spoke well of his youthful appearance. Only the gray at his temples protested, *Well, maybe not so young as once.* Colin shared his father's good looks, though his complexion was not so dark. Where was Hannah's big brother now?

She hopped to her feet. "Hello, Papa!"

A grin broke across his face, and he wrapped her up into a smothering hug without dislodging his paper. "How's the Hannah lass today?"

"Extra fine, Papa. We had half holiday from school; the plumbing went crook and flooded the halls, so we all came home." She followed him through the doorway.

"When I was your age, I would have given anything for a holiday like that. Now that I know better, I say 'too bad!' School is important."

"So the headmaster says, Papa. That is because you and the headmaster need not learn sewing. You cannot imagine how tedious is sewing!"

"Something a girl has to know, though." He hung his hat on the hall tree. Usually he tossed his paper onto his overstuffed chair before heading for the kitchen. Tonight he kept it tucked under his arm.

Did the paper say anything about the bishop's drive this morning? A twinge of worry darkened Hannah's immediate future.

She followed. "When I sew I'll have a sewing machine, like Mum. I won't ever put in a seam by hand. Old Miss Broaditch teaches us hand sewing. Medieval sewing, Papa!"

He stopped suddenly and turned. He was grinning impishly. "Go ahead. Say it."

She grinned, too. "Because Miss Broaditch is left over from medieval days."

"What?!" Mum—tall, slim, beautiful Mum—stood in the kitchen doorway staring. The sunshine from the kitchen windows made a sort of halo behind her soft auburn hair. She wore her hair in a short bob like most other women did, but it didn't lie quite flat. "I didn't hear that, did I?"

"Of course not." Papa gave her a hug and a surreptitious pat on the backside. Mum's cheeks flushed a bit. She glanced at Hannah, who pretended, as always, that she hadn't noticed. He sniffed. "What's for dinner, Sam?"

"Lamb left over from the dark ages and potatoes from a peck Chaucer dug at Canterbury. The child is supposed to be learning respect, and you're abetting insolence."

"Chaucer didn't have potatoes; they're New World, and she's growing up just fine." Papa opened the oven door slightly, the better to appreciate the aroma of the succulent lamb.

Mum shook her head in dismay. "Hannah, call Edan and Mary Aileen to the table. Dinner's ready."

"Yes'm." Hannah hurried out the door, just as Edan came down the hall. "Edan, go tell Mary Aileen to come to the table, Mum says."

He turned and headed back the other way.

No longer having anything to do, Hannah stood outside the door to listen, just in case the bishop's name came up.

Papa's voice dropped from lilting to sober. "Your eldest son made the paper. National news."

Hannah heard the newspaper rattle, being opened and folded. *Colin? Was Colin in the newspaper?*

She heard Mum gasp and could not resist peeking. Mum stood by the stove, reading where Papa indicated, her hand pressed to her mouth. "Cole! By all rights he could be at the bottom of the sea now, and we'd never know where—or how—" She shuddered.

Curiosity got the best of Hannah. She arranged her face and came bouncing into the kitchen. "I called them." She stopped. "What's wrong?" She hurried over to Mum. "May I see? Please?"

"Go sit down. Grace, you may serve now." Mum handed the paper back to Papa and left the room.

Papa tossed the paper carelessly onto the kitchen table. Hannah followed him out to the dining room and took her place. Edan flopped into his seat and Mary Aileen perched in hers. When Mum entered the room her eyes were a bit wet. Papa held her chair for her.

Grace came in carrying the leg of lamb, surrounded by red-skinned potatoes cooked to tasty perfection. Grace made breakfast and lunch and cleaned up in the kitchen, but Papa liked Mum to cook dinner. "Her cooking is what I hired her for," he would tease, "and why I married her."

Hannah looked at her hands. "I'm sorry. I forgot to wash up. 'Scuse me, please." She hopped up and hurried out to the kitchen. She grabbed the newspaper and read quickly where Mum had been looking. Cyclone . . . shipwreck . . . a pearl worth thousands . . . and they even spelled his name correctly. She ran back to the dining room and took her seat, "drying" her hands on her skirts.

How absolutely dreadful! How wonderfully romantic! How exotic! Exciting! She thought about Colin's amazing adventure, and then she thought about Miss Broaditch's pre-Renaissance sewing class. The brilliance of his life made her bleak existence look all the bleaker. Her plate was set before her—the lamb, the sliced potatoes, and a mass of dark green chard all prettily arranged. Bleak, yes, but there were a few bright spots. Like dinner. Minuscule bright spots in a sea of humdrum. Sea. Shipwreck. Her heart fluttered with horror and elation.

"Someone pulled a bonzer prank on the bishop today," announced Papa out of the clear blue; Edan choked, spraying partly-chewed potato all over his plate. The boof-head would spoil it yet.

"You mean that sheep skeleton?" Hannah asked.

Papa stared at her. "What do you know about a sheep skeleton?"

"We were on the corner when he drove by, and that thing rattling along behind. Papa, it was *so* comical. You ought to have seen it."

"Skeleton?" Mum's fork paused halfway to her mouth.

Papa smiled. "Tied to the back of the bishop's new car as he drove all over Sydney. Remember how he got on so in the pulpit about the evil of autos? There's a certain delicious poetry there. An irony."

Mum looked at Hannah, at Edan, then Hannah again. "If it was so comical, I'm surprised neither of you mentioned it before now."

Edan's eyes and nose were running. He coughed mightily and croaked, " 'Scuse, please." He left, and just as well; he was no good at keeping secrets, at maintaining an aura of innocence.

Hannah shrugged. "It was disrespectful, was it not? I mean, the bishop being the goat; you know? And you tell us, 'Be respectful.' I didn't know whether it ought to be mentioned atall."

Papa nodded. "Told you she's growing up fine, Sam."

Mum glared at Hannah. There was no such thing as pulling a fast one on Mum.

Hannah finished her dinner in silence, excused herself and pretended to study. But her mind wasn't on the conjugation of French verbs. It dwelt instead upon her brother so far away, and upon his marvelous exploits.

Papa settled himself into his chair with the newspaper, a book and the wireless. Mary Aileen went up to their bedroom where the light was better, for her eyes were none too good and she was working on her needlepoint. Mum read. Edan wandered off, perhaps to bed, perhaps to the back shed where he was building, in his own words, a magnificent scooter with roller skate trucks as wheels. Smoke, the tortoise-shell cat, bounded about the room awhile in a fit of the evening crazies, then curled up to sleep on the horsehair loveseat.

Hannah went upstairs, slipped into her nightie and waited.

Eventually she heard footfalls coming up the stairs, gentle ones. They passed her bedroom door. Quietly Hannah stepped out into the hall and followed Mum to the master bedroom. Moments after Mum closed the door, Hannah knocked at it.

"Come in, Hannah." How did Mum know?

She was standing at her dressing table brushing that rich auburn hair. She studied Hannah a moment, crossed to the window, and sat down in her big wingback chair.

Hannah perched on Mum's lap, hesitantly at first. "I'm sorry, Mum. Are you angry with me?"

"Aye. 'Tis nae so much the bishop business I'm angry about as y'r duplicity with y'r Papa. Ye know y'r guilt, and ye led y'r father down the primrose path." Under normal circumstances Mum carefully suppressed her Irish accent. The Irish were politically unpopular, she said, what with labor unrest and the Irish push for nationalization. Thus her speech usually sounded just like Papa's and everyone else's in Sydney.

But when she was weary either of body or of spirit—when she was truly tired—she slipped back into her old Irish accent of yesteryear. She had no reason to be physically weary tonight, so it must be soul-weariness, and Hannah felt she was the cause of it.

Hannah shrugged. "Remember when we were camping, and I, uh, did that? I confessed to Papa, and he thought I was trying to make an excuse for Colin. He was certain Colin had done it and was being devious. He didn't believe me."

"That be nae reason to live a lie. Tomorrow after school ye shall make apology to the bishop."

"Maybe we won't have any school yet."

"Ye'll go to school, young lady, if ye be up to y'r neck in water. And I'm nae so certain I wish to know how the plumbing failure came about."

"Mum, I'd never do a thing like that."

"Aye, ye would."

Hannah giggled suddenly and curled up close in Mum's lap. A soft, warm arm wrapped around her shoulders. "Perhaps I might, but this time I truly didn't. Mum? Do you suppose that news account was correct—about the shipwreck and storm and that pearl?"

"So ye read it. We didn't want ye troubling y'r head with it. Aye, mostly correct, I suppose. Nae such news item gets *all* the facts right."

Hannah sighed and just lay there a few minutes. "I feel guilty, Mum."

"As well ye should. The bishop, yet!"

"That's just it. Here God spared my brother's life, and then I did that to God's priest. It, ah—it doesn't seem right. Not fair."

"Then ye best apologize to God as well."

"Tell me something true, Mum. I don't mean it disrespectful of the church, or God, but are you just saying that because that's what a Christian ought to say, or do you believe it? I mean, is prayer real? Do you truly think it works?"

Mum sighed heavily and drew her daughter closer. "There was a day in me youth when I thought that when ye prayed ye spoke, at most, to the ceiling. I know now, that 'tis truly communion with God. Aye, 'tis real. 'Tis what's kept y'r brother alive when we knew naething of his whereabouts or health. I'm convinced of that."

"But you didn't know he was in trouble, not until that newspaper item. And you prayed for him anyway?"

"Constantly. And y'r father does as well, make nae mistake. Sure'n he's wildly angry with Colin—ye know how volatile y'r father can be—but he loves the lad, too. Aye, he prays, just as does meself."

"Wish I were with Colin."

Mum stretched around to look at Hannah's face. "Hannah, Hannah, Hannah. Y're far too headstrong for y'r own good. Don't even dream of joining y'r brother. For one thing, since ye read the article, ye know they quoted the captain as saying Colin had left Broome. That leaves the whole continent. He could be anywhere. More important, a sixteen-year-old lad is big enough and man enough to make his way out there. A twelve-year-old girl cannae."

"I'd almost rather run off than face the bishop tomorrow."

"Ye had y'r fun. Now ye'll take the responsibility that goes with it. Next time, think first, aye?"

Hannah curled tighter, savoring the warmth, the closeness, the press of Mum's arm and the soft rise and fall of her breathing. *Next time, I just won't let Edan in on it. Then I won't get caught.*

CHAPTER FIVE

LILY

Many miles to the west lay the sea and Eighty Mile Beach, that narrow strip of sand drawing the line between land and water. Forever to the east stretched desert nearly as flat as the sea. Behind them, Broome; before them, the dusty track. And thus it had been for three days. Now Colin lay in sweet green grass beneath a quandong tree and listened to the horses munching nearby.

A gunshot echoed off the low hills to the west. The dun raised its head briefly and went back to grazing. Either Dizzy had encountered trouble, or their dinner was in the bag. The notion of trouble seemed too remote to investigate. Colin dozed off again.

"Hey! I do the shooting, you do the cooking, remember?" Dizzy stood towering above him. Casually he dropped a brown body at Colin's feet and flopped into the shady grass beside him. He stretched out and dragged his hat forward over his face. "This is the life, Col. Take it easy, live off the land, see the world. Wake me up when dinner's served, eh?"

"But of course, Señor Romales. And do you wish candlelight, or the soft, twinkling light of a crystal chandelier?"

"Is gonna be moonlight, you don' get started, eh?"

Good point. Colin lurched to his feet, leaving the

sparse shade to the hunter home from the hill. His hip joints argued every time he rose to stand, but at least they didn't ache like they had. Though he had ridden horses for years, he had gotten away from it during his boating job, and his body told him about it after three days in the saddle.

He dressed out the wallaby, pausing only to examine the curious fingernail-like tip on the creature's tail. After hanging the carcass to cool, he started a fire.

This was the life, all right. No commitments. No responsibilities. No worries.

Ironically, the storm that littered Eighty Mile Beach with wreckage and left four men dead, including Sake Tamemoto, had dumped so much fresh rain on the interior that the dormant desert was springing to vibrant life. Charming little flowers popped up amid the new grass, and here and there trees and bushes bloomed.

Colin watched his fire leap and dance. When it died down to coals, he would roast their meat. He dug a couple of turnips out of his saddlebag.

The lump in the shade stirred. "Eh, Col. Save the liver 'til morning, eh? Slice or two of fried liver for breakfast would be good."

"Let me tell you about some stuff called porridge. It'll revolutionize your life."

"Naw, tha's the stuff they use to stick wallpaper. You shouldn't eat stuff like that, Col."

"Find any water when you were back there?"

"Lotsa water. A *tinaja* 'bout quarter mile off."

"What's a tee-nah-hah?"

"Waterhole. Rain water caught in the rocks."

"Good-oh. Then I can use some of our water here to keep your liver cool."

Liver! Gag. What would Mum say to liver for breakfast?

Colin thought about Mum's cooking. Sparkling, bounding little Hannah. Quiet Edan. Sober Mary Aileen.

And Papa. Colin could feel his heart tugging at him, drawing him home in a sudden, exquisite pique of homesickness, simultaneously yanking on him to get away. *Don't let Papa suck you in!* The war in his heart contrasted so vividly with the peace and quiet of this bucolic outback. Why couldn't life be simple?

He split the carcass and propped it over the coals to cook. Then he nestled the turnips in among the ring of stones to roast slowly. He poured fresh water over a towel, next he would gather the liver and heart into the towel and hang it from a tree in the breeze. If he wet down the towel now and then, Dizzy's breakfast liver would stay cool and fresh until morning.

"Diz! Where's the liver?"

"Look inside."

"I left the entrails right here and they're gone."

Dizzy sat up scowling. "Right where?"

Colin pointed to a spot under the tree.

Dizzy hopped to his feet lightning quick and squatted down near the sparse grass where his breakfast had been lying moments ago. He traced in the dirt with his finger. "Dog. A bloody dog rob us! How come you don' hear it, Col?"

"I was right here. He couldn't have."

"Tracks go off that way, see?" Dizzy straightened and pointed.

No, Colin didn't see. Dizzy could probably track a soaring eagle back to the egg it hatched from. Colin had no such expertise. "I heard dingoes are wily, but this is amazing."

"Ain' no dingo. I seen dingo tracks. This is a dog." Dizzy snapped erect and pulled his long-barreled revolver out from the back of his belt. He moved in closer beside Colin. " 'Fore we go chasing, we just look awhile, eh? Which way the wind blowing?"

He picked up a pinch of dust and tossed it in the air. It drifted ever so casually to the northeast as it dissipated.

"Good," Diz grunted. "Best shot if we keep downwind of him."

"There. Beyond those yellow bushes." Colin might not be good at tracking, but he was very good at looking.

"Sí!" Dizzy raised his revolver slowly, carefully, aiming with both hands securely grasping the butt of the gun.

Colin got a better, albeit fleeting, look. He yelled and shoved Dizzy's hands upward; the gun blasted harmlessly in the air. "It's a person, Diz! I saw a person."

"*Que?!*" Dizzy broke into a run toward the bushes. Colin swung out wide to come at whoever it was from a different angle.

A dark, blue-gray shadow darted out of the scrub this side of the bushes and raced away, a bloody something in its mouth.

"If tha's a person, I eat my hat!" Dizzy poured on more speed.

They ran past the yellow bushes, past the wallaby innards strewn about in the hot red dirt. Dizzy got a shot off at the dog just as it ducked behind a tree.

"Who'd think a dog be 'way out here! Took my breakfast, too!" Dizzy swung a fist at the air and gave up the chase. Wearily, he turned back toward camp.

Colin fell in beside him. "Hey!" He gasped and broke into a run. In the distance by their fire, a boy had grabbed half the roasting carcass and was running away.

Huffing and puffing, Dizzy ran as far as the fire and stopped. "I'll guard what's left," he panted.

Bonzer. Just bonzer. Colin would never catch up to that fleet-footed lad. Besides, half a wallaby would serve two. Why did he bother? Because it made him mad.

The thief slowed down, stumbling. He glanced over his shoulder, dropped the side of meat and lurched back into a faltering run. Colin ignored the meat and kept going. A few hundred yards further, when he'd about caught up, the thief could manage no more than a rapid, shuffling walk.

Suddenly the thief stopped and wheeled, brandishing a small pocket knife; its blade no more than three inches long. He was left-handed. "Stay back," he wheezed.

"No worries, mate. I'll just stand here 'til you drop over. Who do you think you are, to come sneaking into camp and steal our food? You only needed to ask, you know. Instead you send in the dog to decoy us away, eh?"

The thief stood wavering, as if confused by the impasse. A head shorter than Colin, he was probably five-one or five-two, just a frail lad. He looked young and tender and very vulnerable despite his tanned skin, weathered by the sun. His cheeks glowed scarlet from the exertion of his escape. His skin color told Colin some dark ancestor lurked in his background, and a raven-black wisp of hair had slipped from under his hat, pasting to his sweaty forehead.

"I don't—" The hand that held the little pocket knife drooped. "Let me go, please? Won't bother you no more. Just let me go."

Colin stepped back and raised his hands. "All right. I'll let you go. You can turn and run away to nowhere, or you can follow me into camp and have dinner with us. There's enough for all of us; even your dog—that is, if Diz isn't too ropeable about his breakfast. Anyway, you're invited. It's your choice." He turned slowly and started back.

Twenty feet separated them, when Colin noticed from the corner of his eye the thief's shadow begin to move. With tortured, shuffling steps the boy followed. He was obviously worn out, or dried out, or both. Why would he wear that ragged tan jacket on a warm summer evening? Colin wondered.

Colin picked up the half-roasted wallaby side on the way in. They really would be eating by moonlight at this rate.

Dizzy stared at the thief. He bolted to his feet and pulled his battered old hat off his head. "Desiderio Romales, *a sus ordenes*. Col, you invite her to dinner, eh? Tha's good."

"Her?!" Colin wheeled to stare. A look of pure panic flashed across the thief's face. Those bright black eyes darted from man to man.

Dizzy stuffed his hat back on and sat down by the fire. "We don' touch you, *Señorita*, we promise. You safe here. Come, eat. You can go, stay, what you want. 'Cept that dog of yours. I beat the tar outta that dog, I catch him. He took my breakfast."

What was happening inside that little head? Colin tried to read her face and could not; perhaps she herself didn't know. And how did Dizzy know it was a she? She wore a man's shirt miles too big for her. Her mens' trousers hung so loose and baggy the cuffs were rolled tight, and the rope that served as a belt pinched the waistband into wads of overlap. That hat, every bit as tattered as Dizzy's, sat down around her ears.

Her knees buckled, and she suddenly flopped to the ground, still a rod away from the fire. She stared vacantly at the sizzling slab of wallaby.

Colin turned the meat and shoved another turnip among the stones, this one closer to the fire. His duties as cook temporarily abated, he could sit and stare back at her. He could even take a nap, but he didn't quite trust her enough for that yet. Maybe Dizzy was wrong—this could be just a boy with a feminine face. Whatever; whether he or she, the kid was obviously very hungry.

Normally, Dizzy zipped from place to place, from moment to moment, with an endless energy. Not now. Slowly, casually, he stood up. He sauntered to the tree where his waterbag hung. He poured a cup of water and ambled over to the thief.

He handed her the cup. "Sip it, eh? You look pretty dry."

She downed it in three swallows.

"Col? How 'bout you fill it up again, eh?" He handed Colin the cup and sat down in the grass beside her, facing her. He pressed both hands on her face and she made only a token effort to duck away. He pulled her hat off. A long coil of black hair dropped down her back. It looked a little like Hannah's hair, but Hannah's was not nearly so dark.

"You don' get all that fever being sick, eh? What happen to you?"

She sat silent, staring at the fire.

"I watch you flash that knife at Col. Cacky-handed. Maybe you flash your knife at somebody else, they cut you, eh? Lemme see your other arm, please."

"Let me alone, please? Don't bother with me."

Dizzy's excruciating English purred gently. "Hey, we don' hurt you more. You need some help, we here. Ain' no bother. What else we do 'til the meat's done, eh? Lemme look. *Por favor?*"

She looked at him, really looked at him, for the first time. "Filipino."

"Tha's what they keep telling me." Without asking, he laid a hand on her arm just above her elbow; she caught her breath. Diz's voice purred on. "Col, in my near saddlebag, a bottle I was saving for a special time. This time as special as any, eh?"

Colin handed him the cup and hunkered down beside Dizzy's saddle to rifle through his left saddlebag. Here it was, a small, flat bottle of amber whiskey. Strange; neither in Broome nor aboard Captain Foulard's boat had Colin ever seen Dizzy drink whiskey.

Dizzy had peeled the jacket off her right arm and was rolling a blood-stained shirtsleeve high. She had wrapped a grimy handkerchief around what had to be the world's most painful gash. It seeped yellow pus. It burned an ugly red. With the sleeve up, it smelled like a dead rat.

"You don' look out, you gonna end up with blood poison or gangrene," Dizzy muttered, then raised his voice, "Col, get the waterbag, too, and my other shirt."

She shook her head. "Don't use your water up on this."

"Got lotsa water. No worries."

She frowned. "Where?"

He nodded toward the low hills to the east. "You don' know that? I thought maybe you hang around here because of the water."

"I didn't know. No." She sighed. "Just traveling, like you, I guess. Did I miss Broome? Did I go too far?"

"Naw, you going fine. Wha's in Broome? Family?"

"Nothing. Just a place."

"Is a place, all right."

Colin was not a medical man. But Dizzy appeared to be, at least in practical matters such as this. The erstwhile thief settled to an air of acceptance, perhaps even complacency. She made no comment or protest as the near-doctor and his reluctant assistant spent half an hour cleaning the horrid wound.

Dizzy used his whiskey not to drink, but as an antiseptic, literally pouring it in. He discoursed in fractured English on the existence of germs, and how he'd learned from experience that sauerkraut juice, obnoxious though it may be, will not kill them.

Colin tried to reconcile what he saw but could not. The girl was perhaps fifteen, sixteen at most. Mary Aileen's age. A little darker than Hannah's coloring. Like his sisters, she was totally female and should have been subject to weeping. And yet, despite the searing pain Dizzy caused her, gentle as he tried to be, her cheeks remained dry. Her eyes glistened a few times, but that was all.

Dizzy sat back and washed his hands with the last of the water from the bag. "I go fill this up again 'fore we eat, eh? Dinner 'bout ready, cook?"

"Oughta be."

"Hey." Dizzy dipped his head toward the thief. "Sorry I take a shot at your dog, eh? I was angry."

"You keep saying *my* dog. Isn't that *your* dog?"

Colin scowled. "Why you think it's our dog?"

"He stays near that bay mare. I saw him last night, following behind you. He stopped when you stopped here, and he's been here all day today."

Colin and Dizzy stared at each other.

"Naw. Couldn' be." Dizzy wagged his head.

"You said he didn't belong to the owner. Maybe he chums with one of the horses we bought?" Colin hopped to his feet and went looking. The wallaby head and hide were missing now. The entrails had been scattered further. Colin walked out to the horses and stood around awhile watching, examining all the bushes about, looking hard at the pink earth and the gentle green.

There. A hundred feet away. Watching suspiciously with steely eyes, so still it appeared as nothing more than a blue-gray mass in the shade of a shrub, lay Max.

CHAPTER SIX

BLUE MOUNTAINS WONGA

A three-foot length of wool yarn thrown into the air and let fall as it may would lie no more serpentine than this mountain road. Mary Aileen did not have so much a tendency to motion sickness as did Mum; still, the twisty track upset her stomach. Edan sat beside her in the rumble seat, wrapped in his own unfathomable cloak of thoughts. The rough track didn't seem to bother him, but with Edan you never knew.

Hannah, in the front seat between Papa and Mum, squirmed for the thousandth time. Her dark head bobbed. Could Hannah never sit still?

Papa shifted into first gear and urged their touring car up the final steep grade. Drab dust rolled out behind them. "At last!" Mum heaved an audible sigh. They topped the rise and rolled the remaining quarter of a mile to their traditional family camping ground.

Mary Aileen was born to camp out. She loved this secluded site, though not the ride to it. She loved simply to sit and absorb the silent strength of these mountains. She enjoyed the picnicking and the tenting. The night sounds fascinated her.

Papa unloaded the heavy canvas tent as Edan and Mary Aileen measured out its space and drove stakes. In the past, Colin had driven the stakes. He enjoyed camping almost as much as she. Where was he now? Her heart ached. Hannah began complaining right on schedule as she wandered about the campsite doing the odd jobs requested of her. By now she was always either tired or hungry or bored or all three.

Within the hour Mum had dug out her little kitchen and was heating a casserole of ham and beans over an open fire. Edan and Papa went off to set up the latrine. Hannah curled up in the dust beside Mum to watch the flames play. Mary Aileen carried bedding into the tent and rolled it out. She heard Papa speaking sharply to Edan somewhere beyond the trees.

As her own blanket roll fell open, her sketch pad and pencils dropped out. She sat a few minutes, pretending she was thinking when, in fact, she wasn't at all. Then she scooped up her sketching materials and walked out into the waning sun of autumn.

Some of the cliffs and canyons in these Blue Mountains dropped precipitously even as others flowed away in gentle undulations. Their campsite nestled on the crest of one of the long rolling hills. Mary Aileen walked the hundred yards to her favorite perch, an outcrop hanging on the brink of forever. She crawled out onto the smooth hard stone and sat down.

Behind her, overhanging gum trees shielded her from the sky. Beyond her the vault arched blue and endless over the gaping canyon. Why did the sky here seem far deeper and bigger than the sky over Sydney? Near the horizon it melted into a gentle gray to match the autumn haze. Sometimes it was difficult to see where sky ended and land began. Tonight the rolling gray-purple mountains drew distinct lines against infinity.

Mary Aileen sketched outlines she had sketched many times before—the rounded hills to the east, the ragged ridge across the canyon from her perch here, the weird knob out on the west end of the ridge. Should she sketch the knob this time, or should she not? At least several hundred feet high, it was a protrusion of wrinkled and gnarled granite, like an ugly wart on an otherwise graceful landscape. When she drew it exactly the way it looked, her picture appeared amateurish, unnatural. If she left it out, her sketch looked more refined, but inaccurate.

Aha! She had a sudden idea she'd never had before. She drew a tree where the knob ought to be. Mother Nature would surely plant a tree to hide that knob sooner or later. Mary Aileen would make it sooner. She sketched the tree after the form of the trees beside her.

On the crest of the mountain here, the trees spaced themselves at orderly intervals, making them easy to sketch individually. Below, in the wet gorge, they crowded each other, forming a dense green mat seemingly to protect the canyon from prying eyes. Living things were hidden in that canyon, wonderful things—lyrebirds and bowerbirds, orioles and pardalotes, platypuses and snakes. She wished she could walk among them unfeared!

Wee-ooo. A bowerbird called in the forest below her. Silence. Something on the forest floor must have startled a flock of king parrots; with their noisy *chack, chack!*, red birds and green spurted up from the hillside opposite. Kookaburras laughed a hearty *g'day* to the waning sun. Beside Mary Aileen's front-row seat, a restless little rock warbler rattled the dry leaves. Wagging its tail side to side, it hopped and skittered about.

The dinner bell clanged, muffled by the trees behind her. Mary Aileen scrambled reluctantly to her feet, turned her back on her marvelous view of nature, and walked down to camp.

Papa bowed his head for the blessing as soon as Mary Aileen entered the circle. He thanked God for the food, and for the opportunity they had to retreat like this for a few days of rest and renewal. He acknowledged God's hand in everything, and as soon as he said "Amen," Hannah dived for the food.

Mary Aileen waited while Edan filled his plate. Then she scooped out her own serving, privately wishing there weren't quite so many onions in the dish. She settled on the ground near the fire, her warm plate in her lap, and ate in silence, missing Colin.

Mum glanced at Mary Aileen's sketchbook. "See anything out there this evening?"

"The usual things. A very pretty flight of king parrots."

In the distance to the north, a mournful sound began: *Wonk. Wonk. Wonk. Wonk.* The litany continued unvarying through the minutes of otherwise silence.

Mum frowned. "That bird calling—you told me what it was and I've forgotten."

"It's a wonga pigeon," Mary Aileen smiled. "A white-faced gray pigeon with a few marks. We saw one last year and you remarked on its size; it's larger than a crested pigeon."

"I remember now." Mum nodded. "When first I came to this country I was fascinated by the exotic birds. Erin has nothing like these. I always wondered what their names were, and I never learned them, for some reason. It pleases me that you've mastered them all, dear."

"Not them all, Mum."

"Near enough. You've a gift for it; apparently a gift I lack, although I do remember the first bird I learned by name. Your father identified it for me." And she looked across at Papa.

An almost misty look came across his face. "A kingfisher. In that crocodile pool beyond Sugarlea. We've seen some country since then."

"Haven't we." The memories misted Mum's face, too.

"Mum, why don't you ever tell us stories about before you were married?" Hannah popped the last of her dinner into her mouth and extended her plate. "More, please."

"You may ask again after your mouth is empty."

Papa lost any mistiness he may have had. "The past is

past, Hannah. You're the future. There wasn't that much of interest anyway."

"Surely there was." Mary Aileen felt her nerve fail. You never contradict Papa. But she pressed on. "I remember once Mum said you hired her and Aunt Meg and Aunt Linnet; that's how you met her. She would still be in Ireland but for you, and where would we be? You see? The past is ours as well as the future."

"And you already know as much about it as you need to." Papa turned his full attention to his plate. The conversation was ended.

Mary Aileen glanced at Mum. She was fully absorbed in eating her dinner also.

"Might I have some more?" Hannah took silence as a yes and refilled her plate.

Edan lurched to his feet. "May I be excused?"

Mum nodded.

Papa scowled. "Stay close where you can hear if we call you. I don't want you wandering off daydreaming."

Edan mumbled something. He folded his napkin, carried his dish to the washtub and walked off into the bush.

Mary Aileen finished quickly, excused herself, and laid her dish in the washtub as she hurried after Edan. Out here at camp, without Grace the maid to wash dishes, the task almost always fell to Mary Aileen. *Let Hannah get them tonight*, she thought.

"Edan! Wait! I want to see, too." Mary Aileen caught up to him just beyond the boulders they often manned as a fort. She fell in beside her brother and marveled at how silently wise he seemed at only ten years old. She tried to picture Papa being ten. She could not. And yet Edan, like Hannah, had inherited his father's piercing dark eyes and good looks. It should not be such a difficult thing to look at Edan and see Papa in the past.

The past is past, Papa'd said. If that was so, why was she memorizing all those dates in history class?

Edan kicked at a stone in the path. "What do you think they're trying to hide?"

"I don't know. But I know it's not something bad, you know—immoral, or anything. When Mum explained the facts of life to me, she said she and Papa didn't—" Mary Aileen glanced at her little brother. "You know what I mean—nothing before the wedding night. That may not mean much to you yet, Edan, but it's very important to older people."

"You don't suppose Papa's a convict or something?"

Mary Aileen gasped. "I can't imagine that! He goes to church every week and seems to like it. He has a spotless business reputation, Mum says. He gives money to the church and to charities. He's much too good to have been a convict. Mum too. Even in the old country, Mum couldn't have done anything too terribly wrong."

Edan led the way down over the rocky precipice, picking his way as he went. To their left, the forested canyon fell away, shimmering in the golden light of evening. "Maybe it's the aunts and uncles they're ashamed of."

" 'Tis true that Aunt Linnet is a musical performer. But there's nothing wrong with that, surely—she's been married to Uncle Chris all these years, and happy. Uncle Aidan and Uncle Liam out in Kalgoorlie are gold miners. That's an honest occupation. Uncle Ellis is still back in Ireland; we never hear about him much. And Aunt Meg and Uncle Luke—Papa's very proud of them, Uncle Luke being in the ministry and all, with his large parish."

"Papa's proud of everyone, save me," Edan blurted.

"Oh, Edan, he just doesn't understand you fully yet. When you get older and he gets to know you better, he'll like you more. It worked that way with me."

"Not with Colin."

What could she say? He was absolutely right.

That wonga pigeon began its monotonous call again—*wonk, wonk, wonk*. She was supposed to be the nature lover, but the wonga annoyed her now. The annoyance made her angry, not because it was there, but because she could not control it. She knew she could not turn off the pigeon, but she thought she should be able to turn off the irritation.

Wonk, wonk, wonk, wonk. . . .

Cautiously, Edan traversed the narrow ledge from the pathway to the cave. He stepped into the soft, powdery dirt of the cave and began craning his neck, peering here and there.

Actually, it wasn't exactly a cave—it was an overhang, a bulging, brittle slab of dark rock that protruded twenty feet from the side of the mountain. Under its jutting nose, the "cave," at least fifteen feet high at the front, extended thirty feet back into the side of the mountain. Its roof tapered down until only Edan's body fit between floor and ceiling, and finally, in its very nether recesses, not even Edan could go.

Darkness slithered out from the rear of the recess now, inching forward as the sunlight waned.

"There it is." Edan pointed straight up.

Matted and plaited of sticks, grasses, moss and spider webs, a rock warbler's nest hung suspended in a great wad from the cave roof. Like all rock warbler nests, it drooped in a clumsy ovoid glob from its attachments at either end.

"Do you suppose there's something in it?" Edan strained his neck in an effort to see it better.

"Not this time of year, surely. It's winter, or nearly. Here, let me lift you up and perhaps you can get your finger through the hole there and feel about for eggs." Mary Aileen knelt low in the powdery dust and clasped her arms around Edan's legs.

Tilting and teetering she lurched to her feet. His legs were pressed against her face, his hand gripping her hair for balance. She could neither see nor move her head. "Are you high enough?"

"I think so. Step back. To the left. No, too far. To the right. That's it. A bit higher?"

Mary Aileen stretched as high as she dared, on tiptoe. Who would imagine such a small lad could weigh so much? "Don't wiggle!"

"I'm not; I'm reaching. Almost . . . There! It's all soft inside, 'Leen. Don't move around so much!"

"I can't keep my balance. Don't; I—." She lurched uncontrollably sideways. The whole teetering weight of him threw her off, and he came crashing down with her.

The nest, a dry, crackly wad of debris, splacked down on Mary Aileen's head, spraying a million bits of dust all over her face. She'd be forever brushing it out of her hair.

Edan snapped around to his knees and stared aghast at the fallen nest. "We ruined it! I didn't mean to pull it down, 'Leen! Oh, look! There's no way we can hang it back up there."

"You needn't feel bad; you didn't mean to."

He glared at her and she was surprised to see tears in his eyes. " 'Course I didn't mean to, but I did it. It happened."

"Edan—" Why was he so upset? What could she say to soothe him? "Edan, there are many, many rock warblers around and lots of nests. It's not a great tragedy."

" 'Tis!" He lifted the shattered pile of woven trash as if it were someone's baby. He looked up at the ceiling, then back at the nest; tears coursed down his cheeks. "It's always a tragedy, 'Leen, when somebody's home gets torn apart."

And now her own eyes burned hot and wet.

Colin.

CHAPTER SEVEN

KALGOORLIE

"Max? Hey, Max! Come on! Get moving!" Colin twisted in the saddle to look back. It wasn't easy; Lily rode right behind him and he had to crane his neck to see around her.

Reluctantly, the brindled dog lurched to its feet and padded out onto the track, twenty yards behind them.

Satisfied that her chum had joined them, Colin's horse quit dancing around and settled to the track. Animals! Weird animals. Why could not Dizzy have chosen ordinary dim-witted horses, horses who placidly plod through life? Colin's bay mare possessed in the hulking body of a plough horse the brain of a bandicoot. A charitable observer might call the horse "positive," or "an optimist." Colin knew her true colors; he was condemned to ride the length of the Madman's Track and then some on a happy, half-ton twit.

Dizzy's dun gelding possessed no brain at all. As good feed and fresh grass fattened it and honed its spirit, it grew more and more fidgety. Only when its mates, the bay and the ugly dog, traveled nearby did it behave at all well.

And Max. In the nearly two months on this track, Max had not once come within an arm's length of a human being. "If I hadn' took that shot at it and scared it good," Dizzy would say, "it'd be coming up and biting us now, I vow."

No contest. Colin agreed. And so they traveled south, the fizz-brained horses and the skulking dog.

Not to mention Lily. Apparently her plans to find Broome died aborning, for when the men moved on, she fell in with them and went south. She was a part of them, yet not a part of them. She kept to herself, said little, volunteered no information. When they camped come evening, she always took it upon herself to gather firewood. Sometimes she added to the menu berries, roots or fish. She had a talent for catching fish with her bare hands. Whenever the rare opportunity presented itself, she would even wash the men's clothes, and afterwards, her own.

There her participation ended. She allowed the men to let her ride—on Colin's horse in the morning, on Dizzy's in the afternoon, so as not to wear either horse down carrying double-dink. She never asked to be taken aboard. One morning Colin deliberately neglected to invite her up behind him, and she simply started walking, with the same mindless acceptance as Max. In camp she remained apart, much the same as did Max, off to herself, wrapped in her own dark dreams.

The land undulated gently now, shaping itself into low orange hills. Smoky green mulga spread in broad patches across the hills and flats.

As they rode beneath a grove of the straight, slim trees, Colin asked over his shoulder, "What's mulga good for, Lily?"

"Lots of things. Eat the seeds. Start fires with the bark. Make digging sticks and boomerangs; good strong wood. Sometimes it has galls. They're big round lumps that're good to eat."

"You know all this stuff. You're really smart. You got some Aboriginal blood in you, right? Is that where you learned all this?"

Silence.

"So why won't you tell us anything about yourself? All we know is your first name. And why did you try to steal from us, instead of just asking?"

"You asked me that before; I didn't tell you then and I'm not talking about it now."

That pretty much ended that. Colin gave up the conversation.

The trees ended, too. Dirt tracks crisscrossed the barren hills. Abandoned mullock piles stuck out like boils here and there. For some reason they saw rabbits but not kangaroos or wallabies. And even the rabbits looked scrawny. It was dismal countryside.

Hours later Dizzy pointed beyond the hill ahead. "Dust up there, or smoke. I think maybe we come up on Kalgoorlie, eh?"

On the horizon ahead, a gray cloud stained the sky.

Kalgoorlie! Now Colin would see adventure of a profitable sort, maybe even lucrative. Deep in the earth below Kalgoorlie ran a network of veins, half a mile wide and two miles long, a lode of gold ore so rich they called the strip The Golden Mile. And Colin's uncles owned a bit of that mile.

Dizzy twisted himself around in the saddle, the better to converse. "I'm getting a bad feeling 'bout this, Col."

"Why?"

"Lookit all these little towns we gone through, eh? Some of them clear dead. Empty houses and boarded-up mines. Some of them only a coupla houses left. Leonora's got all those dead mines, save one. Menzies ain' hardly nothing no more, less'n a hunnert people. Goongarrie. Broad Arrow. You hear the folks there talk 'bout how they used to be big towns. Ghost towns they are now. I think we're on the wrong end of the boom, *compadre*."

"You worry too much, *amigo*."

"Eh, maybe. What you think of Paddington, where we just been through? Six hotels there once, Col. We couldn' even buy lunch!"

"But Kalgoorlie's still going strong, Diz. My uncles have been there for as long as I can remember. It's apples."

Dizzy might have his misgivings; Colin certainly did not. Colin and Dizzy would do well as miners, he was sure, but what about Lily?

Well? What about Lily? She wasn't Colin's responsibility, nor Dizzy's. She wasn't anyone's, really. Did that make her everyone's?

She coiled her hair up under her hat as they passed still another scraggly, abandoned claim. Sheets of corrugated tin lay about, pocked with rust. A weathered, broken stool sat atilt near the tiny shelter that must have once been home to someone. What did the erstwhile owner dream as he sat by his door on that stool contemplating the evening? They rode on past, almost reverently.

Of all the big and small towns spread throughout Australia, Kalgoorlie boasted the wildest, headiest of reputations. According to the stories, every gambler and shill in Australia graduated from her famous Two-Up school. Lurid tales professed that every girl and woman in the town was absolutely gorgeous, and available for a price. If the yarns were halfway credible, life in this remote mining town roared and hooted, laughed heartily, ended violently, thumbed its nose at the proper world outside. Kalgoorlie's reputation promised howling Saturday nights in some of the world's wildest pubs.

For half an hour, as they rode from Kalgoorlie's scattered outskirts inward, Colin waited with bated breath for the fabled town to flame into the deliciously exciting life it was famous for. Amid the constant drone of flies, Kalgoorlie seemed to doze.

Dizzy drew his dun to a halt in front of the postal station. "Don' know, Col. Think ever'body here decide to be respectable and moved to Perth?"

"Maybe they're all at work."

"Wheels on the poppethead out there haven't turned

since I started watching them. And half the stores and houses look boarded up. *Muerto*. Dead. Plain and simple."

"What's the poppethead?"

Dizzy turned in his saddle and pointed. A wooden skeleton five stories tall towered beyond the sheet-iron roofs. Built like a railway trestle and shaped like a gigantic windmill, its open lattice-work of wooden beams supported not vanes but huge wheels at the top. Various horizontal structures, like shored-up railway trestles, angled off near roof level, carrying mine buckets or cars. It all looked very industrious, and larger than life.

"They use it to bring up ore from deep down. The wheels, they're like pulleys, y'know?"

"I've seen three or four of these around the area."

"Sí, and none of 'em moving, you notice."

Colin swung his leg forward over his horse's neck to avoid Lily, who sat motionless behind the saddle. He slid to the ground and tried the post office door. Locked.

"Good thing we ain' in no hurry. Le's wait, eh?"

"Yair, guess so. Coming on suppertime, anyway."

On the assumption that it would be the establishment the locals favored, and therefore have the best food, they chose a pub with the most motor cars parked out front. Colin avoided disturbing Lily again by walking his bay the short distance, and tied the animal to a porch post two doors down from the pub.

Heading for the door, he stopped short. Lily remained back by the horses, watching Dizzy and Colin with those huge, dark, gamin eyes.

"Coming?" Colin called.

"I don't have any money," she shrugged.

"That's all right. Diz here, he doesn't have any money, either."

With the same passivity she shared with Max, Lily let herself be escorted emotionless into the pub between her two traveling companions.

As Colin stepped from sun into gloom he wondered if entering this pub with Lily was a mistake. She appeared to be the only female in the establishment—not even a barmaid could be seen in this male bastion of ale and noise. Dizzy had seen through her little-boy masquerade instantly. Would these grizzled ruffians also?

No worries. Nobody paid any attention to the newcomers. The two dozen men in this stuffy little pub sat at the tables with their backs turned to the door, or hung off the bar, watching some speaker in the corner. A miner by dress and language, the orator harangued about the shabby way all those t'other-siders treated Westralians, calling them sandgropers and ignoring their unique needs, and how the Perth people made no effort to help. Perth was as bad as Sydney, when it came to support. "Secede!" bellowed the orator. "They claim they need us, but they're not ready to do anything for us. We abso-bloody-lutely don't need them!"

Colin led the way to the only available table in the place, a little round wobbly one in the back corner. He flopped in a chair, grateful to be sitting on something that didn't require straddling. Lily sat down with her back to the room.

Dizzy smirked, "Always heard there's lots happening in Kalgoorlie, but if I knew it was politics I woulda stayed home. I find someone to wait on us." And he wandered off to the bar.

Did Lily seem nervous? It looked so to Colin. He took off his hat and hung it on his knee. He ran his fingers through his dirty hair. Tonight he would purchase hotel rooms, a single for each of them—bathing facilities, a comfortable bed with sheets and a real pillow, electric lights.

Dizzy was back. "They got mutton stew or beef and potatoes. Whatya want?"

"Beef." Colin looked at Lily. She hesitated, then nodded. "And tea. Get a big pot of tea."

Dizzy grinned. "This is gonna be pretty good; get to eat something I didn' hafta shoot first." He walked away. Perhaps Dizzy missed civilization as much as Colin did.

Civilization. Colin thought of the family camping he had once known; how Mum and Papa enjoyed getting away from town for a while. Colin wondered where they'd come from originally. None of Papa's current friends had known him as a youth. Either he had cashed in his old friends on a complete set of new ones, or he came from somewhere other than Sydney. Colin didn't know. He did feel Mum had been a city girl back in Ireland, many years ago—before she knew Papa.

His family had camped occasionally as a form of relaxation from the busyness of city life. Colin had just spent the last nine weeks camping and now looked forward to a comfortable respite in this city. Fate behaved as weirdly as their animals.

Dizzy returned with a pint of ale. He settled in a chair to watch the political process that made Australia unique—oratory lubricated liberally with alcohol.

He finally removed his hat to scratch his head. When Colin mentioned a hotel with a bath, a broad grin spread across Dizzy's tanned features. He leaned forward. "I asked where all the trees north of town went. They said they all got cut down for firewood to stoke the deesa, deeso—the plant where they take the salt outta the water. All the water here is salty."

"Desalinizing plant. *Every* tree, you say?"

"Looks so. Tha's a lotta water to distill."

The tea came, and eventually plates mounded high with beef, potatoes and carrots. Colin was not fond of carrots, but right now they looked good.

As he picked up his fork, his conscience was pricked. He had not asked a blessing on his food—something he never did anymore. Somehow, out on the track, it didn't seem quite so important. Here at a table, with silverware and plates and the other accouterments of civilization, the sin of omission smarted fiercely. He closed his eyes a moment and hypocritically prayed to a God he was not the least sure existed. Then he dug in, and theological considerations slipped away. Real gravy. Aaahh.

Presently Colin became aware of a hulking form near his elbow. A burly miner was standing at their table. He stared at Lily. "Don't I know ye from somewhere?" Irish. He had the same accent Colin's mum used when she was very tired.

The huge eyes glanced up and quickly flicked away. Lily muttered, "No, sir. I'm new here."

The miner reached out suddenly and yanked her hat off. Her long black hair tumbled down her back. "I knew it! Harry, tell me if this ain't Niel's Lillipilli."

A voice from another table roared, "Sure is!"

The miner leered. "Ye got muckle nerve, lass, running off from y'r husband like that."

"He's not my husband!" Lily's eyes, big as saucers, flitted with terror from Colin to Dizzy.

"He put a twenty-pound reward out for ye. Say g'day to y'r friends, little lady; y're going home now." And the fellow started to lift her out of her chair by one arm.

Before Colin could stand up, Dizzy's chair was already flying, tipped over, and Dizzy was on his feet. He held a long-barreled revolver steady, solidly pointed at the miner's heart. So swift was he, Colin had not even seen him pull it out of his belt.

The fellow stared at Dizzy for a long moment. "This is a runaway bride. Ask anybody here."

The rest of the room was staring now, too. Even the orator had ceased, and the silence hung heavier than the cigarette smoke.

Lily started to speak, but Dizzy held up a hand. Soft as rain his voice crooned, and that gun never wavered. "Have a seat, frien', and join us, while I ask anybody here. Col, loan him your chair, eh?"

Colin stood up and stepped aside. Warily, as if afraid it would collapse beneath him, the miner sat down.

"Ta. Now. Before you blokes get thinking 'bout rewards, le's ask the lady's side of it, eh? Lily, you never talked about yourself; tha's all right. But now's the time you tell your side. Speak up."

Her hands trembled. She licked her lips and spoke directly to Dizzy. Her eyes never left his face, as if to seek strength there, and his eyes never left the miner's.

"My mum died last year down behind Kambalda, so I went into Coolgardie to find a job. I got a job right away with Othniel Banks, cleaning and cooking. A few weeks later he said he wanted more than cleaning and cooking, he wanted—" She shuddered. "I wouldn't. So he locked me in a closet for a couple of days—to show me who's the boss, he said. Then he—uh, he made me be his mistress. He locked me up in his cellar whenever he was away from the house. It was seven months before he got careless about the lock, and I could get away. But I never married him. He's not my husband."

Dipping his head toward the crowd in general, as was his habit, Dizzy's voice continued firm and gentle, "There now. Which of you blokes attended this lady's wedding, eh? Got any witnesses?"

Silence, thick and brooding.

Dizzy kept his eyes on the miner, then stole a glance at Lily. "Did you steal from him?"

"I took eight pounds," her voice quavered.

"How much did he pay you—wages?"

"Nothing. He never paid me."

"What's a good cook worth, Col? Twenty pounds a month? That's a hunnert-forty. So this Othniel still owes her a hunnert thirty-two, eh? He the one who cut your arm?"

A constable came bursting in the door and stopped cold, uncertain what was in the air, what to do.

She nodded. "The morning I got away, before he went to work. He was mad at me. Usually he just hit me, but this time—"

"Stand up an' show the gentlemen here your arm, señorita."

She hesitated. Her eyes moved to the constable.

"Do it."

Reluctantly she rose, peeled her jacket off and rolled up her sleeve. The raw scar flashed in the gloom.

Abruptly, Dizzy tipped his gun away toward the ceiling. He stuffed it in his belt at the small of his back and sat down. "If you still intend to take her back, I guess you will. I can't keep her safe forever. But any man here who collects twenty pounds for her is so low a snake'd hafta duck to get under him. Anybody disagree with that?"

No one stirred. Lily stood like a slave on an auction block, her head down, studying the floor. Tears welled in her eyes and coursed down her cheeks, the first tears Colin had ever seen her shed.

The constable finally ambled forward, addressing not Dizzy but the miner. "You wish to press charges, sir?"

"No." The miner wagged his head. "No. Let it pass." He looked at Lily. "Niel said ye stole more than jus' money from 'im."

"These clothes I'm wearing," she barely murmured.

"Them rags?" The miner stood up suddenly. "Sure'n he shoulda paid ye to take 'em." And he walked away from the table shaking his head.

Conversation picked up in patches, here and there. The constable chided Dizzy for a couple of minutes about exposing a gun in a public place, but he didn't confiscate it. Colin watched Lily's face as she sat down; the familiar look of resignation had returned, the expression that said she didn't care what anyone did to her. Her nose and eyes were wet, and he handed her his handkerchief. The constable turned and left without further comment.

Dizzy picked up his overturned chair as if nothing had happened and sat down again, returning to finish his cold dinner. "This Othniel, *es un gordo, no*? He's a fat man?"

Lily nodded. "How did you know?"

"Y'r clothes, they big enough my horse can wear 'em."

She muffled a giggle and smiled. It was the first smile the men had seen on her face. First the tears, then the smile, the first cracks in her dark armor.

"How'd you get so far so fast, eh? Your wound was maybe a week old when we found you, all infected like it was."

"I rode the stagecoaches until my money ran out," she whispered, her head down. "I even rode with a camel train awhile, until one of the camel drivers started getting personal with me. I went on foot another two days and then I ran into you."

Dizzy nodded. "What's next?"

"I don't know."

"I don' either. Col here, he wants us to take a bath so we don' offend the horses, and get some sleep. Tomorrow, I guess we all look for jobs, eh?"

Colin laughed. "What'd that miner call you? Lillipilli? Know what that is, Diz?"

"No. Wha's a lillipilli?"

Lily said nothing, so Colin answered. "A sweet fruit from a gum tree, like a cherry. Mum buys them from the Aboriginal women for pie."

"Sweet fruit. Mmm." Dizzy looked at Lily and nodded. "Yeah, it fits." He swallowed the last of his dinner, as if it might be awhile before he ate again, and pushed his plate away. "Now, Lily, you listen. I spoke the truth when I said I can't protect you forever. But you draw us a map, show us where this Othniel's place be. Maybe he still come around for you, y'know? You turn up missing, we go look for you, eh? And you let us know where you are if you get a job. Let us check it out for you."

She nodded, looking grateful for the first time, then whispered, "I'm sorry."

" 'Bout what?" Dizzy reached for the teapot.

"Causing you trouble."

"You did'n cause no trouble. You did'n ask for none o' this, eh?" He poured himself a cup of tea, draining the pot. "Now. One other thing. You read and write good?"

She shook her head. "Not very good."

"You'll need that, y'know. But I can't do it for you, jus' like I can't protect you forever. You decide to take the respons'bility, you come to me. I help you learn to read and write better. Col, too. He's smart. But him, me, we can't do it for you. You gotta do it for yourself, y'know?"

Those huge dark eyes studied Diz, and Colin detected a spark in them. "Why are you doing all this for me?" she asked.

Dizzy stared at the teapot awhile. Was he trying to choose the right words, or was he groping for an answer? He looked up. "You still a kid, y'know? Lotsa bad things happen to you, and you still a kid. Maybe you need some help yet, getting started in the world, I mean. Me, I'm here, I can help. So why not, eh? People done me lotsa favors. Now I pass 'em along. Someday you pass 'em along to someone else."

She propped both elbows on the table and sat silently for a few minutes. Her eyes glistened again. "The first day you found me, you said I was safe with you. I really am. You can't know how good it is to feel safe when you're a girl." Her eyes rose to meet his. "Thank you." She looked at Colin. "You, too. You've been very good, both of you."

Very good? Colin pondered the words. He enraged his father, broke his mum's heart, literally ripped his family apart. Very good? How could those words refer to him?

Dizzy finished his tea in one gulp and stood up. "Let's go find that hotel room with a bath. Then we gotta find Col's uncles. If we're gonna get rich mining gold, we wanna smell good, eh?"

Colin stood too, feeling suddenly relieved, as if a great stone were lifted from his back. Others still weighed him down, but he somehow felt better about himself. "What's the best way to go about finding my uncles, do you think, Diz?"

"Two ways." Dizzy offered Lily a hand, but she didn't take it, rising herself and smoothing her baggy clothes. "I can put a bullet in the ceiling, and when the constable come running in we can ask him. Or, we can promise the barman we don' shoot holes in his ceiling if he tell us where to find 'em."

"Let's try the quiet way first." Colin stepped up to the bar, and addressed the tender. "We're looking for a Liam or Aidan Sloan. They own a mine here, I'm told."

The man nodded, gesturing toward a nearby table, "You already met their foreman, Flannery."

Colin twisted around to gaze at the man who was now looking right at him. They had indeed met. A few minutes ago, Dizzy had pointed his revolver square at him. Now what?

Colin's father had often accused him of deviousness and indecision. This was no time for either. He crossed boldly to the miner and extended his hand. "Mr. Flannery, sir, if our friendship keeps on as it began, I expect we're in for one bonzer time of it. I'm Colin Sloan, your bosses' nephew."

The big man stared at him. "And meself is good and sorry I ever got out o' bed this morning."

CHAPTER EIGHT

BLOOD AND WATER

In twenty years the Golden Horseshoe had yielded over one hundred tons of gold, though its owners claimed that these days, in 1925, the mine was hardly paying its way. The Great Boulder had produced nearly four million ounces so far. The Perseverance and the great and mighty Ivanhoe put over a million ounces of gold apiece into their owners' pockets. The Sloan brothers' Southern Star provided, at most, a bit of sugar for their tea.

Colin stood on the decking of the Southern Star's shaft and gawked at the view spread out before him in the clear, golden light of morning. Jumbles of tin-roofed buildings, some very large and others mere shanties, cluttered the rolling landscape that swept down from the mine and up the next rise. Midway, an enormous black smokestack rose several hundred feet straight up. Colin counted five great poppetheads, the only ones he could see from this angle. Elevated tram trestles spread out like spider legs from the poppetheads. On the far rise stood a rank of tall, cylindrical water tanks—the desalinizing plant. He could see not a single tree.

Most of the equipment looked rusted, much of it in disuse or abandoned, but Kalgoorlie was still Kalgoorlie, the town on the fabulous Golden Mile. Colin felt an excitement here, an anticipation. Here he felt he would find what he was seeking. Here his soul, or at least his pocketbook, would triumph.

It must be the fact that mines are hidden away below ground that makes them less than impressive on the surface, thought Colin. The Southern Star boasted no towering poppethead, no elevated tram tracks, no jaw crusher or stamp mill. A simple tin roof on one-story stilts covered the shaft and supported some pulleys under its rafters. Twenty feet away, its only power source stood waiting for some action. There a stout post perhaps fifteen feet high held a huge horizontal reel, and an old gray horse in harness stood in a circular path beneath the reel, ready to turn it. A system of heavy ropes connected the reel with the pulleys at the shaft.

Flannery tugged on a rope by the shaft. Seconds later a brass bell up in the rafters responded with a dull clank. Flannery walked out to the gray horse and swatted it on the rump. It lurched forward and began to plod around its circle. The heavy ropes wound ever so slowly from down the shaft up through the pulleys and onto the reel. The pulleys creaked; it all seemed so primitive.

A rusty cage rose slowly out of the shaft. When a stopper knot in the rope hit the pulleys the stoic old horse quit plodding. Out of the cage stepped a fat, balding little man with a red nose. If he'd had a beard, he would have been the perfect image of Father Christmas in grimy overalls.

He scowled, and exploded to Flannery, "You bloody galah! If you'd been down there where you're supposed to be, this never woulda happened!"

Flannery scowled back. "So, you changing my day off again?"

"What?"

"Anytime something goes wrong below, it's on my day off. Then you change my day off to another day. So what is it now?"

"You're getting a bit mouthy, Flannery." The fat man stopped and stared at Colin. "I oughta know you."

"Colin. Cole Sloan's son, out from Sydney."

"Well, you don't say. My, oh my, oh my!" The fat man turned and yanked on the rope Flannery had just pulled. "Gotta get Liam up here. My, oh my!"

If he's going for Uncle Liam, then he must be Aidan, Colin figured. Flannery turned the gray horse around and ran the cage back down the shaft.

"So, you're Colin! Look at them Sloan eyes. Bet your papa's right proud o' *you.*"

Proud of me? He can't tell me often enough how rotten I am, Colin thought bitterly.

Colin waved a hand toward Dizzy. "Let me introduce my mate, Desiderio Romales."

Dizzy extended a hand. If Uncle Aidan saw it he ignored it. "Howd'y'do, Romales." Then he wrapped an arm around Colin's shoulders. "What brings you out to Kalgoorlie, lad? Not bad news from home, I hope."

"No, sir. Mum and Papa are fine. I just didn't want to work in Sydney, and was hoping perhaps there'd be work out here for me."

Uncle Aidan paused, studying him with bleary eyes. "Perhaps there is. Perhaps there is." For the first time he looked—really looked—at Dizzy. "Understand, the price of gold is down, and the Southern Star isn't what she used to be. We can put on maybe one man, but not two."

Dizzy pursed his lips. "Sure, I unnerstan', Mr. Sloan. I unnerstan' better'n you think."

Colin frowned. Dizzy didn't usually read in prejudice that wasn't there. Surely he was wrong.

Dizzy nodded toward Colin. "Think I go look aroun' some, Col. You and your uncles, you got lots to talk about. Come by this evening maybe, eh?"

"Right-o." Colin watched his friend saunter away toward the horses.

Uncle Aidan was watching, too. In fact he watched quite intently as Dizzy mounted and rode away on the dun. The bay mare threw her head high and whinnied after her old track mate.

The bell clanked and Flannery whacked the gray horse, winding the cage rope up again. *How do they get up and down when there is no one on the surface to run the reel?* Colin wondered.

Slowly, laboriously, the old cage emerged with a man who looked far more like Papa than the tubby Uncle Aidan. Colin was introduced to his Uncle Liam, who was quite a magnificent spectacle. Apparently he was prepared to spend the day below, and yet he was dressed in his Sunday best. His patent leather shoes shone, and a necktie in the very latest style gleamed on his crisp white shirt. He had Papa's lithe build and graceful movement. Colin calculated him to be nearly six years younger than Papa, and yet he seemed older.

"Looking for work," Uncle Liam mused. He raised his voice. "Flannery! While you were off merrily doing the block, the boko did a perish. We're strapped. Go close up down on three. Where were you, anyway?"

"Sitting in the Exchange, thinking of ways to poison the nag," Flannery snarled. He climbed into the cage and hooked up a thin rope with well-spaced knots the length of it. Then he unhooked the heavy rope, and began lowering himself down into the black hole, hand over hand with the knotted rope.

So that's how they do it, Colin thought.

Uncle Liam glowered at the descending cage. Under his breath he described the Irish Flannery with adjectives Colin would not dare speak at home.

"When would you be prepared to commence work, lad?" Uncle Aidan sounded ebullient. It was nice to be welcomed as a responsible adult instead of an errant child!

Colin shrugged. "Immediately, sir."

"No, no. Not 'sir.' I'm your Uncle Aidan. Call me Uncle." His voice dropped a notch. "Colin, we'd love to hire you immediately, but there's a problem."

"More than one," grumbled Uncle Liam.

"True," Uncle Aidan pressed on. "The most recent, and most disastrous, occurred totally beyond our control. You see, Colin, we find the use of horses to be more economically sound than to employ engines requiring costly fuels. The gray mare over there is our above-ground animal. The below-ground animal, a lovely blood bay gelding, died of unknown causes just this morning."

"Sorry to hear it." Colin tried to picture getting a horse down that shaft and could not. They must have taken the blood bay down by some other route.

Uncle Aidan went on. "We'll show you the whole operation, of course. Proud of it. Briefly, we dig on any of five levels and load sledges with the ore. The below-ground horse draws the ore to the shaft here, where we transfer it to buckets and haul it to the surface."

"Using the gray horse."

"Precisely. Every week, according to schedule, we haul the ore to a stamp mill. The mill processes it for a percentage of the final yield. Much more economical for us in the long run than to build and operate our own stamp mill."

"So you get your whole week's income at once."

"Clever boy! Dinkum lad! Yes. Now you see our problem. Without a below-ground horse, we can't move the sledges, which means we can't get the ore to the shaft to be raised. We'll not be able to send our ore to the mill on schedule—the whole thing is thrown off, don't you see?"

"So, you'll buy another horse."

"Too right. But the Southern Star operates on a very narrow edge. Expenses have eaten up last week's income. Perhaps we can sell something. But until we get ore out and money in, you see, we'll have to forego employing you. Or even paying Flannery, for that matter."

Uncle Liam scowled at the thought. "Why the fair cow had to up and die now—of all the rotten timing. Last week would have been less cruel, or next. But this week, when we're low—"

Colin saw where his duty lay, and he hated to do it. With his mare below ground for a week he'd have to walk anywhere he wanted to go. Around town wouldn't be too bad, but what if Diz or Lily got jobs down in Boulder or somewhere? He'd be walking for miles! Stone the crows!

Ah, well. Blood is thicker than water. And they really needed the help. "If all you want her for is a week or so, there's your below-ground horse." Colin nodded toward his bay mare.

"Oh, my. No, we couldn't." Uncle Aidan wagged his head, and his jowls jiggled.

"Why not?" Uncle Liam's voice seemed tuned to a perpetual whine.

"True, it's only for a week or so. A fortnight at most. Still, Liam, it's a serious imposition, particularly for a flash young fellow like this who's wanting to get out and about on a Saturday night." Uncle Aidan tossed Colin an exaggerated wink.

Colin grinned. "I'm loaning you my horse; you loan me your above-ground horse if I need it."

"Ah. Well. That would work, wouldn't it? Perhaps. Perhaps." Uncle Aidan wrapped his arm once more around Colin's shoulders. "Lad, we're glad you've honored us by coming."

They walked together down to the house, an extremely modest little bungalow with a tin roof. Whitewash flaked in great patches from the bricks. "Coolgardie brick," Uncle Liam explained. "Rotten stuff. You try to put a hole in it, it disintegrates. Won't hold paint."

Uncle Aidan seemed to claim one side of the cottage and Uncle Liam the other. Colin refrained from asking why they avoided trespassing on each other's holding; it was, after all, such a small house. They set Colin up with a pallet in the back room, a pantry attached to the kitchen. It would serve well enough; he didn't plan to be home much anyway, and it was free.

After a light lunch of porridge, they returned to the mine.

Whatever Colin expected a mine to be—close, dark and stuffy—this was worse. Miles worse. Uncle Aidan worked the reel as Uncle Liam and Colin descended from sun to gloom to blackness. Liam led Colin from level to level, through one drift then another, and they all looked the same—rough and gritchy pitch dark walls that closed in tight all around. Colin knew he could never work down here; not only would he be lost instantly in this blinding maze, he'd go daft from the grasping closeness.

He followed Uncle Liam down still another level, and thought about the endless windswept sea. Much as he disliked his former job opening shell, nothing could surpass the working conditions on that lovely open deck. Where was Captain Foulard now? he wondered. Had he launched his brand new lugger yet?

Uncle Liam stopped in front of a rope strung loosely across the tunnel. "The Star ends here, and the Hard Yakka goes on down the drift. Don't know who owns it now; went into receivership. They say you can walk the two miles from Boulder to the top end of Kal without once coming to the surface. So many of the claims interconnect like this."

"It all looks alike to me," Colin said. "How do you know whose property you're on?"

"Mostly common sense, a good compass and a measuring tape." Uncle Liam turned his back on the rope and the Hard Yakka and started up the drift the way they had come. When he turned right into a side tunnel Colin felt completely lost and disoriented. They came upon a little wood-and-iron rock sled. "Here's where we're working at the moment." Uncle Liam hefted a pickaxe and swung it into the chunky, eroding wall ahead.

Colin stepped up for a closer look. In the light of Uncle Liam's headlamp a few specks glinted in the rock. "That's gold? That's what we're looking for?"

Gold! He was staring at his first gold. Somehow he had imagined the gold in mines to simply lie about ready to be picked up, or the bright nuggets were chipped easily from the walls. He had forgotten that ore is solid rock, and that you must break it up to shape a tunnel and retrieve the gold peppered through it.

"About ready to blast again, soon as we can afford the gelignite. Here, you can lend a hand. Load the stone boat."

Colin in those first hours became a true gold miner, loading the wooden sled with chunks of rock. Opening shell never looked better.

They quit only when Uncle Liam ran out of protrusions to strike with his pick axe. The wall, now flat and featureless, no longer provided an easy target for breaking chunks away. They left the stone boat where it stood and climbed through the steep and constant blackness of a side drift. Suddenly they popped out into a wider tunnel. Uncle Liam turned right and followed the new channel to a wider passage. The enlargement, ceiling-less, penetrated upward, upward, Colin wondered how far. Then Uncle Liam tugged at a rope near the wall.

Clanking and scratching far above told Colin they had returned to the main shaft. Here came the open cage. They stepped in and tugged the rope. The cage jerked roughly and they were on their way up. Ragged, rocky walls brushed past close on all sides, sometimes nudging the cage, causing it to lurch. Colin wished it had some sort of enclosing protection. Uncle Liam blew out his light and they continued the ascent in utter darkness.

Minutes later, a white blip overhead widened until it became the bright, open light of the surface. They finally reached it, and Colin rushed gratefully into open air.

He was surprised to see the sun so low. They must have been hours in that timeless gloom. Uncle Aidan was tying a harness made of rope around Colin's bay mare.

His heart thumped. When he'd volunteered his horse for the below-ground work, he had not yet been below ground. He couldn't have realized how penetratingly black it was down there *all* the time. Nor was he fully ready to see the horse go down.

Uncle Aidan smiled toward him. "Ah, there he is. What's her name, lad?"

Colin shrugged. "She really belongs to the dog. We'll call her Max's Lady."

"Of course." Uncle Aidan looked at him oddly. "Liam, I'll take care of her below. You get her headed down right and Colin here can handle the reel." Uncle Aidan ambled over to the cage and let himself down the shaft.

Max. Come to think of it, Colin hadn't seen Max since they arrived in town. Had the brindled dog given up on his unrequited love?

Then Dizzy was riding toward him in the fading light. He swung down, waving with a grin. He stepped in beside Colin and watched the cage rope descending, and Uncle Liam making the last knots in the mare's makeshift harness. His grin faded.

Dizzy shook his head. "Col, you definitely don' wanna do this."

"Their below-ground horse died today, Diz. It's just for a week or so until they can buy another one."

"No, Col. You don' realize. Once that mare goes down, she ain' never gonna come back up."

"Sure she is." But a seed of doubt buried itself in Colin's thoughts. Uncle Aidan was blood, after all, his father's brother. Papa would never deceive or take advantage. Neither would Uncle Aidan. Would he?

Diz watched grimly, despairingly, as Uncle Liam attached the heavy reel rope to the ungainly harness. Then he tied the lead line from the mare's halter to the rope above her head. The bell clanked. Uncle Liam nodded to Colin. "Run her clockwise."

Colin walked out to the reel and urged the gray horse into lethargic action. The great reel wound slowly.

The bay mare's eyes grew wide. They rolled until the whites showed as her front end rose. She pawed the air and shook her head. And now her hind legs left the ground. She pulled them up close to her belly. Suddenly she thrashed mightily, her head flaying from side to side. She swayed back and forth, hung vertically above the open shaft.

The lead line dragged at the mare's head until her nose pointed straight up. She squealed, terrified, but the sound was choked off by the stretch in her neck.

"Uncle Liam, she's going to kill herself!"

"S'all right, lad. No worries. Let 'er down."

Dizzy gasped and Uncle Liam yelled as a gray mass hurtled across the open dirt between reel and shaft. Max took a lunge for Uncle Liam, slamming into him like a cannonball. The man staggered back and fell against a roof support. Dizzy was there in a flash, his long-barreled pistol in hand. He kicked Max two feet across the dry dirt and fired his gun in the air. The dog dropped back snarling. Dizzy fired again, and the dog ran off.

"Kill that thing! Kill it!" Uncle Liam was shrieking.

With casual composure, Dizzy helped the man to his feet. "You realize how far a stray bullet travels? Don' dare fire into town. Too dangerous. Might hit somebody, eh?"

"That was your dog!"

"Naw, tha's *her* dog." Dizzy tipped his head toward the struggling mare. "That was Max."

Uncle Liam stared at him, then Colin, then the mare. Max had ripped Liam's white shirt sleeve, and the blood on it said he'd ripped his arm, too. "Get her down below," he snarled.

Colin reversed the gray horse and sent it on its endless circle. Inch by inch the mare's backside disappeared down the shaft. Colin's heart ached. He didn't want this. What if Dizzy was right and she was doomed to darkness forever? What if she destroyed herself on the way down? She thrashed about some more; what if in her struggle she broke her neck? Colin thought about the hundreds of hours he'd spent on her back, about her happy-go-lucky disposition she'd developed on the trail. As she continued her descent below ground level, he ran over to the deck.

Only the whites of her eyes showed in the darkness, then faded. He could hear rocks falling, jarred loose as she flung herself against the sides of the shaft. Now and then a hoof would strike a timber. The big twit was absolutely terrified, and it was Colin's fault; he'd agreed to all this.

What seemed a long time later, the heavy rope went slack. The bell clanked. Colin stopped the gray horse. For better or worse, the deed was done.

Dizzy still stood in the same place, wagging his head. "Hope you're right, Col."

"Me too. How's Lily doing?"

"Got a job already. Working in a factory that makes cordial. Used to be eight cordial factories in town, they say; now there's only two. But it's still the good stuff, I guess. Famous, they say."

"And you—did you find a job?"

"Plenty of miners around. They don' need no miners." Dizzy grinned with twinkling eyes. "What you think, you see the old Diz in an apron?"

"An apron!?"

"Sí! The Perseverance need a cook, and I tell 'em, ain' no better cook than me. I made lunch to prove it and got the job."

"If you're such a dinkum cook, how come I had to do all the cooking on the track?"

"Me, I'm there already. You needed the practice yet. 'Sides, look how good a cook you are now, after I taught you everything I know!"

Colin punched Dizzy's arm. All his life he'd heard about the bond of mateship in the outback. He had it now, right here. Dizzy accepted him exactly as he was, and old Diz, the only known Texan in Australia, came as near to perfect as a friend could come.

A thought suddenly robbed him of his pleasure. He sobered. "I suppose you'll be saving up to head home one of these days."

"Maybe." Diz shrugged. "Who knows? Say, Saturday night, eh? Maybe you come around the Exchange, we eat supper together."

"Sounds good. See you there, Cookie."

Dizzy chuckled. "You know what they call cooks in the outback, eh? Baitlayers. Tha's me! Later, Col." And he walked off to his new job, leaving Colin to this one—a genuine Kalgoorlie miner.

CHAPTER NINE

UNDESERVING WORM

Hannah gathered the little sheaf of envelopes out of the mailbox on her way in the door. She abandoned her book-bag in the hallway and went off seeking Mum. She would look first in the kitchen because that's where she most frequently found her.

Grace the cook sat at the kitchen table peeling potatoes while Mum hovered over the oven.

She glanced up and grinned brightly. "There she is! How did school go today?"

Hannah flopped down in the other chair at the table and tossed the mail down. "Not so good." She leafed absently through the envelopes. Business letters; nothing looked interesting or exciting.

"Oh? And what went crook on you?"

She might as well get it all told and over with. "The water pipes did it again, Mum; you know, like before? Flooded the halls and two of the rooms. We were all wading about to get from place to place. And they say I did it!"

Sam stiffened. "Is that right'?"

"No, Mum! Not this time. Nor the other time, either. I would not do something that would cause so much damage. You know that."

"No, I don't know that. But I'll accept your word for it. I suppose the abbess wants to see me in her office tomorrow?"

"No, Mum. I'm suspended."

Mum stared at her in disbelief. "Isn't that a bit drastic? What has convinced them so thoroughly that you're responsible?"

Hannah shrugged. Her eyes burned, and if she didn't get control of herself, she'd be blubbering in a moment. "When I pro—protested my innocence, the abbess said that if it's true that I didn't do this—and she thinks I did—that there are lots of other things I've done that I never got caught for, so the punishment is still due. Then I got lecture number three."

"What is lecture number three?"

"The abbess has three lectures she gives us girls who end up in her office. Number one is for the first time you show up, and she tells you about the folly of sin. The second is if your transgression is more severe; it's about the evils of a dissipated life. This one was about penance and purgatory. We all have them memorized."

"Too bad none of them have made an actual dent in your conscience."

"The abbess and I don't see sin in the same light, Mum. I think sin is swearing and lying and things like that. She thinks it's going down the up stairwell."

Mum was silent, and Hannah turned again to the mail. The last letter on the pile was from Kalgoorlie. "Look, Mum—a letter from Uncle Aidan! We haven't heard from him in a long time, have we? I mean, not even at Christmas!"

"That's true. I hope it doesn't mean bad news." Mum peeked once more into the oven, then swung it open fully and reached for the hot pads.

"Might I open it, Mum?"

"The pie or the letter?" Mum smiled, reaching into the oven.

Hannah grinned. "Both."

Mum carried the steaming pie to the table. "The pie waits for dinner. You may open the letter."

"Lillipilli pie! My favorite! Ta, Mum!" Hannah ripped into the letter.

What scratchy, tortured writing! Hannah would receive a failing mark were she to write a letter like this for class. Obviously, Uncle Aidan considered punctuation an option rather than a necessity. Was she reading this right? "Mum, look!"

Mum sat down at the table. Hannah handed her the letter and peered over her shoulder.

There was a scowl on her face as she read, "Dear Cole you'll be pleased to know your son is safe here with us however we have fallen on hard times recently with the drop in gold prices and cannot afford an extra mouth for very long we would appreciate a donation from you toward the support of your son he's welcome of course good to see him sincerely Aidan." It was a breathless reading without the punctuation.

Hannah looked into her mother's smokey gray-green eyes and saw there a mix of hope and pain. "He's safe. Your prayers are still working, right, Mum?"

Samantha gave her daughter a one-armed hug and dropped the letter on the table. "Too right. Your suspension and now this. Your father is going to be livid."

Hannah flopped back into her chair. "Mum? Colin must be ill or hurt. If he weren't, he'd work for his keep, surely; Uncle Aidan wouldn't have to go begging."

"I don't know. I just don't know." The glint of hope in her eyes had fled and Mum suddenly looked very weary.

Hannah studied the pie without really seeing it. She was sure much of Mum's pain was derived from Hannah herself. Even when she was innocent, she caused Mum pain, and Papa, too. Take the mess at school, for example. If she had actually caused the pipe problem, would she have been the one to report it? Of course not! Apparently, her mistake was to tell the nearest sister the moment she discovered it—or discovering the leak at all.

And now, Papa would surely make a big scene of it. He'd go storming to the school and cause a fuss. At home he'd rant and rave again about Colin's sneaky streak and stubbornness. That hurt worst of all, for Hannah knew the torture in her brother's heart, and that it had driven him from home. And now that same pain of alienation was torturing her.

Colin ill? That probability stabbed at her too.

She wandered back to the hallway and hefted her bookbag. She climbed the stairs to her room. By the time she reached the landing at the top she knew what she would do.

But how to do it?

Dinner that night began predictably unpleasant and slid downhill from there. Papa fumed. Mum ate in grim silence. Mary Aileen pushed her food around on her plate as if she were responsible for all the family's ills. From time to time she'd glance at Papa with a hangdog look of fear and worry. And Edan? Like always, he simply stepped inside himself and closed the door. He sat, he ate, he excused himself, he left. No comment, no spark of life. Papa said he was dull. Hannah knew better. Edan soared, she was quite certain, but never where anyone could see it.

She finished her meal. The questions with which she had come to this table had resolved themselves into answers. The plan spread before her mind's eye, flawless.

She folded her napkin. "May I be excused?"

Mum nodded. Mary Aileen glanced at Hannah's plate enviously. Mary Aileen was condemned to sit there until she finished her food.

"Papa, there's a—an, uh—a—an *alternative.* That's it. The abbess says I may serve a detention, if you prefer. That means I must stay three hours past school each day and not go out at noon or recess, and I'll receive extra work to do. Papa, please might I serve detention a few days and *then*—"

"No!"

"And *then* you could apply to the abbess. 'Twill give you a bit of time to cool off, and her as well. Her even more; the floor will be dried out by then. Please, Papa? Your meeting with her will go so much more amicably, don't you see? And I'll not miss any school."

She hoped she had used the word *amicably* correctly.

Apparently she had. He studied her and she held his eye.

"No child of mine will take punishment she doesn't deserve."

Hannah shrugged. "Mary's child Jesus did."

Mum hid a smile behind her napkin. Mary Aileen watched intently, with great, liquid eyes.

"I'll discuss it with your mother." When Papa said that, it equaled a delayed yes! She'd done it!

She hurried around the table, bumping Mary Aileen's chair, and threw her arms about Papa's neck. "Thank you, Papa!" She ran to the stairs.

The first part of her plan had concluded splendidly. Now for the second. She hurried to her room and closed her door behind her. She dumped out her books and stacked them in the back of her clothes press. She dug out the papers, and the notes from her teachers that Mum never saw, the pens and pencil stubs, the dry, rounded erasers, and the compass and protractor she had not yet used this year.

In her bookbag she carefully packed her striped blue dress and the brown cotton one, all the stockings she owned, what underwear she had, the blue and black hair ribbons, her other pair of shoes, and her hairbrush. What else did she need? Books were too heavy, toys too childish. She found no room for Emily, the little rag doll that had been her companion her whole life. She would pack her nightie in the morning. She closed up the bookbag and set it by her little writing table.

Late that evening, as soon as the house settled into its night quiet, Hannah slipped downstairs. Moonlight painted white rectangles on the kitchen floor as it streamed through the windows. The light glinted on two eyes. Smoke the cat hopped up onto the kitchen counter and curled into a watchful ball. In the darkness of the night, the little tortoise-shell cat was always watching.

Hannah climbed up to Mum's sugar bowl and robbed it of all its coins. Only Smoke knew. In the parlor she opened up the secret compartment in the secretary and took the money Papa kept there for emergencies when the banks were closed.

The next morning Hannah put on her uniform, kissed Mum and Papa goodbye, and hurried out of the house with her bookbag. She hastened past the church, behind the school, down the busy streets to the railway station.

The price of her ticket took all but two shillings. Very well, she would go without food. Undaunted she sat on the cold iron bench beside the equally cold iron posting box to wait. Rain began, misty and soft at first, then hard and pounding.

She suffered less than an hour's wait for the train, and suffering it was. Did anyone ever sin as Hannah had just sinned? Because of the high incidence of strikes and riots downtown, especially on the waterfront, Hannah was forbidden to walk alone any farther than the school. Here she sat, blocks and blocks beyond where she was allowed to be.

But that was the least of her transgressions. The detention option was a lie, a device to keep Papa away from the school and give Hannah a few extra hours for her escape. She remained, today as yesterday, *persona non grata* to the abbess. She'd lied about the abbess, a woman ordained for God's work. She'd lied to her own family and Papa in particular, dear Papa who loved her so. What an undeserving worm she was! No wonder God left her with two shillings for a week's food! She didn't merit that much.

By the time Samantha glanced at the hall clock, wondering when her errant daughter might return, Hannah had crossed the border from New South Wales into Victoria, the first leg of her long, long journey to Kalgoorlie.

CHAPTER TEN

PERFIDY

On a whim, Colin turned aside from Lionel Street into MacDonald Street and followed it the few blocks to the racecourse. He slipped through the gate and walked out to the rail. Long gray shadows stretched out across churned dirt. A waning sun turned the red-ochre track to fire. Colin wandered not up into the grandstand but out to the horse barns in back. Here was his turf, his familiar ground. Silence. No, not quite silence—the flies buzzed, the constant flies. The track sat vacant, between race days now, the race days themselves much farther apart now that Kalgoorlie no longer boomed. Colin thought about his adventures with Papa at Sydney's racecourse, among its venerable barns. There is a grand excitement among the barns, the owners and trainers, that patrons and bettors will never know. Good times, those.

He left the peaceful, empty racing grounds and continued up into Hannan Street.

Half a block this side of the Exchange he saw a familiar form sitting on a bench beneath a streetlight. He crossed the street to say hello.

Lily smiled at him. "Good to see you."

He plopped down on the bench beside her. "Good to see you. What are you doing out here?"

"Waiting for Dizzy. I'll let him walk me home when he

gets out of the Exchange over there." She nodded toward the pub across the street.

"Why not come along in? I'm going there right now to have supper with him."

"No." She shook her head. "It's not—" She took a deep breath and started over. "This last week has been brand new for me, Colin. I have a good job, and a nice room with a nice old lady in a comfortable little bungalow over on Dugan Street. All nice and comfortable, Colin, you see? That's new for me. And I like it."

"I see. And nice girls don't go into the pubs?" He smiled. "You're not the same girl who stole that side of wallaby a couple of months ago."

"She's a stranger." The huge eyes turned to him full force. "You and Dizzy, you changed me. Helped me change, I mean. You were gentlemen. And you treated me like a real person. Dizzy says he won't do things for me I ought to be doing for myself, and I'm starting to see how wise that is of him." She brightened. "The landlady and Dizzy are both helping me learn to read and write better."

"I'm really glad for you, Lily. I'm glad the 'stranger' is gone."

"Dizzy says you sent your mare down below in the mine. He's quite worried about that. Is she still there? I guess so; here you are, on foot."

"Just for another week. We took ore to the mill today, so my uncles will have the money for a new horse this week. And the gray horse is so tired from hauling ore out that she needed a rest. Otherwise I would have ridden her up here."

"Do you like mining?"

Colin shrugged. "Now that I've been at it a week it's a little better. It's a lot of hard work, but I don't mind that. They don't feed the horses enough, though, so I bought some extra feed with my own money. And the first thing we did when my mare went below was drag the dead horse off to an abandoned shaft. They just pushed it in. I didn't like that much."

"Mmm." She wrapped herself in her own thoughts, and changed the subject. "Colin? You grew up in the city among polite society. When is it proper for a nice girl to get married?"

"You mean, what age, or what time of year?"

"Age. Both, I guess."

"Well, let's see. It's all changed now. You see, up until the war, girls were formally introduced into society, and then they were courted a year or two before they got married. But after the war, those formalities were set aside. Now girls get married any time, and sometimes they don't even get that formal introduction into society. Mum says it all started when women's hemlines were raised almost to their knees. That's when it all changed."

"You mean my dress isn't proper?"

Colin studied what she was wearing for the first time. It was not exactly a flapper dress, and it looked very pretty on her. It was made of a silky-looking blue fabric, and draped from her shoulders in graceful folds. The waistband came not at her waist but at her hips, like every other girl's dress. The hem just barely covered her knees.

"Your dress looks very much the same style as my mother and sister would wear, so I'd say it's perfectly proper."

"And you're saying a nice girl can marry when she wants?"

"Pretty much so."

"Are there any rules for it?"

"Rules? For getting married? I don't know. I've never thought much about getting married. I guess one sure rule is that if you're a woman you cry at the wedding—unless of course you're the bride. And don't sneeze in the punch bowl!" He laughed lightly, but Lily was pensive again.

"Mmm."

"You sure you want to just sit out here alone, Lily?"

"Yes. Yes, this is fine."

"Well, uh, then I guess I'd better get going. Diz is prob-ably waiting for me in there." Colin stood up. "Uh, see you later. *Sure* you don't want to come?"

"No. I'm fine." And she smiled again. It was the second smile in five minutes that she offered voluntarily, a drastic change from the waif he'd met two months ago.

Colin waved to her and headed back across the street.

The Exchange Hotel pub rumbled tonight with the hubbub of scores of milling, sweating, jostling miners and shopkeepers. A few well-dressed girls circulated among them; still, Kalgoorlie hardly seemed the den of iniquity its reputation painted. Colin paused a few minutes at the doors, looking for Dizzy. There was no sign of the Perse-verance mine's new cook.

Wait! There he was, bellied up to the bar, laughing and talking with a man in a white suit. Colin threaded be-tween the busy tables and shouldered himself a place—a very narrow place—beside Dizzy at the bar.

"*Buenos dias, amigo.*" It was practically the only Span-ish Colin knew.

"Eh! *Aquí está mi compadre! Qué tal?*" Dizzy stepped back a few inches. "Mr. Newport, my frien' and fellow trav-eler Colin Sloan, from Sydney. Col, Mr. Newport is assis-tant manager at the Perseverance."

Colin reached past Dizzy to shake his hand. "How do you do, Mr. Newport." The man looked every bit a manager of sorts, with a splendid handlebar mustache that divided his long, lean face. He stood half a foot taller than Dizzy. "Mr. Sloan. Related to the mine owners?"

"Nephew, sir."

"That explains a lot." The man nodded curiously and motioned to the barman. A moment later a pint appeared at Colin's elbow.

Colin felt his cheeks flush. "Uh, I'm sorry, sir. I deeply

appreciate your generosity and friendship, but, uh, I don't drink, sir."

Someone punched Colin in the right side. He grunted and slammed against Dizzy on his left. "That's rude, lad," bellowed a familiar voice. "He shouts you a drink, you drink."

Flannery, the big Irishman, hovered at Colin's right.

Dizzy looked positively amused. "Lemme know if you need help on this one, Col."

What was going on here? Colin looked wildly at Dizzy, then at Mr. Newport, who appeared equally amused, and at the hulking Irishman. Mr. Flannery looked downright hostile. Colin found himself stuttering. "Uh, er, welcome, sir. Join us."

"Join us, the lad says! Like ye joined the Star, and now y're looking to move up in the world, aye? Mayhap join the Perseverance next. Ye need a lesson or two in respect, lad, and a bonzer lesson in the purpose for union rules regarding seniority."

This was all going over Colin's head. Flannery's mates were calling to him to relax, but the admonitions only infuriated the man further. Without warning he drew back a big fist and swung at Colin. *A fight?* The last fight Colin could remember being a part of was a childish match at the age of six with his sister Mary Aileen over a paintbox. That ended in a draw. This fight would not end in a draw. With horror Colin perceived that this man could beat him to a bloody pulp.

With the whirl of thoughts and memories, in the same moment Colin ducked away from the blow. The Irishman's fist caught him a glancing thump on the shoulder and sent him sprawling. Now the huge foot, shod in a heavy brogan, was pulling back to kick him and he was twisted at such an angle as to make him unable to avoid it. Colin's heart screamed, *Help me!* even as his head frantically sought a way out.

A wiry leg whipped out lightning-fast and hooked Flannery's ankle. The Irishman flipped onto a table of spectators, wearing a look of utter amazement.

His two chums came boiling up out of their chairs to take over. Dizzy had joined the fracas, so apparently it was in order for Flannery's mates to offer assistance. Colin had no idea how the rules of bar brawls worked, but Dizzy needed help. Colin scrambled up from the floor, laced his fingers together and used the double fist to wallop the nearest brawler on the back of the neck. The fellow's knees buckled, and he dropped to the floor.

Dizzy had sunk to a squat on the floor, but apparently had not been struck. As he rose suddenly he had his arms wrapped around the third fellow's legs. He kept rising steadily and with a mighty heave sent the fellow straight up and over the bar head-first. As the fellow plunged downward on the other side, his boots caught the shelves of bottles and smashed them into the huge mirror. Shattered glass was everywhere.

Flannery was back up and coming toward them; Dizzy flattened him again with a body blow and a solid right. The Irish fell back against the same table of onlookers and collapsed to a sprawling pile on the floor. He put the back of his hand to his nose, and blood spurted all over his white shirt.

Dizzy raised an arm in the air. "Is over!" Then he placed a hand on the small of his back, where everyone knew he kept his gun. He didn't have to produce it. Then he pointed directly at Flannery. "Nex' time, you think better'n to bung on a blue with a Tejano, ch? Ain' nobody better with a gun. We're the best-shooting, fastest riding, smartest drovers there ever was, 'cause we got the fastest, smartest cattle in the world. Half-devil, them Texas longhorns. So don' you go risking your life messing with no Texan, eh? Goes for your mates, too."

Colin found himself coiled tense as a spring. He stood

up to his full height, and forced his fists to unclench. "Thanks, amigo."

"Was nothing, compadre." Dizzy turned to Mr. Newport. "You look like a cat with canary breath, eh? You know wha's going on, no?"

Mr. Newport smirked. "Flannery was by to see me today, asking for a job. Seems the Sloans sacked him. Replaced him with young Colin here. I didn't know your last name, lad, but it's all clear now."

Everything was clearer now to more than just Mr. Newport. Colin eyed Flannery for a moment, wondering about the best approach. The Irishman remained where he'd fallen, dripping blood and looking bewildered.

Colin took a deep breath and a big, big chance. He stepped toward Flannery and extended his hand. "I had no idea when they said they had room for me that they were letting you go, sir. I'm sorry."

Rolling heavily to his feet, Flannery looked at Colin, and beyond his shoulder to Dizzy, "I don't believe ye," and walked away.

Colin turned to Dizzy with a questioning look.

The Tejano shrugged. "You tried, eh?"

"I tried."

———

After an enjoyable dinner with Dizzy that night, Colin listened to all his stories about the picky diners at the Perseverance and about the way Lily was brightening into an interesting young lady. He did not relate his own conversation with her; it seemed to be a confidence not to be betrayed, not even to Diz.

Returning home very late, Colin tossed on his cot awhile and then dropped off to a fitful sleep. He was rousted out of bed at the usual early hour, to the realization that the work week had begun in earnest.

Uncle Aidan stayed home to pore over accounts, while Uncle Liam walked uptown to tend to business. Colin, now a reasonable hand at mining, headed for the Star alone. He gave the gray mare an extra quart of oats and hitched her up, then greased the pulleys, a regular first-of-the-week chore. Putting the bay mare's feed in the cage, he reached for the knotted rope to let himself down the shaft, and froze in the action.

In the shadow of the tool shed crouched Max the dog. The snapping black eyes seemed to survey Colin's every move. Was there sadness in them, or was Colin reading too much into the surly dog's face?

"Max, I despise you and you despise me, but I know your mate's underground and you miss her. Come on. Promise you won't chew me apart on the way down, and I'll take you with me."

The dog's head lifted slightly.

"Come on, Max. This is your only chance. If Uncle Liam learns I let you down, he'll sack me. Do you want to go or not?"

The dog stood up. Colin called to him again, jiggled the cage and let it drop a few inches. The dog moved forward, cringed, moved a few feet further and slunk to the ground.

This was silly, almost comical. Why did Colin bother? The dog would never trust him enough to get into the cage. If he did, he'd probably leap out again the moment it started to descend—maybe take Colin's arm with him. Dizzy had the dog pegged right; he'd bite at any opportunity.

Colin started to move the cage again. The dog crept over to the decking. Colin stopped the descent. "Last chance, Max. Now or never."

The dog whined, its tail flat on the ground. Slowly, hesitantly, it crawled out onto the cage at Colin's feet.

Colin turned on his headlamp and started down, from gloom to blackness. He glanced down at Max. The dog lay bellied out on the cage floor, as flat could be.

It took exactly two minutes and ten seconds to travel from the bright sunlight to nether darkness; Colin had it timed. And for those two minutes, Max moved not a muscle. Not even a whimper escaped him; Colin admired that. When the cage reached within six feet of the bottom Max leaped out. He barked, the first real bark Colin had ever heard from the dog, and the noise of it reverberated down the tunnels.

"Max, you'll get us both in trouble! Keep quiet!"

Max's Lady whinnied exuberantly from her side-drift stall in the distance. Was she pleased to see Colin, the oats, or the dog? It was hard to say. She squirreled around joyously as all three arrived. Colin admired the mates' reunion, dropped the hay and oats in her manger, and walked off down the tunnels to work. Max was on his own now.

Just how would he get his horse out of this hole? He thought about the terrible scuffs and scrapes she suffered coming down, abrasions not yet healed. Uncle Aidan assured him it would work out fine, yet he'd also assured him they would purchase a horse promptly, and he would be paid his salary. So far, neither had happened. Ah, well. Give it another week.

The week passed, bathed in honest sweat. A lot of sweat.

On Saturday morning, Colin hauled four and a half wagon loads of ore to the mill—five trips. "I do say someone's working hard. Twice your usual run," commented the mill clerk.

By eleven a.m. Colin was unharnessing the gray mare after her morning toil. The rest of the day would be his own. And he'd be paid today. He might wander up to the Perseverance and help Dizzy fry sausages. Perhaps he could travel down to Kambalda and Lake Lefroy. He'd heard about the ghost town and the vast salt pan beside it. Now was his chance to see it.

He forked hay into the gray mare's manger and reached for the curry brush. It wasn't there. Now, where—

Colin laughed. "Diz, if you get any sneakier, you'll be giving tiptoe lessons to mice. How long have you been here?"

"Jus' a minute." Dizzy grinned. With the purloined brush he began rubbing the gray mare down, quickly, expertly. The Texan was a natural horseman. His face turned serious. "Col, how much you making here?"

"Two quid and change. Why?"

"Flannery was pulling seven; didya know that?"

"No." The ramifications of the fact flooded Colin's thoughts. "Of course I'm not an experienced miner like Flannery. You sure about that?"

"Sí, am sure. How much 'sperience it take to break your back and sweat?"

"I agree what I'm doing isn't very challenging. But still—" Colin licked his lips. "They're family, Diz."

"They taking advantage of you, blood or no blood. Tha's all I see, and it makes me mad. Got your horse back yet?"

"This next week."

"Mr. Newport, he don' think they can get her back up outta there. 'Specially, he says, 'cause their shaft's too small. He says there's union regulations, and the Sloan mine ain' meeting 'em, but nobody sends inspectors around to the little places no more."

"It's not a very profitable operation. Not like I expected it to be."

"Tha's for sure." Dizzy ran the metal comb through the mare's tail. He grinned suddenly. "Col, maybe if I'm lucky I be a mine owner one day."

"I thought you were going home to Texas."

Dizzy stopped and leaned thoughtfully against the horse's rump. "Been thinking 'bout that, Col. Texas is a good place. Best place in the world, eh? But this place ain' so bad. I got steady work here, and a chance to get ahead if I can just buy into that claim. Make a good life for myself. Is what I come to Australia for, a fair go, no?" Off-handedly, he added, "And Lily's here."

Colin stared in disbelief. "Diz, you're in love!"

"Maybe." The weather-worn Tejano grinned like a bashful schoolboy. "Been thinking 'bout that, too. Can't do no better'n her. Gonna let it go awhile. If we still think is good idea, maybe I marry her, and—well, just been thinking about it, is all."

"That's great! God bless you both." Colin blurted, then froze. Why did he say that? He seriously doubted God existed, let alone blessed men in their everyday business.

If Dizzy noticed anything he didn't mention it. He lurched erect and hung up the brush and curry. "I was hoping you were making what Flannery made; maybe put the bite on you for a loan."

"To buy a gold mine?"

"A small claim. Feller's wife is sick. He's moving to Perth. First one puts the money in his hand gets the dig, so I gotta do it fast. I saved eighteen pounds ten so far."

"In two weeks? That's a lot of money!"

"Ain' hard, you stay outta the pubs. But it's 'bout as much as I can save, week to week. Will take me three months at this rate. That might be too late, eh?"

"Let's walk down to my place. See if I can rustle some change from under a pillow or something." Colin's heart sang. It soared. He still had over a hundred and thirty of his two hundred pounds from Captain Foulard. He didn't need the money just now. He could lend Dizzy a hundred, knowing he'd get it back in time. He could help his mate build a new and promising life, at no real cost to himself. He would not have thought the simple act of helping a friend could generate such joy.

Dizzy eyed him suspiciously as he fell in beside. "Col, you got a look about you. How much change you 'specting under your pillow?"

"Will a hundred pounds do it?"

"*Ai, Chihuahua!*"

"What does eye chee-wah-wah mean?"

"It mean I never think you got that much."

"Courtesy of Captain Foulard. I've been wanting to put it safely in a bank, but I've been down in that mine every minute of banking hours. It's still in my room."

"You sure you wanna do this? Tha's a lotta money. Besides, you keep saying that dun is mine, but I keep thinking I ought to pay you for it, eh?"

"A gift is a gift, Diz."

"But not the money. Tha's a loan, or I don' do it."

"It's a loan."

All the way to the bungalow, Dizzy waxed enthusiastic about the mining claim. He described every inch of it and Colin began to realize how miserly and poor was the Sloan mine. Dizzy spoke of electric lights in the passages, and a generator and donkey engine. He told how many tram tracks ran below. Were the Sloans to move ore with a tram on tracks instead of that cheap stone boat, they wouldn't need a horse below. A man can push a tram car about with one hand. Maybe Colin could get a better job working for Dizzy.

Colin led the way through the small, rusty iron gate and into the house. He stepped from the cheerful winter sun to cool gloom. "Uncle Aidan? Uncle Liam?"

No response.

"Rats!" Colin headed for his little room. "I was hoping they'd be home so they could pay me." He paused. "What am I supposed to say when I invite you in?"

"*Mi casa es su casa*. But it ain' your casa, so don' worry 'bout it, eh?" Dizzy followed him through his door, laughing.

"Looks like I better do laundry today, instead of traveling around to the ghost towns." Colin dropped to his knees in the corner. "It's right here, under my spare shirt in this box."

In fact, until he got to an actual bank, Colin did all his banking in the bottom of this box. He brushed the shillings and pence aside. Here was the one-pound note all wadded up, leftover from that strange night at the Exchange last week. The envelope with the—

The envelope with all his money, his minor fortune from his life as a pearler. . . .

The envelope was gone.

CHAPTER ELEVEN

ESCAPE

Colin sat still in a hard wooden chair, trying to conceal his nervousness. Across the desk from him, constable Nigel Bowden filled out yet another form.

The constable raised his eyes to glare at Colin. "You are certain the money is missing? You searched the room thoroughly?"

"It's not that big a place, sir. Yes, sir. The small change was still there. The envelope with the larger amount of money was missing."

"Have you any notion who took it?"

"No sir. We don't lock the house, but nobody comes by there."

"No suspects? How about that little Filipino with the revolver?"

"Dizzy. He's not Filipino, and he's not capable of that. No."

"What proof can you give that the sum exists?"

"What?"

"How do I know you didn't fabricate this claim, perhaps to accuse your uncles and milk more money out of them? I happen to know you receive less pay than your predecessor."

"I wouldn't do that, sir! No, sir. It's exactly the way you have it on that complaint."

"But you can't prove the money existed, was actually in your possession?"

"I—" Colin sighed. Not even Dizzy had known about it. "No. I have no witnesses."

Constable Bowden leaned back in his chair. "When a complaint is made I am required by law to file it. I shall do so. But in this case, until and unless you can provide a more substantial claim, I am forced to conclude that the complaint may well be spurious. Do you understand what I'm saying?"

"It means you're not going to do anything about it."

He slipped the form into a folder. "I suggest you look first to that dark little foreigner you associate with."

"Thanks for the help." Colin rose from his chair and turned to walk out into the cold, hard afternoon. What now?

Dizzy, casually conformed to a porch post, launched himself to vertical and fell in beside his friend. "You don' look like the law was kind to you, amigo."

"You're the person they tell me I should suspect first. You're dark and foreign."

"Guess I'm glad I ain' Chinese, then. I'd be in jail, eh?" He started off down the street a step ahead of Colin.

Colin followed blindly. He didn't care where he was going. "Who do you think, Diz—?"

"You don' wanna know who I think."

"Diz, they wouldn't do that. They wouldn't rob their own nephew."

"And why you think not?"

"They're Sloans. Like Papa. He's as trustworthy as a man can be, and they're—well, they're Sloans. That's all."

"Who else gonna muck around the house all day while you work underground? Who would go through your stuff in that back room? If some stranger come by, he look for the silver and gold in all the places riches be kept. Not where some two-quid miner sleeps. And wouldn' he take *all* the valuables, not just yours?"

"Unless he was just after cash. If you steal goods you have to sell them. That's not so easy in a town like this, without being detected. And my uncles don't have any cash, let alone any valuables."

"Maybe." Dizzy sounded totally unconvinced.

Colin felt just as unconvinced, but these men *were* his family. He was almost sure they wouldn't do such a thing. And because they were family, he would defend them before the world. That's what family was all about.

A light dawned in Colin's muddled brain. "What about Flannery? He knows the house; when we'd be below at the mine, my uncles' ins and outs. And he's sure not all that fond of me!"

"Eh, maybe." Dizzy walked on in silence thinking. "Y'know Col, I didn' say thank you yet for helping me. You're a dinkum mate. I 'preciate it."

"I didn't help you."

"You wanted to. That means a lot to me. A whole lot. Whether you actually do or not, sometimes tha's chance. You defended me; tha's real friendship and I, uh. . . . " He lowered his head. "You know what I mean?"

"Yair, I know. If you don't get this mine, if you can't make the offer in time, are you still gunner marry Lily?"

"That ain' settled yet. First, I hafta be making good 'nuf money to raise kids. A big 'sponsibility, Col—kids. Then we see."

Somehow they drifted toward the rooming house where Lily lived. They spent the rest of the afternoon with her, sitting in the back yard drinking cider she'd made from berries, and reminiscing about the old times and the journey south. Colin was beginning to miss his hulking bay mare terribly.

The three of them ate supper at a little cafe where it was proper for young ladies to be seen. Colin was amused watching the lovebirds. Who could have dreamed of such a match. It made Colin think about who his love would be, and when would she come into his life?

The two left Lily at her house well after dark and then stopped by the Exchange for a drink to mourn Colin's loss. Dizzy called for a pint of bitters and shouted for Colin's straight soda. A curious reversal, this; Dizzy with money and Colin with none. And yet their friendship had not suffered the least bit of change. Colin thought of all his fair-weather friends in Sydney who measured friendship in pounds sterling, who were with you or shunned you according to your present financial situation.

He pondered, too, the compelling lure of the pub that brought so many men out every night. Colin leaned both elbows on the bar and tried to figure it out. It couldn't be the atmosphere, so full of smoke you could slice it. Nor the alcohol, for few men quaffed more than one. Couldn't be the darts, not that many actually played. It might be the good food, but then not many actually took their meals here.

One of the girls pushed her way between them. She nodded to Diz, to Colin. "Good evening, gentlemen." Her smile, carefully calculated to dazzle, did just that. "Which of you would be willing to buy a maid a drink?"

Dizzy shuffled his feet and mumbled in an accent much thicker than usual, "Eh, uh, don' speaka English. Mebbe Col here, eh? He talk good."

Was that the game? Colin mimicked Dizzy's fractured speech. "Sí, but he don' have no money, *comprende*?"

She looked from face to face. "All right, which of you two is bunging on the act? It's gotta be you!" She smiled at Colin. "You speak the king's English better than I do, right?"

"Eh, mebbe." Colin shrugged. He enjoyed this game immensely, but where would Dizzy take it? Colin had no expertise at all in this sort of banter.

She turned to Dizzy. "Say something to me in whatever language it is you speak."

Dizzy's crackling black eyes studied hers. He ran a finger down her cheek as his voice breathed in her ear, "*Eh,*

*señorita, corazón, tu tienes un ojo de vidrio. Y la pierna,
qué lástima; la pierna es de madera.*"

Whatever he said, it absolutely devastated her. She
stood, her mouth agape, her cheeks flushed.

"Is too bad I don' got no money. Sorry, señorita. Nex'
time mebbe, eh?"

The girl looked from face to face, but dwelt on Diz.
"Right-o, mates. Next time." She left for greener pastures,
still glancing back at Dizzy.

Colin moved in closer. "Crikey, Diz! What'd you say to
her?"

"Can' tell you, Col. Too dangerous."

"Don't toy with me, mate. What'd you say?"

"No, Col, couldn' do that to you. I mean, you don' give
no little baby no loaded gun, eh? Might get hisself hurt.
You just a kid yet, too young to handle the power."

"Break it down, Diz. What did you say?"

"Eh, well. . . . " Dizzy hesitated, and the twinkle in his
eye threatened to ignite the hardwood. "Careful how you
use it now, Col, lad. What I tell her, I said, 'Eh, sweetheart,
you got a glass eye and a wooden leg.' "

———

Rats. The cage was at the bottom of the mine. Colin
stood on the decking and studied the knotted rope a few
moments. With a sigh, he began hauling it up. Minutes
later the cage clanked and swayed to the surface. He
tossed in the horse feed and Max's ration, and stepped in
himself. He flicked on his headlamp and began the slow
descent into the blackness.

Max's Lady greeted her breakfast—and presumably
Colin—with a delighted whinny. The cage at the bottom
meant that either Uncle Liam or Uncle Aidan had already
descended. Colin wanted neither of them to know Max
was down here, so he tossed the bone and the dog food
carelessly into the back of the mare's stall, and began
scratching her ears.

Her scuffs and wounds still were not healing well. They needed sunlight to clear up, not this perpetual night. Colin smeared more petroleum jelly on them and took up his tools. Time to go to work. He descended to the lowest level, hating the closeness, the confinement, the darkness.

He rounded the final, most recent curve of the tunnel, then stopped cold and gasped. In the feeble light of his headlamp he saw Uncle Liam. Either by accident or design, the miner had hacked out a chair-shaped ledge in the drift. He sat sprawled in it now, as a man might sit in his parlor. With a glass in one hand and a bottle in the other he scowled at Colin. "You're late."

"Not unless the clock in the kitchen is slow. How long have you been here, Uncle Liam?"

"That's none of your affair. You should've brought the horse. I got a load here. Go get the horse."

"Yes, sir." Colin knew the mare wasn't finished eating yet. How could he give her an extra few minutes? He turned as if to do as he was bidden, then stopped and turned back again. "Uncle Liam? I hate this darkness; it really weighs on me. And you seem to like it. What do you think about, sitting here like this in the blackness?"

"What business is it of yours?"

"Something must draw you to it. Maybe if I find out what's good about it, I won't hate it as much."

"Nothing good about it. But it's better than up there." He poured himself another drink and downed half of it. He muttered, "Better than up in the world."

Colin waited.

Uncle Liam studied the rock wall beyond his nephew. "Not a thing good about it. Your Uncle Aidan up there; now that you know him, what do you think of him?"

"Seems to enjoy fiddling around with books and accounts. Cheerful and friendly, in his way."

Uncle Liam nodded. "All the qualities of leadership a

man needs to be great. There but for an accident of birth walks the Prime Minister of Australia, lad."

Colin moved in closer and hunkered down, leaning against the tunnel wall opposite. "What do you mean?"

"Your Papa told you how he took over Sugarlea and we came out here. Bet he didn't tell you the complete truth."

"He's never told us anything at all."

"Don't blame him a bit. Your Papa was the dinkum son, the lad who could do no wrong. The firstborn and our father's pet. If there was a favor to be given or a gift bestowed, he got it. Aidan and I got what was left, precious little. His closest flesh and blood, and he gave us leavings. He has much to be ashamed of, I tell you."

Here was a chance to get some family history. Colin must press carefully, keep Uncle Liam talking. "Where did you grow up?"

"Sydney. He never told you? Aidan and Cole were born at Sugarlea. I was born in Sydney. Your grandmum was quite a society figure in the city. She had all the connections. She could have made quite a nice place for Aidan and me, but she let Father poison her mind against us. Didn't do a bloody thing for us."

"And Papa went up to Sugarlea. When? When my grandfather died?"

Uncle Liam drained his glass. His voice was getting louder, thicker. "Your father got the plantation, the office in Sydney—everything. We got nothing. We coulda made something of our lives if we had half the breaks he got. Now there he sits in Sydney, a fine preening bird, while we struggle against dirt and debt in the armpit of Australia. Father's pet."

Colin wanted to learn more, so much more. But the tone of Uncle Liam's voice was turning hostile. Perhaps this was not the best time to pry further into Papa's past. He hopped to his feet. "I'll get the horse now."

"You were supposed to do that already. And you're late." His voice got still louder, yet harder to understand. "You know, lad, you're not a blasted bit better than your old man. You know that? You grew up being the apple of everybody's eye and now you expect it. Well, around here that's not gunner be! You toe the mark here like any Chow off the boat. You got that?"

"Yes, sir." Colin started to leave.

"Don't you go prancing off when I'm talking to you, boy! You supposed to have that horse down here already. And you don't come waltzing in late like everything's apples."

"I wasn't late, sir. I was here by half past six and had tha—"

His voice roared. "Don't you ever contradict me, Cole!" As he lurched to his feet a cold sliver of fear sliced through Colin's heart. He had no experience at all dealing with drunks. What would he do to avert trouble? He had no idea.

"I'll try not to do it again, sir."

"Quit giving me that 'sir' truck. You think you can smooth-talk the way your Papa always did. Say what makes 'em happy. Get all the breaks going your own way. It don't work here."

"Yes, sir. I mean, Uncle Liam. I'll go get the horse."

Uncle Liam was not to be stayed by words. He moved forward, a pure, raw hatred burning in his eyes. *Why is he turning on me?* Colin wondered. *His fight is with Papa.*

"Neither does your bludging go well here," he roared. "You need a little discipline. You need to learn life isn't just pretty presents from your father. Running around the country with hundreds of pounds while your uncles sink into debt."

Colin sucked in the stale air. "It *was* you! You stole money from your own blood!"

"Don't bash Bibles at me, you bloody little wowser! Your father has the scruples of a sewer rat. He robbed us and he'd rob you!"

"That's not true! And here I thought Flannery took my money."

Uncle Liam fired three expletives in a row. "Flannery, that Mick! Cole married a Mick; you're one, too!" Here he came at Colin.

Colin backed up and slammed against the rough-chopped wall. He turned to run, but Uncle Liam's backhand caught him in the ear and sent him ricocheting against the opposite wall. He threw up his arms for protection, knowing even as he did it that there would be no protection from this raging shicker. He cried out, knowing no one would hear.

Uncle Liam shouted a surprised, gurgling yell. In the uncertain light of Colin's headlamp beam he slammed backwards, sprawling on the ground. Max, snarling and growling, churned about on top of him.

Colin bolted up the tunnel. He stopped and wheeled. "Max! Come on! Come, Max!" He turned again and ran. If he reached the cage first he could hoist himself up and out of harm's way.

But his was not the only safety at stake now.

He took the cage instead to the upper level, to Max's Lady. He untied the startled horse and led her out of her black stall. The tunnel ceilings were far too low; he could never ride her in here without braining himself. Leading her, he urged her to a trot and turned down into the side drift that he hoped would lead him below; the shortcut. Or was it? He still became confused in this rat's maze. What if he were running right into Uncle Liam?

Reaching the lowest level by means of drifts and adits took a while. It also took knowing the correct ones. Finally Colin reached what he hoped was the lowest level, the confused horse jogging behind.

The light from his headlamp bobbed and whipped about ahead of him. The constantly shifting shadows made him nauseous—or perhaps the truth was making him sick. His own uncles! Then he realized he was sobbing. Fiercely he brushed the tears out of his eyes. *You're a man Colin! Act like one.*

He stopped suddenly. Before him lay not a T but a chickenfoot, not two ways to go but three as he left this side drift. Why had he never noticed the other tunnel? He looked at the ground; it told him nothing. No sledge scrapes or footprints hinted at the path to take.

"Max! There you are!"

The brindled dog trotted past him and continued right on down another drift. That particular tunnel would not have been Colin's first choice. He followed, though, having no better suggestion of his own. They came shortly upon the rope strung across the tunnel. Max trotted under it and on into the darkness beyond.

The Hard Yakka mine. Colin undid the rope enough to let the horse step over and led her forward, out of the Southern Star, into the absolute unknown.

Did Uncle Liam know his way around the Hard Yakka? Probably. Could he negotiate it in his present drunken condition? Possibly. The cool, clammy walls closed in even tighter here. A stale, musty odor like moldy furniture hung in the blackness. "Max? Where are you?"

He could detect the dog prints in the powdered dirt ahead. Actually, there were many dog prints, going in both directions. Max had been this way before, more than once. Colin stopped. Max's tracks disappeared down a side drift far too narrow for his Lady. Now what? Colin had no choice. He called to Max down the side tunnel and led the horse forward, straight ahead.

Then Max was behind them again, panting slightly. He trotted past Colin, past his Lady and continued ahead. How much did the wise old dog grasp of the situation?

For an hour they threaded from tunnel to tunnel, from level to level, sometimes up, usually down. Where were they, and how deep in the earth? Cold fear gripped Colin's heart and seemed to squeeze life from him. He could never find his way back. His last day on earth might well end hundreds of feet beneath it.

Twice they hit deadends and had to backtrack to some other option. Sometimes Colin led, sometimes the dog. Colin was sure now that Max was just as lost as he was. If only they could have followed the dog through that narrow side drift, maybe that would have been the way out—or would it?

He jerked to a halt so suddenly the mare bumped into him. A chasm yawned, wall to wall, right in front of him. Two planks stretched across it, a terrifying makeshift bridge. Colin flashed his headlamp down; nothing. He looked up. Nothing. Here was an abandoned vertical shaft from some prior mining venture, penetrating to infinity in both directions—and nothing to cross it but two thin boards.

Max trotted briskly across. The planks rattled. He reached ground on the other side, watching, waiting. He seemed to sense the dilemma.

The planks would hold Colin if he didn't lose his nerve or his balance. But could they hold a thousand-pound horse? Even if they could, she'd never cross them. The tunnel was too low for her to jump the hole, too narrow to turn her around. Colin felt the sobbing well up within him again, contrary to his best intentions—tears of frustration and fear.

What choice was there? His mare would die a slow death by starvation, if left to herself, or plunge to an instant death in the gorge below. Back her up? She didn't back well under the best of circumstances. What if she wedged sideways? He'd faced that before.

Then Colin remembered the words of old Captain Foulard: *I feel risky today. Too much happen to that pearl. Charmed, that pearl. I'll win.*

The lusty Kanaka did not shy away from risking everything he had, not just in the matter of the pearl, but daily, on the unpredictable sea. Colin led the mare to the very edge and crossed on the boards, his eyes set firmly upon Max. The planks strained and creaked with his weight.

Colin reveled but a moment in the solid footing of the far side. "Come, girl." He tugged gently at the leadline. "Come on. You're charmed, lass. Come!"

For minutes the mare repeatedly moved forward, hesitated, stopped, shifted her weight back. She took a step onto the planks, stepped back. Colin murmured encouragement, keeping his headlamp shining on the boards.

Suddenly she bolted forward, wide-eyed, clattering, lunging. Her shoulder hit Colin and squashed him against the wall. The glory of that blow struck him: *The mare's shoulder had hit him; she was over here!* The planks clunked and clattered to oblivion down the hole. There was no turning back now; the chasm blocked their return.

Suddenly Colin's spirits soared, without a solid reason in the world to feel exuberant. He urged the horse forward down the tight and narrow drift, Max following at a steady lope.

Beyond a curve up ahead shone a glimmer of pallid light. Light? But wait; it couldn't be the sunlight—not in these depths. Had they somehow doubled back to the Southern Star?

A cheerful voice boomed in the distance, "Why, here's Bluey, mates! Allo, Blue, old boy!"

Colin rounded the shallow curve and came up flush against a gate of dry, dusty timbers. And beyond the gate was the light! Naked, white light bulbs hung from the ceiling of a great, broad tunnel! Max had slipped easily under the gate boards, and bellied out ten feet from the miners, begging for tidbits.

Half a dozen men sat beneath the nearest light bulb, resting at their morning tea. One of them pointed at Colin, "Mmph, thbmmph." Dry crumbs spattered from his mouth.

No longer lost! Safe at last from Uncle Liam's rage! The relief welled up in Colin like a pot boiling over. His eyes and his nose were suddenly wet and the shame nearly blinded him. Here he stood in front of these strangers, strong miners all, blubbering like an infant.

"Saw you in the Exchange Saturday night, lad. Your mate's cooking our lunch. Here to see him, are you?"

It was the Perseverance!

A miner with more presence of mind than the rest finally leaped to his feet. "Don't know how you got here, lad, but you sure must have a tale to tell. Help me here, Smitty, with these timbers; let the lad through. Starve the bardies, he's got a horse with him!"

The succeeding events would become a jumble in Colin's memory. The men tore down the rickety barrier with their bare hands and brought him into the welcome light, wagging their heads over the open wounds and scrapes on Max's Lady. Now that Colin could see them in decent light, his heart wrenched anew to think he was responsible for this!

Then he relayed the whole incredible story, including Dizzy's dream of owning a claim, the reason he'd searched for his money in the first place. The miners marveled over the details of his underground journey from the Star—a horse across the chasm on two narrow planks of wood? Incredible.

"You've the bill of sale for this horse, lad?"

"Here somewhere, I think." Colin dug the worn, folded paper out of his wallet.

The miner studied it and nodded. "Good-o. At least your uncles can't claim ownership of your horse. Now here's what you do, lad. We'll send your horse to the surface up our number two shaft; she should fit. We'll drape her in hessian, to keep from bunging her up worse'n she is. Then you ride straight to the constable's. Show him this bill of sale to confirm the horse is yours. Next, ask him to go with you to your uncles' place. Clean your stuff out of there with the constable at your side for protection. You're not safe there alone. He'll be the witness that you took nothing that wasn't your own. Then you leave the Star behind—for good."

Colin nodded, too tired to disagree. He still felt choked up, and tears still stained his cheeks; but no one chided or teased. Their tolerance surprised and comforted him.

He decided to follow their advice to the letter, and even made some decisions of his own. Saying a brief goodbye to Dizzy on the way out, he promised to send what money he could spare.

Soul-weary and virtually penniless, Colin put Kalgoorlie behind him. By noon he was ten miles east of town, following not a proper track but rather the railway, with Max plodding along fifty feet to the rear.

———————

"When shall we reach Kalgoorlie, please?" Hannah asked the conductor almost in spite of herself, for she'd asked the same question not an hour ago.

He smiled. "Another hour, miss."

"Thank you." Her stomach gurgled. How embarrassing!

She sat staring out the window at the flatness, wishing she had something, anything, to eat.

A horseman rode by in the distance, headed east.

Hannah stared. She shrieked. She leaped from her seat and ran to the front of the car. "Let me off! Let me off! My brother's out there!"

"I'm sorry, miss. Next stop's Kalgoorlie. No doubt you are mistaken and your brother's waiting for you at the depot."

She shoved past the startled man and grabbed the great iron handle on the door. The fellow cried out, yelled at her not to touch it. She wrenched the bar and let go as the door whooshed open.

Rough, dry bushes whipped by the opening, and the endless ochre dirt trundled beneath in a blur. The train was moving so fast! If she paused to think she would lose everything. Frantically she shut her eyes and took the leap.

CHAPTER TWELVE

SLEEPERS

Mary Aileen picked at the food on her plate, but she certainly didn't feel like eating. She glanced over at Edan. He was putting his potatoes and lamb away stoically, quietly, the way he did everything else. Two chairs empty at the table tonight—she secretly rejoiced that Mum successfully resisted Papa when he decreed that the chairs be removed. Colin and Hannah were part of this family. Mary Aileen had a tremendous fear that they would be dismissed and forgotten. Could Papa do such a thing? She wasn't really sure. He was so incredibly hurt and angry.

Edan excused himself and left the table. Mary Aileen thought about an American nursery rhyme she'd read in a schoolbook, "Ten Little Indians." One by one misfortune befell them "until there were none." She might be glad the chairs remained, but she could not bear to look at them.

Mum finished her meal and laid her silverware methodically across the plate. "Have you heard yet from the constable in Kalgoorlie, Cole?"

"His wire arrived this afternoon. He says Colin left town and no one resembling Hannah detrained. He's investigating, though."

"She'd be there by now if that's where she were bound. Cole, where else would she go?"

"I wired Chris in Adelaide. She hasn't shown up on their doorstep. That leaves Meg and Luke in Queensland."

Sam stared at the centerpiece on the table. "Unless—Cole, you've never wanted to talk to the children about our past. Could she have gone on a pilgrimage to Sugarlea, to seek it?"

He frowned and shook his head. "Kids don't care about past history—I can't imagine it."

"Yes, we do." Mary Aileen laid a fork across her plate even though she hadn't finished her supper. She couldn't eat. "We're afraid, Papa. Afraid you did something terrible and don't want anyone to know. We don't even know where you were born. It's not just your history, you know. It's ours, too."

Those wonderful rich, dark eyes studied her. What a handsome man, her father!

"What are you hiding, Papa?"

His mouth tightened. "When I committed myself to Jesus Christ nineteen years ago, I was not a worthy man. That was the old Cole Sloan, a different person. Not trustworthy. Not the man who fathered you. I spent several years making restitution for the past, as best I could. And with God's help, I've followed a new way of life. God forgave the old Cole Sloan. I've put him away. I don't want him resurrected."

There were still questions to ask, and the right way to ask them, and Mary Aileen did not know how. Suddenly she envied Hannah, especially Hannah's ability to read her father and draw the desired response from him. She looked at Mum.

Mum glanced briefly at Papa. "Your father asked for my hand on two occasions. On the first, I felt that because of his devious ways I could never trust him. But as he says, he changed. When he asked again I accepted. But I had to learn to trust him; I knew perhaps a bit too much of his past." She raised her voice, and sounded confident, "I've never been disappointed, Mary Aileen. Never in our marriage has he betrayed my trust. This is the man you should know and emulate, not the man he was before."

"But still I want to know—we all want to know."

"Perhaps someday, when you're old enough to understand."

"Colin is old enough to understand. He's old enough for lots of things—things you didn't seem to want him to do." Mary Aileen scrambled ahead with the questions that so long crouched in the back of her mind. "Papa, are you afraid Colin might turn out like the old Cole Sloan? Is that why you constantly told him he was doing everything wrong? Were you trying to make him an exact copy of the new Cole Sloan? He's not you at all, Papa. He's Colin."

"I think that will be quite enough, Mary Aileen." Cole's eyes were dark, full of pain and obvious distress.

"Papa, he's not like you now, but he's not like you say you used to be either. He's not devious, and he's certainly not a bad person."

"That's enough!" Papa's voice bellowed.

Mum's voice was hard as flint, "You may be excused, even though you've not finished."

Mary Aileen looked from face to face. The conversation had ended. "Thank you," she mumbled, carrying her plate to the kitchen.

The doorbell rang as she was headed for the stairs, so she answered it.

A telegraph messenger stood in the night rain. "Cole Sloan, please?"

"Come in." She led him to the dining room. "Papa, a telegram for you." Papa signed it without saying a word, and Mary Aileen saw the lad back to the door.

She peered into the dining room and stopped cold at the door. Mum's head was hung down and Papa's face and neck were turning red.

He stood up so abruptly his chair slammed backwards. "Not a bad person, she says!" He stormed out of the room.

Mum melted forward, her elbows on the table, and buried her face in her hands, sobbing.

Mary Aileen's heart froze in her breast. *Whatever . . .?*
She crossed silently to the table and read the telegram.

*YOUR SON STOLE OUR BAY MARE STOP SEND ONE
HUNDRED POUNDS TO COVER LOSS STOP AIDAN
SLOAN*

———————

*If this is the winter sun, what a frying pan the sum-
mer sun must be!* Colin tugged his hat forward and closed
his eyes. Max's Lady slogged along at a constant pace, her
ears flopping with each stride. She was probably walking
in her sleep; Colin was pretty much riding in his.

He glanced back. Staring straight ahead, old Max came
along at a numb, ground-eating dog-trot, his tongue dan-
gling out the side of his mouth. Colin guessed it was high
time he stop again to rest the animals. Max's weeks of ease
in Kalgoorlie had softened the old bitzer. Plenty of trees
lined the railway here, but their gangling crowns and thin
leaves offered scant protection. The only really good shade
moved along the ground under the belly of his mare.

Max broke stride and turned suddenly, poised to see
what came behind. Was it Uncle Aidan or Uncle Liam? A
thump of fear hit Colin in the breast.

In the far distance a lone walker came this way. What
would a traveler be doing on foot along the railway right-
of-way? Colin couldn't remember a hiker behind him earlier, but then, he hadn't really looked back since he'd left
Kalgoorlie. It looked as if the walker would soon catch up.
A man on foot, faster than a man on horseback? That
wasn't hard when the horse was Max's Lady. Colin could
walk faster than this old plug. On the track she'd always
trailed twenty paces behind Dizzy's dun.

*Dizzy, old pal. How is the love-struck little cook do-
ing?* Colin wondered. He descended his mount and let the
lead go slack. Max slumped to the ground in grateful resignation, and Max's Lady dropped her nose until her
sleepy head touched the ground.

After a few minutes rest and musing, Colin shaded his brow and looked again after the hiker. He had gained a bit. He—no, it appeared to be a woman! The traveler employed a strange gait, more than a walk but not quite a trot, as if in a hurry and yet ready to drop. Colin decided to wait. The animals needed the break, if he didn't.

The traveler stumbled, quickened her pace. *Surely Lily wouldn't be coming out here.* The long, dark hair . . . the diminuitive form. . . . Colin gaped, stunned. It couldn't be!

She wouldn't be out here alone! Where was the rest of his family?

Hannah's weary voice called plaintively, "Colin? Is it you?"

Colin mounted the mare and jerked her head in the direction they'd come, awaking her to action. He jammed his heels into her ribs and she lunged forward in a brisk canter.

"Oh, Colin! It *is* you! I was so afraid! Thank you, God! Oh, thank you, God!" Hannah, frail little determined Hannah, lurched into a disconnected run.

Colin leaped from the mare's back and wrapped his arms around his little sister. Sobbing, she fell against him and clung tight.

Colin would not have thought he had any more tears after the frightening, twisted events of this terrible day. But a few fell unbidden before he could put up his guard. No matter. Hannah was weeping in earnest now, babbling incoherently. With her face buried against his chest she wouldn't see his tears at all.

He looked about desperately for any sign of solid shade. Trying to pry her loose from her vise-like grip, he murmured, "Hannah, Hannah. Under here, come on." He pushed her down to sitting under the mare's broad belly and leaned her against the stout front legs. Max's Lady stood still, as if she knew somehow her protection was needed.

Colin sat down in the dirt beside Hannah and shook his head. "What a mess you are!" He recalled how Hannah had spent a good deal of her childhood with scuffed knees, the price of being a tomboy. But they were more than scuffed now; her shins were covered with dried, blackened blood, her knees torn and raw. The palms of her hands were scraped too, and gravel stuck to the caked blood. Dirt smudged her face from eyebrow to chin.

Her blue-striped frock was torn and dirty—another throwback from her childhood. He handed her his handkerchief, and she blew more blood from her nose and attempted to clean some of the grime from her face.

"You came out here alone, Hannah?"

She nodded. "After I jumped from the train and started running this way I had an awful thought. What if I was wrong? What if it wasn't you after all that I'd seen from the window, and I should have ridden into Kalgoorlie like the conductor insisted? And then I thought, what if I can't catch up to your horse? Oh, Colin, I had such horrible thoughts."

"*You jumped off the train?* Hannah, it passed miles ago, and it was *moving*—I mean really moving!"

She nodded. "So I started praying to God. It works for Mum, so I tried it. Mum said once you mustn't make deals with God. I wanted to so bad, but I decided I better do it her way. I didn't say, 'God, if you'll help me catch up to Colin—and it better be Colin and not some stranger, I'll be good forever for you,' but I wanted to. But He heard me and He did it. Don't you see? He did it!"

"Hannah, *why* did you do this?"

She shrugged. "I don't know. I just did. I wanted to find you."

Colin barked, "No! You better start giving me the dinkum oil, because I'm this close to riding away and leaving you." He held up two fingers, pinched together. "*This close!*"

"You wouldn't."

"I didn't invite you here. You're not my responsibility."

Her eyes grew big. "You've changed, Colin."

"Maybe. I've seen the world—like you wouldn't believe. Death and betrayal—deceit, greed, tragedy. *Noble Sake Tamemoto; ignoble uncles!* Of course I've changed. So have you. You used to pull funny little tricks and pranks. But this isn't a bit funny, Hannah."

"Colin, everything's wrong at home since you left."

"It was wrong before I left."

Her huge dark eyes pored over him. "When Uncle Aidan wrote and asked Papa to send money—"

"He *what*?"

"To help feed you. I was afraid you were terribly sick or hurt and couldn't work. I thought you must be all alone out here. You didn't have anybody. I had to come." The child in Hannah Sloan spoke through the face of a woman. Softly she implored, "Please don't be mad at me, Colin."

His hat kept brushing the horse's belly. He dragged it off and tossed it aside. Wearily he rubbed his face with both hands.

"I'm so sorry," she murmured.

"I'm not mad at you, Hannah." Colin drew his knees up to give his elbows something to hang on to. I can't believe—yair, I guess I can, too. Dizzy was right. When they put the mare down that shaft they knew she'd never come up again. I worked for them for weeks, and I'm sure now they never intended to pay me, not even at the reduced wage. They stole my money, and then they had the gall to ask Papa for still more. Those wretches!"

Hannah looked at him blankly.

Colin gazed into Hannah's sweet little face and wished he could find some answers there. "They're scoundrels, Hannah. They're not even ambitious scoundrels. They're lazy scoundrels. And Uncle Liam says Papa is the worst. I can't believe anything he says, but if he's even half right— Hannah, what if I'm that way and just won't admit it? Or don't know it? Maybe I *am* as sneaky and crooked as Papa says I am."

"No! You're the genuine article, Colin. Don't even think that!"

"I'm past thinking. My loaf doesn't function anymore." Colin rolled out from under the mare and gained his feet. He held out a hand. "Come on. I don't have enough water to clean you up. Let's go on to the next settlement and civilize you."

Hannah giggled and lurched erect stiffly. "Can't be done, else Mum would've managed it years ago. Right?"

"Dead set!" Colin boosted her up into his saddle, laughing.

Hannah's poor knees spent another twenty-four hours unattended, for they did not reach a settlement that day. At dusk they left the railway for a quarter of a mile to a cluster of sandalwood trees and there found a seep with water enough for Max but not quite enough for Max's Lady.

They camped without a fire. During the night headlights from a motor car or truck rattled east in the distance by the tracks. Hours later the lights passed again heading west.

Late the next afternoon Colin and Hannah reached a little shantytown, a spiritless cluster of cramped, tin-roofed buildings. The settlement existed for no other reason than to house the fettlers who maintained this particular stretch of the Trans.

The Trans. Colin thought often about this desolate, magnificent railway linking east to west—Adelaide and Port Augusta to Kalgoorlie and eventually Perth. All the history books told the heroic tale of its construction. How often had he read about the blood, sweat, and tears—the very lives of men and camels that went into it? But that was just head knowledge. Riding alongside its tracks became for him a heart experience, for he had just spent over two days in the saddle, and he was not even a tiny fraction of the way across. There is distance, and there is distance. And then there is the distance the Trans covers.

The only accommodation in this village could not really be called a pub, but it boasted a toilet out back. Hannah spent twenty minutes in the ladies' facility washing off blood and dirt. When she joined Colin she didn't look a whole lot better, but certainly cleaner.

She flopped into a chair and drank a glass of water in three gulps. "Do we have enough money for a nice dinner? I'd so love a nice dinner."

"Yair, but we can't stay here. We'll camp outside tonight, like last night."

She shrugged. "I didn't get too cold, I guess. How much money do we have?"

"Two quid seven. Dizzy insisted I take it when we parted. I'll have to make it last."

"I made two shillings last clear to Adelaide, almost." She pondered the bare wooden table before them, "Colin? Perhaps we could get jobs here. If we made enough money for trainfare we could go anywhere we wish."

"You're going home."

"Colin, please don't send me back."

"I won't send you. I wish I could, but I can't. I'll take you, at least to the city line. It'd be too dangerous, a little girl traveling alone."

"I'm not a *little* girl!"

"You *are* a little girl. It's a miracle you got this far." *Miracle.* There he was, using God-words again.

"You travel all over. So can I."

"It's different with a girl, Hannah. I'm a man and I'm older."

"What's different? I'm as fast as you are, and as smart. I proved I can travel; I got here, didn't I?"

"With a girl, there's the chance that something might—" He studied her a minute, holding those huge dark eyes with his. "Never mind. Just take my word for it, it's different."

"No." She shook her stubborn little head. "No. I'll stay with you. If you go off and leave me I'll make a way. But I'm not going back unless you do." The dark eyes blazed. "And that is the end of that!"

That indeed was the end of that. Never in his life could Colin outargue his little sister. Why bother trying? Their beef stew (the only dish on the menu) did not taste nearly as good as meals at the Exchange. Or perhaps Colin's fate had soured his taste buds. His responsibilities in Kalgoorlie no doubt improved the flavor of those pleasant meals with Diz and Lily.

There was one way out. He could send a letter to Papa and ask for the money to come home.

He'd die first.

"Hee, lads; your ear." A grizzled mountain of a fellow stepped up to the bar and turned to address the room.

"Not you again, Brekke," yelled someone from the far side of the room.

"You're all aware we're short-handed, and we're short of sleepers in the bargain. I'll shout for any man here who agrees to come with me down south for sleepers. Twill be extra work; I'll not take any fettlers off the tracks." He looked around expectantly.

Hannah leaned forward. "What're sleepers?"

"The wooden cross-ties that hold the railway tracks."

"How long?" asked the heckler across the room.

"Fortnight."

"Last time you said 'fortnight' we were gone three weeks. Not I, Brekke."

"Come, lads. Bonus of five quid a head if you see it through to the end. What say?"

Muttering and a spate of laughter seemed to be all they had to say. Then a fellow rose and walked to the bar. He spat out an unholy epithet. "Brekke, you ratbag, you know I'll do anything for a free ale. Sign me up. Pay by the week; Saturday without fail. None of this 'fortnight' foolery."

"Pay by the week it is, Jack. I've got one. Who's next?"

Colin found himself speaking up. "You've two, if my little sister can find boarding with a decent family here; I can't leave her here alone."

The huge man studied them both a moment. "Bit hard, mate; not much here. We'll take her along, if she can cook."

"I can, sir!" Hannah blurted without a second's hesitation.

"She can't!" Colin shot back.

"I can! I'll sew on buttons and such too if I may go along."

"I've two and a cook," cried Brekke. "Who's next?"

"Why'd you do that?" Colin scolded. "You're not going! Do you realize how tough these ruffians are? Men who wouldn't think twice about—"

She cut him off. "You go adventuring. So can I. Besides, you know we need the money, and with two of us working we'll get it twice as fast." Those big dark eyes softened. "You've been halfway 'round the world, and your shipwreck on the pearl boat and all, so trav—"

"How do you know about that?"

" 'Twas in the newspaper. So traveling and jobs are old hat to you, but I've never been out of New South Wales. I've never ever had a true job. This is so exciting, Colin!"

Exciting? Lovely. Just lovely.

Brekke was roaring, "You, lad! You have a horse, eh? That bay out front. Does she pull?"

"Yes, sir."

"I'll hire her, too. We'll need a horse for the close work."

"There! See, Colin? We'll make pounds of money!"

It took Mr. Brekke all night to finish assembling a crew. Next morning they caught a westbound freight into Kal, detrained at the yards east of town and clambered up into the back of a big, rumbling stakeside lorry—Max's Lady, Max and all.

Colin had somehow expected to take the train all the way; after all, these were workers for the railway. On the other hand, he'd never before ridden any distance in the back of a truck. It was exhilarating somehow, albeit dusty.

Hannah glowed like Christmas. All smiles and excitement, she hung on the stakesides to watch the road ahead, her hair tumbling on the wind, or sat at the rear simply to stare at the pall of bulldust boiling out behind. What was going on in the child's mind? What was she planning next? Colin hated to think about it.

They made good time in this thing, bounding along down the flat, dry track. They would have easily covered three hundred miles that day if the truck hadn't broken down in Kambalda. Mr. Brekke was four hours by the roadside before getting a ride back to Kal with a traveler who happened along in a Ford touring car.

Colin knew nothing of mechanical repair other than what Dizzy had taught him about the air pumps on pearl boats. With nothing to do but stay out of the way, he wandered around the abandoned settlement, poking and exploring and admonishing Hannah to stay close by. She stayed so close she was right on top of him all morning. He wished she hadn't taken him quite so literally.

Thirty years ago, Kambalda enjoyed prosperity as the gold fields' population center, with Kalgoorlie the upstart town. Now Kambalda sat totally abandoned under the hot, dry sun. Colin probed the ruins of the Red Hill mine and saw in its dusty past the future of the Southern Star and possibly even of such venerable giants as the Ivanhoe and Perseverance.

Hannah didn't do too badly at preparing lunch. She made lots of sandwiches, while the bread was still fresh. Colin helped. In fact, all three crewmen seemed very helpful. They laughed at Hannah, they laughed with Hannah, they teased her and encouraged her. The sun had drifted past three p.m. before Hannah got the lunch leftovers cleared and stowed.

Mr. Brekke arrived after five that evening with the necessary parts and a repair truck from the yards. The driver started up a welding rig in the truck bed, and the crew pitched in to commence repairs.

Mr. Brekke beckoned to Hannah. "You. You jumped off the train, didn't you?"

She nodded. Fear sparked in her big, dark eyes.

"The conductor reported it to the yardmaster, as he ought, and the yardmaster was of the opinion you were on your own. Then constable Bowden came looking for you. Next thing, they had search parties out all up and down the line. Still out there, some of them. They stopped by the settlement the night you detrained."

She hung her head. "I'm sorry I caused so much fuss. I wasn't thinking. I only wanted to reach my brother Colin."

Colin sighed. *There goes our freedom.* "You knew who she was when you hired us, didn't you?"

"Knew when I walked into the pub who you were." He glared at Hannah. "Today I told the constable you're safe and that you'd left town. Didn't tell him you're with us, o' course. I couldn't get your bag from him else he'd suspect. All he needs to know is that you're not lost or hurt. If he found you here, I'd lose your brother, too, and it's too short a crew to lose another man. You got any plans to jump overboard again?"

"Oh, no, sir! I promised I'd work for you, and I will. I'll do my best for you, sir." Her voice dropped to a shy mumble, " 'Tis my very first job, sir, and I'm indebted to you for hiring me."

Mr. Brekke glared at Colin. "What about you?"

"I, uh . . . I'm pleased you took care of it as you did, sir. Thank you."

The huge man looked from face to face. The gruff countenance softened. "Good enough." He walked away.

Colin gave Hannah plenty of help preparing supper for the hardy crew. After all, the cook at the Perseverance taught him everything he knew. He smiled again at the thought, and at his memories of the stalwart little Tejano.

It was nearly dark when they finished up. Colin had never considered how endless a task cooking could be—all the preparation work and constant clean up, and in the end nothing to show for it but a clean kitchen—only to repeat the process in a few hours.

The moon, entering its first quarter, was rising already, impatiently chasing the dying sun. Just to give her some exercise, Colin rode Max's Lady out to Lake Lefroy, with Hannah darting about on foot—with him, yet not with him. The "lake" was a salt flat, totally dry, stretching and glistening as far as the eye could see. Australia was level; Lake Lefroy was a kitchen floor.

"Look here, Colin! Look what I've found!" Hannah stuck her head back into a tin shed. The sign over the door said BICYCLES FOR RENT.

She rolled one out. "It has the old-fashioned solid tires. Bet it's still ridable. Come on, Colin! Choose one and ride with me!"

Colin dismounted and took a look inside. A score or more of abandoned bicycles leaned against each other in the musty shop. He chose one randomly and wheeled it out into the orange glow of sunset. He climbed aboard. Nothing gave way, so he pushed it forward with his feet on the ground. It creaked, then whispered in rhythm from a dozen rubbing joints. The sprocket turned, but not without protest. He shoved off and began pedaling. What glorious freedom!

Hannah, fifty feet ahead, had already bumped down the slope out onto the world's greatest cycling arena— Lake Lefroy. Colin was sure all the bikes had tasted Lake Lefroy salt; the salt pan was probably the very reason the rental had existed. He had to pedal hard to catch up with Hannah.

The sun dropped away, leaving only the feeble moon to cast its light, but the salt flat was so brightly reflective, it was as if the moon were full. They rode in a wide loop for miles, it seemed, across a crystalline crust as smooth as linoleum.

Except for the crackling whisper of tires on salt, and the creaks attendant to bicycles so long ungreased, they rode in silence. Beside Colin, Hannah began to pedal faster. Faster. Faster. She flung her head back and closed her eyes, and the wind ran like fingers through her long hair.

An hour after they returned to the truck, the crew was on the track again. They rode all night trying to make up lost time, and the next day ate at a little pub called the Golden Dream in a tiny, nearly abandoned town.

Hannah chose not to eat. She took Colin's last quid into a ramshackle hairdressing emporium, and emerged half an hour later, her dark hair shorn to a short bob. The child had become a woman.

CHAPTER THIRTEEN

JARRAH

Slim as a telephone pole and taller than a Sydney office building, it stood with its feet firmly in the earth and its lacy head halfway to heaven, snubbing mortal men. Colin stood at its base gazing up openmouthed. Never had he seen a tree so absolutely awesome as this one. Cut it down? Unthinkable.

"Gunner study nature, or make a quid?" Mr. Brekke's voice boomed out across the open woodland. He came striding over and paused beside Colin.

Colin shrugged and grinned. "Guess I can't do both."

Brekke tilted his head back. "Quite a sight, eh? Jarrah, this one is. Jarrah and karri—king karri—finest trees in the world, right here in Western Australia."

"Back east it's red gum they all crow about."

"Crikey, lad, that's just 'cause they never saw these." He waved an arm nearly as thick as the tree trunk. "Jack and Woppo over there—go help them cut up that stick. And stay away from Woppo. When he's off his turps, he's mean."

"Yes, sir." Colin shouldered his crosscut saw and set off beneath the mighty trees. Out on the ends of the eight-foot blade, the saw handles bounced gently up and down in rhythm with his strides. The undulating blade hummed a faint chant in his ear; *whonnnn, whonnnn,*

whonnnn. Ferns and shrubs grabbed at his ankles now and then. The ground gooshed in places, soggy from the winter rains.

Like carefully placed chessmen, the tall, straight trees stood evenly spaced some yards apart, as if aligned in rows by the hand of man. Their loose, open crowns let through nearly all the sunlight. Colin remembered reading in a geography book about the rainforests of South America, and how the trees there screened out ninety-five percent of the light from the humid floor. He could not perceive a forest so dark and close.

Jack and Woppo were hacking away at a tree that must have been felled several years before. Why would someone cut down a tree and then leave it to rot? Colin laid his saw aside and took up Jack's measuring stick. With it he marked off the length of a sleeper and set his saw on the mark. He drew it across.

The stakeside was chugging this way from somewhere; Colin could hear it behind him.

"Alo-o, Colin!" Hannah's cheery soprano sang out above the thrum of the motor.

Colin wheeled. She waved from the driver's side, a swift and hasty wave. Instantly her hand darted back to the wheel, and just in time. The truck lurched over a small, half-rotted fallen tree and rumbled on away through the greenwood.

Colin gaped. "She's driving! And she's alone!"

"Why not?" Jack gripped the nether end of Colin's saw and drew it towards himself.

"She's just a little girl!"

Jack stared at him a moment. "Look again, lad."

Numbly Colin dragged back on the saw. It yanked away from him; he pulled it back. Forth and back, forth and back. Hannah was twelve. She wouldn't be thirteen for another three months. Hannah, with a hair bob just like Mum's and Mary Aileen's. Hannah, driving that huge, ungainly stakeside . . . traveling three thousand miles alone and penniless . . . and making it.

"Quit riding the saw, lad. Wake up!" Jack gave his end an extra tug. "I've had to work with that bugger Woppo all morning; I'm in no mood to offer charity." Jack, snaggle-toothed and middle-aged, was an average rouseabout. He bent his back to any work placed in front of him, though never with much enthusiasm. He earned the sugar in his tea, and apparently that's all that interested him. Had he never married? What sort of family had he come from? No one seemed to know much about him, and no one, as far as Colin knew, ever dared ask. It was just Jack—no last name ever given. He'd drifted about, working here and there as opportunity arose, like so many Australian men since the Great War.

Is this my destiny? Empty as Jack's? Colin wondered. *I am, after all, doing the same thing.* But was Jack's life empty? He went where he wished and did as he pleased. He earned his way, contributing his share, turning the wheels of progress. No worries. No chains to tie him where he didn't want to be.

No love, either.

"Git off the saw, Drongo!"

"Sorry."

Back and forth, back and forth, back and forth.

Colin couldn't help wondering if anyone loved him. Hannah, obviously. But, Mum? She said she did, but then why did she consistently side with Papa? Did Papa love him anymore? Did he ever love him? Colin was not certain the man was capable of love. Duty, yes. Affection, yes, especially toward Mum. But clear, strong, undying love? For anyone?

Am I capable of that sort of undying love? Perhaps I'm too much my father's son—unable to love completely. If that be so, a wandering life doesn't fall so far off the mark.

The saw rasped within a few inches of bottom. "Hold it," said Jack, breaking Colin's reverie. He hooked a peavey in the log and rolled it a quarter turn. They cut it through, measured off the next length, and began the interminable back and forth motion once again.

The truck horn tooted in the distance and the stakeside appeared again, staggering through the bush, threading among the trees.

"Time to eat!" Jack abandoned his end. Gratefully Colin walked away from his.

Hannah bounded down from the cab seat—quite a bound for such a small frame. She hopped back to the flatbed, full of eager enthusiasm, and gathered up three sack lunches. "This is the last stop, so I can join you." She dipped herself a tin mug of water from a large pail on the flatbed and settled under a tree.

Colin sat down beside her, opened his sack and looked in. Two apples and a sandwich. "When do you think Mr. Brekke is gunner find out you can't cook after all?" he teased.

Jack plopped down at Hannah's other side. "Stay off her, Sloan. Mebbe she has some learning to do yet, but she ain't no blacksmith."

Hannah frowned. "What does that mean?"

"A blacksmith is a rotten cook." Colin bit into his sandwich. Mutton. He was not overly fond of mutton. "When did you learn to drive a truck?"

"This morning. Mr. Brekke says that with me driving the truck, that leaves one more man free to cut wood. So he sent Les and Max's Lady off across the creek where the truck can't go. Some good sticks there, he says."

"I can't believe he'd trust you with the truck."

"Well he did. *He* doesn't think I'm a little girl." She tossed her head and her freshly cropped hair floated out like a halo. "Soon as we're back to work I drive about gathering spools. Mr. Brekke showed me how to tell the boggy places and stay away from them. He's setting up the donkey engine and mill. Then Mr. Brekke will haul the sleepers to the railway. 'Tis a long way. Colin, this is so glorious!"

"Yair. Glorious. 'Til you take out the front end driving over logs." He envied her enthusiasm. He enjoyed her ebullience. So why did a sense of danger and dread, of foreboding, hang over his head? What did he feel that he could not put his finger on?

Hannah popped the last of her sandwich into her mouth and bounced to her feet. "I'll see you later." Absolutely glowing, she scrambled up into the truck cab. The electric starter groaned a couple of times before the motor kicked in. No doubt Hannah believed herself to be an expert driver already. What would she do when she ended up in the driver's seat of a vehicle she had to crank? The gears ground. Suddenly the old stakeside lunged forward. She needed practice with the clutch, too.

Jack watched the stakeside waddle out across the forest floor. "Quite a bobby-dazzler, the little lady. Them dark eyes—"

Colin wheeled toward him. "Don't even think about her. She's too young."

Jack studied him with a steady eye. He smirked. "She's safe from me, lad, but not because you're protecting her. I can beat the tar outta you anytime I care to. It's Brekke's got his eye on her, and I know better'n to tangle with that hunk of a Norwegian. Fights like a threshing machine. Get to work now, Warb." He sauntered off, looking not the least bit concerned.

Brekke!

Suddenly the amorphous mass of foreboding in Colin's brain took on a hideous shape. Little Hannah had no idea whatever of the dangers lurking about, and Colin had seriously underestimated them. Brekke. And if not Brekke, Jack or someone else. Colin had to get Hannah out of here. He had to help her reach safety in Sydney under her father's roof.

Under her father's roof. Safety. A sudden remorse flooded him—or was it homesickness? He wanted to be under his father's roof as well, even with all the friction and anger and irritation. He didn't want to be stranded a continent away, cutting up trees, with his little sister in imminent danger. He wanted Mum's good cooking and Edan's quiet support and Mary Aileen's constant, critical, watchdog eye. He wanted home.

The stakeside was back. Hannah pulled up alongside him. "Mr. Brekke says you're to help Les load spools."

Colin grabbed the door handle, wrenched it open and climbed inside. He flopped in the seat. "So what else does Mr. Brekke say to you?"

Hannah shoved the stick into first. They lurched violently into motion. "He says don't run over any stumps. Colin, what's a spool?"

"The sections of tree trunks that we sawed up. The sleeper-length pieces."

"Oh, of course. All right."

"Look at that. Another good stick just lying there abandoned. They wouldn't dare waste this much wood in the eastern forests."

"Mr. Brekke says we'll cut up this downed timber first. He's going to bring some men over from the logging camp tomorrow and have them fell us the rest of what we need."

Mr. Brekke. Brekke this. Brekke that. Part of the fear in Colin's heart was turning to anger.

Hannah brought the truck to a lurching halt beside a sawed-up log. Les sat on it, and beside him, Max's Lady dozed with one hind foot cocked. "There's a meeting tonight in the logging camp down the track. Let's go, Colin."

Colin slid out his side as Hannah jumped down out of hers. "What kind of meeting?"

"Some kind of preacher. Mr. Brekke says he's very good."

"Naw. I'm not interested in going to hear no preacher."

"Suit yourself. I'm going."

"With Mr. Brekke?"

"And Jack and some others, I think.."

That did it. Colin would go too.

It was a good thing Mr. Brekke, not Hannah, drove his truckful of sleeper cutters that evening. A cold, drizzling rain fell, making the slippery track nearly impossible. With the skill of an old hand, Brekke drove a snaking, twisting path through the trees, often in the track, sometimes leaving it.

He forded the puddled low spots by shoving it into first gear and speeding up. As the men whooped, the motor howled, and Hannah shrieked, they hit the fens full tilt, spraying muddy water ten feet high on both sides. Only one time did they bog to a stop. Everyone hopped out and pushed, and then ran like sixty to clamber back on, for once the truck got moving, Mr. Brekke stopped for no one. Colin found himself sharing with the others a wild and heady glee as they rattled and slogged the four miles to the logging camp. This was living, rain and all!

The Marri Creek logging camp looked like a war zone, if Colin had any notion what a war zone looked like. Huge stumps stuck out wherever you turned. Wilting, drying branches littered the ground. The earth itself, with no protective covering of grass, had been churned to the consistency of a newly plowed field by the hooves of scores of bullocks and horses.

The loggers' only sleeping accommodation was a grayed tarpaulin stretched between trees, the only kitchen a tin safe and the open fire. Colin hopped down; he had to run to keep up with his eager little sister.

Mr. Brekke hailed the boss. "Brought you blokes a bit of fresh meat and some tomatoes. Even brought the cook, if you've a need for one." He nodded toward Hannah.

"A sheila! Our baitlayer's sixty years old and can't see outta one eye. How'd you rate so high, Brekke?" Laughing, the boss shook Mr. Brekke's hand. He doffed his battered hat to Hannah. Colin instantly regretted letting her come.

"Our man of God here." The boss waved a hand toward the fellow who apparently would speak tonight. "James Otis."

The young fellow smiled and nodded in an unassuming way. He was younger than Colin would have guessed—still in his teens—and much more cheerful. One might expect a preacher to be old and somber and set in his ways, to wear black clerical garb. This lad dressed like a logger. James Otis looked to be a half-caste—Aboriginal and white. Whatever Colin had expected, this young man certainly wasn't it.

He approached Hannah boldly. "You surely have a Christian name; what do they call you besides 'the cook?' "

"Hannah Sloan." She smiled, and for the hundredth time Colin regretted everything about this venture. "Do you really preach?"

"Yes, mum, I really do. But I'm a logger by trade. Top disposal mostly."

"You dispose of tops?" Her voice sounded so childlike.

"Yes, mum, exactly that. After the fallers drop a tree and others take the wood, there's still the leafy crowns to be gathered and burned—or cut for firewood." He smiled, and the charm in his smile neatly circumvented Colin's determination to dislike the man.

The last of the bullock teams came plodding in, bedraggled and muddy. Hannah watched wide-eyed as the ungainly, waddling beasts made their way through the camp to a makeshift paddock on the edge of the wood. And then, smoothly, before Colin was quite aware of it, the preacher lad was leading Hannah about showing her this and that. He was talking about bullock teams; the leaders, body bullocks, pinners and polers; terms all as foreign to Colin as Dizzy's bursts of Spanish; and Otis obviously knew what he was talking about. Hannah followed, absolutely enthralled.

"Once they're cut, the logs are all moved by bullock teams, or horses." He gestured as he spoke. "Trucks and tractors need a bit of a track, you see, and their tires slip and slide in weather like this. The bullocks can go anywhere, climb over anything. It may take them forever, but they get there."

Colin could not wedge himself between Hannah and Otis; she was pressed too close. So he stepped in at her other side. "You from around here?"

"No. New South Wales, down on the Murray. My father ran a mission to the Aboriginals there for many years."

"Red gum, right? Murray red gum trees and Murray cod. My father brokers the lumber and salted fish from there. That where you learned logging?"

The dark man smiled again, rather sadly. "I'm sure my father had seminary in mind for me, but I wanted to be on my own. Went off to work in the Barmah forests east of Echuca when I was fourteen. I love working with my hands. Of course, I love the Lord, too."

"And you think loggers need preaching?"

He laughed. "Do you doubt it?"

"Not for a minute." Colin was careful to stay on guard against this brash young fellow who was so obviously playing up to Hannah. Why didn't he dislike the bloke more?

That evening, the loggers and the railway sleeper-cutters ate their meal together—not Hannah's cooking, but that of the one-eyed camp cook. With the rain drumming harder than ever, they built a roaring fire as close to the tarp as possible, then lowered its back end nearly to the ground in an effort to trap the warmth.

It didn't really work, but it looked as though it ought to, so you felt just a bit warmer. Colin mused upon the tricks the mind can play.

Here was another mind trick. Standing before the men seated under the marquee, his back to the fire, young Otis looked much taller than before, more dignified. Hannah sat right up front, Colin at her side, as close to the fire as anyone, but she shivered all the same. Reluctantly Colin removed his own coat and wrapped it around her.

Otis smiled in his own disarming way. "I learned bullocking from my father, as well as a lot of other practical skills. He's a very religious man, in the best sense of the word. He loves God and he loves serving God."

Religious man. Colin thought. *Could Papa out-religion Otis's father? He'd come close!*

"Being a man of God, my father doesn't use the foul language bullock drivers are known for, even when angry or frustrated. I remember when once our bullock cart bogged near the river, bringing a load up from the dock. The riverboat skipper, Gus Runyan, came upon him in the track, laughed at the struggling bullocks and asked, 'How they doing?' My father replied, 'All they do is puff, piddle and poop.' It was the worst language I ever heard him use."

Colin found himself laughing. Papa knew some language, too, pretty rough words—picked up around stables and such, but he never used it—at least not in Colin's presence.

"My father was a good lad when he was small and a good man when he grew up. He was the kind of person every woman wants her son to be. But, my friends—" Otis paused, looking about. "He was not a Christian! Being good doesn't make you a God-fearing man. Fearing God does. Being good doesn't make you a Christian. Trusting Christ does."

Hannah leaned over and stretched up to whisper in Colin's ear, "Then what is Papa? And what was he before?" She was obviously listening, hanging on every word.

Otis launched into a series of stories then, entertaining yarns that were more jokes than tales, about his youth and his father's youth. He spoke of Ellen, his Aboriginal mother, of her enduring faith, and of the way she kept the mission running even when his father preached out on the circuit.

He told about his father's joy and embarrassment years ago when a lovely red-haired woman virtually proposed marriage to him. Twelve hours later another woman confessed her love for him—a double whack between the eyes with a red gum board, Otis called it. A sharp twist of envy wrenched Colin's heart. Young Otis here was apparently privy to minute details of his father's life. The line about the red gum plank was surely his father's phrasing as he bared his past to an eager, listening son. Colin sighed. The humorous, intimate tales continued. Otis was a good storyteller.

"I hope none of you has ever stood in the dock, being tried for a crime. I think you all know, though, what a witness does at a trial. A witness delivers his testimony, telling what he saw and knows. This is my testimony; it is what I've seen, and what I know.

"At thirteen, as soon as I could quit school, I left my home to work in the forests nearby. It was not what my parents wanted for me, but I was determined. I'm sure all of you can understand a boy who's anxious to grow up. Two years later, I decided I was not far enough from home. My father knew all the loggers. In fact, many of them worshiped at the mission. I was always under his eye one way or other. So I came out here to where the trees are legends. Pemberton, and the king karri." He breathed an almost reverent sigh, "Oh, how grand," and a dozen loggers nodded in complete agreement.

"It was near lunch time, and the fallers were working on one last stick before breaking. I was thinking about something else, not paying attention. Every one of you knows that can be fatal in the forest. I heard the crack and the whoosh. I could feel it coming. I heard the fallers shouting. Its shadow fell across me. I was doomed and I knew it.

"I whirled and looked up. It was right there! All I could do was cry out to God, 'Please, God, save me!' "

A charming grin spread across his face. "I'm standing before you, so you know how my story ended. But let me tell you how God saved me. First, the crown of that falling tree caught in the branches of a plain, trashy old marri. That threw the log off plumb. It spun on its base and fell five feet away from me. The second way He saved me was to open my eyes, right then and there, to the fact that He *does* exist, and He *does* care about me.

"I'd been hearing the Gospel my whole life. Jesus came into the world as a man, died on the cross as a sacrifice to pay for my sins, rose from the dead, entered heaven, and promised to bring His believers to paradise with Him. But only at that moment, when death had just brushed me with her skirts, did I realize how very personal that Gospel is. God, a person—and me, a person.

"It wasn't a catechism that saved me that day, or a precept or a fact. It was a person saving me. A *person*. Do you see? That is my testimony. That is what I have seen and know.

"And now God wants to deal with each one of you, person to person, if He has not already—just the way He became real to me. If you do not yet know Him, I want to talk to you. We can discuss it together, and further see what salvation means personally."

Otis stepped forward into the seated audience, casually squatting down to talk to one here, another over there. He was congratulated by others for an entertaining message. Hannah studied the wet ground between her and the fire, staring motionless at the dripping water.

Personal. A lot this Otis knew. And yet, he said he *did* know. Colin's brain spun itself dizzy with fruitless thinking.

———

Because of the constant rain and fierce wind the crew

opted to stay overnight at Marri Creek. As always, Hannah slept in the truck cab; everyone else huddled under the soggy tarp.

At dawn they started back, Mr. Brekke's crew and two fallers on loan. The lumbering stakeside bogged down frequently and Colin had to walk the last mile back to camp to fetch Max's Lady. She pulled and the men pushed to free the truck from the sucking slop.

The truck rolled into the camp twenty minutes before Colin got there on Max's Lady. The fallers had already begun their work, hacking in synchronization at the base of a tall jarrah, one to the left and one to the right. *Chik chuk chik chuk chik.* They cut a wedge-shaped notch in the tree trunk—putting an address on the tree, Mr. Brekke called it.

Opposite the notch they set their crosscut saw and began cutting. Colin walked down to the creek. Why did the doom of this tree—a mere spiritless timber—affect him so?

The creek ran muddy from last night's rain. It was reshaping its bank here and there, eating away a bit at one point, laying a shallow mud bar somewhere else. There on the bend it had washed away half the soil from beneath a jarrah. The washout must have occurred many years ago. Robbed of its underpinning, the sapling had tipped over nearly horizontal, hanging above the flowing water. But the tops of trees are constrained by nature to grow upward, reaching for the light. And so it grew—straight up toward the sky like any other tree, its lacy crown nearly as high as its mates'. Only the L-shaped angle at the very bottom of its trunk remained as evidence of its victory over the destructive vagaries of the meandering brown creek.

Men yelled in the distance. In spite of himself, Colin turned to watch. Cracking and rattling, the tall jarrah leaned in the direction of the wedgecut. The whole tree shuddered, poised on the edge of death. Slowly, with an air of stately resignation, it began its first and final fall. Its leafy top whooshed, brushing through the crowns of luckier trees. Down it came, faster, faster. Dignity abandoned, with a roaring, shattering thud it shook the spongy earth.

Small mortal men swarmed over the giant, instantly at the task of reducing its immensity to narrow strips to be slipped beneath iron rails. Colin joined the other mortals in butchering a tree because he was paid to do it. Here was the most heinous of all the miserable, unpleasant jobs Colin had worked at in the last year. To cut up this inert titan into sleepers, to fell so noble a symbol of—

Of what? Philosophy escaped him, his thoughts were as jumbled as they were yesterday—indeed, as they were for many days. They tumbled about in his head, chaotic and disjointed.

Hannah arrived with the noon meal. Work ceased, but not the confusion, or the haunting, pounding memory of the falling jarrah.

CHAPTER FOURTEEN

AN EVENING IN TOWN

Smoke the tortoise-shell cat curled up in Mary Aileen's lap, making knitting impossible. Mary Aileen had to either shoo the cat or abandon her handwork. She laid her knitting aside, then heard the front door close downstairs. *It's Papa.* She picked up Smoke and carried the limp, warm creature out of the room with her. She paused, watching from the top of the stairs.

Below in the foyer, Papa shook out his great coat. "I know we need the rain, but this is too much of a good thing. Edan home yet?"

"Probably around dark." Mum stepped up to him for a hello kiss. "Carl rang up this afternoon. He praised Edan's work and asked to take him along to get hay. He expects to return late. Says he'll drop Edan off here on his way in."

Papa nodded. "Little bite before supper?"

"Grace is bringing a tray of fruit and string cheese."

"None of that fresh raisin bread left from breakfast?"

"Edan took the last of it in his lunch. Come, sit." Mum led the way to the parlor. Mary Aileen glided downstairs and followed at a discreet distance. Papa looked weary, perhaps even heavyhearted. What else could be going wrong?

Papa flopped into his favorite chair and rubbed his face with both hands. "I got some returns today on the inquiries I sent out. No sign of Hannah or Colin anywhere around Kal. Aidan and Liam are looking; they want me to reimburse them for expenses. The area railway superintendent says he's on the lookout. He found a schoolbag with a girl's school uniform, brown frock and underwear. No name. He thinks it's hers, and he gave it to the constable. She can't retrieve it except through him. And certain unidentified railway workmen say Hannah and Colin found each other. They're together, somewhere. Sam, I'm half tempted to go out there."

Mum sighed and settled into her rocking chair, tipping it back. "To what end? If they travel east they must come by railway. That's covered. You've far less chance of finding them than the locals who know the area. And you've responsibilities here."

Papa sagged forward, his elbows on his knees, and stared at the ornate Persian rug. "Why, Sam? We did our best to raise them well. They're fine children. Why?"

Mum studied him intently, gently. Her face softened and she slipped into her comfortable old Irish brogue. "Be ye saying ye truly want to know, Cole? Or be y'r 'why' rhetorical?"

Papa lifted his head and looked at her. His voice rumbled, sounding very, very sad. "I really want to know."

Mum sat back in her rocker, and her voice took on the lightness of air, the gravity of earth. Mary Aileen marveled at the strength and authority that cloaked Mum now. "Ye be nae the man I married. Certainly ye be nae the man who indentured me out of the auld country those many years ago. Ye were crafty then, and devious, a man not to be trusted. As well ye had to be, for ye were sore beset by problems, scarcely any of y'r own making."

He waved his hand as if to brush away her words. "Those were the days, weren't they? Trying to keep Sugarlea afloat with no money to float her with. If Liam and Aidan had just helped—if only they'd taken over the Sydney office—I wouldn't have started out with such heavy debts. I don't think I ever told you how badly they milked the estate. My father left debts behind at his death, but we could have righted them if all three of us had worked together. Instead, they trebled the indebtedness and then got gold fever."

"And I daresay they're still milking any cow they can lay a hand to."

He nodded. "I doubt they've changed. They wanted nothing to do with Sugarlea. I gave up trying to get them involved. Then the ruined cane crop. And the Kanaka labor woes." He shook his head. "Don't know how I carried it all, as I look back on it."

Grace slipped quietly past Mary Aileen, set a tray on the coffee table, and left the room.

"Ye carried it bravely because y'r the strongest man I've ever known. And a fighter who will nae quit, no matter what. Y'r strength and will to fight helped ye bend y'rself to God's will, too. Today y're an infinitely better man, in God's eyes and in me own. I cannae tell ye how proud I am of ye, and of the distance y've come as a Christian."

"But—?"

"But y've forgotten y'r past, Cole Sloan. Y're in such a fret to put away the flaws, ye left behind the good as well. Remembering what ye were aids in what ye become."

"There was no good."

"There was much good, but I'll not argue it, now. I tell ye this: God did nae make the new Cole Sloan out of new clay; He used the old Cole Sloan. Y've come on a long journey, and y'r past has shaped y'r future."

Papa smiled. "I remember long ago you talked about the force of history in our lives. I didn't see it then."

"Ye still seem to ignore it, Cole. And ye expect Colin in particular, for he's the eldest and most like yourself, to start his own journey—not where y'rself did, but where y've lately come; not at the beginning of the journey y'rself took, but at the end of it. He cannae do that, Cole. Ye can show him the best way, but ye cannae force him to take it.

He must choose his own way, just as ye did back then. If he arrives where you've come, praise be to God. But *he* must do it. Ye can but watch and pray."

"Are you saying I should have been more lenient?"

"Nae regarding sin, nae, of course not. But more understanding. This moment, ye ken nae what y'r youngest son's hopes and dreams might be. Ye only see Edan as a miniature of what y'rself thinks he ought to become."

"I'm his father, Sam. Of course I know him."

Mum went on, "Nor Hannah either. Hannah's an imp and a tease, guilty of most all the pranks ye blamed upon her brothers."

"No."

"Aye. The camping incident, for example."

"Which one?"

"All of them, no doubt. But the one I nearly caught her at was Baylors' tent. 'Twas Hannah who tied the pony to the main pole. In the middle of the night when the moon was high, she stepped outside our tent and waved a white towel. The pony saw it and bolted, shaking the tent and frightening the poor beast further. Away it went, tent and all."

"You *knew* it was Hannah? Why didn't you tell me?"

"Ye were already punishing Colin. Besides, ye fain would have believed me. Ye did nae believe Hannah when she confessed, and she knew ye wouldn't. Ye thought she was trying to save her brother. Ye dinnae believe me now. Do ye?"

"Hannah." He wagged his head. "I've been good to her. You're a fine mother, Sam. Why would she run away?"

"She loves her brother, Cole. She fears for his health and safety."

"What about *her* health and safety?"

"Cole, she's almost thirteen. When y're that young y're immortal. At least ye think ye be. Naething can touch ye; charmed ye are. Everything comes out all right, every ending be happy. She simply went off to help her brother."

"All right. Tell me, why did her brother leave?"

"I aver to find for himself what ye were trying to force him to accept." Mum closed her eyes then, and began to quietly rock back and forth, the sadness of the world etched in her face.

————

"Here he comes!" Jack dropped his end of the crosscut saw and fought his way through undergrowth out toward the track. The stakeside came slooshing and sliding down the miry trail. Colin left the saw where it was, buried half-way in a fallen jarrah. He waded out to the track also, through the drizzling rain and the tangled wet weeds clawing at his shins and ankles. Les and Woppo emerged from the bush and joined him for the final quarter mile hike into camp.

Under the big canvas tarp that served as kitchen, dining hall, office, and men's dorm, Mr. Brekke sat thumbing through a ledger. "Come on, you coves. Payday."

Jack stepped in front of Mr. Brekke, first in line, his big hand out flat. Brekke counted out several bills and handed them not to Jack but to Hannah behind him. "Here you go, cook."

She beamed. "Thank you, Mr. Brekke." She looked beyond Les and Woppo to Colin at the end of the line. Her smile spoke volumes. *My first job! My first pay! Be happy with me!* She glowed, so utterly pleased that Colin could do nothing else but join in her enthusiasm. He grinned broadly.

As each received his week's pay, Colin watched Hannah back at her work. She had removed the top and bottom from a tin can to make a biscuit cutter. She patted out the mass of dough with the heels of her hands, for she had no rolling pin to do it properly. She pressed the tin into the dough, smoothly and deftly cutting the neat white circles. Actually, her biscuits weren't bad. Two wallaby haunches roasted by the fire and six potatoes nestled in the stones around the firepit. Colin had taught her everything she knew about cooking on an open fire.

"Gunner give us a lift into town, Brekke?" Jack counted his pay a second time.

"I'm goin' to the big town. You coves want to ride in the back of the truck, that's your affair. But when the truck returns tonight, you'd better be on it or you walk. And if you're late for work in the morning, I'll dock you." He made a few final marks in his ledger and closed it.

Then he rifled around in a hessian sack. "Brought a bonus for all you hard-working lads." Bottles clonked together as he pulled them from the bag.

"This better not replace the five quid you promised us at the end." Jack watched him suspiciously.

"Naaah. We cut half again as many sleepers as I'd expect from a crew this size. Just a little thanks from the boss. Here you go, cook." Brekke handed a bottle of ale to Hannah.

She glanced wide-eyed at Colin, surprise written on her face. "Th-thank you, Mr. Brekke, but I don't touch spirits."

"Sure you do." He laughed. "You're a big girl now, making your own way. Ain't gunner hurt you none. Give it a try."

"No, sir, really. Um, thank you. . . . " Her eyes flashed again to Colin. *Help me, please!*

But it was Jack who sprang to her defense. "Give it up, Brekke. If the cook's shickered, we eat worse than usual. She's right and you're wrong."

Brekke glared at Jack, but he withdrew the bottle and his offer, handing it instead to Colin who passed it on to Jack.

Colin shrugged and grinned. "If I get stinko, I'll forget which log I buried the crosscut in."

"Three pen'worth of God help us," the burly Norwegian muttered, and it was not a supplication.

By common consent the sleeper-cutters quit work early that Saturday afternoon. By equal consent, they hid the stakeside's distributor cap, just to make certain Brekke would not leave for town without them. Woppo asked to borrow the horse, so Colin saddled Max's Lady and they ran her up a plank into the stakeside. Snapping and snarling at anyone nearby, Max scrambled up behind the horse and lay cowering at her clumsy feet.

Brekke invited Hannah into the cab with him. Hastily and firmly she insisted upon riding in the back with her brother. Was she afraid of him, of some recent confrontation? Colin felt a heavy sense of dread again. Brekke fumed and sulked, but couldn't force her in front of the others. He asked a few more times, but she insisted no, and Jack and Colin backed her up. She rode in back.

The old stakeside galloped full tilt down the dusty, ragged track. Max's Lady splayed her feet and braced herself, white-eyed. Everyone bounced along, laughing and falling against one another. Colin quickly and gleefully got caught up in the carefree atmosphere. "Where are you going that you need a horse, Woppo?"

"Cakeshop first, then the pubs, in that order. Never been to Ravensthorpe before."

"A cake shop!" Hannah grinned. "I've not had sweets in ever so long! Let's stop, Colin, please!"

Jack shook his head and growled at Woppo, "You watch what you say in front of the little lady. You know better'n that."

Hannah frowned, looking confused.

"A cakeshop ain't what you think," Jack stammered.

Hannah shook her head. "I don't understand."

Jack nodded. "And you keep it that way, milady. You're a fine lass, Hannah, brought up right; stay that way. And one other thing—when we get a few pints under our belts, we ain't always the gentlemen we oughta be. So if one of us gets to pestering you—Nels Brekke in particular—you just call on one of us to protect you. Y're a fair dinkum young lady—I come to know that this week, watching you—and we don't want to see you spoiled."

Hannah looked at Colin, more perplexed than ever.

"We'll talk about it later," Colin assured her, but he couldn't stop thinking about Brekke.

Everyone clambered out the back of the truck as soon as they arrived in Ravensthorpe, babbling about real cooked meals. Woppo disappeared on Max's Lady. Down the dirty little town's main street came a truck even sorrier and noisier than the stakeside. Three men in the open cab laughed and waved as they passed, and the four in the back shouted something unintelligible.

Brekke yelled something back at them, laying a huge hand on Hannah's shoulder, and headed for a pub. "This way, lads. The blackfeller who drays our sleepers from Lake King to the railway claims this is the best around."

The best around lacked certain amenities. Chairs, for instance. Patrons arrayed themselves on stools and benches. And cleanliness. The bare tables sorely needed wiping. What the place lacked in furnishing and cleanliness it made up for in multilegged creatures. Spiders had laced the sooty ceiling end to end with webs. Flies easily outnumbered customers ten to one, maintaining a steady drone above the normal hum of conversation.

Brekke paid for Hannah's dinner, then tried in vain to get her to take a drink, whether it was his shout or not. Eventually Jack and Les went for a game of pool in the back room. Colin felt suddenly alone and out of sorts.

Brekke hoisted his bulk to his feet and announced, "Hannah and me, we're gunner go find a picture show. You stay here, Sloan," he winked, "and make sure you're back at the truck in time."

"My sister's too young to be in your company. Either she stays here, or I go with you."

"Crikey, lad, it's just a flaming picture show. Any man here will agree she ain't no little girl, but there's nothing to go butchers about. C'mon, cookie."

"Mr. Brekke, s-sir." Hannah stammered a moment, torn with decision. "I told you yesterday, and the day before, I'm only the cook and the driver. I refuse to begin any sort of—uh, er—a more personal relationship with you. I can't call you Nels, like you suggested, and I really don't think I ought to—"

"Look, do you wanna see a flick, or not?"

"Well, yes, I do, but—"

"Well, that's all we're gunner do. C'mon."

"Uh, well. . . . " She looked at Colin. Brekke jerked her arm suddenly, and they were out the door.

Panic welled up in Colin's head and chest. He couldn't handle Brekke alone. He ran to the back room. "Where's Les and Jack? The two woodcutters who just came in for a game?"

A bleary-eyed pool patron wagged his head. "Met a couple girls and left out the back way. Didn't even shoot their round."

Colin jolted back to the main room and out the front door. Night had settled in, making it difficult to discern direction. The meager light from the windows along streetside were not enough to illuminate the way. He peered up and down the broad dark track in vain. Where could Brekke have gone so quickly; a man his size would be hard to miss. He couldn't have gone far.

A block away upstreet, Max's Lady stood dozing by a corner pub, barely visible in the gloom. Colin sprinted, covering the whole block in seconds. He didn't see Max around, but that didn't mean he wasn't nearby. "Max!" He whistled, "C'mon!" He vaulted into the saddle, twisting the mare's head around in one motion.

On horseback he'd cover the town in no time—every alley and back street. He started by looking down the alleyways closest to the pub he'd just left. Out of nowhere a leanaway came staggering up the street in front of him.

"Hey, you!" Colin called. "Where's the picture show? The cinema."

"Picture show?" The man stopped and shook his head. "Don't bother, mate. Film's the same the last four weeks."

"*Where is it?!*"

"Up that way," he dragged a pointing finger, "two squares and over one. Can't miss it. Big corrugated tin sign."

Colin headed north. Suddenly he dragged the mare to a stop; a familiar roar in the distance behind him told him someone had just revved the engine of the stakeside! *Brekke. It has to be Brekke!* He whirled the mare south again. *If I can just make it in time. . . .*

There it was, rumbling onto main street, sputtering in low gear. Turning away from him, it rounded a corner, and chugged off to the west, spouting gray exhaust against the darkness.

Colin thunked his heels into the mare's ribs. He abandoned the stirrups, drew his knees up to her shoulders and hunched down into her mane. Instantly caught up in the thrill of the chase, the horse lurched forward, extending herself in a laborious, rocking-horse gallop. Under normal circumstances, Colin could just about outrun this pudgy old mare, but at this pace he might be able to at least keep the truck in sight.

Then from the west beyond town, out of nowhere, headlights appeared. Colin could see the black bulk of the stakeside between himself and the lights. Horns blared, headlights swerved, and both vehicles lurched to a halt.

He could hear voices shouting lustily back and forth. The stakeside door flew open and Hannah leaped out into the glare of the headlights. Someone called to her, then an arm reached out and grabbed her.

It was the rattletrap truck Colin had seen earlier, with the load of ruffians! Hannah was leaping from the frying pan to the fire!

Brekke's voice boomed above the cacophony, shouting at Hannah and at the young larrikins. The second truck pulled out easily around the stakeside and continued eastbound. Colin dragged Max's Lady to a halt as the headlights bore down on him, robbing him of what little night vision he'd had.

The rattletrap slowed somewhat as it passed Colin, and he could hear Hannah call something from the back. Still laughing like kookaburras, the three larrikins in the seat motioned to him. "Come along, mate!"

He glanced at the stakeside as it finally jerked into motion. Without hesitation, he spun the mare on her hindquarters and whipped her forward with the reins. The doover truck ahead had no back bumper, no tailgate. Hannah and the blokes were all shouting to him at once now, barracking him on.

The rattletrap truck slowed nearly to a halt, and Colin remembered how once not so long ago the gangly mare had leaped the wide mine shaft with only two narrow boards to aid her. He called upon her now, urging and driving. She gathered herself in a leap, her muscles bunched between Colin's knees, and flung herself up into the darkness.

Colin heard her feet hit the wooden truck bed. Max's Lady squirmed beneath him. Without his stirrups, he started to slip; he grabbed a handful of mane, too late. He slid forward and sideways as the mare lurched wildly, shaking him loose.

Rollicking laughter rang in his ears as he fell. Who on earth were these no-hopers who had nothing better to do than to cackle incessantly? Colin cried out as a clumsy horse foot stepped on his leg.

Now the laughter and cheering redoubled itself as Hannah's exuberant voice called out, "Max! Good, Max! C'mon, boy!"

A solid, warm furry body slammed into Colin's face. The familiar growl and snarl snapped right by his nose.

They were aboard. They were all aboard, even Max. The rattletrap truck heaved forward, picking up speed as half a dozen men's voices chattered gleefully.

The stakeside was hot on their heels. If they could just evade Brekke and his designs on Hannah, at least one danger would lie behind them. But what were these ruffians up to?

CHAPTER FIFTEEN

BAA BAA BLACK SHEEP

"Here you go, Edan." Mary Aileen refolded the newspaper in order to read it more easily. "Pencil and paper ready?"

"Yair." Edan didn't sound all that ready. He shifted on his daytime sickbed, the horsehair settee in the parlor.

"Papa says the nation's population is about six million. For convenience use six million even. It says here there are over twelve hundred cinemas in Australia now. How many persons per cinema is that?" She listened to the pencil scritch on his pad as he copied the problem.

"Next?"

"This one's easy. The article reports over sixty films are produced in Australia each year. What is the per capita?"

"How many people per picture, or how many pictures per person?"

"Work it both ways. This is arithmetic practice. Next?"

"Go ahead," he muttered sullenly. Arithmetic was not his favorite subject.

"On the 9th of June, a train derailment at Traveston, Queensland, claimed nine lives. What percentage of the population died in that tragedy?"

"Come on, 'Leen! That's too hard! I'm getting Mum to make up the problems."

"Work on it. See how well you do."

"I hate percent problems."

"I've noticed." Mary Aileen stood up and stretched. "You've missed almost a week of school, Edan. You don't want to fall too far behind." She walked out into the kitchen.

Mum sat in her kitchen rocker, reading the rotogravure.

Mary Aileen plucked an apple from the fruit basket on the table. "Anything in there we can turn into an arithmetic problem for Edan? He's on portions and percentages."

Mum frowned. "You'd really have to scrape. It's amazing some of the things they put in here. What they call human interest stories. Designed to warm the heart, they say."

"Warming the heart does very little for arithmetic." Mary Aileen swung a chair around to face Mum and sat down. "Particularly Edan's heart." She took a big juicy bite; she loved the crisp apples that came from Bendigo.

Mum pursed her lips. "I detest when men and boys get sick. Even a mere chest cold, like Edan's. They're such babies."

"What sort of heart-warming are you reading about?"

"Well, there's this item from a Perth paper about a Filipino. Seems he wanted to marry, but couldn't support a family on his current job. So his white mate offered to lend him a hundred pounds to help him buy into a gold mine in Kalgoorlie. Turns out the white mate's own uncles robbed him of his stash before he could make the loan. Some local miners who knew them both heard of their misfortune and contributed to a loan fund, interest free, from their own pockets. The man has his bride and his gold mine."

"Is there a picture, Mum?" Mary Aileen got up to peer over her shoulder. "Oh, quite a nice-looking man, isn't he. And she's a sweet-looking lass. Just look at their happy smiles!" She stretched and took another bite of her apple. "Stealing from your own nephew. Sounds like something *my* uncles might do!" She froze at her own words.

Mum's mouth dropped open as she gazed in disbelief at her oldest daughter. Mary Aileen shook her head. "It couldn't be, could it, Mum?"

"No. No, of course not." Mum stood up and started for the door.

"Where are you going?"

"To write a letter to—" She glanced again at the paper and pronounced the name by syllable, "Des-i-der-i-o Roma-les." She looked at Mary Aileen with haunted eyes. "Just in case."

———

Colin crooked his fingers and raked his hand across Max's Lady's rump, for lack of a curry to brush her with. The scuffs and gouge wounds on her backside and legs were healing well, now that they had bathed in the wholesome light and air. The hair around the scars was coming in white, though. How old was she, anyway? Her teeth revealed "over twelve, less than eighteen," but the quality of forage affects a horse's teeth as much as age does. It is difficult to tell once they pass ten years.

"Breakfast, mate."

Colin left the mare to browse in the bush and walked back to the campfire.

All seven men sat around the fire eating Hannah's biscuits, and she was hard at work cutting out another batch. Her grimy, blue-striped frock would never come clean, Colin thought absently. He settled down beside Joe Fitzroy.

Joe handed him the tin pan of bacon. "Bacon and biscuits it is, mate, 'til we get somewhere there's chickens."

"Bacon and biscuits are just fine." Colin helped himself to three rashers.

"Y'need more than that to keep alive."

"Ta." Colin took three more. "Hannah and I never really thanked you properly for helping us out last night." He passed the pan to Pot Dabney on his left.

Hannah nestled the iron Dutch oven into the coals.

"She makes better thick-milk biscuits than Horace ever did." Pot waved his half-eaten biscuit in the air. "That's thanks enough." He popped it in his mouth.

"Jarrah-jerker." Joe chuckled. "Always happy to pull one off on some jarrah-jerker. We don't warm up to timber people too much." He sat in the cold of early morning in nothing but a shortsleeved shirt, yet Colin could see no sign of shivering or gooseflesh. The big man looked powerful, his bulging muscles making his clothes seem tight. His hands were huge. Curious hands. Here sat a hard-working man, yet his burly hands looked remarkably soft, almost like a woman's.

"Then you're not foresters. What do you do?" Colin took a big bite of the hard, stringy bacon.

Joe watched him intently. "We eat rabbit the other two meals. If you think the bacon's tough, wait 'til lunch. We're sheep shearers. Headed for Victoria, eventually, with maybe a short cut near Adelaide. Then on to Gundagai, if the truck makes it that far."

"It'll make it," Mike said, reaching past Ray for another rasher of bacon. Mike and Ray looked to be brothers, Colin figured; they shared the same sandy-brown hair and gray-green eyes. And they both sounded vaguely American. "Got us this far, didn't it?"

"Running on baling wire and Hail Marys. Mike, there, is our mechanic." Joe wagged a finger toward Hannah. "What's the story with you two? Black sheep on the run or something?"

"My father will tell you I'm a black sheep, but my mum would say not. So it depends who you talk to. Hannah here is my sister." Colin took another bite and tried to talk around it, "I'm trying to get her safely home to Sydney. She'll be thirteen in October."

Joe wagged his head. "Bit young, I'd say."

"Not for Nels Brekke. He was the one driving that stake-side you forced off the road. You men saved her. I could never have caught up."

"Good-oh!" Pot cackled. "Weren't a real cheery sort, were he? 'Specially when we crumpled his intentions. Don't mind a bit that we crueled that bloke's plans." Pot's hands looked unusually soft too.

"Seeing that horse jump into the moving truck was worth the price of admission." Hungrily, Jackie Jump, a small, lean Aborigine, watched Hannah peek into the Dutch oven. "Never seen a horse do something like that. And that blue dog; he's a bottler." Jackie looked around. "Where is he, anyway? Didn't quit us, did he?"

"He's nearby. Stays with the mare." Colin watched Hannah at the oven, too. "Thanks for feeding him."

"Don't thank us for that. That meat was so bad we were gunner throw it out anyhow. In fact, the dog thought twice about eating it." Jackie reminded Colin of Dizzy in some respects—the quick, lithe way he moved, and his tough, wiry build.

Colin pondered the feeble flames dancing about on the coals. "Shearers. 'Spose we could join up with you, maybe find work on the stations? We've a few pounds to help on the trip."

Joe nodded. "I was just about to ask if you'd like to join us. Ever do any stock work?"

"Just horses at the racecourse in Sydney. Pretty good with horses, actually. That's all." Colin smiled. "And I can shuck oysters like nobody's business."

"Don't muster a lot of oysters in Victoria. Racecourse in Sydney. That where you got that jumping horse?"

Colin laughed. "Bought her in Broome last fall. A genuine Texan Yank picked her out for me."

"Here now! You oughta talk to these two Wooloomooloo yanks!" Joe waved toward Mike and Ray. "Up to putty nine months of the year, but when it comes to undressing a sheep they're the best there is. Always acting like they're Americanized—they're as Aussie as thee and me."

Hannah giggled. Her eyes—her whole face—sparkled with delight. She seemed totally comfortable with these itinerants, far more so than Colin. Colin would not in a dozen years have thought of approaching these rough-hewn fellows for help last night. Either Hannah was an intuitive, shrewd judge of character or she was very, very lucky.

Suddenly, without warning, thoughts of God flashed across Colin's mind. Might God have directed their paths thus far? Colin thought about Otis's claim to have met God. That didn't mean Otis couldn't be mistaken. Besides, even if Otis were right, Colin wasn't at all ready to attribute every stroke of fortune to Papa's all-in-all God.

Joe was still ranting on about how Mike and Ray put on such a Yankee act.

Hannah peeked for the third time into the Dutch oven. "Another minute or two."

"What does your Texan cobber sound like when he talks?" Mike asked.

"Let's see. I'd talk about a mob of horses and he'd say, 'tha's a remuda.' Or I'd point out a horse tailer and he'd say 'tha's a wrangler.' A mob of cattle rushing were 'a herd stampeding.' Muster is a 'round-up.' While he's talking, you keep translating from Yankese to Strine. Uh, 'caramba, compadre!' And 'buenos días.' "

"Don't he speak English?"

"Not good English. Spanish, mostly. He gets along."

"Now you gunner learn Spanish, Mike?" Joe laughed a hearty "Har, har, har."

Hannah was smiling at Colin now, with an expression of curiosity and wonder. One more peek and she lifted the oven off the coals. Using towels, she popped the rack out and handed it to Mike to be passed around. Her face fell as she watched the biscuit rack empty. With a sigh she started mixing up another batch.

It took the truck all day long to reach Esperance, about a hundred and ninety miles. They ate restaurant food there, and bought eggs. Colin purchased extra water tanks for the horse. Then, loaded to the gunwales, the old truck rolled northeast.

The land began to flatten out. Trees were shorter, the bush sparse. For hundreds of miles across this ruler-line landscape, the tallest things in sight were the telegraph poles—and a few wild camels Colin saw in the distance on several occasions. Hannah's nose, unaccustomed to desert sun, fried to a raw red and began to peel.

When he first saw them, Colin would not have given a brass razoo for this whole canty bunch. But as the days passed and he got to know them better, he began to almost enjoy them. They treated Hannah with every courtesy, yet not distant enough to keep her outside their circle of friendship. Wiser this time around, Colin kept a sharper eye for leers or unwelcome attention. None of these men seemed to see her as Brekke had; no one teased or harassed her. He wondered if that would change.

Twice between Balladonia and Cocklebiddy the old truck blew out tires. In Sydney, when Colin's father had a tire problem, he simply hopped aboard a trolley or bus to complete his trip, then rang up his mechanic to come pick up his car. Here on the flat, endless track, Colin found himself dismantling the whole wheel, scraping the damaged inner tube, cutting a patch and cementing it on, reassembling the wheel, and pumping it up with a tire pump in dire need of lubricant to reduce air leakage.

Why did Colin end up repairing the flats? He was the only person who didn't drive, and no one bothered to instruct him. Even Hannah drove her share. To Colin therefore, in the scheme of labor division, fell the non-driving tasks of minor and mindless repairs. Besides, it was Colin's half-ton horse that put so much extra load on the ancient junker.

Cocklebiddy behind them, they followed the telegraph east along the southernmost edge of the continent. Colin had never been anywhere near the Nullarbor, for he had crossed to Broome by the far north route. Australia is basically flat, but this part of the country somehow magnified that sheer flatness. To their right rolled the southern ocean. They could hear the breakers from camp some nights. To the left stretched a gentle ridge paralleling the coast, and beyond it.

When, a hundred miles west of Eucla, a gasket in the water pump gave way, Mike cut a new one from the lining of Hannah's shoe. Colin noticed her shoes appeared too small for her feet, not to mention how worn they were becoming.

While they were stopped Max caught still another rabbit. Half a dinner. Lunch and dinner were always rabbit. Colin was becoming excessively bored with rabbit, but it was food. And it was free.

Sand, too, became bothersome. Mile after mile the wind sent fine white sand scudding across the track. After days of lying beside them, the ridge now crossed their track. They climbed through a winding gap in the ridge and out onto its top.

They pulled up to the petrol pump in Eucla late on the fourth day. As far as they could see, the white sand drifted up against the trunks of small, dead shrubs. It lay in ripples across the open land and hung poised in dunes along the crest of the rise.

Hannah jumped down out of the back of the truck. "Train travel is so different. You just roll on day and night. You don't realize what a distance you've covered, until you have to cover every inch of it in an open truck."

Colin fell in beside her. It was such a nice change to walk around and stretch your legs instead of sitting and jiggling, and hanging on to your hat. He pointed into the distance. "The cliffs along the bight. You see pictures of them in books. Here's the real thing."

"I remember stories about Edward Eyre coming through these parts," Hannah added. "Can you imagine traveling this whole bight without so much as a camel? The truck is bad enough, but at least we can make two hundred miles a day. And the telegraph."

"The telegraph is the only reason Eucla's here." Colin ran Max's Lady off the truck to stretch her legs. With Max jogging fifty feet behind, he led the mare up past the telegraph station. The simple stone building stood amid the blowing white sand, a tiny blip of modern technology in a vast and hostile primal land. The building had stood there forty-eight years. Why hadn't it been buried in the sand by now?

Hannah stopped to gaze at the structure. "Joe says that before federation, they couldn't send a telegram between states. So an operator on the Western Australia side of the building copied the message down, then passed it through a window to a fellow on the South Australia side, who in turn sent it on its way. Can you imagine anything so silly?"

Joe says— Colin's neck prickled. Was the same thing happening again? Hannah was so naive.

Hannah headed back toward the truck. "And he says there used to be a score of people working here. But now most of it is automatic, and there's only four or five employees."

Joe waved toward Colin as they returned to the truck. The burly shearer held out a tennis-racket-sized hand. "Got ten bob, mate? Petrol here costs more than rubies and pearls."

What price pearls? The thought from the past jolted Colin. He dug into his pocket. "Got a carpet here. The pot owes me ten."

"Good enough. Wanna eat more rabbit, or pay an arm and a leg to eat in their roadhouse here? What's your fancy?"

"The poorhouse is worth it if we can eat something besides rabbit. Anything but rabbit."

"Hannah?"

"I'll take the roadhouse," she said without hesitation.

Joe nodded. "We're unanimous. See you inside."

Colin tied the mare on a long lead to the back of the truck, but she would find no grass or browse in this desolate land. She was starting to look nearly as scrawny as when he had first seen her in the paddock above Broome. There wasn't much choice. She cocked a hind leg and dozed off, with only her tail showing signs of life as it snapped and flailed at the ubiquitous flies.

Hannah followed Joe inside. No doubt the others already sat in the gloom of what had to be the nation's smallest, poorest roadhouse. Colin found himself walking away from the restaurant, south, out to the crest of the steep bluff. Directly ahead of him the bluff fell away to the flat shelf below. A mile beyond, the sparkling turquoise ocean lapped quietly at the shore. Shoreline and white beach extended as far as he could see to the west. Here at Eucla, the sharp ridge they had been keeping on their left came angling southeast to the water and plunged in. To the east, that ridge, in the form of ragged cliffs, dropped precipitously to the water below. No beach there, no friendly sand. The surf crashed hard against the wall. Colin knew, too, that that vertical wall separating land and sea extended over a hundred miles along the featureless coast.

Black sheep? Perhaps he was. If he weren't, he could go home again. He'd swallow his pride and telegraph his father for money to whisk Hannah directly home, instead of subjecting her to this torturous, dangerous journey.

But he couldn't. He just couldn't. Maybe he was, after all, a black sheep. A prodigal.

He turned his back to the ocean and its perpetual movement. Before him to the north, with the sun in his face, a desolate land rolled away. A whole continent of desert, of blowing sand as pale as death, stretched beyond. For several minutes he stood there between the empty desert and the restless sea, and felt the world's bitter sadness seep into his soul.

BROUHAHA

"So you see, maybe God made rabbits and maybe He didn't. Don't matter. What matters is that stupid people turned them loose on us. Whitefeller know-it-alls brought rabbits in for sporting when there never should have been any rabbits in the land. Now they're all over the continent. Rabbit fences don't stop them. I helped build rabbit fences up north on the Murchison and up behind Port Hedland. Had rabbits on both sides of it before we could get the wire up. 'Scourge of God' ain't nearly it. 'Scourge of fools,' is more like it."

Colin watched the grand philosopher, Jackie Jump, wave a roasted rabbit drumstick high. Colin was getting pretty tired of eating rabbit, like everyone else, but he hadn't yet made the furry creatures a topic of philosophical discussion.

With huge white teeth, Jackie stripped the meat from his rabbit leg. "You saw Eucla, Colin, what it looks like now. Didn't used to look like that. When I was just a nipper traveling with my uncles, we'd stop at Eucla on the way 'cross. Green it was then, with trees and birds singing— wrens, willy wagtails, big white cockatoos with tinges of pink. Most beautiful birds in the world, them major mitchells. Don't ever see them no more 'round there."

"Why the change?" Colin finished his rabbit forequarter and tossed the bone into the fire.

"Rabbits. Mobs and mobs of rabbits. They ate everything green, then the bark off the trees. They even ate the wood. Then they starved, thousands of them, 'cause nothing was left to eat. They're still out there, as you well know. Go out and shoot dinner anytime you get hungry. But not so many now. Not after they ruined the whole face of the land."

"You mean twenty years ago there wasn't this loose sand blowing around Eucla?"

"Twenty, thirty. Too right. Always the wind was blowing; the trees all lean away from windward, you notice. But not all this sand. Droughts didn't mean as much then, 'cause the land came back with the rain. Now the droughts hit harder, and they hit suddenly. We've three years of drought right now in Victoria here. You see how the paddocks look."

"So the desert is man-made."

"Man-made. 'Course, now there's men making a living off it. Killing rabbits is big business. Lot of the larger stations hire blokes full time just to kill rabbits. And there's other rabbiters who go from station to station, stay maybe a month or six weeks, cut the rabbit population back, and move on—they serve stations too small to hire a rabbiter year 'round."

"They shoot them?"

"Poison them. Too 'spensive to shoot them. You're talking hundreds. They put out phosphorized wheat, but it's slow. They suffer for days. There's stuff called 'Toxa' that kills them right away, but it's expensive. Lotta rabbiters use apples soaked in strychnine. Lay a trail of poisoned apples, come along the next day and gather up the bunnies. They throw away the meat now. In the old days, you wouldn't do that—throw anything away."

"What did you eat when you were traveling, if there weren't any rabbits?" Colin finished the last of his potato.

"Possums, 'roos, wombat now and then, wallabies.

Lotsa things. They're all gone, too, just like the birds. Worse'n the birds. Ain't none left of some of them."

"Mmm." *A desert of man's own making,* Colin thought. Vacant. Barren. Arid. In a way, it was like the desert Colin felt within himself. Or was he being too pensive, poetic? He pushed the thought aside.

"Let's go, lads!" Joe's voice boomed from the veranda of the government house two hundred yards away. Colin lurched to his feet and wiped his greasy hands off on his trousers. He picked up his mare's reins and led her to the house.

"The shed hands and classer are here, but Clarke's people are still out mustering, so we'll start with this mob." Joe waved an arm. "Let the truck through that gate. Hannah can start them this way with the truck and you run 'em into the pen, Colin."

Run them into the pen. It sounded so easy. Never in his life had Colin ever seen a sheep up close, let alone try to bend an ovine will to his own. He mounted the mare with some uncertainty and rode her through the gate.

Eagerly Hannah drove out into the paddock. Much of the dirt had been pounded to soft powder by thousands of little hooves. Fine bulldust boiled up behind the truck.

Just as eager as Hannah, the brainless old mare flung herself forward into her rocking-horse canter. She was sweaty and blowing before they reached the far end.

A mob of wool balls on spindly legs came bursting out of the truck's drifting dust, creating a dust-wall of their own. Colin reined the mare aside and swung her around beside them. He urged her forward. She set her ears and leaned into the bit, loving every minute of this sheep-run.

It was so easy! As they neared the holding pens Colin would simply crowd the mare in closer, haze the mob right where he wanted them to go. They were near the pen now. Suddenly a suffocating cloud of dust wrapped him tight. He choked; he couldn't see. When finally he cleared his eyes enough to open them, the mob was clattering down the paddock, behind the truck and back to the far end.

"Gimme the horse!" snarled Pot Dabney. Colin slid down from the saddle barely in time to avoid being yanked out of it. Pot swung aboard and wrenched the mare savagely aside. He galloped her away into the dusty gloom.

Within moments, the mob was back again. Colin heard Joe's foghorn voice call, "Stay put, Colin!" Colin stayed put, though the mob bore down hard upon him. The mare no longer ran free and happy with these sheep. Pot was jerking her this way and that, twisting and turning, threatening the sheep with mayhem beneath the horse's clumsy feet. Colin yelled and waved his arms. The tumbling, bounding sea of wool angled away from him, veered away from Joe close beside him, and thundered into the chute to the holding pens.

"Tea time's over!" Joe roared. "Get to work."

Covered with dust and grinning radiantly, Hannah parked the truck by the shearing shed and clambered to the ground. She ran inside and was waiting on the shearing floor with a broom in her hand by the time Colin got inside.

Jackie Jump had already hazed a few dozen sheep into the small holding stanchions inside the shed. Carelessly he laid his black hands on the nearest wide-eyed ewe. In an instant she flipped onto her backside, her legs sticking straight out. Jackie dragged her out onto the floor in that inelegant position and ran his shears down the center of her belly. Colin was amazed that she did not struggle more.

Joe's shears buzzed to life behind Colin, and then Pot Dabney's and old, bearded Horace Hamm's. Curtis Carew, thirty-five years a shearer, wrenched his ewe to a sitting position and went to work. Scrawny, weathered Curtis weighed at most a hundred and ten pounds; the sheep outweighed him by five stone.

Ray turned out his first clipped sheep. Already Mike was sharpening and oiling blades, tending the donkey engine that powered the shears, minding the creaky, complaining overhead belts. Colin watched, rapt. These men, so easy to label *riffraff* when they were swagging it, had become an efficient, closely-knit team.

"Don't stand there like a stunned mullet, lad. Take this to the table." Joe left his fleece on the floor and went for another sheep. Colin did not in the least feel like a part of this team.

Hannah seemed to. She was right there in her role as broomie boy, sweeping up the rapidly forming flecks and loose balls of wool. She absolutely glowed with enthusiasm.

Colin scooped up the fleece and tossed it onto the table at the end of the floor. Instantly a shed hand materialized at Colin's side, spreading the fleece wide, expertly snatching away this wad of wool and that from the edges. Swiftly he folded it here and there and rolled it into a ball. The classer gave it a passing glance and tossed it into one of several bins, the first of the day's harvest.

The shed hand scowled at Colin. "Where's the next, lad?"

Colin jogged out onto the floor. He grabbed up Jackie's and Curtis's fleeces and ran to the table. He ran back again to fetch Horace's fleece and Joe's next.

"Tar boy!" barked Joe. Hannah dropped her broom. From the shoulder-high wall sill she snatched up an open can and with a paintbrush smeared black gooey salve on a cut in the sheep's flank. Obviously, Joe had instructed her ahead of time as to her duties. He had not said a word to Colin.

Two more fleeces lay on the board. Colin was sweating now. He picked them up and walked them to the table.

Joe did not so much as appear warm. He announced loudly even as he worked, "With this drought, Mr. Clarke's going to slaughter all his age-cast ewes or anything close, so keep them out separate. Stags, also."

"Got a broken-mouth here," Jackie called.

"Oughta throw away the concertinas, too," muttered Curtis. He struggled with a particularly wrinkled old sheep between his knees.

In a daze, Colin gathered more fleeces to the table. Terminology flew about his ears, an alien language that meant nothing to a humble lad from Sydney with a knack for opening oyster shell. In moments the classer and shed hand would fling a fleece out across the table, trim it, roll it and toss it aside. Colin, the mindless rouseabout, ran, hard-pressed to keep up.

"Smoke-oh!" called Joe, and work ceased.

Hannah led the way out to the gum tree behind the shed and flopped down, looking utterly spent. "Colin, this is so grand!"

He collapsed near her in the shade and stretched out. The flies found his sweaty face instantly. "It's work like you wouldn't read about. We were crazy to join up with a mob of shearers. Daft."

"Oh, no! It's perfect. In school you read in history books and geography books about Australia's primary industry, but it's all just reading. Like the shearers' strikes. Twenty-five years ago, in Barcaldine, remember? And they were doing just what we're doing, except they didn't get paid but a skerrick of what we're earning. Same hard work. And now I can understand what the strikes were about, to work so hard like this and not earn a decent quid. And all the work that goes into wool. It's not just something in the schoolbooks, you see? Suddenly it's real."

"It's real, all right." Colin drew his hat over his face to hold the flies at bay. He envied her enthusiasm. Why couldn't more of it rub off on him?

" 'Twas real then, too." Ancient Horace Hamm settled down beside them in the shade. He sat cross-legged, building a sorry excuse of a cigarette from a pouch of tobacco and a yellow bit of paper. "Good for you, lass, to appreciate the sweat, blood and tears we paid for our privileges. Not many youngsters do."

Hannah turned her head to stare at him. "You took part in the shearers' strikes?"

"Ay-uh. Barcaldine. I was there. Shearing time's midsummer there—January, February. The rainy months, up in Queensland. 'Twas a thousand of us strikers there in March, refusing to cut without a contract, when they called the military in. Torchlight parades most every night, the army flexing its muscles and we shaking our fists. We had a strike headquarters in Ash Street, and we lived in a tent camp at Lagoon Creek. The military pitched their tents by the courthouse. Then the railway workers struck, and it was all gone to Hades in a handbasket from there."

Hannah sat up wide-eyed, watching him. Colin knew for a fact that old Horace was cleaning up his language considerably in her presence.

Horace lit his cigarette. The paper flared into bright flame until the fire reached tobacco. Horace's cigarettes, ample and bulging in the middle, left much to be desired at either end.

He continued, his voice a quiet drone muffled in memories. "The wallopers arrested the leaders. Then some pastoralists tried to bring in nonunion shearers; met them along the railway with bullock carts. A hundred of us rode out there to stop them. Lots of shots fired. What a brouhaha! Ah, 'twas a heady time. We lost that skirmish, but we all sat down at the bargaining table come June and worked out a truce. I still recall one of them, a pastoralist named Frobel. Wise man—did a lot to smooth the waters. Funny, the people you remember. And a loud bloke named Sheldon. Worth putty, that Sheldon. But y'know, I can't remember the names of my own mates in that adventure. Mind's getting rickety."

"It must have been terribly exciting!" Hannah beamed.

He chuckled. "We won in the end, I'd say. The pastoral-ists hire union shearers at a decent wage today. Times have changed, and for the better. Except the men are still the same." He puffed on his acrid cigarette. "You, lass. Aren't you frightened about being out here so far from home with these ruffians?"

She laughed. "Ruffians? Heavens no! Besides, we're not so far from home anymore. Not like when we were clear over by Perth. No, I'm not frightened. I'm with Colin and God's taking care of us."

Colin pulled his hat off his face to stare at her. Was she making sport? No. She sat in casual repose, watching the dancing leaves overhead.

Horace stood up and wandered off.

Hannah drew her knees up and crossed her arms over them. "Colin, I'm so sorry Uncle Chris and Aunt Linnet weren't in Adelaide. I would have loved to see them. London and Paris. Isn't that something, to simply up and travel to Europe?"

I'm sorry, too, that they're out of the country, Colin thought. *I could turn you over to their care and be free of the responsibility of you. I didn't ask you to join me.* But she had acted in love. Colin would refrain from speaking his thoughts out loud. "I'm sorry that cut near Adelaide fell through, too. If Joe had signed us up for that job, I'd have found out then what kind of work this is."

She snapped her head around toward him, frowning. "You wouldn't quit, would you? It's not that bad. You'll get used to it."

"Easy for you to say. You're pushing a broom. I'm run-ning full out, like a chicken without a head."

"Let's get back to it, laddies," Joe bellowed. "Don't wan-ner disappoint all them sheep." He led the way into the shed. By the time Colin got inside Joe had already shorn a ram, and was shouting, "Where's the fleecy?" Colin was the fleecy. He picked up the ungainly wad of wool and toted it to the table. Onerous as opening shell used to be, at least you could do it sitting down.

Mr. Clarke appeared directly; his musterers had brought in several mobs of sheep. He stood about for most of a day, watching, obviously waiting for a chance to criticize. Eventually he went back to his government house and left Joe's crew in peace, if all-out hard work be peace. They turned out the cobbler—the term for the last sheep to be shorn, Colin learned—six days after they signed on.

Mr. Clarke balked at giving Hannah pay equal to the men's. Joe protested, threatening union action, and Mr. Clarke gave in. She had, after all, done a young man's work, Joe fumed; Mr. Clarke was getting full value and then some. Colin stood back and watched. How much of Joe's tirade was grounded in justice, and how much in an unhealthy interest in Hannah? He couldn't tell.

"Which'll it be, lads?" Joe asked, as he distributed pay all around. "The big town or the nearest pub?"

"Nearest pub now, big town tomorrow, then on to the next cut. Up in Shepparton, ain't it?" Pot stuffed his money in his pocket with a flourish.

Joe nodded. "So be it. Pile in, lads."

Colin saddled Max's Lady and ran her up into the back. He didn't bother to notice whether Max got in or not. He was crooked on that old dog anyway. The mutt barked at the sheep and stirred them up, making them all the harder to handle, never doing much of anything useful.

The rest of the crew took so long washing up, Colin found himself luxuriating up front in the seat for once, instead of bouncing around in the back. Joe climbed behind the wheel. Hannah hopped in beside Colin. They were off.

Joe should have been happy. The first cut of the season brought them a nice check. Why was he so quiet?

He smiled suddenly at Hannah. "So how do you like shearing, lass?"

"I love it." She sobered. "Are we going to have to argue with the pastoralist every time I get paid?"

Joe grimaced. "No. Clarke's so flooting worried about union trouble you can wear him down to get just about anything you want. He's a softy, but every other pastoralist we work for will be tough. Arguing won't work. We won't be able to shout 'em down to get you the pay you deserve. And you deserve it. You work hard as any man. You did a fine job."

"Thank you. Who's broomie boy when you don't have a girl?"

"Some boy your age. But, you see, a pastoralist will hire a hundred boys on the shearing floor before he'll give the time of day to a girl. It's a man's world there, lass. If you manage to earn five shillings a week this season, that'll be a shilling I don't know about."

Colin scowled. "We're saving up to get her back to Sydney. Won't get far on five bob."

The truck rattled into a sleepy little village. Colin noticed up ahead that it supported not one but two pubs, facing each other on alternate corners of the town's only cross street.

"Stop, Joe!" Hannah bounced up and down in place, pointing. "That shop is still open!"

Joe guffawed loudly as he slammed on the brakes. "Women! They can't stand the noise of two coins rubbing 'gainst each other."

"Thank you, Joe!" Hannah leaped to the ground even as Colin made a wild, lunging grab for her.

"No, Hannah! We're saving our money, remember?"

An iron grip locked Colin's arm in place. Joe didn't sound hostile but he certainly sounded definite. "Now, that young lady worked hard for her money. It's all hers, not yours, and she'll spend it as she cares to. Understand?"

Colin understood perfectly. With dismay he watched Hannah disappear into a small draper's shop.

The pub they entered offered rabbit on its menu, but everyone declined. Ray and Mike hung themselves on the bar for some serious drinking. Joe, Pot, Horace, Curtis, Jackie Jump and Colin crowded around the largest table in the place and ordered steaks. Steaks. Beef. Colin could hardly wait.

"So you're the boofheads put a brush on the board!" a rather young man with slicked-back hair called to them from the bar.

Colin leaned toward Pot. "What'd he say?"

"We're the idiots who put a girl in the shearing shed."

Someone else cackled, "Smart, them shearers."

As one, the men at Colin's table rose. The sudden anger in their faces frightened him. Joe purred menacingly, "She's a sister, and innocent. You'll mind what you say."

"Here, you blokes!" the bartender barked. "No trouble, or out you all go."

About half the room glared back and forth at each other. Colin's companions sat down again.

"Gotta expect some of that," old Horace grumbled. "Letting Hannah work on the board is gunner draw some comment. Just ain't done, you know."

Colin glanced at Joe. "Even when she works as hard as any man?"

"That ain't it, lad. She's a sheila. Mosta the stations won't let her near at all."

"Mmm." Maybe shearing was not the trade for them after all. But where else would they find work? "How far to the nearest large town?"

"Five miles. Bendigo."

"Joe! Colin! Look!" Hannah's soprano voice warbled. Colin twisted around. She approached the table, proudly wearing a new frock—straight lines, a waistless dress with a very feminine flounce at the bottom. The latest style. As she stepped in beside Colin he noticed she also wore new black shoes. They were definitely a woman's shoe.

Pot waved his glass aloft. "We ordered steak all around, lass. What'll you have?"

"Oh," she giggled. "Steak! Haven't had steak in ages, have we, Colin. I'll order mine. Is there room here for me?"

"Always, lass." Pot drained the last of his glass.

She ran off to ask the bartender for another steak.

Joe reached over and poked him. "Put the turps aside awhile, Pot. You've had more'n enough."

Jackie Jump grinned at Colin. "That's why his name, you see. Least little drop makes him drunk. A man who gets drunk so easy, they call him a two-pot screamer. Pot, here, for short."

"Oh." Colin had it all wrong. He'd assumed the nickname *Pot* meant the man could hold his alcohol. For a bit there he had felt as if he were one with this crew, and now suddenly he felt quite naive again and out of place.

Joe bolted to his feet and lunged for the bar. Colin jumped in surprise. Now Pot roared and leaped to the fray. A leering, laughing larrikin at the bar had wrapped an arm around Hannah's shoulders. She was squirming to release herself from his embrace. In no time half the men in the hot, stuffy room were on their feet and shouting at once.

Colin's heart jammed itself into his throat. What now? What could he do? Before his eyes the whole pub erupted into a melee such as only the legends record. Men were pushing and shoving and roaring at one other, as if the least provocation was all they needed. The bartender bellowed for a halt to the nonsense.

Decrepit, paunchy, profane old Horace could still fight a tiger to a standstill, and Curtis Carew, weighing in at no more than a hundred and ten pounds, was tough as fencing wire. Every man in the pub was as strong as these shearers or stronger. Colin was no match for the least of them.

As nearly as Colin could tell, Pot started it. He punched the fellow with Hannah in the face, and a man with slicked-back hair turned on Pot and slugged him. Hannah! *Where is she?* Colin's brain screamed. *She's still trapped in this mess.*

Jackie Jump disappeared into the mad rush along with every other man Colin knew by name. Suddenly, a face Colin had never seen before loomed directly in front of him, swinging. Colin didn't even feel the blow connect; he simply sprawled numb and confused in the wreckage of the table, glasses and ale, contemplating the water stains on the ceiling as pandemonium burgeoned elsewhere.

Then the whole side of his face began to burn with pain. His brain woke up. *Hannah!* He struggled to sit up, leaned too hard on a shattered table leg, and fell back when it rolled out from under him. *Hannah!* He regained strength in his knees and tottered to his feet.

Suddenly a hole opened in the churning mass of belligerents. Colin froze, openmouthed. Jackie Jump, like the axle of a wheel, rotated in the middle of the hole, creating it as he moved. He swung a huge slab bench in rapid circles, parting the waters, mowing down the opposition. He was working his way toward the door. Beneath the spinning bench, Hannah crawled on her hands and knees, safe in the eye of the storm.

"Run, lass!" Jackie cried.

Hannah bolted for the door. From nowhere a grizzled drover seized her arm, yanking her to a halt. Above the thunder of the brawl Colin heard his snarling speech. "Slut!"

Colin lurched forward and grabbed the blackguard by the nearest appendage—his ear. He jerked the warrigal back, slamming the man in the side, and connecting solidly with a punch in the face. Before the fellow hit the floor, Colin had his arm around Hannah, dragging her out the door.

The cool night air hit his sweaty face with a jolt. He latched on to a porch post and hung there gasping, still gripping Hannah, as his lungs worked to catch up.

The constable and his assistant stood by the window, billies in hand, peering in cautiously. "What you think, Chester?" asked the assistant. "Looks a bit wild yet, eh?"

"Duty-sworn to protect the public we are, but it appears the only two left to protect have just escaped the melee—the lad and lass here. What's the hurry to rush in?"

"Couldn't agree more, constable. Coo! Lookit that king hit, willya!"

Hannah sobbed bitterly on Colin's shoulder. He drew her closer. What could he say? He had no idea what words to speak to a terrified little girl.

The whole side of his face throbbed, and Colin couldn't help thinking what Papa would have done in such a situation. The real question was why he should *care* what Papa would do. He had left home a full year ago; what Papa might have done should be the farthest thing from his mind. It no longer interested him. He was done with Papa, and with trying to please the man. Or was he?

He patted Hannah's shoulder. "You're safe now. It's all right."

But her weeping continued unabated.

"You don't have to be frightened anymore, Hannah. It's over."

"I'm not," she wailed. "And I wasn't." Her dark head shook. Her voice stammered, riddled with sobs. "I was never frightened with you and Joe there. When I was crawling, I tore my new dress!"

CHAPTER SEVENTEEN

RATS!

Hannah huddled in closer against Colin. They were pressed deep in the doorway of a butcher shop, trying in vain to escape the predawn chill.

It's curious, thought Hannah, *how much warmer a Sydney spring morn is than this in Bendigo.* Never in Sydney had she felt such damp, penetrating cold. She began to muse about her warm, soft bed at home. How she wished she were in it! She missed Mum and Papa and Edan and Mary Aileen. She even missed Smoke. But she couldn't tell Colin, not in a million years. He'd have more reason than ever to make her go home.

In a way, she wished this adventuring would go on and on. In another way she wanted to be safe at home. *You can't eat your cake and have it, too,* Mum always said. This must be what she meant.

Out in the street Max's Lady dozed, her nose nearly touching ground, her hind foot cocked in its peculiar way. Max lay curled against the shop wall ten feet away. When would the butcher arrive for work? Hannah was beginning to despair.

At last, as the sky grew gray with the creeping dawn, he came. He wore a flat straw hat and clean white shirt that shone in the semi-darkness. A frighteningly large man, he appeared as wide as he was tall. He frowned at Colin, then

Hannah, but said nothing. Hannah stood up straight, and looked to Colin to do the talking.

"Good morning, sir." Colin tipped his head as he removed his battered hat. "My sister and I have a favor to ask of you. Two favors, really."

"What makes you think I'm running a special on favors today?" The man turned his back to them and unlocked the door.

Undaunted, Colin pressed his request. "Our dog Max here hasn't eaten for quite awhile and we're hoping you might have a bone for him, maybe some scraps."

"That ugly dog?" The man stared at Max.

"Too right, sir. Bad tempered, too."

The man's eyes flitted to Colin. Did they twinkle? A smile seemed to creep to his lips. "I think I might have a bone. Is that one of your favors?"

"Yes, sir. The other is employment. We're willing to do any work you might have available."

"No work. Come in; I'll give you some scraps." The man pushed the door open and twisted the electric light switch.

Hannah yelped. "Rats! A rat just ran across the floor!"

The man shrugged. "Butcher shops and rats. They're made for each other."

A blue streak whipped past Hannah's knees. In a stroke, Max crossed the open floor and seized the brown furry creature in his mouth. He shook his head wildly and tossed it aside. Hannah felt her stomach turn over. His nose to the floor, Max set off in search of more.

The butcher stared at the dog in disbelief. "You know, I don't have work for you two, but maybe for that dog, I do. Good ratter, he is."

Colin smiled. "I'm very happy to hear that, sir. I never could see the worth of the mutt, until now. He's tried the same with sheep."

"Doesn't make the shepherd very happy, I'll wager." The

man seemed friendlier now. He disappeared into a back room and emerged with a bulging hessian sack.

Hannah's mind raced as she watched Max explore a rathole in the baseboard. It was the fourth hole he'd found in just minutes. "Sir, how much would you hire Max for?"

"What?" The man laughed. "How would he sign for his pay?"

"You said you may have work for him. Perhaps. . . . " She paused. "I know! You could pay a sum for each rat caught in your shop. You could lock him in here at night and let him work."

"Lock a dog in a meat market?" The man guffawed.

But Colin had caught the vision. "Sir, the evening before last, some very good personal friends were involved in a . . . er, an altercation. We spent the last of our shearing wage helping them pay their fines. But if you'll advance us the money for food today and some bricks, we'll set Max to catching rats for you. And you can pay per head."

The butcher studied Colin a few moments. "A shilling for each dozen rats and scraps for the dog."

Hannah licked her lips. "That's a lot of rats, sir."

Colin didn't seem the least worried about the number. He nodded. "How about twelve rats per shilling for the first hundred—no! For the first ninety-six—and eight rats a shilling for any over ninety-six?"

The man chuckled. "Shrewd lad. A deal it is. And the money for—for bricks, did you say?—is an advance against wages, not a gift."

"Agreed, sir!"

Hannah's breastbone tickled. Now, what were they getting into? At least with their five-shilling advance they could eat breakfast. Colin fed Max from the hessian sack of scraps; Hannah had never seen the sullen old dog so near ecstasy. The blue-brindled curmudgeon even wagged his tail once. For him, that single flap of the tail was a paroxysm of delight.

They rode double-dink down to the pottery after breakfast. Colin turned Max's Lady into a vacant lot nearby to graze. For a few pence he bought broken bricks and potsherds as Hannah wandered about marveling at the stolid old buildings, the ancient kilns. Then Colin scooped dirt from the lot into the hessian sack, explaining his plan to Hannah. While the horse tried to fill up on the sparse grass, they chose several stout sticks to serve as clubs.

Their next stop was a small inn on a back street near a livery stable where they took two rooms. Hannah already looked forward to a good night's sleep on a real bed.

By closing time they had returned to the butcher shop. The stout man locked his door and began the daily task of counting his till. "This I gotta see," he kept saying.

As Max located the ratholes, Colin and Hannah plugged them with bricks and sherds. It took them nearly an hour before they were satisfied only one hole remained, just one way for the rats to enter the shop from beneath the floor or within the walls—a hole beside the wrapping counter. Colin poised the hessian sack of dirt on the counter edge above the hole and ran the mare's long lead-line from the sack to the door. When the line proved five feet short he begged some twine from the butcher to complete the trap. Then he strewed the last of the scraps from Max's breakfast, and everyone stepped outside—the butcher closing the door behind them.

"Colin?" Hannah was curious. "How can you be sure there are so many rats about?"

"Remember Clyde Armbruster? No, I guess you wouldn't. You were too small yet when he died. Anyway, he said once if you see one rat in daytime, there's a hundred hiding."

"So, you really think your plan will work?"

"I really think so. I wouldn't waste my time if I didn't. Here's a bob. Go buy a loaf of bread for supper."

Hannah didn't need any coaxing. She ran down to the bakery, ravenous. No one lauding the life of exploration and discovery had ever mentioned that a large part of adventuring is going hungry.

Then they waited, watching, hovering by the door of the shop until past eight. "Now," Colin whispered, and just in time; Hannah could wait no longer. Carefully Colin inched the door open, his cudgel poised at ready. He yanked on the leadline. The hessian sack went *thwuck!* in the blackness.

Then he slipped through the door with Hannah close behind, and twisted the light switch. Hannah shut the door and squealed. Rats—dozens of them, scores of them—poured across the floor in every direction, headed for the plugged holes. And Max! The brindled beast went mad with delight, seizing rats then worrying them, tossing them aside to chase the next.

Rats scampered up the walls. They scurried along the overhead bars from which the butcher hung carcasses and sides. They teetered like acrobats, balancing as their tails whipped in wide circles. Eyes glinted red from every dark corner. Hannah's excitement was matched only by revulsion. *Rats! What could be more gruesome?*

Colin clubbed the creatures that ran overhead, while Hannah only flailed at them. She never could quite hit them. Maybe it was because with every swing she squeezed her eyes shut tightly. The frenzy slowed. Max ran back and forth, still seeking any movement.

Instinctively, the dog stuffed his nose under the hessian sack. A slim brown rat bolted out from beneath it and zipped across the room. Max made a lunge for it. Without slowing, the furry creature darted up the closest haven of safety—Colin's pant leg!

Colin jumped and howled. Grabbing his pant leg above the knee with both hands, he tried to keep the rat from climbing further.

"I'll get it!" Hannah swung her club at the wiggling bulge.

Colin yelled; she'd missed. Her second blow dislodged the rat and Max completed the task.

"We did it, Colin!" Carefully, squeamishly, Hannah picked up a dead rat by its bony tail. The bristly, furless appendage felt differently than she would have imagined—and it was cold. Gleefully she stacked rats in piles of ten. "Two hundred thirty-eight! Colin, how much is that?"

Colin studied the floor a moment, muttering and wiggling his fingers. "One pound, six." His serious expression broke into a happy grin. "Over a pound for one night's work!"

Exhausted, Hannah plopped down beside her brother in the middle of the floor. "Look at your poor leg. Hope that won't happen every night. Maybe you should tie butcher's twine around your pant legs, though!"

"Not maybe, Hannah. Definitely." A green lump on his shin was rapidly turning purple. Little red clawmarks made a curious pattern up and down his leg.

"We missed a hole behind the counter. Some of them escaped down it. Did you see? Do you suppose we'll catch as many tomorrow night?"

"I don't know. Probably not. Some, though, for sure."

Max tossed another rat in the air, number two hundred thirty-nine. He ferreted out a few more, but essentially the hunt was over. Max, jubilant in his own misanthropic way, curled up near his Lady at the livery on the edge of town, and the tired but happy hunters retired to their rooms at the inn.

A real bed. Genuine bedsheets. Hannah burrowed into the unaccustomed softness. Still, it took her a long time to fall asleep. Her dreams that night were marred by myriads of ghastly little creatures—what *were* those things—that pursued her through the family's camping ground on that distant, familiar ridge in the Blue Mountains.

After receiving his pay from the butcher, Colin sold the rats, all hundred and fifty-seven pounds of them, to the knackerman as tankage, to be rendered for fertilizer. Three shillings ten pence more is three shillings ten pence more.

The next night they caught another hundred and seventy-four, earning eighteen shillings four from the butcher plus two shillings tuppence from the knackerman.

Hannah visited two other butcher shops the next day, describing in lurid detail how well their rat-catching system worked and how safe it was, for it used no traps or poisons. One shop agreed to let them come in. The other butcher seemed all ready to sign them up until he erred by asking his wife's opinion. Aghast, she loudly proclaimed there were no rats to catch in their elite establishment. Hannah spotted three holes from where she stood by the counter, but she knew better than to argue. Let them live with their rats.

The third night their harvest, as Colin called it, was sixty-seven. Five shillings and a few pence. What with food and lodging and stabling for Max's Lady, it didn't quite meet expenses. They helped the happy butcher plug all his holes and lay bait for the few remaining pests, and moved on to the next job.

From the second butcher shop, a more extensive operation with three large rooms, they reaped four pounds two in five days. A fortnight after they began the rat-catching business, they had successfully put themselves out of work.

Hannah gave Colin nearly all her part of the earnings, because he asked it of her. With her bit remaining she purchased undergarments and stockings at a lovely little shop. *In what forgotten nook does my schoolbag lie?* she wondered. It seemed so very, very long ago that she'd lost it. She also found a modest little carpetbag with a leather handle long enough to hang over the saddle horn.

She bought a strawberry sundae and sat at a white, wrought-iron table outside an ice cream parlor. Bendigo was such a pleasant town, notwithstanding the one butcher's wife. The ice cream was so cold and smooth. She paused to savor the last plump, red strawberry. She sat shaded by a gaily striped canvas awning, and thought about the weathered canvas marquee in the jarrah forest on the other side of the continent, beneath which young James Otis had preached so fervently. He knew God. Mum knew God. Clearly, Papa knew Him. Hannah, though not quite certain she *knew* Him as such, had learned quite well that she could ask Him for help and get it. Why did Colin resist Him so?

In her mind she reviewed her first awful bit of treachery when she lied to her parents, stole from them, and ran away. Did God sufficiently forgive her for that? How would she know when the slate had been sponged clean?

Perhaps she might consider her life these last few months as evidence of His forgiveness. She left home in the fear that Colin lay ill or worse; he was healthy and strong. She had envied his exciting travel and adventures; now she was taking part in them. True, adventuring was not altogether comfortable, but the cold rain and mud of the forest, the parched sand along the bight, the hot, stuffy shearing shed all seemed a universe distant from this gentle place. Adventuring had its delightful moments as well as its sweat and tears. She was truly blessed.

That was it! She was blessed! Blessings equated to God patting you on the head and saying, "It's all right, lass." Colin partook of the blessing with her. Did that mean he, too, basked in God's grace and mercy? She scraped the last of the ice cream from the bottom of her dish and licked the spoon.

"There you are!" Colin came riding up at a jog. He swung down, tied Max's Lady to a lamppost, and plopped into the chair beside her. "How much money do you have?"

"Two bob, and you can't have it."

"Not enough anyway. How do you manage to spend so much?"

"Me? You had all the balance of it."

Colin absolutely glowed. "I stopped by the feedstore for hay for the mare and happened to fall to talking with a pastoralist from up north. He needs a rabbiter."

"Max can catch rabbits."

"No, a full-out rabbiter. He says they're the worst this spring he's ever seen them. He's willing to hire us for six weeks. Give me your two bob, and we'll buy as many apples as we can. Last year's will be cheap because of the drought—they're all going soft. Then we'll use the proceeds to buy more apples to finish the job. It promises a handsome profit, they say, at the end of it."

"Up north. Near Shepparton? That's where Joe and the crew are. Perhaps we can visit them. Wouldn't that be lovely?"

Colin shook his head. "They're moved on by now. Planned to finish the season near Gundagai, remember?"

"Well, we can ask, anyway."

"Give me your two bob. I'll be meeting Mr. Slotemaker later and he'll haul the apples. He has his truck down here. We can be on the road and making money by tomorrow morning."

Reluctantly, very reluctantly, Hannah handed the sum over to him. As he disappeared up the street on Max's Lady, she fingered the coins that remained. Seven pence. Here was another facet of adventuring no one ever mentioned—one never got wealthy at it.

Hannah returned her empty dish to the parlor, and walked back to her little room. Rat-catching lay in the past, and good riddance. For all the money made, rats were still vermin, a most disgusting creature. Now rabbit-killing lay in her future, with its promise of good money and further adventure. She looked forward to working in the great outdoors, the profit and the exciting life of a rabbiter. Why, then, did her spirit languish so under this gentle spring sun? With a heavy sigh she climbed the stairs to the home that was not home and packed her bag.

CHAPTER EIGHTEEN

GHOSTS

"See those trees up ahead? That's Echuca. We'll stop and get a bite to eat there."

Colin watched the thick green smudge of red gum wave and bounce in the distance beyond the windshield of an ancient farm truck. On his left Hannah bobbed jerkily. If springs once existed in this old truck, they no longer functioned with any efficiency. Every rut and hole in the road communicated itself to their aching backsides.

On Colin's right, Emory Slotemaker clung tenaciously to the rickety steering wheel. Wooden shoes were all he lacked to complete the image of the perfect Dutchman. His gray, thinning hair looked to have been blond once. His gnarled hands told the world he worked hard; his ample midriff the fact that his wife fed him well. "You tads ever been around the River Murray before?"

"No, sir." Colin glanced at the wall of dust they were kicking up behind them.

"I was," Hannah chimed in. "My train from Sydney to Perth crossed the river at Albury."

"Ah, yes. Any family around here?"

"Not very near." Her head jerked about as they bounced along, and Colin wondered if she was nodding. "Our aunt and uncle live in Adelaide, but they're out of the country until fall."

"Farmers?"

"Musicians, sir. He's a rather famous organist and she sings. Chris Yorke and Linnet Connolly. She's Mrs. Yorke, of course, but she uses her maiden name because she's known by it. Uncle Chris says professional people often do that."

"The Adelaide Lark!" Mr. Slotemaker cackled happily. "Why, I saw her on her first tour down the Murray. When was that, now? Aught seven, I think, or perhaps aught eight. Around there somewhere. Adele and I happened to be in town at the time, and we went to the showboat to hear Miss Connolly. Sweet, sweet voice. I understand her sister lived in Echuca for a while."

Colin looked at Hannah and she looked back. "Here?" Colin asked. "Samantha or Margaret?"

"Not Margaret, I don't think. Must have been Samantha, then. Didn't stay around very long. Married and moved away, like so many do."

Colin's brain whirled. *Mum, here! But, why? What brought her from Queensland and the shadow world of Sugarlea?* He and Hannah both barraged him with questions all the way into town, but Mr. Slotemaker, though he tried, could recall nothing more.

The rabbiter recruiter parked his rattletrap truck on what he called the Esplanade. As he left them, he instructed his new rabbiters to get lunch and be back at the truck in an hour.

Neither Colin nor Hannah had any money left. They would have to remain hungry until they reached the station. Colin ran the mare off the truck to give her a rest and tied her to a gum tree between the broad open avenue and the river. He grabbed half a dozen soft, bruised apples out of what would soon be rabbit bait. He handed three to Hannah.

Mum, here? Colin wandered out onto a wide wharf to gaze at the amazing river below. A complex crisscross of beams and diagonals, the wharf stood nearly thirty feet high, its footings in the water and its top level with the

town and esplanade. Below, the yellow river wound a lei-
surely course in a big S-curve among a mass of trees and
beached boat hulks.

Hannah murmured, "I can't imagine Mum standing
here just as we are now, but I suppose she did."

"Me either. Mr. Slotemaker said she married and
moved away. That means Papa would have been here, too.
Or passed through, at least."

"I've never even seen this place before. Why does it
make me feel homesick?"

"That's odd. Me, too." Colin's little sister had just put
into words what Colin felt but couldn't express. Homesick.
In a strange, inexplicable way, that was it. *Mum was here.*

"All right," Mr. Slotemaker's voice boomed behind
them. Colin jumped. "What is the story with you two
youngsters? You asked all those questions, and now you
find the wharf more interesting than food. What troubles
you?"

Colin didn't care to bare his soul to a stranger. "Not
troubled, sir. Just surprised. We never knew our mother
came this way, or lived here. It's, ah—it's very interesting."

"Interesting! Absolutely. I was hoping the *Adelaide*
would come through with a load of red gum from the Barmah, so you could see a paddle steamer in action. The
Adelaide is one of the very few left anymore, though the
trade is picking up a little. The government's building
dams, flood control weirs, and the river steamers haul the
materials."

"The Barmah Forest?" Hannah looked around Colin to
Mr. Slotemaker. "Someone we met south of Kalgoorlie
worked there. A preacher lad—James Otis, by name."

"Otis! Of course. Half-caste he is. His father started the
Barmah Mission upriver from here." The farmer frowned.
"I'm trying to recall the connection. I think perhaps your
mother was involved at one time with the mission, too. Of
course that was a long time ago."

"She's very religious. It could be possible." Hannah nodded vigorously.

Colin's head swam. *Did Mum ride in a paddle steamer? Did she visit the mission? Did Papa? This man couldn't know, but Mum would.* How could he break the wall of silence? Did he want to? Through his mind flashed plots of Victorian novels he'd read—by George MacDonald and others—wherein the son discovers secret relatives, long-lost brothers. Romantic as they were, such things never *really* happened, or *did* they?

"Here now, listen! You'll see a paddle steamer after all." Mr. Slotemaker pointed to the bend beyond the east end of the wharf. Colin could hear it now, a chugging noise like a locomotive and the sound of paddles flogging the water. Then she appeared from beyond the bend, flailing her way toward them. Colin was accustomed to the great, deepwater freighters in Sydney Harbor. This was such a tiny boat, hardly more than twenty-four feet long. Her wide deck sprawled out flat on the water and Colin could just barely see a paddle wheel slap at the river from beneath its housing. Spewing smoke, she chugged past the wharf. Her pilot waved and hooted her whistle. Colin found himself waving back exuberantly. Infectious, these little boats!

"That's the *Etona*," Mr. Slotemaker announced, though the name on her pilothouse was plain to see. "Built with mission funds from Eton college in England, many years ago. She served as a missions boat until churches were established all up and down the river. The mission board sold her. Now her owners use her for fishing, over around Boundary Bend, I believe."

Hannah mused aloud, " 'Follow me and I will make you fishers of men.' The *Etona* did it backwards. Fishers of men first and then fishers of fish."

"Never thought of that," Mr. Slotemaker chuckled. "True, though." He watched the departing boat, lost in thought, until it disappeared. "The river used to flood regularly. Usually twenty feet or so. But occasionally a real banker would come through—a thirty-foot crest. Never happens anymore with the weirs holding the water back. Let's move on. You say you find the place interesting. I'll show you the waterfront. The railways nearly put the paddle steamers out of business for a while. The town almost died for a few years. But after the Great War, a lot of veterans settled in the area. Selectors, businessmen. Echuca's much livelier than she used to be."

For another hour, while Colin's stomach churned with hunger, they walked the streets of Echuca. Mr. Slotemaker showed them the old mills on the east end. They talked about the great cranes, only a few of which still worked, that lifted tons of wool and timber from the river to the rails. They passed a vacant lot with a crumbled arbor and tangled weeds, said to have been an elegant tea garden serving the best scones in town.

They visited a hotel across the Esplanade from the wharf, and with a knowing wink, Mr. Slotemaker took them downstairs to an old sly-grog shop in the basement. He showed them the dank, narrow passageway to the surface where customers could escape, should the police come raiding. It smacked of intrigue and excitement. Colin could not imagine either Mum or Papa even knowing about this colorful bit of Echuca's past.

Back at the truck, Colin loaded the mare and climbed into the cab. Mr. Slotemaker drove out the east end of town and over a great iron bridge into New South Wales. Colin hadn't thought to ask if Slotemaker's holding was in Victoria. Did it really matter? They were on their way again.

They pressed north toward Deniliquin. The countryside lay flat and smooth, unending. Patches of scrub braided in and out to break the monotony. The sun poured down and glanced up from the parched ground; the hot brilliance forcing Colin's eyes into a narrow squint. Despite the constant jostling, Hannah dozed off and leaned hard against him.

About suppertime she awoke, long after they had left Deniliquin behind. The apples they'd munched on were gone. Colin thought surely she suffered hunger pangs as much as he did. Why didn't he stop this nonsense immediately? A telegram to Papa in Sydney would end the odyssey. Hannah would return safely to her mother's arms. What anger, what pride of heart drove him to endanger her like this?

And yet, he had never asked for this responsibility. It was she who flung herself across the continent without thinking of the consequences. She was fortunate he let her tag along. The tug-of-war that raged in his heart served only to confuse and frustrate him.

In a blaze of blood-red glory, the sun died. The truck's headlamps painted bouncing waves of light on the bush. Kangaroos came out like ghosts, and with flashing orange eyes bounded across the road ahead, dodging the light.

At ten that night, the truck lurched into the dooryard at Dresden Downs. "Turn your mare into that paddock beyond the henhouse." Mr. Slotemaker pointed into sheer darkness. "You'll have to unload your apples tonight; the cargo for the missus is stowed behind them. You can stash 'em in the henhouse so the 'roos and possums can't find them."

"Thank you, sir." Colin ran the mare down the gangway and handed her off to Hannah. Let Hannah find the paddock beyond the henhouse in the darkness. He watched Mr. Slotemaker disappearing into the house and muttered, "Wish they'd invite us to supper."

Hannah murmured, "They will. I prayed for it." And off she went into the blackness with the mare in tow. Max looked half asleep as he followed his lady friend.

What a colossal nerve, to expect divine results in spite of their own foolishness. But she was a child; Colin must excuse her ignorance on that score if none other. He scooted his ten fifty-pound hessian sacks of apples one at a time to the back of the truck bed and dropped them over the side. Then he dragged them two at a time to the hen-house. He felt weary. Pound weary. Stone weary.

Mr. Slotemaker called from his veranda, "The missus says you two will eat with us tonight."

"Thank you, sir. Coming." Colin stared at the house. He stared into the darkness that had swallowed Hannah. He stared at the invisible God somewhere above him. *They will. I prayed for it.* She had said it so matter-of-factly.

Hannah joined him presently, waiting for him to close up the last of his apples. She followed him to the house, looking more than a bit trailworn. The sturdy Dutchman appeared and held the door open for them. He led the way through a formal dining room and into a warm, friendly kitchen.

Mrs. Slotemaker looked exactly as Hannah expected she would. No modern, urban bob—her wavy blonde hair was pulled back very loosely into a pile of gold-and-silver braids. She was rather short and square, but by no means fat or even pudgy. She was a solid, strong woman exuding a radiant happiness.

She looked at Hannah, then Colin. "My word! What a ride from Echuca will do to you—let alone from Bendigo. Miss Sloan, you'll sleep up at the house here; there's a daybed on the back porch. You three wash up now. The dumplings just went into the pot, and dinner's almost ready."

They stepped out the back door to a washbasin. Colin waited for Hannah. A hazy gray form, barely visible in the light from the kitchen, bobbed in the darkness. Mr. Slotemaker took a carrot from a bag on a hook and stepped into the gloom. Colin followed out of curiosity.

An ancient, bony gray horse hung its head over the paddock rail and nickered for his treat. Mr. Slotemaker snapped the carrot into pieces and hand-fed them bit by bit from his palm. "Hector here is my past," he smiled. "This horse is twenty-nine years old. Dresden Downs was brand new when he was young, and we lived in a stringy-bark shack. He cleared the land. He drove sheep. He pulled the wagons and the plow. He taught my children to ride—" his voice choked a bit, "and most of all, he taught them to trust. He's as much a part of the downs as the house itself. More. He's older'n the house."

"I don't expect he does much around the place any-more."

"No. But then, neither does my uncle. And I don't have the heart to let either one of them go." Chuckling, the man strolled back to the porch to wash up.

Colin rubbed the horse's warm velvet nose and dug his fingers into the loose flesh behind his gangly ears. It was awhile before he realized his desire to touch the horse didn't come from any affection for the animal; he desperately yearned to lay his hands on the past, to find out what yesterday felt like. It felt remarkably like today.

What a drongo you are, Colin Sloan! Such silly thoughts and childish whims. You should be thinking more like a man!

They settled at the kitchen table, with the Slotemakers at either end. Colin and Hannah faced each other. A glorious pot of bubbling lamb stew and dumplings sat before them. Without asking, their hostess had poured milk for Colin and Hannah and strong coffee for herself and her husband.

The pleasant woman looked briefly from face to face, smiling. "Our youngest, Marie, married and moved away last year. She was the last to leave the nest. It's wonderful to have young people around the table again." She held out both hands. Hesitantly Colin took her left hand as Hannah took her right.

Even more hesitantly, Colin took the man's extended hand. Mr. Slotemaker closed his eyes. "Dear Lord, we praise your holy name. We thank you for these two delight-ful young people you brought among us, and ask your hand and blessing upon them. Now bless ye please this

food and us to your service. Amen." The grip let go. He ladled stew for Hannah.

Hannah expressed her thanks and began to chat ami-
ably with Mrs. Slotemaker, while the woman filled her own
plate. The men followed suit and began to eat as though
they were starved. Colin knew he was.

Hannah talked with Mrs. Slotemaker as one cook to another, asking how to keep bacon fresh longer, and in what
ways you might use sour milk. The two were old friends—
and equals—in moments.

Colin could not put the Dutchman's prayer out of his
mind. Papa had always said grace, or asked Colin or Mary
Aileen to do so. But they'd never joined hands. Somehow
that simple difference made these humble folks' prayer
something other than mere table grace. It left Colin with a
strange yearning.

"Help yourself to more," Mr. Slotemaker offered, refill-
ing his own plate. "So, this will be your first job rabbiting."

"Yes, sir. I talked about it some with one of the shearers
I worked with, and the chemist in Bendigo where I bought
the strychnine."

"Real nuisance this year, worse than usual. I'll be moving my rams up out of that south paddock—I'll show you
where tomorrow. The wethers are already in. While we're
shearing, you can bait the south paddocks, and when I
bring in the ewes and lambs, you can do the north side."

Colin nodded, and helped himself to more stew. Mrs.
Slotemaker's cooking was almost as good as Mum's.

The next morning, though his whole body protested
strongly, Colin rose before dawn to cut a hundred pounds
of apples into wedges and soak them in the strychnine so-
lution. At three in the afternoon he rode out to lay his first
bait trail as a professional rabbiter. Almost a full day later,
the memory of that warm, clasping table prayer still
haunted him.

CHAPTER NINETEEN

EAGLES

It was either old age, or he was going soft. Cole Sloan prided himself on being inured to hardship and long travel. But this train ride across the width of the continent was almost more than he could take. It was hard to imagine his little girl making it. He stepped out onto the bleak platform and looked around. Nothing, absolutely nothing welcomed him to Kalgoorlie. He was depressed already, and he'd only now stepped both feet onto solid ground.

He walked from the railway station, periodically shifting his carpetbag from hand to hand, even though taxis and carts stood by for hire. He desperately needed the exercise. The constable's office, just a block off Hannan Street, proved easy to find. He stepped from the hot sun into stuffy gloom and set his bag down just inside the door.

An officer in a black wool tunic stood up at his desk. "Can I help you?"

"I hope so. Nigel Bowden? Cole Sloan, from Sydney." He extended his hand in a firm shake.

The man's expression clouded. "Oh—. I do hope you haven't come all this way on a wild goose chase, sir. We have not located your daughter, and from what we can gather she is no longer in the area." He cleared his throat and loosened his collar.

Cole pulled a letter from his pocket. "A man here called Desiderio—Desiderio Romales wrote to me concerning my son. I'd like to meet him, if I can, and then claim my daughter's schoolbag."

"Of course. Yes. Uh, do be seated." Constable Bowden waved toward the chair opposite his desk, and sat back into his own. He folded his hands and leaned forward. "I have questioned Romales several times myself—even put him in jail to soften him up. His friends at the Perseverance mine bailed him immediately and threatened legal mayhem if he were further detained. I doubt he can be of any help to us. He persistently maintains he knows nothing, and never so much as met your daughter."

"And the railway hasn't seen her since her jump?"

"Correct. So, she's not headed east. We would get word the moment she boarded a train. I've heard rumors she's joined her brother down south around Pemberton or Albany, but officials there haven't actually spotted her. Every office in Western Australia has her description and her brother's. Sooner or later, Mr. Sloan. They have to turn up sooner or later."

"And I immensely appreciate your thoroughness, believe me. Where might I find this Romales?"

"I'll take you by there now, if you wish. Will you take your daughter's bag now, or come by for it later?"

"If I may, I'd like to get it later, and leave my bag here as well."

"Certainly!" The man was on his feet bellowing for his assistant, "Hooper!"

From a back room a tall, scrawny fellow appeared, his tunic flapping wide open.

"I'll be out for a while, Hooper. Take over. And button your tunic." The constable picked up his hat and charged out the door. Sloan had to step lively to keep up. "Hooper," the man grumbled, "is not a pretty reflection on the department, but what a fighter—Rafferty's rules, especially.

Very handy fellow to send in first when quelling a punch-up."

Sloan chuckled. "I suppose you get calls like that frequently." They crossed a busy street and climbed into a shiny black two-seater.

"Not so much as the old days. Kalgoorlie's got her colorful sorts, though, make no mistake." The car started with some difficulty. The engine was apparently not kept in the same bright shape as the exterior.

"Such as?"

"Oh, the usual low-grade criminals attracted by the Two-up School; gambling seems to be in Kalgoorlie's bones. And people like Jack the Pickpocket. Specializes in drunken miners, but he'll tap anybody close by. Then he'll turn around and buy groceries anonymously for widows and orphans."

"The Robin Hood of Kalgoorlie."

"Indeed. Myself would dearly love to play Sheriff of Nottingham to him, but we can't catch him in the act. We won't let him near the racecourse. Too many well-lined pockets in one place. I'll not be one to encourage theft."

"Speaking of theft, my brothers tell me my son stole their horse—a bay mare, I believe. I'd like to see the police report of the incident, if possible."

"Your son st—" Constable Bowden gawked briefly, then returned his attention to driving. "They told you your son stole that horse?"

"Yes. And then requested remuneration for it."

"Indeed. Indeed." He wagged his head. "Frankly, sir, when you walked into my office I would never have identified you as a Sloan, knowing your brothers. Let me tell you about the incident in question."

The drive to the little Romales cottage took a mere ten minutes. During the brief interlude, Cole learned more than he ever wanted to know about Aidan and Liam, things he had pushed from his memory through the years. His blood boiled. But then, he was not surprised.

No one answered their knock on the door. Sloan sent the constable on his way with repeated reassurances, and settled on the front veranda steps to wait. He spent some time studying the tiny dwelling. It had been recently painted, and an old bullnose porch covered the veranda. Though not an expensive place, someone maintained it well.

Restless, Cole wandered around to the back. A dun horse strolled out from under its protective tin roof and stuck its head over the paddock fence. He rubbed its face. The animal looked sleek and clean, well kept, like the house.

He walked out front and perched himself again on the veranda rail.

Up the road a happy-looking couple approached. The slim, swarthy fellow looked foreign. The little lady walked with a free and lilting step, a happy woman, if Sloan be any judge at all. Their banter ceased the instant the pair spied him.

The fellow stepped onto his veranda boldly and extended a hand. "Desiderio Romales, *a sus ordenes.*"

Sloan stood erect and received the handshake smiling. "Cole Sloan, Colin's father."

The dark face lit up in a happy grin. "*Claro!* Your eyes are his eyes. *Bienvenido! Mi casa es su casa.* Come in. Come in!" He led the way through the unlocked front door.

Sloan stepped into the cool room. The furniture was simple—four straight-backed chairs and a table. The newlyweds were apparently just setting up housekeeping.

Romales put a hand on his wife's shoulder. "My wife Lily. Lily, mebbe some of that good cider, eh?"

"If it hasn't turned yet. Let me look." Her warm, dark eyes and coffee-and-cream skin suggested Aboriginal blood. Her sparkle was purely that of a new bride.

Romales indicated a chair. "Siddown, please. Hope you join us for dinner, eh?" He sat casually on another chair and draped himself loosely on the edge of the table. "So, you seen Colin lately? How he's doing, eh?"

Sloan settled onto the hard chair as he shook his head. "I just arrived. First, I want to thank you very much for answering my wife's letter. She wept with happiness when she read it. When you spoke so highly of our son, you bestowed us with a beautiful gift."

Romales studied Sloan a moment with penetrating eyes. His voice was soft but firm. There would be no small talk from this man. "I don' speak highly of him so's I make you feel good. I speak highly 'cause Col, he got lotsa good stuff to speak highly of. He's honest and solid and willing to work. You can depend on him; ain' many men you can say that about. And he knows how to be a true frien'. Ain' many men you can say *that* about, either."

"I'm glad you think so."

"You don' get my point, Señor Sloan. Ain' me jus' *thinking* so. What I think don' count. Iss the way it is; the way *he* is. Tha's what counts. An' Col got this notion, I think mebbe iss true, that you can't see any of the good in him."

"You're getting a bit personal, aren't you?"

"Mebbe time somebody did, eh?"

Sloan had to force his body not to move until he decided how to move. He wanted sorely to leave. To stay. To punch this brash, irreverent dill in the nose. To hear and learn more. He flashed a swift, earnest prayer heavenward: *Help me, Lord! I don't know what to do.* And quite as swiftly came the clear reply, *Stay. Learn.* Reluctantly he forced himself to relax and sit back.

"You told my wife in your letter that you spent two months on the track with our son. That's longer than I've ever spent with him, at least all at once. Tell me, what did the two of you talk about?"

Romales sat casually also, but there was tension in his manner, like a cat's. "Lotsa things, sometimes nothing at all, eh? Tha's how you learn to know a person's heart."

Romales' wife entered with the cider and three glasses. She wore a worried expression, as she poured the refreshment. "Are you sure you want to talk so freely with this man, Dizzy?" There were no veiled references with her—she clearly spoke her mind. Sloan smiled, as she sat down to join them.

"Sí!" Romales answered her. "Once he talk to his brothers he get all the wrong ideas. Better we talk to him first, eh? So he gets the truth."

He turned to Sloan. "Top of the track, we just starting, Col, he had all the money. I don' got nothin', eh? Not even the horse. He bought the horses and the food. Down here, when he s'pose to get paid and didn', I had all the money and pay for ev'rythin'. Didn' make no difference, y' know? Friendship, it don' change. One pays one time, other the nex' time; nobody keeps count. Tha's real—uh, amigos. Compadres. What you call it?"

"Mates. Cobbers."

Lily gazed at Cole with her deep, dark eyes. "Dizzy didn't mention to you, I don't think, that they let me travel down with them. They shared their food and water supply and let me ride. With them I felt safe, Mr. Sloan. Neither Col nor Dizzy made any suggestions, or wanted anything. I had to hide inside myself at first until I finally realized I was truly safe. They protected me and they never asked anything. You're big and strong, Mr. Sloan. You probably don't realize how wonderful it is to feel safe and protected with someone."

Romales commanded attention with his low, rumbling voice. "Lately we been goin' to a little stone-block church over to the other side, corner of Porter and Egan. Preacher there say just las' week that a man's character is what he does when no one's watching. Col, he got that kind of character. He's a real man, and a gen'leman. He's a son to be proud of."

A real man? A son to be proud of? Colin wasn't a man, he was just a kid. Why, the stuff he pulled at home—Sloan could hardly feel proud. He studied the self-assured man before him, one who seemed to know a Colin Sloan that Cole didn't know at all.

Lily stood up. "Dizzy put two rabbits in the meat safe just last night. Rabbit stew with cornbread coming up. I hope you'll stay for dinner." She smiled and those black eyes snapped from dark to bright. "Maybe Dizzy will turn us some tortillas."

Romales nodded at her and was silent, giving Sloan space to think. He welcomed that, even though his thoughts would not come together. He sighed heavily and leaned on the table. "I had plans for my son, Mr. Romales, but—"

"Dizzy, eh?"

"Dizzy. Cole, please. My plans for him were spiritual, plans for his growth as a Christian. But he wouldn't fit into those plans. He fought me. Refused me. Fought God. He went clear off course, Dizzy, and neither his mother nor I. . . . Nothing we said or did seemed to help or make any difference. Now, our daughter Hannah—" Sloan stopped midsentence.

Romales studied him intently, searching for the right words. Sloan wished he could read the man better. Romales relaxed further. "Know what I see? I see a man hurtin', an' that bothers me, 'cause mi compadre—my mate—he loves that man. Col never said that, but I can tell iss true, eh? And my mate, he's hurtin' too. I know that for a fact."

"Can you see what I should do?"

"No. I can' say what you should do." His tortured English purred gently. "But mebbe Lily and me, we can help you find out, eh?"

———

Wide blue sky arched over a hushed gray-green landscape. A black penstroke, hardly more than the line across a capital T, circled in the limitless sky. Another appeared. The lines thickened as they spiraled, growing until Colin could discern their kind. Eaglehawks. He picked up another rabbit from beneath a bush and headed back toward the horsecart.

He tossed two handfuls of rabbits onto the back of the cart, disturbing the cloud of flies. He would pick up the remaining bait this time around, too. Mr. Slotemaker would be turning his wethers out into the paddock soon. No bait could remain for the sheep to find.

Max barked sharply. Colin walked toward the sound as Max's Lady dozed in the spring sun. Sometimes Max brought the poisoned rabbits in, sometimes he simply stood there barking at them. Colin could not discern why the dog would touch one and not another.

"Good dog, Max." Colin picked up the limp animal. There was a bit of yellow yarn in a tree, marking bait, but Colin could find no chunk of yellow-dyed apple. He pulled the yarn and continued on his trail. He'd have to hurry. The circling eaglehawks would rob him of his harvest if he wasn't quick.

In a week Hannah would turn thirteen. Colin thought he should arrange some sort of observance. Were she at home, Mum would have a special party or tea in her honor. Mum would know just what to do. Colin hadn't the slightest notion how to begin.

He smiled to himself. A week ago he had passed his seventeenth birthday. Hannah made no comment. She obviously had not remembered. Quite probably she didn't even know what day it was. It was easy to lose track of time out here on the swag. Seventeen. Making his own way. *Watch me, Papa!*

He brought four more rabbits back to the cart and led the mare a few hundred feet down to a dry creekbed. He tied her to a massive white gum tree, and she dozed again.

The eaglehawks were settled beyond the trees.

Smoke-oh time. Colin didn't smoke, as most of the shearers did, but he relished the traditional rest anyway. Shearers broke every two hours. Colin had no timepiece with which to judge his breaks. Out here in the sun-drenched reaches, time slipped by on tiptoe, and who could know when an hour passed? But it seemed about time for a break, and he stretched out prostrate beneath an ancient, sprawling gum, covering his face with his hat to thwart the flies.

Now this was the life! No onerous responsibilities. No problems. His mind drifted to that ride down the Madman's Track with Dizzy. It seemed so long ago. Good old Diz. The man kept his eyes open. He watched for opportunity, was open to change, tackled anything he did with a determination to do it the best he knew how. Whether he was tending the shell diver who depended utterly upon him, cooking for the bosses at the Perseverance, or hunting meat and water on the trail, he didn't drag his feet wishing for something else.

He probably would have done very well below ground in the mines. Now in retrospect, Colin regretted not giving it more of a fair go. Did he tend to give up too soon? It seemed that way. Perhaps he'd be on his way to wealth now, had he only stuck to it.

On the other hand, he was on his way to some kind of wealth now, and enjoying the open sunlight in the bargain. On Tuesday, Wednesday and Thursday, he'd re-fed his bait trail, then he and Hannah gathered the corpses. Three hundred rabbits a day for three days. With today's harvest they'd have well over a thousand. Sell the skins in Bendigo or Melbourne, sell the carcasses for tankage at the fertilizer plant, buy more apples—he'd still make a handsome profit.

No profit to those who sit on their hands. Colin climbed to his feet. Smoke-oh was over. Back to work. He led the mare down the dry creek to where the bankside trees opened enough to let the cart pass through. He led her out and across the arid flats.

From the northeast he could hear Max's bark. Colin left the mare to rest again and headed in that direction. Max nosed a stiff rabbit beneath a bush. When Colin picked it up, the dog trotted off dutifully.

Here lay another nearby, just recently died, for the carcass was warm. The rabbit's thick lips had drawn back into a grotesque smile, those huge yellow teeth showing clear to the gums. Somehow strychnine tightened all the muscles at once; the rabbit's back arched unnaturally and its legs protruded stiffly. Jackie Jump claimed that the poison made all the heart's muscles contract at the same moment so that with one convulsive beat it wadded up into a cardiac fist. How long did it take a rabbit to die thusly? Jackie Jump claimed "right away," but that could mean any amount of time, were time measured at all in this land of vivid sun.

Max was wandering somewhere to Colin's left. Suddenly he bolted past, yapping furiously, and disappeared into the bush ahead. Seconds later a pair of glossy black eaglehawks squirted up from beyond the trees. Eight feet of wingspan barely got the birds airborne. With heavy flapping they jerked themselves back up into the freedom of the skies.

Colin grinned. What bravado Max must have feigned to drive away two such birds of prey! Every dog should experience that sublime thrill once in a lifetime.

The grin fled. "Max, no!" Colin lunged forward at a dead run. "No! Get away!" The eagles had torn a rabbit apart, strewing it about. Max had laid claim to a portion of it.

"Max, don't eat that!" Colin flung his rabbit carcasses at the dog. "Get away!"

Snarling, Max ducked the carcasses and held his ground. Colin kicked at the dog. The crazy bitzer snapped back. His teeth sank into Colin's leg just above his shoe. The dog grabbed a piece of the entrails and ran off two rods.

Colin raced after him. He could see nothing to throw. "Max! Get back! No! Please, no!"

The dog turned and loped into the bush, dragging his dinner with him.

Colin would never find him now. He should not have yelled and attacked. He should have called the dog instead. But calling the dog never worked either, the stubborn mutt.

"Max! Please come! *Max!*"

No response.

Colin gathered up what he could of the remains and retrieved his rabbits. Quite probably Max got none of the poison. Much of a poisoned rabbit's body is not tainted. He collected the yellow yarn and the last of the bait. Half an hour passed.

"Max? Hey, Max! I'm headed home now. Better come along."

Colin climbed into the box and woke Max's Lady. He urged the horse forward, watching the bush around him.

His happy shout startled the mare. Max had appeared suddenly, trotting off alone to the west, headed home! Max's Lady tossed her head and picked up the stride. Why had Colin worried?

The dog stopped suddenly and shuddered.

Colin dragged the mare to a halt. "Max?"

The dog shuddered again. He jerked convulsively. Colin jumped down and ran toward him. Max snarled and backed off.

"This is no time to be belligerent, old friend. I won't hurt you." He took another step forward. The dog growled and fell to the ground. Gently Colin reached out. The dog's teeth broke the skin on two of his fingers. "Max, no. . . . "

A violent convulsion seized the old dog, sending every muscle into spasm. Max's lips drew back so tightly into a horrid grin that they disappeared. His head reared back, the spine arched. He lay quivering, then relaxed. He dragged air into his tortured lungs in huge gulps.

Again Colin tried to reach out. Again the snapping jaws drove him away. He thought of Max's patient leading, hundreds of feet below Kalgoorlie. Possibly on that occasion Max was leading his lady friend to safety and Colin was, literally, along for the ride. But then, he thought about the way Max had sprung to his defense when his uncle accosted him. In his strange, warped way, Max cared about Colin. Why wouldn't he let Colin approach now?

Another convulsion. The dog's eyes glassed over. Only as the old warrior's life ebbed out was Colin able to drag the dog into his arms and hold its head and weep.

OCEANS OF OPPORTUNITY

"Edan," Mary Aileen suggested, "why don't you go curl up and nap on that bench until the train comes?"

"I'm not sleepy," her brother lied.

Edan never got to stay up this late. Mary Aileen hardly ever did. She was glad Mum let them come along, even if her own eyes were getting heavy. The electric lights along the platform here would have made it look like day, were it not for all that blackness beyond. Where the train platform ended, the lights—and any semblance of a normal day— ended. The spring night could not be called warm, but it felt quite mild and pleasant. Mary Aileen let her shawl hang loose.

Mum approached from the far end, pacing more than strolling. Mum did not wait well. She smiled at them. "Why don't you go sit on the bench, Edan? If you fall asleep we'll wake you when the train comes."

He shook his head. "I want to see it come."

Mum stood close beside Mary Aileen. "I trust you're not getting your hopes up. If he found them he would have wired ahead."

"I know. Mum, have you or Papa ever been to Kalgoorlie before?"

"No."

"Then he's not seen my uncles in many years."

"Not since they went west and he took over Sugarlea. That was well over twenty years ago. Of course, he didn't go now for a family reunion, but it's nice he could visit with them again." Mum turned away. It was all she had to say about it.

Mary Aileen wondered how Kalgoorlie compared to Sydney. Would she ever travel? It was a wistful dream in her mind and heart.

"Here it comes!" Edan perked up instantly.

A light appeared in the distance; the locomotive was turning a corner somewhere several blocks down, and now the light approached. Mary Aileen listened to the measured huff and puff, the song of power. Black in the blackness the engine loomed, hissing and spitting steam. The platform lights bathed its black flanks in brightness and made its steel handrails glow. The churning wheels rolled by; what a din! On up the way the locomotive roared, past the lights into darkness. The cars behind it drifted to a stop.

Instantly rouseabouts were passing great canvas sacks to and from the mail car. The baggage cars opened as porters rolled wheeled carts into place. Loading and unloading one train out of many—and getting everything right—must be an incredibly intricate task. But see how each person did a small portion of the whole, and how it all came together. Mary Aileen watched rapt.

"There he is!" Edan dropped Mary Aileen's hand and raced off down the platform. Mum hastened after him. Mary Aileen tried to hurry and look dignified, as befits a girl fifteen. She couldn't do both so she sacrificed the dignity.

Gum-tree tall, Papa came striding up the platform toward them, a bag in each hand. Edan reached him first. Papa set a bag down to give Edan a hug. Mum was all ready to embrace him also when she spied his other bag. She stopped dead as if poleaxed.

Hannah's schoolbag!

Mum stared at it the longest moment. Then quietly she covered her face with her hands and began to sob as Papa drew her in and pressed her to himself.

———————

"Happy birthday!" Colin joined the general chorus of well-wishers. It wasn't hard to get a crowd for a birthday party on this remote sheep station; just mention a piece of Mrs. Slotemaker's cake. The ringers, shearers and rouse-abouts all milled around the veranda of Slotemakers' government house. The guest of honor blushed, thanked everyone, and cut the cake.

Mrs. Slotemaker helped her serve it up on small plates, while Colin passed them to the guests. Mr. Slotemaker poured cool punch and served it to the thirsty crowd.

Mrs. Slotemaker cut the last of it. "I baked three sheet cakes, since the shearers are in; I knew we'd use at least that much. I've never seen men eat the way shearers eat."

Colin grinned. "Hard yakka, mum. We know; Hannah and I worked with a shearing crew for a while."

"Oh my!" Mrs. Slotemaker stared at Hannah. "You were on the boards, child?"

"I was broomie boy, yes'm." Hannah grinned. "And tarboy. A cut down by Eaglehawk, near Bendigo. A lot of dust, sweat and flies, but I enjoyed it."

She smiled. "I imagine you enjoy most of what you do."

"That's right, except—" and her bright grin faded, "killing rabbits. Since we buried Max I've thought about all the suffering that's caused killing all those rabbits. It really hurts me."

The farmer's wife stood a moment, thinking. "Colin, after we finish here, hitch up the cart and bolt the seat down in back. I want to take a drive."

Colin finished his cake, and helped collect the dishes into a big washpan. Then he hurried out to the barns to harness up Max's Lady. He wondered as he worked if she missed the brindled old curmudgeon at all. She nuzzled his pockets for a treat of apple slices. So far as Colin could see, Max's love had gone totally unrequited.

He dusted off the upholstered seat that fit into the open cart, bolted it to its brackets, and drove up to the house. The shearers had returned to the shed. Mr. Slotemaker had gone into the house, and the other hands were dispersing gradually, still licking icing off their fingers, talking and laughing.

"We'll leave the dishes for now. Hop in, Hannah." The Dutchman's lady left her apron on the veranda rail and climbed into the cart. She settled onto the upholstered seat. "Drive east a way, Colin, then turn north up that lane beyond the first paddock."

Colin clucked to the bay mare. They jogged out of the yard onto the faint track. With half an ear he listened to the women talk, while his mind was swallowed up in thought about poor Max. Mr. Slotemaker had told him that strychnine didn't usually spread through the whole animal, because it was so fast-acting. Dingoes often ate poisoned rabbits without effect. Max must have eaten just the bit of stomach or liver most affected by the poison. Bad luck more than bad meat. If only the eaglehawks hadn't torn the carcass apart. . . .

He turned north onto a feeble track.

"Beyond that big gum tree, go right."

Colin did so. They left any semblance of track, and bounced over rough ground.

"Stop here." Mrs. Slotemaker stood up in the cart and pointed to a mound of disturbed dirt extending nearly a quarter mile. Grass and weeds had started to grow over the area here and there. Some plants that didn't take hold stuck out of the ground leafless and bent.

"That's a grave, Hannah. It holds over two thousand sheep and cattle and fifty horses. They didn't die quickly, as from strychnine. They died of starvation over a period of several months. There was nothing we could do for them but stand by and watch them suffer. Even if we could have afforded to buy hay for feed, there was none to be had. Every grazier in the district was facing the same horror.

"When it was clear that even a break in the weather wouldn't save them, Emory brought in a steam shovel and dug the channel. We drove the dying animals into it and shot them."

Hannah's mouth hung open. "The drought caused this?"

"Rabbits. Swarms of rabbits covered the land and ate everything in sight. There wasn't enough left for the grazing animals, and not enough rain to replenish the land fast enough. All those animals would have survived, had it not been for the rabbits. They wouldn't have suffered such terrible agony."

"Jackie Jump said the area's in drought time again," Hannah said, settling back down on the cart seat.

"He's right, and the forage is nearly gone again. I know what you and Colin are doing seems very unpleasant. It is. But you aren't really causing animals to suffer. You're saving animals from suffering. In fact, during drought when the grass and browse are gone, the rabbits and 'roos starve, too."

For a moment Hannah studied her hands in her lap. She turned suddenly to Mrs. Slotemaker and smiled. "Thank you."

Colin turned Max's Lady around and started back. He had entered this line of work for the money. It had never until this moment occurred to him that there might be some greater end to be attained, something worthwhile beyond money. It cast a whole new light on things.

What about Papa? Was what his father did as helpful? Colin quite frankly was uncertain how his father supported the family, much less whether his work had purpose or usefulness.

Papa, Papa. Over and over, Colin's thoughts and memories returned to the man he'd walked away from. That part of his life had ended. Wasn't he an adult now, making his own way in the world? Wasn't he proving himself? Why did ghosts of the past haunt him so?

They rattled into the yard a few feet ahead of their cloud of dust. It caught up to them as Colin drew the mare to a halt by the veranda rail. As it drifted by, Hannah and Mrs. Slotemaker descended, coughing.

When the dust had settled, she asked Hannah, "If you could do anything you wished today on your birthday, what would it be?"

"To sit in the shade and read a book. I've not done that in ever so long."

"Very well. Choose a book from the shelf in the parlor, any one you like. I recommend the gum tree out by the spring house, unless you've seen a better spot."

Hannah curtsied. "Why, thank you, but I'll help you with all those dishes. Colin has his apples to cut and soak. We're doing the last paddock tomorrow."

"Colin will help me with the dishes. You go and read now. This is your day. Enjoy it. No arguments."

Hannah's dark eyes flitted past Mrs. Slotemaker to Colin. They asked unspoken questions.

Colin grinned. "We don't question the boss's orders. Go."

She hugged Mrs. Slotemaker. She hugged her brother. She went.

Mrs. Slotemaker started for the tub of dirty dishes but Colin reached it first. He scooped it up lightly, pretending it wasn't nearly so heavy as it was, then toted it into the big summer kitchen out behind the house.

Mrs. Slotemaker put on an extra kettle of water to heat, and directed her black housemaid about beginning preparations for dinner.

As Colin shaved soap into the pan, he reflected on the enormous quantities of dishes, pots and pans he had washed since leaving home. The job had fallen to him on Captain Foulard's boat, on the Madman's Track, at his uncles' cottage, in the forest with Nels Brekke's crew, and nearly every meal with the shearers. Even when Hannah was designated cook, he washed dishes. Why should it be any different here? He poured boiling water into the pan, added as much cold, and set the kettle back to reheat for the rinse.

Mrs. Slotemaker handed him a towel and plunged her arms into the soapy water. "You've been moping about ever since you buried your dog. It's not hard to understand. He wasn't the most lovable, but even the ugliest dog can tug at your heart. They have a knack for that."

"Unlovable. You got that right. He wouldn't let me get near him most of the time—not even at the end." Colin glanced at the teeth wounds in his fingers and secretly rejoiced that Mrs. Slotemaker was the one submerging her hands into the water.

"I imagine it would have been much easier if you could have said goodbye. Reconciled, I suppose is the word."

Colin thought about that a moment. "Yair, I think you're right."

Mrs. Slotemaker turned the plates one by one to drain on the sideboard, without looking at Colin. "Hannah alluded to the fact that you and your father don't get along very well either."

Silence.

Bitter, penetrating silence. Reconcile. Growl. Snap and snarl. Eyes burning with hostility until they dulled and emptied. "Scuse me a moment; I'll be right back to finish here."

Colin draped the towel by the drainboard and hurried out back to the dunny.

He stepped inside the dark, stinking little two-holer and latched the door, but he didn't really use it. He wiped his hot and burning eyes. He blew his nose. He wiped his eyes again. His act more or less in order, he returned to the summer kitchen.

His hostess was humming a tune Colin had heard before in the church back home. If she noticed his reddened eyes, she didn't let on. Colin suddenly felt very wary of this woman. Like Mum, it seemed she could read his thoughts. Perhaps all women could perform that magic with men's minds.

She set a handful of forks on the drainboard. "Hannah and I had a delightful talk this morning while we were baking. What a lovely child she is. You two both have had a good upbringing, I can tell."

"Thank you Mu'm."

"We talked about God quite a bit. Hannah had some remarkably mature questions. For instance, she asked me if I knew *when* God's forgiveness is complete for specific sins."

"She, ah, never mentioned that to me."

"Perhaps it just never came up." She laid out more flatware to dry. "She felt guilty about specific things, like lying to her parents and running away. Legitimate guilt, actually. And she worried about how long God would let her live in her sins before He forgave her. An excellent question."

"Yes'm. She can be very grown-up." He hoped his response was vague enough that she would understand he didn't want to talk about it.

"I explained to her what the Word of God says about it," Mrs. Slotemaker persisted. "You simply confess your sins—sincere about it, of course. He forgives them instantly, and then He forgets about them. Hannah seemed immensely relieved. We knelt and prayed right there and took care of the matter."

He was still searching madly for the right words to respond when she began talking again.

"Your sister was also unclear about what makes a person a Christian. No surprise there. Many adults, even in the church, don't understand that. She's a wise young lady to ask such important questions."

"Yes'm." Confusion. A desire to get away. Colin quit looking for correct responses and started seeking a graceful way out.

"And so," Mrs. Slotemaker continued, "I explained that to her also. I told her that a Christian is someone who believes in Jesus—what He says and who He is. That person confesses his belief aloud, and embraces it in his heart, taking the living person of Christ into his heart. That is a real Christian."

"Yes'm."

Mrs. Slotemaker looked Colin squarely in the eye. There was no way he could leave the room now. "Hannah did that this morning, Colin. I've known and loved Jesus for many years; he's a personal friend and Savior to me. Today Hannah committed herself to Him also. She's a Christian now."

"Yes'm. That's very good. Uh, Mum will be pleased." *A personal friend and Savior? A living person?* Here was a woman not in the least like James Otis, who made exactly the same claims, but in a different way. A rush of conflicting thoughts muddled Colin's poor, tired brain.

She turned again to the basin. "Hannah says your parents are godly people. Christians. Wouldn't it be tragic if you refused God, not because you thought it was the right choice for you, but because it was the opposite of your parents choice? I'm sure you'd not be so foolish. God must be accepted or rejected on His own merits, not because someone else accepts or rejects Him. Don't you agree?"

"Yes'm." Colin's ears burned. Nay, more than his ears burned, his very heart burned. He dried the last of the flatware and emptied the dishwater out by the garden. As quickly as possible, he excused himself from the summer kitchen and took refuge in his poisoned apples.

———

It took Colin and Hannah four days to work the last paddock, laying the bait trail, re-feeding it, gathering the rabbit carcasses. Without Max the work took much longer. Colin would never have dreamed he could feel so sad over such a surly, ugly, old dog. They gathered in the last of the bait, the yarn, and the harvest late on a Monday afternoon.

Tuesday they completed skinning. They loaded the skins and the barrels of carcasses onto Mr. Slotemaker's borrowed truck. Hannah showed Colin how to work the gears and drive as they drove their last load out to the railway station in Deniliquin. Thursday afternoon they returned to the Slotemakers' with their cash in hand, thanks to the wonder of modern telegraphy.

Colin paid for the use of the truck and accepted Mr. Slotemaker's check in payment for services. He felt quite professional and businesslike.

"Where are you headed now?" Mrs. Slotemaker asked.

Hannah looked at Colin. "We've talked about Gundagai. We have some shearer friends who should be there by now."

"It'll bring us closer to Sydney. We can pick up the railway there, and take Hannah home." Now that it appeared within reach, Colin had trouble believing it.

Mr. Slotemaker nodded knowingly. "Got a letter from a friend north of Wagga near Junee. Jim Barnes. Just a small cocky with a few hundred thousand acres. He mentioned a serious rabbit problem, so I wrote him back about you. Might find work if you head up that way."

"Oceans of opportunity there," Mrs. Slotemaker added. "Rabbits everywhere and not enough men available to handle the problem."

"Thanks for the tip!" Colin said, genuinely grateful. They all sat about on the veranda for another hour in casual conversation. Colin secretly hoped Hannah and Mrs. Slotemaker wouldn't get off onto the subject of God again.

By dawn Hannah and Colin were headed northeast, on their way to Junee.

CHAPTER TWENTY-ONE

OCEANS OF RABBITS

"Know what I'm going to buy with our next check, Colin?" Hannah braced her perch on the top rail of the stakeside. She was getting pretty good at riding in the backs of stock trucks. Newly shorn sheep crowded at her feet, packed so closely none could move or lie down. The truck hit a dip in a dry creek. She clung to the corner post.

"A railway ticket to Sydney."

"Trousers. I'm tired of having my legs and knees constantly scuffed. Heavy drill pants like yours, or dungarees."

"Not a bit ladylike."

"Neither is trying to stay modest on the horse, or when we're bouncing along in the back of a truck like this. Trousers are *more* modest for the things we're doing."

"Still, it's not proper."

Proper! Easy for Colin to say. He doesn't have to remember to keep his knees together. Look at him with one leg hooked over the rail, all neatly braced, hanging on with one hand. Men! They just don't understand. Hannah watched the dry countryside. An hour ago they had wound through low hills and gentle rises, much more interesting than the flats they traversed now.

"I wish Joe and the others had made it to Gundagai," she sighed.

"Good thing they didn't. What a mess that flood left! They'll be forever digging the place out. At least only the river drainage flooded when the dam broke. There'll be shearing on the flatland above the flood."

Hannah counted her forty-second rabbit on this leg of the trip. She and Colin would be sorely needed at the Colfax station, just as they had been at Slotemakers' and Barnes'. She pondered deep thoughts about death and killing. There were the rabbits, of course, but people were saying several men had died in the Murrumbidgee flood.

She didn't have any answers. Either she didn't know enough about the subject or she didn't know enough about life. These farmers' lives and livelihoods depended upon keeping the rabbits at bay. She and Colin were performing a valuable service. The revulsion she originally felt about killing the soft bunnies abated considerably as she beheld the hideous suffering and destruction they caused.

The truck slowed, crossed a creekbed and rumbled up the far bank. "Colin, if you had lots of money, what would you buy?"

"Our own stakeside. Or at least one of those little half-ton trucks—something to drive from place to place and haul Max's Lady in."

"If it weren't for the horse, we could have accepted a ride in at least a couple of different vehicles. We could have been sitting inside, on real seats."

"We need the horse, Hannah."

"I know." She thought about how they'd sometimes needed Max, too. He had been so good at seeking out rabbits, which in their final moments had hidden in the bush. They needed Max to catch rats, were they to take up that particular line of work again. She missed dear, nasty old Max terribly.

The truck lumbered into a wide, bleak yard of beaten earth. Ramshackle sheds with stretched canvas roofs huddled precariously at the far end, laced together by bonds of rail fence. A smokehouse, a meat safe, and an outhouse—all the accouterments of country living—stood about in attendance to a most dismal-looking government house. It was built like a small box, with a couple of lean-to's attached to one end. A loose stone chimney indicated the kitchen. Its walls were vertical slabs of timber with the bark still intact. Weathered canvas formed the roof. Scattered about was a lot of just plain trash—bits and pieces of boxes and things. The crude, primitive nature of the buildings aside, this station lacked the crisp cleanliness of the Slotemaker place, the casual friendliness that had greeted them at the Barneses'. There was a feeling of desperation here, though Hannah had not yet seen a human face.

"It's Uncle Edgar!" a soprano voice called out. Three ragamuffin children came tumbling out of the government house, followed by a fourth about Edan's age, though he was scrawnier than Edan and much tanner from the sun.

Edgar Colfax drove the truck into a small paddock by the main barn. He walked toward the house, closing the gate behind him. As children lined the top rail watching, Colin dropped the tailgate and ran the ramp down. Max's Lady, literally up to her belly in sheep, wheeled and bolted down the ramp unbidden. She had endured the whole trip with sheep jammed under her and pressed against her legs. It had obviously affected her disposition. She stood off to a corner now, glistening with sweat and wild-eyed.

Hannah called and waved her arms, trying to herd the sheep into some semblance of order. The shorn animals milled about, bumping into each other as they poured down off the truck. They shifted aimlessly about the paddock in a tight bunch. *Sheep are so stupid*, Hannah thought.

The oldest boy jumped down into the paddock and crawled up onto the driver's seat. The children opened the gate, and he drove the truck out into the wide dooryard. A lad Edan's age, driving the big stakeside—and Hannah had felt so proud of herself for having driven in the jarrah forest! She walked over to the gate, slipped through behind Colin, and followed him toward the house.

"You hired a couple of kids?" A tenor voice, thin and reedy, stormed from inside the house. "If I wanted kids doing the work, I'd send my own out." Hannah paused outside the rickety fly-screen door, uncertain if she should enter.

"They're experienced rabbiters. Did a good job down south around Deniliquin and Wagga Wagga." Uncle Edgar was speaking.

"Don't be crazy, Duncan. I don't want our kids fooling around with strychnine," came a weary woman's voice.

The four children captured Hannah's full attention outside, asking who she and Colin were and where they came from, and why she wasn't married. She was trying to explain that just-turned-thirteen is really too young to marry when a voice bellowed from the house and Colin tapped her arm. She followed him inside.

The children trailed behind. A tired-looking, skinny woman with dark circles under her eyes snapped, "You kids run outside. Go!" The children reluctantly turned and left.

The woman's dark, stringy, shoulder-length hair could use a washing. Actually, Hannah thought, a cut and a style would help too. On her hip she carried a baby of perhaps nine or ten months.

Duncan must be her husband, the man of the house. He didn't have the same tired look as his wife. He certainly had none of the open joviality that made Mr. Slotemaker so delightful.

He frowned suspiciously at Colin and Hannah as Uncle Edgar introduced them. "Got a thousand pounds of soft apples waiting for you in the wheat shed," he announced. "You two think you can handle the job?"

"Yes, sir." Colin sounded mature and confident. Hannah felt very proud of him. "We used sixteen hundred pounds at Slotemakers' and two tons at the Barnes station. We saw a lot of rabbits as we were coming in here. We can start with a thousand pounds, but we'll likely need more."

"That's all there is and all there's going to be. You'd best be sparing of them."

"Yes, sir." Colin dipped his head. "No better investment you can make on the land than rabbit control, sir. Saves the browse and grass, particularly in dry weather."

"Investment means money, and that we don't have. Do your best with what's here."

"Yes'r." Colin started for the door, and Hannah silently followed; there would be no friendly chitchat with the Colfaxes.

Colin pulled his swag out from the passenger side of the truck and handed Hannah her traveling bag. He addressed the oldest Colfax child, Gerald. "When we were hired, your uncle said we could have the use of a horse cart. Where might that be?"

"I'll show you." Gerald led off across the wide yard. "You gunner hire us to help you?"

"No. I happen to know your mum doesn't want you messing around the poison we use. She'd be angry if you did."

"I'm ten now. I can handle it."

"The answer's still no."

"That cart there." Gerald pointed. He didn't seem the least upset that no job loomed in the offing after all. "Needs grease, but it'll do. You gunner put that bay mare to it?"

"Yair." Colin gripped the shafts and pulled. The cart creaked pitifully. "Gunner have to pull both wheels and grease the bearings to get this doover in shape again."

"I'll show you where the grease is if you'll let us help you."

Colin stopped and studied him. "How much?"

The boy shrugged. "Bob a day."

"Hafta think about that." Colin busied himself with the cart wheels.

Hannah was already off in search of it. Where would they keep axle grease? Main barn, most likely. There was the little girl who called herself Mitzy, hanging up diapers. "Mitzy, how old are you?" Hannah picked up a wad of wet diapers and started pinning them to the line.

"Eight. I'll be nine after Christmas."

"A birthday right near Christmas? Do you win or lose?"

"Lose, mostly. Bryan usually gets a birthday present. His is in July."

Hannah hung up two more. "I'm supposed to find some axle grease. Do you know where it is?"

"Sure." Mitzy trotted off.

Hannah hurried behind her. Two minutes later she triumphantly carried the grease pot to the carriage shed.

Early next morning, rather than mix up strychnine where the children might get into it, Hannah and Colin carted apples, poison and all out to the paddocks where they'd be working. Hannah found cutting up apples to be a mindless, not unpleasant task. They cut the apples into particularly small slices to make them go further; that took longer than usual.

"Colin? Are we really going home after this?"

"Think of all the school you're missing."

"Do you know what I'd be doing this very minute? Sewing, by hand. With Miss Broaditch scowling at us."

"So instead you're cutting up apples by hand with a total stranger—Mr. Colfax—scowling at you. I don't see any big improvement there."

"I don't get paid to sew by hand."

"You're not learning anything, either."

"I've learned ever so much!" Hannah protested. "Things I never dreamed of. And think of all the places I've been that I'd never seen before."

"You're still going back."

She threw an apple at him and continued slicing bait. It bounced off his shoulder and rolled aside. She didn't want to go home. And yet a small voice deep inside kept whispering, faintly, *Oh, yes you do!*

She stopped suddenly. "Colin, look. Beyond you. That rabbit is just sitting there staring at us. You don't suppose it knows, do you?"

Colin turned to watch the creature as it paused less than fifteen feet from him.

The living rabbit looked much larger than the stiff corpses they collected. It perched, loosely hunched, on its big, broad feet, and twitched its nose. Except when a fly lighted on its eye and it blinked, it made no other move.

"Go!" Colin waved his arm.

The rabbit sat quietly, flaccid in the warmth of the afternoon.

Colin threw an apple half at it. The piece struck its flank. With long, flowing hops it moved forward three feet and stopped again. It made no attempt to investigate the apple, and paid no attention to Colin or Hannah. A few minutes later it casually hopped away to the east.

Hannah and Colin looked at each other, shrugging. They resumed their work without comment.

The first day's trail was finished very late and they got back after dark. No one invited them to dinner. No one offered them a place to stay.

"What did Edgar say about accommodations when you made the agreement to come?" Hannah asked.

"I forgot to discuss it."

"Lovely business manager you are."

Colin rolled his swag out on the shearing floor, and Hannah slept on the seat of the stakeside truck.

The next morning they rode out in eager anticipation of the vast harvest promised by the many rabbits they had seen about the day before. Nothing. The bait lay undisturbed but for a few pieces kangaroos had gotten into. They found the kangaroos and skinned them.

On the way back that afternoon they passed four apparently healthy rabbits along the paddock line. None of the creatures evinced the least fear or attempted to move away.

Uncle Edgar was crossing from the barn as they drove Max's Lady into the yard. He coughed violently and paused as they approached. "Any luck today?"

Colin grimaced. "They're not taking the bait. Not at all. You sure those apples are all right? We never had a problem like this before."

"Apples is apples, I always thought. Don't tell me them rabbits have expensive tastes." He snorted and continued toward the house. Hannah heard him coughing even after the door closed.

"Friendly folk," Colin muttered. He drove the mare over to the paddock. Hannah jumped down to open the gate.

"Wait a minute!" Colin stood up in the cart. "Look at the paddock there. There's not a speck of feed."

Hannah climbed the rails. The naked sheep stood all around, mindlessly bumping into one another, bleating occasionally. "I don't see any hay at all."

"Right. I don't think they're feeding the sheep enough. If we turn the mare in there and feed her, the sheep will take the hay before she can get any. Let's put her out behind the barn on the longline."

Hannah scrambled into the back of the cart and dangled her feet over the side as Colin drove around the barn. Dust rolled high, and they weren't going fast at all. They rattled past a dried-up old leather shoe. Mrs. Slotemaker would never leave trash like that lying about. Hannah thought about the tidy farm down south, and how peaceful the couple had seemed. Content. She wanted that kind of a life when she grew up—after she'd done with all her adventuring, of course. She tried to imagine Mrs. Slotemaker out adventuring. She could not.

Hannah had an interesting thought just then. *Mrs. Slotemaker enjoys high adventure—spiritually. To her,*

Jesus is an exciting person, a friend to be feared and honored. To her, preparing for heaven is just as immediate a concern as preparing for the next jaunt into Deniliquin.

Hannah was forgiven. God didn't even remember Hannah lied to her parents. What a wonderful thought! Mrs. Slotemaker had carefully counseled her not to make light of such forgiveness. Hannah could understand that; her forgiveness had been made possible with a heavy price—Jesus's life and blood. Hannah could also see how she must not glibly take advantage of such instant forgiveness by lying again. Ah, but it felt good to have the slate clean.

That was it! A great light dawned in Hannah's mind. The Slotemakers were happy and content, not because they kept their station clean and in perfect order, but because they were forgiven. And they knew they were forgiven because they knew God. It all fit together. They were walking alongside God instead of running away from Him, like Colin, or constantly bumping into Him, like Hannah.

Hannah knew God personally now. That was the first step. She was forgiven. She had every reason to be content. Why wasn't she? She stood by watching Colin unhitch Max's Lady, without really seeing him. She was absorbed in her thoughts. She wanted to be home. Suddenly, more than anything else in the world, she wanted to be home!

"Colin? Don't you ever want to go home again?"

"I don't know."

"You've thought about it, haven't you?"

"Yair." He stopped and leaned against the patient mare's rump. She shifted her weight slightly to accommodate him. "I'm thinking I don't have any way to take you home and know you'll get there except if I take you to the door. So when I go home, I want to have a pocketful of money. I'm gunner show Mum and Papa that I can make it fine, and do it honorably, too. Not shifty, like Papa thinks I am, or dishonest like my uncles. We've got a nice bit from the last jobs, and this will net us plenty more."

"If the rabbits ever start taking the bait."

"It must be the apples. I'll send for more apples; a different kind. There are plenty of rabbits here to make us a very neat profit. I'm gunner walk in the door at home with new clothes on and money in my pocket. You, too. I'll show Papa he's wrong, and then I can walk out again any time I care to."

"Independently wealthy, like they say."

"That's it." Colin snapped the lead line onto the mare's halter.

"You're afraid I won't go home if you just drop me off somewhere."

"Do you blame me?"

"I guess not." He was right; Hannah knew that. But she hated to hear him say he didn't trust her. Being forgiven and being trusted, obviously, were two very different things.

A familiar child's voice called from the far end of the hospital paddock. Gerald hauled himself over the fence rail and approached at a dragging, slogging pace. He carried a rifle on his shoulder and his left hand gripped at least three dead rabbits by the ears.

He came up to them grinning. "I shot four rabbits. How many'd you get today?" He dropped the rabbits by the barn door and propped his gun against the slab siding.

"Four less than you." Colin brought out an armload of loose hay. The mare nickered enthusiastically.

"None atall?" Gerald cackled. "Maybe you oughta shoot 'em, 'stead of feedin' 'em apples. I can take you out tomorrow and show you where they are." Very grown-up-like, the boy leaned against the siding and pulled a pouch from his pocket. He proceeded to roll a cigarette—in fact, a better-looking cigarette than old Horace Hamm ever rolled. Hannah gaped, dumbstruck.

"We already know where they are. We saw them, all around. They're not taking the bait. It wasn't very hard to shoot those you have, was it? They probably walked right up to you and stood in front of the rifle."

Gerald lurched erect. "They were doing that for you, too?" He frowned. "Don't suppose they're sick with something, do you?"

"I don't know. Never saw rabbits acting like these before." Colin started in the barn door, Hannah close behind.

Gerald followed them into the soft, musty darkness. Colin wheeled suddenly, grabbed the boy's cigarette and stomped it out on the barn floor. "Lad, don't ever take a lighted cigarette into a barn, or a pipe either. Biggest cause of barn fires there is. If you were working the racecourse at Sydney you'd be sacked this minute. Out of a job for good."

"Ain't your barn, nor your place to tell me what to do. Uncle Edgar and Pop don't care if I smoke."

"They care whether the barn smokes, I vow." Colin threw the mashed bumper out the door into the dust. Gerald stared at it, glared at Colin, and walked with them meekly to the house.

Hannah hoped they would get invited to supper when they reported the day's lack of success. They weren't. Uncle Edgar, she learned, had already gone to bed complaining of a headache. Mrs. Colfax acted cross and her husband expressed impatience with his rabbiters. Gerald gave all four of his rabbits to his Mum. The luckless rabbiters ate their last two cans of food—a can of beef and a can of green beans—and retired to their respective places in the shearing shed and the stakeside.

Hannah thought about praying, but somehow didn't have the courage to this time. She mused about the carefree way Mum and Mrs. Slotemaker went about prayer. She thought she'd only just drifted off to sleep, when Colin whomped on the door of the truck. Time to get up already! There was the faithful sun.

She washed up in the sheep's watering trough and wished someone, anyone, would invite her to breakfast. They ate four apples apiece as they hitched up the mare.

Beyond the grove of acacia trees to the north of the house they heard a faint gunshot. Gerald must be out hunting again.

"We should get a gun, Colin, or borrow one. At least we'd have breakfast."

"We're borrowing a dozen horseshoes I found in the tack room. With the rabbits acting like they are, we can knock them down with horseshoes and catch some breakfast. *Then* we'll run the bait trail. I'm starving."

"So much of adventuring seems to be going hungry."

Gerald appeared from the far side of the property, waving wildly and shouting. He ran into the house. Moments later Mitzy burst out of the house. "Hannah!" she squeaked. "Come look!" She came running up to them. "Let me ride with you, can I?"

"Where to?" Colin climbed into the seat and took up the lines. Hannah and Mitzy hopped in the back.

"Beyond the coolibah trees to the northeast, Gerald says. Do hurry!"

"Me too!" Six-year-old Bryan bounded out the screen door and intercepted them. He clambered aboard bright-eyed for so early an hour.

Colin kept the mare at a trot out to the rise a mile beyond the house. On all sides—behind them in the dust, ahead of them crossing the track—rabbits hopped. A constant run of rabbits, scores of them it seemed. Without exception they flowed east, determinedly, mindlessly. As the horsecart topped the gentle slope Hannah heard the stakeside's motor rumbling behind them.

Colin drew the mare in twenty feet short of the east paddock fence. From beyond the trees, from behind the bushes—rabbits, rabbits, and more rabbits.

"They're everywhere! Hundreds of them. Colin, look along the fence!" Impulsively, Hannah jumped to the ground. With Mitzy at her heels she stepped up beside the horse's head. Rabbits passed within a few feet of her. The wire net fence had stopped the silent, inexorable migration. Rabbits crowded against it, milled along it. They continued forward, pressing against each other, pressing into the fencing.

Just this side of a great gum tree a mass of rabbits had surged against the fence. The ones on the bottom had stopped struggling. Others continued to squirm on top of them, and still others scrambled and struggled onto the heap. Hannah stared in disbelief as the pile grew. When the mound reached the top of the fencing, some began to fall over onto the other side, only to continue to the east on their mindless journey.

To the south of where Hannah stood, the fence crossed a dry creek. Another seething mound of rabbits was piling high against the wire in the same fashion as the others. The center post, merely a crooked stick thrust in the sand, cracked under the weight, and snapped in the middle. The wire fence bulged and sagged. The uppermost layer of the scrambling mound of animals tumbled over the top to freedom. The fence collapsed to a barrier two feet high at most, trapping rabbits within its folds.

Waves of rabbits continued to pour over the hill and across the ravine, over the fence or against it. It looked like oceans of rabbits flowing eastward.

Duncan Colfax had pulled his truck abreast of the horse-cart. He stood on his running board and leaned on the door, gawking. "I heard about these migrations when I was a youngster, and rumors of them now and then. Never knew I'd see one. Crikey! Ain't it something!"

Hacking and coughing, Uncle Edgar opened the passenger door, but he didn't stand. He sat there in his pajamas, staring at the incredible spectacle. Mrs. Colfax huddled in the middle of the seat between the men. She held baby Hilda in her lap and balanced four-year-old Ruth on her knee. She was pointing, trying to interest the baby in the sight, but not even young Ruth grasped what she was seeing.

Neither did Hannah, really. "Colin, why? Why would God allow this?"

Mr. Colfax wagged his head. "Good luck for us, Bad luck for you kids. God's sweeping my place clean of rabbits, but I guess that puts you out of a job."

CHAPTER TWENTY-TWO

THE RAINS

Colin wiped the sweat from his forehead with his arm. This was a messy job. He tossed another rabbit skin into the back of the stakeside.

Hannah pinched a tuft of fur on a rabbit corpse and tugged. The hair came out easily in her fingers. She flung the carcass aside. "Colin, there aren't many good ones left. Most all the rabbits that were buried under the others are spoiled."

"Yair. Musta been the warmth. The skins have to stay cool or they slough off right away. We might as well just go with what we got here."

"Subtracting the cost of the petrol, and what Mr. Colfax is charging us to use the truck, we'll still make—" she stood a moment, frowning. "Seven pounds four, at least." Hannah climbed into the passenger side. Colin drove. He stopped a little farther on to skin a few more carcasses, but the sun had pretty much taken its toll on the rest. The damage done, the orange ball retreated behind a thickening overcast.

Flies droned everywhere. Already, tiny maggots infested some of the bodies, and the musty-sweet odor of death hung in the air. They encountered not a single live rabbit in the mile and a half back to the Colfaxes'.

Seven pounds? More like five pounds ten, by Colin's

reckoning. This wasn't near the money he'd hoped to bring to Sydney. Perhaps they ought take one more job. He drove into the yard and parked the stakeside.

Mitzy and Bryan sat under the gum tree arguing about who should feed their baby sister. Little Hilda, oblivious to their banter, lay on her back between them, fussing for her bottle. Hannah plopped down beside them, seeking to settle their disagreement.

Colin rapped on the screen door before entering the house. He pulled his hat off as he stepped into the dimly lit room.

"In the kitchen," Mr. Colfax's reedy voice called out.

Colin found his way there. The messy condition of this shack, untidy beyond primitiveness, bothered and irritated him.

Mr. Colfax sat at the lonely end of a long, rickety table. He stared at his cup. "Tea on the stove. Help yourself."

"Ta." Colin found a mug on the board and poured from the battered kettle. He looked in vain for any sign of sugar. He sat down near Mr. Colfax and reviewed the day's work. "We loaded about all that's salvageable. We don't have a whole lot there. I'd like to get started soon."

Duncan Colfax nodded. "Where you going? Wagga?"

"Yes, sir. Anything I can get there for you?"

He shook his head. "Ever hear of the Spanish influenza?"

"Yes, sir. I was eleven when the epidemic hit Sydney after the war. Hannah was about seven, I guess. My father and another sister were sick with it. The rest of us escaped."

"I was down in Cooma. Left Winnie and the kids alone to volunteer for ambulance service. Buried a lot of strong young men. Lots of babies, too. Babies were the hardest."

"Most of what I remember about it were the restrictions and quarantine. If there was flu in your household they put a yellow flag out front and you couldn't leave your own house until someone came through and certified that everyone was over it. Flu in your family meant you weren't allowed to ride the trains."

Mr. Colfax nodded. "In Cooma, too. The auxiliaries brought food around to the quarantined homes. Shops and businessmen supplied victuals. Did a lot of the cooking in the hotel kitchens. Everybody just sort of worked together. Don't find that kind of community spirit these days. Now everybody's listening to that jazz music and dancing. And the women wear them flimsy clothes. Everybody's thinking about themselves, I reckon."

"Yes, sir." Colin really didn't want to sit talking about the past. He wanted to get his skins to town before any more of them spoiled. "Sure you don't need anything in Wagga Wagga?"

"Fact is, I need everything." The man waved a hand gracelessly. "In late '19 I took this selection as a Soldier Settler. It looked so good. So promising. Raise your kids out in the country where it's healthy, and they'll grow up strong. Be your own man."

"My father said when the government opened the land to selection by returning servicemen, it made a huge mistake."

"Wise man, your father. I'm so deep in debt I'll never see the sun again. And for nothing. If things don't turn around fast I'll lose the land as well. Six years of endless work and deprivation for nothing. And no prospects to look forward to."

Was this an overture for a loan? Was this man about to put the bite on Colin for his rabbit skin money?

Maybe not. Colin drained his cup, waiting further comment. None came. Colin excused himself and left.

Hannah followed him to the truck and climbed in. Half an hour later she had fallen asleep, curled up in the corner with her head thunking against the window.

By late afternoon it started to rain. Only one of the windshield wipers worked, and it wasn't on the driver's side. The road fast became a greasy quagmire. Other traffic churned up the mud. If this kept up, they'd get stuck for sure.

They reached town very late in the day and Colin faced a new set of problems. He had never driven in town before. Even a sleepy town like Wagga Wagga made him nervous, partly because flood damage closed down parts of streets. He couldn't tell when he turned onto a street whether he would be able to drive to the end of it. Colin purchased a room for Hannah at the inn on the corner. To save money, he spent the night in the truck, lulled asleep to the sound of rain drumming on the roof.

———

The broker was late coming in next morning. He finally appeared past ten o'clock. Grumbling, he bought the skins for four pounds two and complained with justification that they were not properly baled. He complained too about having to shovel mud out of his warehouses near the river, and lamented the damage the flooding had caused.

Determined as only a thirteen-year-old girl can be, Hannah bought her trousers, which meant she also had to buy a shirt. Colin added a hat to her purchases to save her poor nose from peeling further. Then she insisted on buying herself a Bible. There went another two bob six right there.

It had begun to rain again—too late now to start back, for the truck's headlamps didn't work well, not to mention the wiper. Colin put Hannah in a room again and curled up on the truck seat to wait out the rain.

Next morning they stocked up on food, bought hay for the horse, filled the petrol tank and headed north. The road had not improved, in fact, it was worse. With the terse explanation, "I've done this before," Hannah took over the wheel. She blasted through the miry ruts and drove alongside the track at the worst spots. Colin had to admit that for all the rain and mud, it was a miracle they weren't bogged yet.

"Colin? Do you know where we're going next?"

"No, but we still have the strychnine and we can probably buy those apples from Mr. Colfax cheaply. Then find a station that wasn't affected by that migration madness and use up our poison bait, I suppose. And on to Sydney."

"So you still want to make some more money before we go home."

"Combining this check with our other money, we're down to six quid and some. I think we need one more job."

After lunch Hannah turned the wheel back over to Colin. She settled down as comfortably as possible in the passenger's seat and pulled out her new Bible. She opened it carefully in the middle, then worked the spine as she had learned in school, opening it to the right of the middle, to the left, a few more pages to the right, a few more to the left. She took great pride in her newest purchase.

Then she closed the book on her lap, running her hand over the soft cover. Opening it at random, she began to read aloud from the book of Haggai. Colin had never even heard of Haggai. He suggested she read silently. In less than an hour she fell asleep again, and her Bible slid off her lap.

They arrived back at the Colfaxes' at half past five. Colin felt very weary. His eyes burned and his head hurt. He parked the truck by the barn and slid out of the seat. "You gunner fix supper, Hannah?"

"If you'll build the fire. Why is it so quiet around here?"

"I was wondering that. Let's unload the mare's hay so Mr. Colfax can use his truck when he needs to." Colin could not have felt less like unloading hay. He tackled the job alone, while Hannah took some things out for their supper, then wandered over to the paddock to check on the animals.

Before he finished, she was at his side, tugging on his shirt. "Colin, you've got to come look at the sheep."

He frowned. "Now what?" He followed her to the barn paddock and climbed the fence to study the shorn creatures.

Hannah hopped up beside him. "They look like they haven't eaten in days. Their flanks are all caved in. And their water trough's dry again. I filled it before we left for town 'cause it was empty. Nobody's done anything for these sheep the whole time we've been here."

"They aren't our responsibility."

"They're suffering! They're hungry and thirsty, and there's no protection from the sun and rain in this paddock."

"They aren't ours, Hannah." He jumped down off the fence and walked to the house, crossing the wide yard. Hannah's blind insistence sometimes rankled him.

No one answered Colin's knock. He heard coughing in the lean-to out back; Edgar must not be over the influenza yet. He waited and tried again. A few feet beyond the screen, four-year-old Ruth appeared. She stood staring at him, bleary-eyed.

"Is your mum or pop here, Ruth? Or Uncle Edgar?"

She shook her head *no* and stood there.

The back of his neck prickled. He knocked again.

A chair clattered in the kitchen. With shuffling steps Mr. Colfax finally appeared. He just looked at Colin a moment. "You're back. Truck okay? Come on in."

Colin stepped inside. "Your truck ran fine, sir, and we filled the tank before we left town."

"You filled the tank? Shouldn'ta done that. Come on back." He turned and walked unsteadily to the kitchen. He flopped down into a chair at the table, ignoring the chair he had tipped over.

Colin picked up the toppled chair and sat in it.

Mr. Colfax's eyes were bloodshot and his cheeks flushed behind a three-day stubble. He had not changed his clothes since Colin left. He still coughed painfully.

"You don't look well, sir."

"We need—we need your help, boy." The man seemed to look steadily into Colin's eyes for the first time. "Take the truck over to Griffith. Look up Dr. Newsome. Got that? There's a couple of sisters and midwives there, but find Newsome. Tell him to come down here to our place. Tell him it's the flu. He might want something on account. Tell him I'll pay him when he gets here."

Colin heard a timid knock out front. The door creaked.

A chorus of coughing erupted somewhere at the back of the house.

"If he won't drive his car down, bring him in the truck."

"Yes, sir." As Colin stood up Hannah appeared in the kitchen doorway, her shirt covered with wisps of hay.

"You say you filled the tank." Mr. Colfax frowned. "There's a hole in it. Past half full, the petrol leaks away. The gauge'll be near empty. We keep the petrol in a drum in back. Take that along and refill the truck tank from that if you need to."

"Yes, sir. Where do you keep the drum?"

"I said. Back of the truck."

"There isn't any drum in back of the truck."

"Edgar said he brought three drums."

"No, sir. Sheep, the mare, Hannah and me. That's all that was in the back."

Mr. Colfax stared at him. "He couldn't have forgot them. He must've forgot them." The man gazed glassy-eyed at nothing in particular. "They're still in Wagga then. Don't matter no more. It's all over anyway. I've given it away. It's all over."

"Mr. Colfax, is your wife sick, too?"

He nodded. "And all the babies 'cept Ruth."

"And Edgar isn't any better?"

"Edgar died yesterday."

Hannah clapped her hands over her mouth.

The man crumpled forward in another vicious spate of coughing. His nose and mouth dripped blood.

What could Colin do? What could he say?

Hannah still stood in the doorway, staring at the man. Colin stepped in front of her to break her gaze and piloted her out into the dark front room.

"Colin—" She wrapped her arms around him, and buried her head into his shoulder. Ruth was tugging at her skirt, and Hannah looked to Colin for direction. They followed where the child led them, silently through the gloomy house.

Colin gasped when they passed a dark side room. Edgar still lay in the dank stillness, his skin blue, his mouth relaxed and open. Colin quietly dropped a curtain over the doorway.

Gerald, Bryan and Mitzy were all crowded in one bed in a corner room. They just lay there, listless. Ruth led them to another room where Mrs. Colfax lay on her side curled around her baby. Ruth climbed into the bed with her. She pushed her away. "No, dear. You go with these people until I'm better. They can take care of you." Her vacant eyes turned to Colin. "Thank God you're here."

Thank God? All this death and misery, and you thank God? Everything in Colin's being rebelled against such a thought. Here was a very sick family facing financial failure, and God didn't seem to be anywhere around. Thank God, indeed.

Hannah lifted Ruth from her mother's bed, in spite of the child's wailing. At least it was a healthy cry. "Come," said Hannah, "I'll bet you're hungry. So am I. Let's make dinner for your mum and family. You can help me."

Colin hurried back out to the front room. He turned to Hannah. "I'll go for help. Think you can feed them and keep things going here?"

She nodded. "I suppose you're upset with me, Colin, but I had to do it."

"Yair, I know. You threw the mare's hay to those sheep." He snorted, more in admiration than in disgust. "I'll get some more in Griffith."

"While you're gone I'll go out and make sure the bait's all taken up out of that northeast paddock. We can turn the sheep out there when you get back, all right?"

"All right. But I'm taking the mare with me. If the truck bogs or runs out of petrol, I don't want to have to walk."

She nodded and stepped back, taking charge of her responsibilities like a woman. As Colin walked out into the damp and lonely evening, he heard Hannah's soft, soothing words to poor, frightened little Ruth.

He ran the mare up into the back of the truck, and tossed the saddle into the cab beside him to keep it out of the rain. As an afterthought he grabbed the tin candle lantern out of the barn and four apples. He was hungry, howling hungry. He'd eat in Griffith, even if it meant begging at someone's door.

The track north was rough, hardly a path. Darkness fell and Colin could barely make out the way. Rain pelted the windshield. The surviving wiper disappeared with a snap. Its broken arm swung back and forth, etching a great arc in the windshield before Colin could find the switch to turn it off. He tried driving with his head out the window. Fumes boiled up from behind the cab aggravating his headache. He had to pull his head in.

The truck coughed and sputtered, drifting to a silent halt. In the dark and the rain Colin could not begin to guess how far he had come or how far he had to go. Disgusted, he ran the mare off the back and saddled her. In the nick of time he remembered to bring the tin candle lantern.

She was stiff and sluggish getting off tonight. He had to work to keep her on the track; she kept wanting to turn back. It took her a good two miles to settle to the trail, stretch her neck out and shift into a ground-eating walk.

Colin was soaked through to his skin and freezing cold. This late in the spring, as hot as it had been last week, it was hard to believe it could be this dreadfully cold. He started shivering uncontrollably. His headache refused to fade, and the constant motion in the saddle seemed to make it worse.

When, an hour later, he was still riding in total blackness, Colin halted the mare to rest her. He loosened the saddle enough to pull out one of two saddle blankets. He left the thinner of the two beneath her saddle to protect her from chafing, and wrapped the larger one across his shoulders to fend off the chilling rain.

After a short time of rest, he lighted the candle lantern and opened its windbreaker door. With some glimpse of the track now, he urged the mare to a jog. When she started to overheat he pulled her back to a walk. Sometime later he dozed off, and awoke with a start when he realized the blanket had slid off his back. The candle lantern had also gone out. Striking a match, he discovered the candle had burned to the socket. Without it, there was no hope of finding the blanket; it wasn't worth going back. The mare was extremely warm again. Was she working too hard?

Where on earth was Griffith? The sky streaked gray as the track leveled out across a barren flat. The trail looked unused. Was he lost after all? The mare could easily have wandered off onto a side track when he fell asleep. No choice now. He must press on. Where would he end up if he missed Griffith? He tried to think of other towns in the area, but none came to mind.

A persistent tickle scratched in his throat, but no amount of coughing could budge it. He began to fear pneumonia in this miserable weather. Was that a town up ahead? The sun was coming up and he could barely discern buildings in the distance. He urged the mare to a canter. She lunged into her rocking-horse gait, dinnerplate feet splacking through the mud.

The ride increased Colin's headache and he began to feel dizzy. Or was he disoriented? The horizon undulated. Max's Lady seemed distanced from him and her head waved weirdly.

She stumbled and very nearly unhorsed him. Colin held her to a dog-trot. By the time they jogged into the main street, the townsfolk were out and about on their daily business. People looked at him oddly.

"Dr. Newsome's office, please?" Colin asked the first person he could stop.

"Left at the next cross street, and three blocks down."

He turned left, but then lost count of the blocks. He found the office by backtracking. A shingle promised Dr. Harold Newsome. No one about. Colin tried the door. Locked. A wave of panic started to rise in his breast. He forced it down and crossed the street. A woman passed and he called to her, "Ma'am, do you know Dr. Newsome's office hours, please? I have to find him."

"Hours? I don't think he has any. Try his home, half a mile out the Rankins Springs Track. You can't miss it."

I wouldn't bank on that. Colin bade her good day and climbed back into the waterlogged saddle. The mare shivered now the way Colin had during the night. What a miserable trip it had been.

Somehow, by sheer luck he thought, he found Rankins Springs Track. The rain began again. The mare groaned and dropped to her knees. Colin pitched forward, slid out of the saddle and down her neck. His ears burned hot with embarrassment. He wondered if anyone had seen this pitiful display of horsemanship. He began coughing again, and urged the mare to her feet.

She took a few steps forward and fell again.

An automobile chugged to a halt in the muddy track. A heavyset fellow in a business suit stepped out. "Who do you think you are, larrikin, to maltreat a horse so!"

"Uh, yes sir . . . " *Maltreat?* He had no intention of mistreating his beloved old mare. *How could the man think such a thing?* "Uh, sir, can you tell me how far to Dr. Newsome's house? I have to find him."

The man stared at him. "I believe you do. Get in."

Colin walked around the front of the auto; he slipped in the mud and lurched momentarily against the car. He climbed into the passenger side as the fellow shifted into gear. "Uh, sir? I can't just leave her. I have to put her up at a stable, or maybe a farm nearby. Let her rest. It's been a hard night."

"I believe you. In your condition, you should have sent someone else."

"I am the someone else, sir. Spanish flu down at the Colfax selection."

"Colfax. Don't know the name. Flu, eh?"

"Yes, sir." Colin felt disoriented again as the auto jiggled roughly along the track.

They pulled into the driveway of a pleasant bungalow. It reminded Colin of the sprawling, airy homes of the pearl dealers in Broome. The businessman beeped his horn.

Colin slid out and thanked the fellow. He stepped under a portico and knocked. The driver loomed behind him.

Dr. Newsome appeared in the doorway, towering above Colin. For some reason, he'd expected the doctor to be short and paunchy. The man before him looked like a heavyweight bare-knuckle boxer. He had to be at least three inches taller than Papa and thirty pounds heavier; not an ounce of it flab.

"Dr. Newsome? Uh, Colin Sloan. We need you. I mean, uh, a family south of here, the Colfaxes. They're—"

"Mmm. Colfax didn't happen to send something on his account, did he? I told him clearly last time I was down, 'I'm not coming again until you pay something on account.'"

"He said he'd pay you something when you arrived."

"Not good enough."

Colin licked his lips. They were feeling very dry and chapped. "Here. I've six pounds. My sister and the Colfaxes' four-year-old are the only two people that aren't sick. They need you now, sir. My sister is only thirteen. She can't handle it herself." He dug into his pocket, handing the wad of money over to the doctor.

The doctor counted the money. "We'll pay yours first and put any extra on the Colfax account. John, please take this young man over to the hospital. Go with him, lad."

"No, sir, you don't understand. I have to go with you. My sister's alone there, and Uncle Edgar died. You'll need help burying him."

The doctor nodded to the businessman. He stepped forward and seized Colin by the arm. "Come with me, lad. The doctor's orders. You've done your part."

"But, my sister—"

"There's help on the way to her. Now, come with me."

Colin had just ridden all night. He was more than ready to sleep. But the mare. . . . "Sir?" His joints ached; he coughed again. "Is there a farmer or a stable for my horse—"

"We'll see to your horse, lad." The brusque driver loaded Colin into the passenger seat, making his head throb. Moments later they passed Max's Lady. She lay in the rain, motionless, where she had fallen. It was all a blur in Colin's mind, and he could not say another word. The next coughing brought blood from his nose.

They pulled up to a low-slung, white clapboard building. A burly woman in a white dress and a brisk young man emerged. The nurse yanked the door of the car open, and the two marched Colin inside. They stripped off his wet clothes, ignoring his protests. He could vaguely hear them speak of influenza; they must be talking about the Colfaxes. Then they lay him in a clean white bed with cool sheets. A genuine bed. He'd not slept in a real bed for months. What was he protesting? He curled up on his side, and between bouts of coughing, he slept like a baby.

CHAPTER TWENTY THREE

THE CALL OF HOME

Sloan settled into his easy chair and kicked off his shoes. *Ah, home.* Whatever the pressures of his trade, at home he could relax. He unfolded the paper and shook it open. Across from him in her rocking chair, Sam picked up her tatting. *Sam.* She wore her rich copper-brown hair bobbed in the latest style. She still carried herself straight and proud on a willowy frame, no more than five pounds heavier than she had been twenty years ago when he met her. A few tiny laugh lines only made her eyes more interesting; her only detectable sign of aging. If Cole Sloan had been told twenty years ago he'd be a one-woman man for eighteen years, he would have laughed out loud. But here he was with that one woman. *Samantha.*

Sam couldn't know he was thinking about her. Yet she glanced at him self-consciously. "So, what's new tonight?"

He scanned the front page. "The Great White Train traveling exhibition. They plan to tour New South Wales for a year, displaying Australian-made goods."

"That will help your business, too."

"Too right. Also, lots of election speculation."

"Bruce will have his way."

"That's what they're saying, but it's taking them half the paper to say it." He spotted an article below the fold. "There's a minor outbreak of influenza down around the

Murrumbidgee, probably a result of unsanitary conditions caused by those severe floods. A couple of deaths."

"It sounds foolish, but I'm glad Colin and Hannah are still on the west side and nowhere near trouble like that."

"We don't know where they are, Sam. They could be right in the middle of it."

She slipped momentarily into her familiar, warm Irish accent. "Sure'n a fine ray of sunshine ye are, Cole Sloan."

He laughed.

Mary Aileen came strolling into the room. She looked more preoccupied than usual. Sam watched her settle onto the loveseat as Smoke left her lap to watch some birds outside the window. Mary Aileen picked up the book she'd been reading all spring and leafed idly through it.

"What's on your mind?" Sam asked quietly.

Mary Aileen looked up sheepishly. "I think perhaps Smoke is in a family way. Her behavior has changed somewhat lately. I read in a book on cat husbandry about such symptoms."

"Kittens! If any of them are tortoise-shells, they'll find a home easily enough, I'm sure. What delightful news." Sam studied her daughter knowingly. "Is there something else?"

"Edan. He was cross with me tonight."

Sloan snorted. "Nothing unusual. He crabs at everybody."

"It's different."

"How?"

Mary Aileen shrugged. "I can't explain. It's—it's just different somehow. I think something's very wrong."

Sam looked at her husband. Cold fear distorted his face. She knew he was thinking of all his children. Colin's flight could be called an aberration, a case of simply not getting along. Then Hannah. Now the water around his youngest was starting to ripple.

Sloan took a deep breath. "Wrong in what way?"

"I don't know. He doesn't talk about things. All he does is get angry. I'm so tired of him getting cross with me all the time."

Cole waited for Sam. She said nothing. Sam had some level of expertise in these areas. Usually she spoke to Edan if there were problems. *Well, the father is the head of the house. Maybe I should—* He nodded. "I'll speak with him." *About what?* Edan didn't usually talk to his papa about anything. He stayed to himself. Cole could respect that in a son. How could he pry into the shell of a boy who had deliberately and consciously closed himself in? For that matter, should he?

Cole's eyes stayed on his paper, but his mind did not. *What could it be with Edan?* Mary Aileen was always so quick to defend her brothers and sister, whatever the charges. Now she herself was being accusatory; it must be serious.

In the past, Mary Aileen had praised virtues she saw in Colin in the same way she supported Hannah and Edan. *She should take up writing advertising promotions. She always sees the good points in everyone and everything.* And then there was this Romales fellow—making almost identical claims about Colin that Mary Aileen made. *Maybe Romales should be the one to talk to Edan!* The Spanish Texan would have the lad eating out of his hand. Hadn't he practically led Sloan down the primrose path?

Or did he? What if Romales was right when he said simply that Sloan ought listen to Colin? Really listen. No preaching, no contradicting, no arguing. *Hah! Wait until Romales has kids of his own and discovers the value of preaching a godly life.*

The thought struck him so forcibly he lay his paper in his lap without thinking. Had he glibly believed he played father to all four of his children magnificently? The family founder—aloof, and yet present for them—counselor and king. It was the way his own father, Conal, had served the post. For the first time Cole gave the fruit of Conal's fatherhood more than a passing thought. Of Conal Sloan's three sons, Aidan was a cowardly crook and Liam an alcoholic. Cole himself would have continued a conniving, disreputable lout, unworthy of the slightest trust or honor, had he not encountered God—and Samantha Connolly.

Of his own four children, two were gone right now—having fled the nest before fully fledged. He was learning *ex post facto* that he may have greatly misjudged them both, in different ways; Colin too harshly and Hannah too leniently. Might he not be just as out of touch with the other two?

Edan! What can I say to him? What can I do? Lord, I try to be the father I perceive you want me to be. It's not working. Show me what I'm doing wrong. Help me.

He sat forward and pulled his shoes on. "Where's your brother now?"

"I don't know. He was in his room an hour ago."

Sam's glowing, understanding eyes watched him leave the parlor. Cole checked upstairs. Nowhere. Maybe the storage shed out back. He heard pounding as he approached. He shoved the shed door open with difficulty. It was sticking worse than ever. *I must remember to send a workman out to repair it.*

Edan was perched on a stool at the potting bench pounding nails into boards. He looked up at his father and returned to his work. Sloan stepped in close and leaned on the bench. It looked like the boy was mass-producing birdhouses. He had drilled tidy holes in a number of boards for the house fronts. Now he was nailing sideboards and floor boards together.

Sloan picked up one of the completed houses. "Well, I'll be. One side is hinged and pegged. For the cat to get in?"

"Papa! So you can open it and clean it every winter. Take out the old nests and brush out the bird lice."

"I see. How many of these are you making?"

"As many as I can."

The narrow shoulders shrugged; the child's head dipped. He seemed suddenly so small and fragile, so easily blown adrift by the winds of fate. Sloan felt desperately like hugging him, encasing him in strong arms and promising him safety.

"Why?"

He shrugged again. "Birds can use them. Especially the sparrows—lots of them around now. They aren't native, you know. People brought them in, like the rabbits, in 1863. Now sparrows are making pests of themselves, same as the rabbits. They take the houses of other birds. So I'm making houses just for them. Understand?"

"I see." *What now? Where do I take the conversation from here? Do I confront him with Mary Aileen's accusation?*

"Hold this, Papa," the lad said simply. He propped one piece upon another. Sloan held it and Edan nailed the two parts together. Silence fell between them, even with the noise of the hammering.

The boy spoke presently, "Are you and Mum going to the Melbourne Cup this year?"

"Plan to. Got reservations through the turf club."

Silence again. Then, "Do you suppose we could go camping? After the Cup, I mean."

"The usual place? I don't know. Hadn't thought about it. I suppose so. I'll discuss it with Mum. She's the one will have to do without a maid."

"I'll do the dishes!"

"That'll be the day!" With difficulty Cole stifled an impulse to take the hammer and do the work himself. He watched Edan, who suffered the clumsiness of a child with poor coordination and hands too small yet to get a good grasp on the tools. He frequently missed the nail heads, bending them over and carving hemispherical dents in his boards. But he succeeded, too. Slowly, but surely, he completed one in the time it would take Sloan to knock four together. He set each aside proudly, and began instantly to work on the next.

"Is this a school project?"

"No." *Bang. Bang. Bang. Bang.* Silence hung awkwardly between them again.

"The way you've been acting lately, I'm wondering if something is bothering you."

"No." The boy tipped his head ever so slightly in Cole's direction.

"Nothing worrying you or making you upset?"

"No."

"Angry at anything or anybody?"

"No!"

"Guess I must have been mistaken." Sloan watched Edan's face intently. No change of expression, no flicker of emotion suggested that Sloan's words had hit home. *Bang. Bang. Bang.*

What had Romales said? *Listen. So what do you do when the child won't speak?* Sloan would like to have scrubbed Romales' weird suggestions, had it not been for a strong, almost divine direction to heed the Texan's advice.

Cole popped open his pocket watch. "Bedtime in half an hour. Come in then."

Edan nodded.

Intensely frustrated, Sloan walked back into the house. He stood in the middle of the kitchen floor, letting his thoughts wander to days gone by. A new Coleman Cooker gleamed in the dim light. Nineteen years ago at Sugarlea, Sam, as cook and houseservant prepared his food on a primitive wood stove, turning out breads, soups and dinners every bit as good as those she served today. Progress. Today she didn't have to split wood and shovel ashes.

"Did you get past the wall?"

He wheeled in the direction of her voice. Sam leaned in the doorway, backlighted, her arms folded. *How long has she been standing there?* She launched herself erect and crossed the floor to his side.

"Aptly spoken." Sloan grimaced. "No."

"I can't crack it either. But I know something unusual is going on."

"What's this birdhouse business?"

"It began a week or two after we returned from camping last."

"He wants to go again."

"Then perhaps we ought to."

"He says he'll do your dishes for you."

"That will be the day."

"That's what I told him!" Sloan laughed suddenly. He gathered this one faithful woman into his arms and hugged her soundly, feeling her warm embrace in return. He kissed her long and happily. This was home.

Surely her tea had steeped sufficiently. Hannah poured a few drops into her cup. Dark enough. She filled the cup, slipped in a spoon of sugar and sat down on the shaky chair at the long table. She felt so very tired. She looked around the kitchen, and thought of what Colin would think. Would he be mad at her? She didn't care. She had brought all their food supplies—the sugar, the tea, potatoes and vegetables—into the kitchen to supplement the Colfax pantry. Actually, it was more than a supplement. The Colfax larder was bare.

Last year Bushell's Tea distributed half a pound of their blend to every home in Sydney as an advertising gesture. They should have sent the tea out to the rest of New South Wales, where it was so sorely needed.

Dr. Newsome's awesome bulk suddenly filled the doorway.

Hannah hopped to her feet. "What can I get you, sir? Tea's steeped."

He waved a ham-sized hand at her. "You sit down, young lady."

She dropped again into her chair.

He wandered casually to the stove, poured himself a cup of tea and sat down near her. He still seemed tall. "Now you listen to me, young lady. Attend to every word I say."

She nodded, fear-struck at his admonition.

"You are not exactly a dynamo of energy. You are a mere girl. I do say you've done splendidly with the tasks left to you so suddenly, but you can't save the whole world. You are going to be sorely tempted to wear yourself out taking care of everyone. But, you must not yield to that temptation, or you'll become ill also."

She didn't understand a bit of this. She nodded anyway.

"When Sister Gertrude tells you to quit and go lie down, or eat something, you are to obey instantly. Is that clear?"

"Yes, sir."

"Good. Trudy is a fine nurse, wise to this kind of illness. And she's a lovely person. I think you'll enjoy her. You'll certainly learn a great deal; you're a bright lass."

"Thank you, sir. May I get you some soup, sir? Turnips and potatoes in mutton broth. It's better than it sounds."

"I'd like that. Thank you."

She bolted to her feet and lifted a serving bowl from the shelf because there were no soup bowls. As she ladled it she inhaled deeply. It smelled quite good, considering she had sufficient onions for it but no garlic.

"You'll have some, too, won't you, Hannah?"

She grinned. "Yes, sir." She ladled her soup into a small saucepan and joined him at the table. She closed her eyes to ask a very hasty blessing, lest he see her and make comment. She sipped the hot broth. Not bad at all. Not Mum's by any means, but not bad. "Colin's eating well, isn't he? I mean—good food?"

"Nourishing, yes. This is quite good, Hannah."

"Thank you, sir. I didn't know what to prepare. Soup seemed best for everyone. Will the sister want some?"

"After she's prepared the body, I'm sure she will. It will be good to have that taken care of. I want you to keep Ruth here in the kitchen when we carry it outside."

Hannah nodded.

Colin. She pictured him suffering as these poor souls did—the racking cough, the chest pain and nausea, the fever and weakness. Poor Mrs. Colfax could not even sit up.

Hannah was getting weary of being here with these dismal strangers. She felt uncomfortable in this cramped, cluttered house with its filth. She didn't like to be around the morose Mr. Colfax, his listless wife, the terrible stench from the dead body in the side room. She wanted to be with Colin. He needed her. She needed him. Why had he left without her? The question was silly as she thought about it.

The soup was losing its savor. She stared at the saucepan, trying to keep her burning eyes from shedding tears.

"Hannah, come here." Dr. Newsome crooked a finger.

She stood to her feet and crossed to his side. "Yes, sir?"

"You have been concerned since I've been here about what I want and what everyone else wants. You've even inquired about your brother. Now I want to know what Hannah Sloan wants."

She shrugged and studied the dirt floor. "I've all I need, sir."

"That's not what I asked. Needs and wants usually differ."

The tears welled up and over. She was behaving most foolishly!

Dr. Newsome's huge, long arms reached out. He drew her into his lap and held her closely, just the way Papa did. "I know one thing you want, possibly two. You want your brother to recover, and you want to be with him."

She bobbed her head and sniffled. She burrowed her head deep into this comforting man's shoulder.

His strong voice, sometimes frightening, settled to a gentle whisper. "Colin is receiving excellent care; you could do nothing for him were you there, and I desperately need you here. The Colfaxes need you. One nurse here is just not enough. I knew that before I left town, but I couldn't afford to bring Hester or Jane, particularly since I'll likely never see a farthing in payment from this family. These Soldier Settler selections never succeed. I'll take you back with me if you wish, but I'm hoping you'll stay."

"I understand. I'll not let you and the sister down." A sudden thought struck her. "Perhaps before you leave, sir, you'll help us drive a mob out to pasture? I doubt the sister and I can do it alone."

"Certainly. What else does Hannah want?"

Thoughts and memories flooded her already confused brain. She snuffled and a sob slipped out. "She wants to go home."

CHAPTER TWENTY-FOUR

FIRES OF HOPE

Three different kinds of perky little honeyeaters flitted in the wattle bush by the veranda rail. Busily they sought out the morsels honeyeaters eat. It couldn't be honey; the wattle had done blooming for the year. Mary Aileen could identify the many varieties of honeyeaters. Colin could not. He would not be bothered with such things. He sat in his canvas chair on the airy veranda now and with nothing else to do, watched the birds' busy activity.

He had heard many horror stories of war hospitals and wretched infirmaries in the hearts of teeming cities. There was legitimate reason to fear and despise hospitals. But this little place was not bad at all. A kindly woman from across the street came to prepare the noon and evening meals—good old-fashioned home cooking like Mum's. The building itself, of vertical clapboard painted white inside and out, sprawled unassumingly across its acreage. It contained two four-bed wards, quarters for the three resident sisters, and several examination rooms.

Colin had one of the wards all to himself. The other ward housed the hospital's only other patient, a ringer named Steve Haynes from north of Goolgowi. A horse had fallen on the poor chap. Colin thought he would wander over and talk to the tough, sandy-haired fellow. He had already enjoyed yarning with the man a few times.

But moving about required energy, and Colin had precious little of that right now. Perhaps he'd just sit awhile and enjoy the late spring warmth.

"Anyone been by for me?" If Mohammed will not go to the mountain, the mountain will come to Mohammed. Steve Haynes stood in the doorway, leaning on his walking stick.

"G'day, mate. No. Expecting visitors?"

"Ride home." Steve settled his square-built frame into a canvas chair and propped his stick against the wall. "I'm discharged. Now if the boss cocky will just come for me, I can quit this place."

"Passing up a lot of good food."

"And a lot of meddling sisters getting professionally personal. I realize it's their job, but I detest being in the hospital. It's belittling."

"Never thought of it quite that way. When will you be back in the saddle? Any predictions?"

"Soon's I can get my leg to fly up over the cantle. There's lot's of work I can do 'til then—driving trucks, building fence, chores."

"Always one more bit of work waiting to be done."

"Too right! Hah!" He pointed out toward the street. A small pick-up truck came rattling to a stop in front of the main entrance. "There's my ride."

Colin lurched to his feet. "Hope our paths cross again. I don't doubt we both have a few stories we didn't get around to telling."

Steve Haynes laughed heartily and initiated a warm, firm handshake. He had to be ten years older than Colin; and yet they were equals in life and experience. Colin relished this moment. He enjoyed being accepted as a man by a man. Diz was that way, too.

With a smile and a wave Steve lumbered out on crutches to his companions and the outside world. He waved again from the open truck window as they left.

Colin sat down again, feeling somewhat lonely and isolated, the only patient in the facility.

After a few moments he stood and shuffled inside. The short trip from the veranda to his own ward left him exhausted. How long would it take to get over the weakness? The cough persisted too, as Sister Hester predicted it would. Bronchitis and other complications often hang on for months, she'd told him.

Sister Hester. She was quite a woman. Built like a water tank, she had the vocabulary of a shorefront rouseabout. She could lift Colin easily; she could even lift the ringer Haynes. She could probably lift a horse without any trouble at all.

Max's Lady! What had happened to her? Was she dead or alive? Colin had asked, but no one seemed to know. They claimed that a man named John would know, but Colin was stuck here in this hospital. There was no way to find John, whoever he was.

He dozed for a while and awoke more restless than usual. The clock at the end of the ward showed eleven o'clock. An hour 'til lunch. He shuffled back out to the veranda. A noisy miner and a pair of blue wrens had replaced the honeyeaters. Complaining fiercely, the noisy miner fled as an auto pulled up out front. Dr. Newsome had arrived on his rounds. *Good! Surely he's brought news of Hannah.* Poor girl, pressed into slave labor all alone in that dreary household. She was much too young for such awesome responsibility, no matter how Dr. Newsome praised her work.

He could hear the doctor's foghorn voice, and twisted around to see if he was coming onto the veranda. Instead, a blur of blue came bursting through the doorway, latching on to him in a sudden embrace. "Oh, Colin!" Hannah wailed, "it was so terrible!"

Eventually, after some urging, she loosened her grip enough to look at her brother. Her nose was peeling, a sure sign her new hat had been no help at all. Her frock looked tight and drawn; Colin realized with a mild shock how quickly she was growing.

"Colin, you look terrible. You're pale and thin. I'm so sorry." The words tumbled out.

"Why are you apologizing? It's not your fault. I got the illness from Uncle Edgar, I suppose."

"I'm not apologizing," she replied testily. "I'm trying to tell you I feel sorry it happened."

"Oh. How is it down there?"

"If Gerald survives the next three or four days, he'll likely make it, but they're not sure. They can't bring him in because they're afraid he wouldn't be able to handle the rough track. The rest are recovering, except Mr. Colfax has a collapsed lung. That's what Sister Jane said. She went down to serve the latest round of duty. Ruth never did get sick, and Sister Trudy muses constantly about why one person gets it and not another. The sheep aren't doing very well, not enough forage; and—" she went on and on, discussing everything from leaks in the worn canvas roofs to the total absence of rabbits.

Colin listened vaguely to her words, but was more engrossed with the speaker. When she first joined him out on the trail, one might have thought Hannah to be impetuous, foolish, quite possibly mad. Now an observer would likely say she was quick to act, self-assured, and quite possibly lacking in deference for one so young. But she was no longer the child who had jumped off the westbound train. Colin tried to decide which Hannah he preferred, the child or the woman. He almost preferred the former. Almost.

She stopped for a breath of air.

"I gave all my money to Dr. Newsome, Hannah. Do you have any left?"

"No. And I gave all our food to the Colfaxes. I didn't bring any up with me," she announced matter-of-factly.

"Are you going back down?"

She shook her head. "Mrs. Colfax wanted me too, but Sister Jane said it was not necessary. They don't really need me anymore. So I brought your swag and my traveling bag with me."

"What about their truck?"

"Dr. Newsome and Sister Jane put some petrol in it and drove it down to them. I told him about the hole in the tank."

Colin nodded, thinking. "I've got a job for you, Hannah. Maybe you can join me for lunch, and then look around town to see if you can find out if the mare's still alive."

Her face fell. "Not Max's Lady, too!"

"The last I saw her she was lying in the road. She looked dead to me, but I was in no condition to be a judge of anything. I just hope the townspeople haven't kept the bad news from me because of my illness. Maybe they really don't know anything."

"I'll find out." There was that simple, gentle, self-assured determination again. The little girl was gone.

————

Hundreds of nearly identical boxed-top automobiles lined the parking field, all sporting their shiny spares at the back. Milling throngs dressed in the season's finest jammed into the stands. They pressed near the outside fence of the racecourse, as the most-favored paraded about the infield.

Of all the events in Australia in any season of the year, this was the place to see and be seen, to strut and admire (or envy), to show off the latest acquisition, be it a bride or a new serge suit. The Melbourne Cup.

Sloan stood apart in the corner of the owners' box and scanned the surging crowd. How many thousands were here because it was the best place to be seen socially, and not for love of the sport itself? As a Christian, Sloan felt constrained to regard all people equally, without respect to station. But he found it difficult to stomach the social climbers, those who did things strictly for the sake of appearance. The Melbourne Cup was certainly a place for that. It was literally jammed with strutters and preeners who had not the least interest in these magnificent horses, the best of the breed, or racing for that matter.

Sam sat relaxing gracefully. Pointing to events on the daily form, she was obviously explaining something to the lady next to her. The other woman nodded. Sloan smiled. Sam was here today for all the right reasons. She loved horses. How many sleepless nights had she spent over the years, helping Sloan tend a sick horse or awaiting the arrival of a foal? She handled horses well, and they responded in kind. The Irish touch with horses was no myth.

Sloan walked past and tapped her knee. "I'm taking a turn through the barns."

"You'll miss the third race."

"Probably." He smiled and she smiled. She knew that the race was the least of it all. He jogged down the steps and out behind the stands, fighting the milling crowd.

Things were less hectic back in the barns, despite the activity of horses being prepared for their moment in the sun. Sloan loved the milieu.

"Cole Sloan! Why, it *is* you!"

Sloan turned. Unabashedly hefty, Mrs. Horvath draped herself in a black silk dinner frock, the extremely narrow skirt requiring that she walk with painfully shortened steps. Her hat, a silver lame cloche, pressed over her head like a giant bell, and she wore a sheer, misty gray shawl over her shoulders.

She came bustling over to him, her feet churning beneath her. "I've wanted for the longest time to chat with you, Cole. Why have you no entry in the Cup this year?"

He took her black-gloved hand in his and kissed the kidskin. "Because, milady, I'm no fool. I've nothing this year close to matching Windbag."

"Windbag! Much overrated! Splendid day, isn't it?"

"Perfect. Should set a record here, or close to it." He disliked small talk, and happened to know Mrs. Horvath never engaged in it for long. On what track was she, really?

She dropped her voice to a hoarse idle, "We heard the sad news that your lovely son decided to go off. Most premature. Delightful lad, but a mind of his own. So like today's youth!" She sighed heavily, as if to let off steam. "Just look at the young women mincing about in next to nothing, their hems practically to the knee! They dare think they can fling the advice of their elders right out the window."

"True, true."

She moved in closer and murmured privately, "And there's a pernicious rumor that your twelve-year-old daughter ran off as well. Surely not true!"

Sloan shook his head gravely and quelled the anger inside. He even smiled. "Pernicious is hardly the word for it. Amazing, sometimes, what rumor mills churn out, isn't it? Tell me, just out of curiosity: where does this rumor claim she went?"

"Why, to Victoria. The shearing sheds north of Bendigo."

He chuckled. "Most rumors have at least a shadow of fact behind them, but that one must have been purely fabricated."

"I'm certainly relieved, of course, that it's groundless, but I must admit I gave it a bit of credence. You see, the granddaughter of one of the ladies in our lawn bowling group attends All Saints Girls' Academy—same school in Sydney your daughter attends. When your child abruptly ceased attending classes, the rumors began to spread."

"Of course."

"And then Mabel—she's another of our lawn bowlers—was visiting her sister in Kangaroo Flat and happened upon an article in the local paper about a fight in an inn in Eaglehawk; a beaut of a blue with the whole pub turned upside down. Two in the hospital, Mabel says, and seventeen fined. And all because of a small, dark-haired girl working on the boards. Well, one rather puts two and two together. And your daughter, known for her quick mind and, well, her prankish ways—"

"No one stopping to think that she's a city girl through and through, as no doubt your friend's granddaughter is, I would assume. Wouldn't know which end of the sheep to apply the shears to, even if she were strong enough."

"Oh, my, yes," she huffed. "Just isn't done, you know, a girl in a shearing shed."

"And with good reason." Sloan nodded sagely. "Certainly not a girl's place. I agree with you heartily on that, but I'm afraid I differ with you on the preferred length of women's dresses. I quite like the new lengths. Not immodest, and certainly more attractive. Aesthetically speaking, of course, Mrs. Horvath."

"I respect your views, Mr. Sloan. Remember, though, that your lovely wife, so tall and slender, is simply made for the new styles. She is one of the few I know who can wear them with dignity. Now Mabel, for example—" On she went, off the subject of Hannah altogether.

Sloan led her along for another five minutes, then mentioned a horse he had entered in the fifth, and needed to check on. He bade her good day, excused himself, and hurried off.

He ducked away from the barns as soon as he left her sight; it was easy to disappear in the crowd. He jogged lightly to the private lounge where the owners and racecourse officials congregated. He pushed inside and threaded between idling, drinking horsemen to the corner table and an easy chair.

He flopped down heavily and snatched up the phone on the table beside it. "Good afternoon, operator. Can you connect me through to the Victorian Police, please? Eaglehawk. If not there, Bendigo. Certainly I'll wait." He slouched back into the chair, the receiver pressed to his ear, as the operator attempted to work her modern magic. The fires of hope raged unquenched in his tortured breast.

CHAPTER TWENTY-FIVE

THE WAY HOME

Everything was gone crook. Hannah stood on the bottom paddock rail, her arms draped over the toprail. The smooth wood pressed warm against her skin. Here in the back paddock of the town's only stable stood Max's Lady, switching her tail. Alive after all, she acted sluggish, lackadaisical. Her ordeal had snuffed her spark.

Colin smiled broadly, but she couldn't tell whether it was her presence or the mare's that generated his happiness right now. His neatly laundered clothes hung slack on him. His face looked thin. Gaunt. The illness had exacted a terrible toll. Hannah shuddered.

Finances. For the first time in her life, Hannah had debts. Dr. Newsome advanced her the price of a room when she returned from the Colfax station. She must repay him, although he hinted broadly that it would not be necessary. To Hannah it was necessary.

"Colin? You still owe money on your hospital bill, right?"

"A little beyond the six pounds I already paid, yair. Part of hospital care is covered by subscription, paid by the locals here. But since we aren't locals, we aren't covered by it."

"I don't like being in debt, Colin."

"Me either." He rubbed the mare's nose.

Mr. Joyce, the hostler, stepped up smiling. He smiled often, but it never seemed quite genuine. His gloomy undercurrent further irritated Hannah. "Where you youngsters going next? More rabbiting?"

Colin shrugged. "We're headed east. See what turns up; rabbiting, perhaps. Yes."

"You'd better take it very easy with the horse. No double dink, no long hauls. She's not up to measure yet." There was that creepy smile again. "I'll go write your bill for her stabling." He walked off toward his small quarters.

Hannah's heart sank still further into the doldrums. Another bill to add to the others, and no receipts.

A large White truck pulled up by the barn just then, and two men climbed down to talk to the hostler as he came from his house. He nodded vigorously and pointed to the side paddock. The men started to walk in that direction.

One of them caught a glimpse of Colin and stopped suddenly. "Sloan!" he called. He turned and walked toward the two as briskly as his limp would allow.

A handsome grin split Colin's countenance. "Steve Haynes! G'day, mate! Meet my sister, Hannah. This is the cobber whose horse fell on him. Spent time in the hospital with me." He shook hands warmly with the stocky young man.

"Pleased to meet you, sir." Hannah was suddenly shy, and didn't know whether to curtsy or shake hands. She did neither, and simply smiled. The ringer smiled back, and Hannah decided the smile was a sufficient greeting.

"Delighted, mum. Heard all manner of good report about you from your brother here." He looked past Colin at the mare. "So this is the beast that made a running jump into a moving truck. Crikey, I'd like to've seen that! She's a meaty horse to be so nimble."

"Nimble." Colin snorted. "I'm afraid she's up to mud at the moment. Still stiff from what I put her through coming into this fair town."

"Eh, I can sure vouch for that! Same problem myself. Not so nimble as I was."

Hannah crowed, "Oh, she's a lovely animal when she's up to grade, and much happier than you see her now."

"She'll be back, I'm sure." Steve scratched Max's Lady behind the ears. The horse leaned into his hand, her eyes half closed. "Bonzer horse."

"What brings you to town?" Colin asked.

"They had to put my horse down—broke a leg when it fell with me. We thought to see what Joyce has here, looking around to buy. This lady doesn't happen to be for sale, I suppose."

"She might be."

Hannah gaped at Colin. He couldn't really be saying that!

He dug into his wallet. "Here's the original bill of sale on her. Purchased in Broome at a reduced price. She wasn't half a hatrack, but she fattened quickly on the track. She's sound and dependable, holds weight well, good disposition, no vices. Tends to barn-sour a little. Good feet; run her barefoot or shod, no problems. Understand, I'll want the saddle to go with her. No use toting that about without a horse under it."

"Here you go." Mr. Joyce appeared from nowhere, handed Colin a bill and hurried off to his side paddock to sell horses.

Colin led the mare out. Hannah stared at him, speechless. He couldn't sell a good friend like this. Her misery was deepening by degrees. He seemed to be serious. The men talked about horses in general, about the Melbourne Cup, the season at the Sydney racecourse and Colin's experience in the barns there. Then they returned to talk of the mare. Steve began a systematic inspection of her, starting at her head, picking up each foot, running his hands down each leg.

Colin jabbed Hannah. "How much did you lug Dr. Newsome's ear for?"

"He gave me three quid. I have some left. But I owe him, Colin."

"Three quid." Colin was oblivious to her protests. He studied the bill in his hand. Hannah knew he was totaling their debts and weighing the options. He nodded to himself. It was all over now. He would sell the mare.

Hannah sighed and wandered off by herself. She liked the big old mare. They'd been through so much together.

Steve left Colin momentarily to talk to his companion.

Hannah felt near tears. She approached Colin again and leaned against the paddock fence next to him. "I don't want you to sell Max's Lady."

"I don't want to either, Hannah, but we need a way home. Besides, you said yourself it's hard to get a ride when she's along. We'll do fine without her, and it's the only way to pay our debts. Steve's a good hand with horses, and he likes her."

"He killed the last one he got upon."

"And I nearly killed her."

It was over so quickly. Steve and his companion loaded the mare into their truck and remarked at how readily she hopped in. Colin settled his bill with Mr. Joyce on the spot. The man was not smiling now, unable to hide his genuine disgust at the turn of events. Colin's sale of Max's Lady terminated any further negotiations for his own horses.

With the remainder of the sale, Colin was able to pay back Dr. Newsome, who only protested mildly. They also cleared the hospital debt, and had enough left to purchase cheap canned goods for their trek—vegetables, fruit, and corned beef. One more night in a city inn and they would be off again.

Hannah packed her traveling bag in the dim light of a bare electric bulb. She grew up with the convenience of electricity in Sydney, and she had it here in town. It was only one of many things she missed while at the Colfaxes'. That and interior plumbing. And dependable water without sand in it. She shouldered her bag, closed the door of her inn room, and took her key down to the desk. They were leaving Griffith at last, and with it the hard memories of illness and separation.

And Max's Lady. Everything they cared for was being stripped away from them. Colin had less money now than when Hannah first joined him east of Kalgoorlie.

They started out southeast of town and ambled slowly along the track—Colin could muster nothing faster than a casual stroll—and watched for a ride east.

"Thought maybe you'd be wearing your fancy trousers out here on the track," Colin said, managing a slight smile.

"I was going to, but I was embarrassed to be seen in them in town. Maybe farther out I'll change."

Colin was huffing and puffing already. "We'll rest here."

"We've come less than a mile! We'll never get anywhere at this rate."

"There're trees here, Hannah. And shade. Can't count on that farther down the track." He flopped beneath a thorn tree.

With a sigh, Hannah found her own shady spot. She dug her Bible out of her bag, dropping it open to Haggai again. She began to read.

Colin was dozing off. She watched him a moment as he fought sleep and lost. He looked unnaturally pale. Somehow, subtly, in the last fortnight their roles had changed. When they'd arrived at the Colfax place, Colin was determined to take Hannah home. Now Hannah was determined to get Colin home. He didn't seem to realize how drastically ill he had been, or how weak he still was. He seemed to be scrambling for enough money to make a jingle in his pocket when they arrived at Papa's. But he'd lost all his eagerness, his spontaneity, in the process, and Hannah missed that. He had changed, and she hated the change.

She returned her concentration to Haggai.

"Colin! This is it! I see it now."

"What?" He blinked and squirmed toward a sitting position.

"It's Haggai. Listen to this: 'Ye have sown much, and bring in little; ye eat, but ye have not enough; ye drink, but ye are not filled with drink; ye clothe yourselves, but there is none warm; and he that earneth wages earneth wages to put it into a bag with holes.' "

Colin smirked. "That's us alright. Holes in our pockets."

"Sister John at the school teaches that Scripture says two things: what it literally says, and the larger, sometimes hidden meaning. It's the church's responsibility to interpret the larger meaning. Now here in Haggai, God is talking about how the Jews should be building His house, but the larger meaning—"

"You aren't the church, Hannah. How can you think you're capable of interpreting the Scriptures?"

"Mrs. Slotemaker says I'm the church. All believers together are the church; that's what the church is," she stated matter-of-factly, and went on, "The larger meaning is, that unless you do what God wants, He doesn't bless anything you're doing. We haven't been doing what God wants, so He's not blessing what we do. See? It's all right here."

"What does He want us to be doing, Miss Preacher?"

"I know what He wants *you* to be doing. He wants you to forget this nonsense that He doesn't even exist, ask Him to forgive your sins, and become a Christian. And until you do that part right, we're not going to get anywhere."

"Really?"

She folded her hands on the Bible on her lap. "Yes, Colin, really. We've been making all manner of mistakes. It's time we started learning from them."

"Yair. I've heard that before somewhere—" He stopped suddenly and stared blankly, trying to recall.

"Colin?"

"Sake Tamemoto. He said it's wise to learn from your mistakes, but better yet to learn without making them. We dragged his body up the beach so it wouldn't wash away."

Her heart lurched as she read the pain in his face. She'd never realized until this moment that her gentle, innocent brother had faced death before—not just Uncle Edgar in the Colfax side room, but violent death in faraway places. "You could have died then, too," she whispered. "And you could have died of the influenza. What if, the next time—I mean—. You could die without ever having made peace with God."

"Hannah, it's not that easy. You're just a very young girl and you don't question things. You're too accepting. I simply can't be sure He even exists."

"Rubbish! James Otis knows Him. Mum and Papa know Him and pray for us. Mr. and Mrs. Slotemaker are Christians. And so am I. You could be if you wanted to. You're just making excuses, and I can't imagine why you're working so hard to avoid Him."

He studied her a few moments and lunged suddenly to his feet. "We have to get going."

She took her time tucking her Bible away. She could catch up to the slowpoke anytime she wished. She glanced behind them at the sound of an approaching vehicle. "Colin! Here comes an auto. Perhaps it's a ride, do you think?" She hopped to her feet.

An awesomely large touring car came rumbling up from the direction of town. It chugged to a halt and trembled as the motor idled. The portly business man at the wheel called, "Get in."

Colin stuffed his swag and Hannah's traveling bag in the trunk. "Hannah, this is the gentleman who gave me a lift to the hospital when the mare collapsed."

Hannah scrambled up into the seat. "Colin has spoken most highly of you, sir. I'm pleased to meet you."

"And I'm pleased to meet you, young lady."

Colin crawled in beside Hannah. They jerked into motion, and were on their way. Hannah had to admit to herself that it was a lot easier getting a ride without the horse.

Beyond the trees the driver left the track, swinging around in a wide circle across the flats. Another hundred yards, and he regained the track, heading toward town.

"Where are we going?" Hannah demanded.

"I'm obeying instructions to return you to Griffith," the man replied simply.

Hannah looked at Colin, searching for an answer in his perplexed face. She was certain they had paid all their bills. They had left nothing behind. Who would instruct this gentleman to bring two innocent travelers back to town? Sure enough, they rumbled down the main street of Griffith, the very street they'd left little more than an hour ago.

Hannah commented on the number of horses and cars parked at the School of Arts. She liked the humble little building. It was nothing more than a single library room with an adjoining meeting hall, but it offered some good books, and a comprehensive atlas. Hannah loved to peruse elaborate maps of exotic places. Their driver parked at its front door.

He hopped out and motioned for the two to follow him.

Hannah was afraid not to. Colin directed questions to the man's back, and tried a feeble protest to no avail. The man ushered them brusquely into the hall.

At least forty townspeople were gathered. They all turned in the direction of Colin and Hannah as they entered the room. "They're here," someone announced abruptly. Hannah felt an intense desire to hide somewhere. Of the whole crowd she recognized only Dr. Newsome and the sisters from the hospital. There was one more familiar face—the new owner of the bay mare, Steve Haynes—standing meekly on the fringe of the crowd. Hannah pressed close to Colin. For some reason she was more frightened than she'd ever been on this whole long, grueling adventure.

They stopped at the very front of the hall, the people crowded behind them. The portly businessman put on a top hat, adjusted it, and stepped up to a red gum lectern. He unrolled a sheet of foolscap and started to read.

"Whereas," he began, "this young man here present, Colin Sloan, a stranger to the town, desperately ill himself, risked life and limb to bring help to our stricken neighbors, sacrificing the health of his only horse in the process; and whereas this young lady, Hannah Sloan, at absolutely no recompense to herself, served tirelessly and ably in the Colfax home, risking her health to restore that of others; and whereas this town seeks wherever possible to reward those who provide the sort of fine example we would want all our own young people to emulate; I, John Stoecker, mayor of this town, hereby proclaim Mr. Colin Sloan and Miss Hannah Sloan honorary citizens of the town, with all the benefits which accrue thereby."

Amid general applause, Hannah felt herself blushing. What benefits accrued? It didn't matter. It was a lovely gesture.

"Colin and Hannah." The top-hatted mayor turned to them. "Both of you quite meticulously cleared your every debt, to the point of selling your horse to pay what was owed. Your sense of responsibility is both exemplary and gratifying. Would that certain adults were so responsible."

Colin mumbled something, a bit embarrassed at the display of honor.

Imperiously, the man raised an arm for quiet and attention. "Bring forth the horse, please."

With a boyish grin Steve Haynes led the bay mare, saddle and all, through a side door. Colin's swag and Hannah's bag hung from the pommel.

The mayor had begun the ceremony duly appearing as a town authority, now he dissolved into pure glee. He was enjoying the gesture immensely. "We took up a public donation to buy the animal back from Mr. Haynes. Citizenship in the town, of course, provides you with the same hospital and health benefits any other citizen enjoys. We're pleased to return to you the payment you made for medical care." The mayor pressed a wad of cash into Colin's hand.

Colin stammered something unintelligible. Hannah could not force herself to do anything but stand there flabbergasted. *What splendid people!*

"Perhaps you've something to say." The mayor gave Colin a nudge forward.

"Yes. I mean—we can't. This is all very generous of you. But we can't accept. We didn't earn it."

"You both most certainly earned it—more than you know. Of course you can accept it," the mayor insisted.

"But we, er—very well, thank you. Thank you very much."

"Hannah?" The mayor's eyes were on the young girl as well as everyone's in the room.

"But we didn't do it for the—the, uh, recognition. We did it because, uh, it ought be done. We don't deserve this." What had she said? She wasn't sure it was the right thing. Maybe they'd agree and retract the offer!

"Of course you didn't do it for the praise of men. That is precisely the sort of example we seek most to set before our youth. And that is why it pleases this town to be able to reward you."

"Uh-huh. . . . " Hannah felt the warmth rise in her face and ears. "Thank you all."

Despite the hostler's warnings about double dink, Colin and Hannah were set upon the horse and sent on their way, down the main aisle and out the front doors. The gathered townspeople cheered and clapped.

Hannah clung to her brother as the mare negotiated the wooden steps off the front porch. They continued down the main street. A few little knots of people clapped as they rode by. They felt like celebrities.

"Colin, I can't believe this."

"It's not what I would have expected in a thousand years."

They rode in silence to the edge of town and onward, out into the flats and rolling hills and woods and bright sun.

"Hannah?" Colin asked eventually. "What was going through your mind when they were—you know, honoring us?"

"I was stunned; of course, I hadn't expected any such thing. I guess the thing I thought about most with all those people staring at us, was how glad I was I hadn't put on those trousers yet!"

CHAPTER TWENTY-SIX

ON THE TRACK AGAIN

Mary Aileen sat on the front stoop and worked at her needlepoint, vaguely aware of the pattern. Her mind kept flying to other things.

There was Papa, pulling to the curb in front of the house. By the time he'd gathered his business papers and the daily newspaper from the front seat, Mary Aileen had stuffed her needlepoint away in its bag. She hastened down the steps to greet him.

"What's all the excitement?"

"You received a telegram an hour ago. We can't wait for you to open it."

"Why didn't Mum open it?" Papa jogged up the steps and held the door for Mary Aileen. It made her feel quite lady-like.

"She never opens things addressed to you."

"Is it about Colin and Hannah, you think?"

"We're hoping so."

Papa greeted Mum in the foyer with the usual kiss. He'd barely put his papers down before she stuffed the yellow envelope into his hand.

He strode to the kitchen window where there was more light, peeking into the pot on the stove on the way. "Beef stew. Smells wonderful!" He ripped the envelope off and studied the paper.

"Well?" Mum prompted him.

"However they came east, it apparently wasn't by train. They're on this side. This is from the constable in Eaglehawk. Colin and Hannah left town right after the blue Mrs. Horvath mentioned, and he has no idea where they went from there."

"That puts them near the Murray during that flu outbreak."

He reached out and gave her a squeeze. "You worry too much. But just to put your mind at ease, I also queried the health officials in both Victoria and New South Wales, asking for the vital statistics. No Sloans among the fatalities. They have estimates of the total number taken ill, but no names."

"To put *my* mind at ease, indeed! You galah!" Mum gave him a playful shove, laughing.

Papa was laughing, too. He nodded. "So they're on this side. I should not have glibly assumed they were still in Westralia, particularly when authorities there heard nothing of them. I'm in the process of sending letters to police magistrates 'round about, for possible word."

"What will you do when you locate them?"

"Thank God. Beyond that, I don't know."

Mary Aileen stood apart, watching. Moments ago Mum had been sober, even grim. Now she bubbled. Papa had gone to some lengths to find out about the death toll from the flu epidemic. They each in their own way conveyed their love for Colin and Hannah.

But isn't love supposed to cement a family together? she thought. *Why is ours torn asunder? Do I even know these two people? They're Mum and Papa, of course—but I hardly know them.* Confusion knotted her thoughts like the tiny twists in her needlepoint wool sometimes knotted.

Quietly, she went to the shed to fetch Edan for dinner.

———

Colin stretched out under a crooked little mallee tree because its lacy foliage cast the only feeble shade around. He ached, bone weary. He still coughed a lot. Would he never get over this?

Hannah lay curled up ten feet away. "Colin? Do you think you should be able to tell a Christian by looking at him?"

"What do you mean? They turn purple or something?"

"You know what I mean. The way they act."

"I don't know. I never thought about it."

"Those people in Griffith. Lots of them weren't Christians—I mean really genuine committed-to-Jesus-Christ Christians, at least not the way Mrs. Slotemaker defines the term. But they did that for us out of the goodness of their hearts."

"True."

"And then there's Mrs. Colfax. All I can remember about her is her face. All drawn and sour. She became absolutely livid when I told her I was leaving there and coming to Griffith to you."

"Livid. Isn't that a little strong?"

"No. She railed at me about my Christian duty. And then Sister Jane told me to leave, that the Colfaxes didn't really need me anymore. Mrs. Colfax claims to be a Christian, but she didn't act like one. She certainly never smiled or said anything positive."

"Mmm." Colin felt himself fading.

"So? Did I owe a Christian duty there? Did I shirk my duty as a Christian by leaving before I ought because Mrs. Colfax, who talks like a Christian but doesn't act like one, said so? Or was I right to leave on the personal advice of Sister Jane, who acts like a Christian, but doesn't profess to have any personal relationship to Jesus Christ? You see how confusing it can be? What were my responsibilities, really, Colin?"

Colin wasn't sure he'd got all that, but he certainly didn't want her to repeat it. In fact, he doubted she could.

A sudden thought popped into his head. "There's a shell sorter in Broome, an Aboriginal fellow. He sits in the middle of a huge pile of shells and sorts them by size; tossing the big ones in one bin, the little ones in another."

"And?"

"Well, he said that sorting the obvious ones—the real big ones and the real little ones—was no trouble. It was all the sizes in between that were hard to sort. You don't have an obvious question there, Hannah, you have one of the muddled ones in the middle, without a clear answer."

"What you're saying is, you don't know the answer."

"That, too."

She moved around, struggling for a comfortable position under the tree. "Colin? You know why God blessed us in Griffith?"

There were several ways he could answer, but none of the answers would be to her liking. Rather than argue he simply said, "Why?"

"Because I was talking to you about Jesus."

"Oh, really?"

"Yes. We were talking about what you had to do to become a Christian. I think what I should do is talk about Jesus more. When I didn't, our pockets had holes in them, when I did speak of Him, we were blessed. See what I mean?"

"So all you have to do is keep talking and we'll get rich?"

"That's blasphemous, Colin! You're deliberately twisting what I say. I don't mean I should do it to bribe God into blessing us. I mean I should do it because it's the right thing to do. I'm supposed to speak of Him. You know what I mean."

"I know what you mean, but that doesn't mean I believe you."

"Stubborn old drongo. You realize, don't you, that being honest and upright gets you rewards here on earth, but you need Jesus to get to heaven."

"Rewards?" He snorted. "If I wasn't so honest, I'd have sold a pearl in Broome for a fortune. I could have gone home in style." His words carried an overtone of arrogance, but his heart wondered if maybe—just maybe—she might be right.

"You didn't want to go home then. It just would've been more to trickle out of your pocket with the hole in it."

He heard pages whisper. She had that Bible out again. She had this burning desire to talk about Jesus. Did that mean she was going to read the Bible out loud from here to Sydney? He opened his mouth to ask her not to.

Too late. "Page ten-seventy-four, Ephesians three, verse four. 'But God, who is rich in mercy, for his great love wherewith he loved us,' Five. . . . "

Her voice droned on. It should be quite easy to block out, she read in such a monotone. Why did Colin keep listening? The words burned like fire in his thoughts.

" ' . . . toward us through Jesus Christ.' Eight. 'For by grace are ye saved through faith; and that not of yourselves; it is the gift of God.' Colin! That's one of the verses Mrs. Slotemaker showed me. She says it's the hardest thing in the world to accept a gift you don't think you've earned. But that's what salvation is. You don't deserve it, but God wants to give it to you anyway."

Mrs. Slotemaker. Colin was getting a bit bored with hearing about Mrs. Slotemaker. Hannah continued with her reading as Colin's sleepy mind skipped through other meadows. *It's the hardest thing in the world to accept a gift you don't think you've earned.* He thought back to the day he insisted Dizzy keep the dun horse Colin had paid for. Dizzy was sure he should pay something for it. Colin was equally sure it was a gift, mate to mate. Old Diz had as much trouble accepting a valued gift as Colin would, were the situation reversed.

And then the affair in Griffith. The first reaction both Colin and Hannah shared was, *We can't accept this; we don't deserve it.* Maybe this Mrs. Slotemaker had the right idea after all.

They hit the track again an hour later. It took all Colin's strength to fling his pack up over the saddle. "You should see what the Bible says about being weak all the time."

"All right, I will. I know you're teasing, but I will." From then on, Hannah had her Bible out every time they stopped, scanning its pages. To Colin's relief, she didn't always read it out loud.

Four days out from Griffith, they stopped at a little crossroads pub for a real meal and private rooms with real beds. Colin relished the temporary comfort.

He knew what the answer might be, but he asked anyway at the bar, "What are the rabbiting prospects out here?"

The barman shook his head negatively. "The two largest stations east of here hire their own rabbiters, then sub-let them out to others. Smaller farmers organized a drive a few weeks ago; killed nearly four hundred thousand. Still plenty of rabbits out there, but they wouldn't have set up the drive if they could afford an exterminator, aye?"

"How about ratting? We've done that too."

"Possibly in Bathhurst."

Bathhurst. Colin and Hannah would be as good as home by then. He'd be content with what jingled in his pocket now and just pray there'd be no more holes.

He paused halfway up the flight of stairs to his room. What was he just thinking? *Pray* there'd be no more holes? What was that book again? Haggai? He'd never really prayed before. Hannah was getting to him.

They were late getting started the next morning. No matter. They were making very slow progress this journey. The initial enthusiasm for travel seemed to be waning. Colin recalled their excitement when they went on the track with the shearers, and the trip north to reduce the

Slotemaker and Barnes rabbit populations. Now travel, once so invigorating, had become a burden.

They came to a curious Y in the road. The official track angled southeast, no doubt to serve some station on the way to the railway town of Young. But the locals obviously left the road at this point and proceeded directly east.

"Which way do we go, Colin?"

"It's not a difficult choice—every five miles we cut off the track is another two hours of travel saved, as slow as we're going."

"But we got directions at the pub."

"Right. They said to cross the first north-south railway spur line. It goes up to Forbes. We want to continue on to the second, in Young. It'll take us into Cowra and Bathhurst."

"Bathhurst. We've been there. That's practically home, by railway."

"Sorry to see the end come?"

"I guess not. Not anymore. Especially seeing you so weak yet. Besides, I've had enough adventuring." She paused. "And I'm still looking for passages about weakness for you in the Bible."

They struck out due east along the defined tire tracks and hoofmarks of the locals. Within half a mile they crossed a gibber plain, a flat paved as tight as asphalt with dark, even pebbles. The horse stumbled frequently. If they hit much of this stuff, Colin was going to have to give up some of his precious money and shoe her.

The wind, fitful before, picked up strength. It churned and swirled, sending willi-willis dancing across the flat land far ahead.

"Colin! Look behind us."

He turned to see a dark, churning, gray-brown wall that filled half the sky. He stared, his mouth agape. "It's coming this way, too. Or else it's growing."

"Fire? Smoke? We're safe out here on the gibbers, aren't we?"

"Just dust, I'd say. We'll know soon. It'll be on us shortly."

Max's Lady raised her head and began moving about uneasily, sidling, pushing into Colin as he led her along.

Hannah pushed in close against him, too. "Colin, I'm so frightened! It looks—" She shuddered. Static electricity made her bobbed hair float out from her head. With the whole gibber plain to walk in, she pressed so close against him he could feel her breathing. Frightened wasn't the word. She was terrified.

So was he.

The wind shifted, whistled, stilled, then came from new directions. The gray swirl closed around them, blotting out the blue sky, driving the sun into hiding, erasing every feature more than twenty feet away.

Colin stopped the nervous horse. "We're going to have to camp right here and wait it out. We can't see; we'll just travel in circles if we keep going." The thick, gritty dust exacerbated his cough. Soon he was hacking so hard that his eyes watered.

He unsaddled the horse and put her on the lead line. With no tree or stake to tie her to, he put a noose in the line and looped it over his arm. Hannah curled up with her bag, but between the darkness and wind she couldn't drag her Bible out.

Dirt scudded swiftly across the gibbers a foot or two off the ground. Dust made breathing so difficult that Hannah put her handkerchief over her nose and mouth. Soon, that didn't serve and her nose and eyes watered and ran as much as Colin's. They resorted to covering their faces with shirttails and skirt hem.

That evening, with a bit of a lull in the storm, Colin opened two cans from their meager stock. They ate cold beans and corned beef straight from the cans, mixed with dust and grit.

"It can't get much worse than this," Colin grumbled.

But he was wrong. Sometime during the night, while Colin slept, the noose around his arm slipped off and the mare wandered away.

CHAPTER TWENTY-SEVEN

BUSHED

If Colin's mouth got any drier, he was sure his tongue would choke him. Hannah was showing the effects of the dust and heat, too. He glanced at their shadow for the hundredth time, making certain they continued east.

Hannah stopped suddenly. "Give me your swag."

Colin let the pack slide off his shoulder into the thick dust. "What do you need?"

"Nothing." She sat down beside it. From her own traveling bag she pulled out a couple of items and her Bible, stuffing them into Colin's swag.

"Hannah, I'm sorry; I'm not sure I can carry all that."

"I'm sure you can't. You've been stumbling about like a blind man, resting every few minutes." She stood up and swung his swag across her own shoulder. "There's nothing left in my bag we can't do without. On we go."

"Now, wait a minute! I'm not letting my little sister carry my swag! How would that look?"

"To whom?" She started off across the hot, dry dirt.

Good point. They'd not seen a living soul in three days, two of those days spent huddled on the ground, hunched against the flying, stinging dust.

He stared a moment at her traveling bag, lying there open in the burning sand. He cupped his brow and gazed out across the invisible wasteland behind them. Somewhere out there lay his saddle too, abandoned yesterday. Would it also soon be buried by this raging dust?

The whipped sand, at the mercy of the wind, had settled into deep dunes and drifts across the flats. It was hard to tell how deep. It was harder to tell what the land had looked like before the storm.

Hannah had gone on ahead, and it took Colin several minutes at a taxing pace to catch up to her. He felt terrible when he reached her, almost nauseous. She slogged along, staring straight ahead. Determination hardened her dirty face into a mask. It didn't look like Hannah.

They crossed one gentle, rolling rise after another, devoid of grass or any sign of life.

"Do you suppose the mare is still alive, Colin?"

"Yair. She's charmed. She was charmed hundreds of feet under the ground and she was charmed in Griffith. I can't see that wearing off."

"But there's nothing for her to eat, and she won't find water either. She's never been out here before."

"Horses can smell water. Dizzy says cattle smell it better, but horses can find it. He told me about horses in Texas smelling it below ground and digging to it in the washes. Gullies."

She didn't look convinced. "All the same I think we better pray about her very hard."

Colin wasn't completely convinced either. Still, the mare was indeed charmed. Anyone who led her through the tunnels from the Southern Star and the Hard Yakka into the Perseverance would agree. Pray for her? Well, actually, why not.

He dared not suggest Hannah ought to be praying for their own survival. He didn't want to worry or alarm her. There was nothing she could do about the situation. The less she knew, the better.

They rested in a crooked little wattle-tree grove through the worst heat of the day. A flock of pink and gray galahs fluttered in, railed at the interlopers, and passed on. Two crested pigeons settled in the branches overhead. Colin drew his hat down over his face to think.

One of the reasons he left home in the first place was to find peace from the constant friction with Papa. Here in the dry and endless outback all the accouterments of peace surrounded him—tranquility, silence, no people to interrupt his reveries. But peace eluded him. His very soul hungered for peace, even in this quiet remoteness.

Late in the afternoon they put the birds and the shade behind them. On the track again.

Except now there was no track. Wherever the locals had traveled on this unofficial roadway, no signs remained. The dust storm had erased everything. It was certain the locals didn't drive their trucks and autos through these rolling slopes. Rock outcrops and soft, sandy dips would hinder any overland driving. Where was the path? Colin hadn't a clue.

Fear, that for so long had nested like an unwelcome little gadfly in a corner of his mind, began to grow until it consumed a large part of his thoughts. They were out of water. They had taken nothing since they drained their only waterbag at sundown the night before. Tomorrow's dawn would see them no closer to survival. Unless they found water soon. . . .

The mare was charmed. But the mare was gone. Until this hour Colin had never really doubted that his own life was charmed. Now he had doubts. For the first time in his life he tried to envision death. He could see only emptiness. You go to sleep, and then what?

If only he had put Hannah on a train; he'd had so many opportunities—Adelaide, Bendigo, Wagga—but his own stubborn pride let those chances slide by. Now she hovered on the very brink of death, and he was responsible. His bitter independence had caused this horror.

The sun would set in half an hour or less; it paused on the flat line behind them, ready for the plunge. The peril of their situation grew within him. He felt suffocated, and outrageously thirsty.

"Colin! Listen. That's not a bellbird, not out here in the dry. It's a bell of some sort."

"I don't hear any—oh, yair."

"Come on!" She was off at a brisk pace, Colin's swag flung across her shoulder. A hundred feet away she turned back impatiently. "Come on, Colin. You'll not improve our position or get any more comfortable by hanging about."

He detested being addressed as if he were a five-year-old, and by a thirteen-year-old, at that! He lurched forward, staggered, and picked up the stride.

She was three hundred feet ahead, the irregular bell sound quite clearly audible, by the time she topped a rise. "There's a fire over among those trees," she called. "Let's see if they have some spare water." She didn't wait for him. She hastened over the hill and out of sight.

Colin heard voices. Voices! Smoke curled in a thin veil up through the trees. He quickened his pace. "Hannah?"

As he reached the top of the rise he heard her say something about her brother. There in a low dip among straight-trunked trees, a campfire burned. A slab of meat—probably a side of wallaby—roasted beside it, and a quart pot nestled in its coals. A worn swag lay open and waiting nearby. Someone had quite comfortably ensconced himself here beneath the frothy green trees. Kookaburras announced the departing day. Where was Hannah? He approached the fire.

Hannah came bounding out from among the trees as if she had not been traveling at all. She grinned brightly; her enthusiasm of yesterday had returned. Colin yearned for it.

"Colin! This gentleman has camels! Three of them. He's freighting with camels. I never dreamed they were so big!"

"Does he have water? That is the question!"

Casually she passed a drovers' glass-lined waterbag to Colin and flopped down by the fire. "Mr. Indjuwa says to drink all you want, there's enough. He's out checking on something."

Colin collapsed beside the fire, delirious with relief. He very nearly drained the waterbag before he realized what he was doing. Sheepishly, he passed it back to Hannah.

From the gathering darkness and the trees emerged the camel driver. Aboriginal, he stood not much taller than Colin, but his solid frame looked twice Colin's width. A charming, dense little gray beard clung close to his face and moved around as he spoke. Between his battered hat and equally battered drover's boots he wore a neat cotton shirt and drill pants.

"Dick Indjuwa. You're Colin, hah?" He plopped down next to him. "You two look bushed."

Hannah grimaced. "Actually, what we are mostly is lost."

"That's what 'bushed' means out here, Hannah." Colin addressed the camel driver, "We're headed for Young to take the railway into Sydney."

The man nodded. "You're going right. Could use some water and tucker, that true?"

"Yes, sir." Colin tried to hide the desperation in his voice.

"Trade you some water and tucker, hah?"

"Sure. But we don't want to short you of what you need for yourself."

The man looked straight up. "This here's a coolibah tree. Know what that means?"

"It means you know a lot more about trees than I do."

Dick Indjuwa threw his head back and laughed long and heartily. "Good, good, good!" He sobered enough to speak. "It means you're sitting on water. Coolibah trees like to keep their feet in water. Either a spring, or dig down short way. Lots of water round here. You won't short me."

"What do you wish to trade?"

"News. Got no news for weeks. You been in town lately?"

"Yes, sir. What do you want to know?"

"Who won the Cup?"

"Windbag under Munro, in three minutes, twenty-two and three-fourths seconds. A track record."

"Good, good. And who won the 'lection?"

"Bruce was returned by a comfortable margin. Nationalist-Country coalition is in now."

"Pah! 'Fraid of that. Rugby League?"

"South Sydney."

"VFL?" The gray beard rearranged itself somewhat.

"Geelong, I think."

"Good as any. Windbag." The man nodded.

Colin was warming to the task now. "A Neville Westerwood and a Mr. Davies are trying to drive all the way around Australia. Last I heard they were still at it. Started in August sometime, I think."

"Fool thing to do. But then, dragging camels across the outback ain't much wiser, hah? Here. Meat's about ready and I have a loaf of bread. Let me fetch it. Ready to eat?"

"Yes, sir!" Hannah beat Colin to an answer.

It was all Colin could do to keep himself sitting upright. He felt absolutely drained, like a tire with the air gone. He lifted his head when he heard hoofbeats.

Hannah squealed. She launched herself across the clearing and wrapped her arms around her friend—

Max's Lady.

Colin couldn't get to his feet. *Of course. The mare wandered off, and this man found her.* He broke into a grin and his dry, chapped lips split. The sudden pain brought tears to his eyes. "Where'd you find her, sir?"

"Walking 'round. She 'preciated a drink. Figured her owner would turn up sooner or later. Here's the bread, Hannah. Want to slice it?"

"Surely, sir."

Mr. Indjuwa dropped the lead line. The mare stood placidly. Colin managed to climb stiffly to his feet and lean against his old friend, to rub the velvet nose, scratch the hard forehead, dig his fingers in behind her ears.

Hannah babbled on about leaving the saddle and bag behind. She explained Colin's bout with Spanish influenza and described the aftermath of the flood on the Murrumbidgee. She related, too, the kindness of the people in Griffith. Mr. Indjuwa blotted up the news and the conversation as a felt hat soaks up the rain. He nodded and commented with his "Good, good, good!" or "Pah!" as the occasion warranted.

Colin left the mare reluctantly and settled down by the fire to dine. Yes, dine was the proper term. Nothing tasted better than to be snatched from a parched death into plenty. Roasted wallaby brought back memories of Madman's Track. He turned around to look at the mare again. Charmed she was.

Mr. Indjuwa and Hannah had a long and pleasant conversation while Colin dozed.

He awoke with a start. The kookaburras with heckling joy were announcing the sun prematurely. He opened his eyes and sat up. The birds weren't actually jumping the gun; the eastern horizon glowed a rosy pink.

What really brought him fully awake were the big condamine bells. The camels were being led into camp, two by Mr. Indjuwa and the third by Hannah.

The tough old gentleman grinned. "Shoulda took the bullfrog bells off them, hah? Let you sleep. Porridge in the quart pot."

"Thank you, sir."

Mr. Indjuwa explained to Hannah how blacksmiths made the big bells out of old crosscut saw blades, and that on a quiet evening you could hear them fifteen miles away.

By the time Colin returned from a visit to the bushes, the boss camel driver was adjusting the load on one of the camel's backs. As he scooped porridge into a tin plate, the driver was saddling another. In theory, Colin knew that camels served as saddle animals, but never had he seen a camel saddle up this close, not to mention the camel. The saddle consisted of a bare, open steel frame in the shape of two boxes. A broad leather strap formed the rider's seat on the rear box. Stirrups hung from that half. Straps and a net bag provided stowage in the front half.

He shuddered to note that the camels were led about not by a halter or bridle but by a wooden peg and a cord looped through a hole in one nostril. Hannah helped Mr. Indjuwa tie the leadline of a pack camel to his saddle. The third camel's line was tied to the second camel's tail.

Everything was set to go. Mr. Indjuwa took up his quart pot, and Colin handed him the tin plate. "Must get on. Good to meet you, Colin." He extended his massive hand to Colin's. He tipped his head toward Hannah. "Miss Sloan, it was a pleasure." Then he climbed aboard his camel and barked, "Hooshta." With a certain stately grace, the animals lurched into long, swaying strides. Dick Indjuwa was on his way again. How timely that he had camped here right when Hannah and Colin needed someone.

"Wait!" Colin called, spying the brown bag by the firepit. "Your waterbag!"

With a cheery grin Mr. Indjuwa waved and continued on.

"He said we could have it. It's full." Hannah walked over to the coolibah tree and rapped her knuckles on it. "Looks like an ordinary tree, as far as I'm concerned."

Colin pulled out his pocket knife and cut off a foot-long branch. "Let's keep this in my swag. We can compare it to other trees."

"Mr. Indjuwa said last night that we were going in the right direction. So, I guess we just keep heading east."

Colin nodded. "Like they said in the pub, cross the first set of tracks, and when we come upon the second, take them either south to Young or north to Cowra. I think unless we see Young in the distance, we go north. We can't miss it."

"Cowra's close to Bathhurst and Bathhurst is close to home," Hannah calculated. "It won't take long."

And being so close, Colin thought to himself, *the railway fare won't take such a big bite out of our few pounds remaining.* Perhaps he could walk in the door at home with money in his pocket, after all.

CHAPTER TWENTY-EIGHT

NESTS

Sloan glanced to his left. On the seat beside him, Sam sat staring straight ahead, her face grim. She did not ride well in automobiles. Pity, because Sloan loved them. Mary Aileen had curled herself into a corner of the back seat, reading. Once in awhile she peeked into the box in the middle of the seat, the box that housed Smoke and her new kittens. Smoke traveled better than Sam did. Sprawled on the other side of the box, Edan watched the passing scenes with the strange, distant stoicism with which he seemed to view all of life.

Sloan kicked the gearshift down into second. Their open touring car ground its way up the steep track beneath feathery gum trees a hundred years old. A mixed flock of honeyeaters, a ragtag cloud of yellow and brown, swarmed from tree to tree across the track ahead of them.

"It's dry up here," Cole ventured.

Sam nodded. "I was noticing that. And warm. We'll not need the extra tent fly."

"Perhaps we won't put up the tent at all, if you don't mind sleeping out."

"I've not done that in ages." She almost smiled. Then it faded.

"What were you just thinking, Sam?"

She shook her head. "What I find myself thinking of a

304

thousand times a day—Hannah and Colin. I wondered just now if they've a roof over their heads."

He reached out impulsively and patted her leg. "This two-week holiday will do you a world of good."

"I don't know. The thoughts come; it doesn't seem to matter where I am."

"Undisciplined thinking. You have to put the past behind you."

"Undisciplined love. I can't put the past behind."

"Too right." He settled back in the driver's seat.

Laboriously the auto climbed out of the vale, past eroded cutbacks onto the near-level mountaintop. They jarred over a worn track that would require major repair within the next few years. Sloan pulled into the familiar opening and killed the engine.

After the cough and rumble of the motor, thundering silence rang in the trees. Sam hopped out with a grateful sigh. Mary Aileen bestirred herself and gathered up her precious box of cats.

"Help with the kitchen, Edan." Sloan opened the trunk and pulled out the larger box. Edan brought over the smaller one. Together they set up Mum's Roost—the portable cooker, the washtub, the condiment box, and pans. Sam unpacked the food, and they were home.

"If we're not setting up the tent," Mary Aileen wondered, "where do I put the sleeping gear?"

Sam went off to ponder the weighty question with her. Sloan would leave sleeping arrangements to the ladies. He dug into the back for lanterns, paused, and stopped.

Edan was wandering away over the ridge, in the direction the children frequently took in the past. Mary Aileen and Sam were looking after the sleeping gear, oblivious. Quietly Sloan closed the trunk, and took off following Edan.

The boy had taken a faint footpath for a hundred yards. He left it and moved away through the open wood. Sloan stayed an inconspicuous distance behind, lest he startle the lad or seem to be spying. Seem to be spying? He *was* spying. If he could not communicate with his son, he would watch him.

Edan crawled out onto a sandstone overlook and hunkered down. Sloan moved in closer. The mountainside fell away at Edan's feet. A deep, densely forested gorge below shimmered in the late-afternoon heat. Blue with haze, the mountains stretched off beyond the gorge toward infinity. What a sublime view.

A ten-year-old boy enthralled with scenery? It was hard to believe. What did the lad see beyond the obvious? Or was he simply wasting his time daydreaming again, as he was so wont to do? Minutes passed. Suddenly Edan bolted to his feet and walked back to the path. Sloan waited conveniently behind a tree until the lad had committed himself to a direction. He headed away from Sloan, farther along the ridge.

Cole moved in a little closer, and not a moment too soon. The boy disappeared to the left of the path. Only the small dark head could be seen, as he slipped down over the side to traverse a faint trail along a very narrow ledge.

If the lad could make it, Sloan could make it. With trepidation, he stepped out on the ledge. He kept his back as close to the steep mountain slope as he could, his face to empty space where the slope dropped away precipitously. He side-stepped along the knife edge, his heels on solid rock and his toes hanging out upon nothing. This surely was not the lad's first trip through here. If Sloan had known years ago where his children trod so dangerously—

A dark, ragged rock outcrop loomed ahead. Sloan watched his son step nimbly from the narrow ledge path into a gaping opening beneath the overhang. A cave. Cole could easily imagine the lure a cave would have for a child his age. In his own youth he would have given anything for a secret place this exotic and remote.

His left foot slipped. For a wild, panic-filled moment he thought he was going to go over. He grasped at the overhanging bush branches, scrambling for balance. His right foot remained firmly on solid stone. He glanced toward Edan.

The boy was staring at him in shocked surprise. *So much for keeping a low profile.* All sense of stealth or secrecy gone, Cole completed the last eighty feet from mountainside ledge to the safety of the cavern with mock confidence.

"Why did you follow me?" It was a legitimate question.

"I wanted to see where you were going."

Surprisingly, the answer seemed to satisfy. Edan turned his attention to the ceiling, scanning the dark recesses, obviously seeking something.

"What are you looking for?"

"Rock warbler nests. They're hard to see unless you know where they are." The boy crossed through powdery dust to a chair-shaped boulder five feet inside. "I'm going to sit here and watch awhile. I heard something up there."

"May I watch, too?"

"If you like." Edan sat down on the rock, crossed his legs and folded them under him.

Not nearly so supple, Sloan sat down beside him and drew his knees up. He leaned his arms across them. "What am I watching for?"

"It's rather like a shrike-thrush or a lady robin, gray on top and reddish below. Moves about very nervously. 'Leen says New South Wales is the only state it lives in, just among mountains here."

"They live here, eh? Ever see one here before?"

Edan's whole demeanor froze. Somehow Sloan had struck a nerve with that innocuous question. Edan shrugged. "Used to."

Sloan watched not the cave entrance but his son. Edan's eyes darted about everywhere at once, but for the most part they lingered on the cave roof. "Edan? This place is so far from anywhere. No one around for miles, except our camp. Ever get scared?"

The boy measured his response. "Sometimes."

"Then why come here?"

"I'm not scared of this place. I feel good here. Colin found it when I was just little. We come here all the time."

"Then what are you afraid of?"

The lad stiffened, straightened. "There!" he whispered. His whole face lit up. A small gray bird paused at the mouth of the cavern. Nervously, it flicked its tail sideways. It hopped across some rocks, wagging its body in an odd way, and fluttered suddenly into the cave.

Sloan lost track of it, but obviously Edan had not. The lad lifted himself silently to his feet and moved catlike across the powdered dirt floor. Sloan followed, a mere spectator to a drama he did not fathom.

"It's back," Edan breathed. Soundlessly he pointed up at the craggy roof. A roundish mass of grass, moss and sticks hung to the sloping roof by attachments at either end. A tiny bird form appeared in a dark hole in its side. Like lightning the bird popped out and flew from the cave.

"Listen." Edan craned his neck. "The babies. You hear them?"

"No, but my ears are considerably older than yours."

Edan beamed. "They're back! There's the nest. I couldn't find it at first, so I let the bird show me. I can tell 'Leen they're back. They built the nest new again. It's okay again." He headed toward the ledge path and stopped. "Want to stay here any longer?"

"Not unless you do."

Edan nodded. Leading the way, he left the cave, tightrope-walking that treacherous path with the nonchalance of an angel. Sloan must have let his apprehension show, for the lad waited for him patiently, perhaps a wee bit smugly, at the upper end. Sloan scrambled to the safety of the crest and they began the walk back to camp.

Sloan grimaced. "One misstep on that ledge and you're at the bottom of the gorge keeping the platypuses company."

"It's not scary once you get used to it."

Here was an opening to resume that aborted conversation. "Obviously, threats to life and limb don't frighten you. What does?"

An exaggerated shrug. "Other things."

"Like . . . ?"

"Like when I'm bigger." The voice sounded very small and distant. "And I get chased out of the house, too."

Sloan felt his mouth fall open and his legs stop walking, and he couldn't do anything about any of it. Finally he forced his feet back into action. *Now what, Romales? You said listen. I listened. Now I don't know how to handle what I've heard.*

Sloan had just as much trouble getting his brain to work as his legs. "When do you think that would happen?"

"I don't know."

Cole needed Sam for this. Mum could soothe fears no one else could. What do you tell a child who would think something like that? How could he think such a thing? Not hard, when you're ten years old and logic is not yet part of your vocabulary. Or perhaps there was a certain twisted logic to it.

Suddenly a certain twisted logic emerged from the birdhouses and the warbler's nest, too. The *aha!* light went on in Sloan's mind. Nests. Home. The boy was obsessed with the fear of losing his nest. How could Sloan mend that nest and thereby allay this innocent little child's fears? He had no idea where Colin and Hannah might be, let alone how to make contact and convince them to return. The covey had scattered; he could see no way to gather it in.

His mind raced. Finally, just short of camp, he wrapped his arm across the fragile little shoulders. "Do me a favor, eh?"

"What?"

"When you feel like you're getting chased out of the

house, stop and talk to me about it before you go, will you?"

―――――――

As far as the eye could see, silver ribbons ran south. To the north, they disappeared around a distant, gentle bend.

"Okay," Hannah announced, "This is the first railway. We cross these tracks and continue to the next set, right?"

"Right." Colin led the mare forward. She stepped gingerly over the rails, planted her feet carefully on the sleepers.

"How far between them?"

"From what I gather, fifteen miles, maybe twenty at the outside. A day's walk; not more."

Hannah didn't have to carry the swag anymore and that felt very good. She draped it around the mare's neck. The mare didn't have the saddle or the traveling bag, and that probably felt good to her. She wasn't in much better shape than Colin. But Hannah did miss the things she had left behind—the trousers, especially. She would have so loved to wear her trousers out in this wilderness.

One of her shoes was wearing out. She could feel a break in the sole right under the ball of her foot. Sand was starting to get in and it was very irritating. By the end of the day the break had widened to a proper hole. She took off her shoe to examine the damage. How battered the poor thing was! On the other hand, she thought of the miles they'd covered.

Colin built a fire and opened two more cans. They ate the last of the bread Mr. Indjuwa had given them, and emptied their waterbag.

"Tomorrow we'll be back in a real town," Colin promised. "We'll dine in style in a real restaurant and sleep in real beds with smooth, cool sheets."

"And I'll have a real bath. I used to hate baths. I can't imagine how I could be so foolish."

"You don't get quite this dirty in school."

"What a blessing! I almost look forward to school again." She pulled out her Bible and went back to work, looking for references to weakness. He agreed to look at the verses in jest. She would show him by producing! Already she had found various references and marked them with gum-leaves. But none struck her as quite right.

The intense heat of day was slow to dissipate as the sun dropped low. Hannah had forgotten how very hot it gets in these hills west of Sydney. She thought about the camping ground in the mountains where her family spent so many happy holidays. Living and sleeping outside a house seemed like such an adventure then.

Colin stretched out and fell asleep where he sat by the fire. The coals crackled and waned.

"Here it is!" Hannah jabbed Colin. He grunted and raised his head. "The abbess preached about this a couple of times in chapel—every time one of the sisters took ill. Listen!" She read by the firelight: " 'There was given me a thorn in the flesh, the messenger of Satan to buffet me, lest I should be exalted above measure.' "

"A what?"

"A thorn in the flesh—a health problem of some sort. The abbess never said exactly what it was. Eight. 'For this thing I besought the Lord thrice, that it might depart from me.' Now listen to this, Colin! Nine. 'And he said unto me, my grace is sufficient for thee; for my strength is made perfect in weakness. Most gladly therefore will I rather glory in my infirmities, that the power of Christ may rest upon me.' Ten. 'Therefore I take pleasure in infirmities, in reproaches, in necessities, in persecutions, in distresses for Christ's sake.' And then Paul ends it with, 'for when I am weak, then am I strong.' "

"I don't get it. When I'm weak, I'm strong? That's nonsense."

Hannah intensely wished she had paid more attention in chapel. Who would ever dream that one might need something from chapel at some later date? What did the abbess say? "If you're strong you start to think you don't need God. When you're weak you depend on Him because you have to. And since He provides what you're not strong enough to provide, the glory goes to Him. When you're weak in the body you're strong in the Lord. Don't you see it?"

He snorted, unconvinced.

She slammed her Bible shut so hard his head snapped around to stare at her. "You were poking fun at me when you said you'd listen to the verses about weakness. Well, there they are. There's all manner of things in the Bible you don't suspect. You've seen that prayer works, over and over. You know lots of people now who say God is real and they know Him. You don't have any excuses, and I am done with talking to a brick wall. You can become a real, true Christian or you will go to hell, but I've done all I can do."

"It's not as simple as you think, Hannah."

"It's even simpler than I think. When I was looking for weakness verses I saw something else way back at the beginning. Matthew somewhere, I think. Jesus said you have to come to Him like a little child. You just accept Him, like Edan would. So do it. Or don't do it. But don't blame me if your pocket gets more holes."

She slipped her Bible under the end of Colin's blanket, just in case dew fell during the night, and curled up in the warm darkness. *Men are so stubborn!*

The next morning they resumed the trek east. Hannah thought about all the comforts and benefits of civilization. Any time soon now! The hills among which they wound grew steeper. They threaded through gum forests and skirted acacia thickets.

At noon they built a small fire and consumed two more cans of food—asparagus and peaches. Only two cans remained.

"Colin, we're bushed again."

"No, we're not."

"They don't build railways in hills this tangled. That first one we crossed had to be the second one, the one we wanted."

"Sure. We just happened to stumble right across a railway without noticing it."

"Something's wrong. We shouldn't be this far into the mountains."

"When I was riding up to Griffith from the Colfaxes in the pouring rain, and the truck quit, I didn't know how far I had yet to go. I kept thinking I'd missed the road, or was on the wrong track, or something. But I just kept going and kept going, and I got there. It's the same now. If we just keep going, we'll get there eventually."

"I think you're wrong. I still think we're much too far east."

"Hannah, you're so stubborn."

"Stubborn!" She hopped to her feet. "You refuse to change your mind about God and Jesus even though the evidence is all for it, but when I don't change my mind because the evidence is all against it, I'm stubborn. You're the one that's stubborn, Colin!"

She rolled the swag, threw it across the startled mare's withers, and picked up the leadline. "Here we go, continuing in the wrong direction. Coming, Colin?"

"Spoiled brat." He struggled to his feet to follow.

Spoiled brat, indeed. And as the day wore on and the hills became ever more confusing, Hannah became ever more firmly convinced.

Colin was horribly, inextricably lost.

CHAPTER TWENTY-NINE

FIRE

"The mare's worn out. We're going to have to rest awhile." Colin was talking about the horse but he might as well be talking about himself. He dragged to a halt, totally, completely exhausted. He flopped onto his back. "You couldn't move me with a bullock team."

He wasn't lying about the horse. She stopped dead in her tracks and dozed off in seconds, her nose drooping to the ground.

Hannah flopped onto the dirt beside her brother. "I guess when I went off adventuring, I thought of it as some sort of lark. Serious, of course—to find you and help if you were ill—but still an adventure. I never gave a thought to the enemy."

"You mean Nels Brekke?"

Hannah shook her head. "No. The country. The land. Floods, dust storms—and distance, just being away from everyone and everything that's familiar." She looked straight into her brother's eyes. "Colin, I'm sure we should go back the way we came. I think we missed the first rail line because it got covered over in the dust storm. In fact, I remember a picture I saw in a book once of a locomotive with a plow in front to clear drifting sand on the Trans. I think we walked right over the first tracks not long before we met Mr. Indjuwa."

"Maybe. Remember how Mr. Indjuwa said we were headed right? No hint or reminder to take the *second* set of tracks we came across, and not the first." He hated the thought of backtracking. Even more he hated admitting his sister might be right.

He changed the subject. "I never thought about the 'enemy.' Yair. Even Brekke had a little bit of conscience. And my uncles had their good points. But the land. It's—" He searched out the word with difficulty. "Mindless. No sense of responsibility, no mercy, no thought of weary travelers. The Enemy. It's what has threatened us most. It's what we've really been fighting."

A dazzling flock of rosellas shot by overhead, babbling. Rosellas are rarely calm little birds, but these seemed particularly agitated. A hawk lifted suddenly out of a gum snag nearly overhead. Colin had not seen it until it was in the air. With heavy wingstrokes it beat its way over the trees and disappeared beyond a ridge.

"Colin, I smell smoke." Hannah wrinkled her red, peeling nose. "And crackling. Listen."

"Can't be. There're no farms or stations in these hills."

"Don't you smell it?"

With a sigh Colin sat up. He inhaled deeply. She might be right. Another camel driver camping? A chimney? Impossible. He looked about for the telltale plume. What he saw was an ominous gray wall. Fear galvanized him and flung him to his feet. "Down the gorge there. Look!"

Bushfire!

Colin had never seen one before, but he knew what he was looking at.

So did Hannah. Her voice was a soft whimper, terror-struck. "Colin . . . ?"

"Which way is the wind moving?" Colin whirled around. In an unexpected flash he remembered Dizzy's trick. He picked up a pinch of dust and lofted it. The powder drifted eastward. "The fire's coming this way, with the wind. We have to get over the ridge, fast! At least find some bare ground."

Either the mare had absorbed their fear or she, too, smelled smoke. She was awake now, her head high, her ears aloft. Colin pulled the swag off her and cast it aside. He swung up on her back and reached out to Hannah. Hannah grabbed his arm and leaped up. Even as she did so, the mare was plunging forward.

At the racecourse in Sydney so long ago, Colin used to exercise his father's horses in the gray mist of dawn. Then, breezing them thrilled him, with their powerful bodies lunging beneath him, their manes stinging his face. This was different. He was riding for his life, and for Hannah's. No thrill—just terror. Colin drew his knees up on the mare's shoulders and buried his face in her mane. He felt Hannah clinging to him, pressing against him, keeping low.

The mare stumbled and clawed up the ridge slope. She staggered in a rocky spot and lurched. They topped out onto a broad tableland studded with short, squat trees.

Hannah twisted behind him. "It's coming! I just saw an orange spot! Colin, are we going to make it?"

The mare's strides lengthened out across the level ground. She extended her neck for serious flying. Hard beside them, a family mob of kangaroos came shooting out from among the trees. They ran abreast like fugitives, the horse and the bounding kangaroos.

Colin didn't have to look behind. He could hear the crackle getting closer, but what was that roar? He glanced back. The fire had crowned out. It leaped now from treetop to treetop, racing across the tableland with—yes, the speed of a running horse. A tree exploded into flame beside them, spraying burning leaves and sparks. The mare veered away in terror. A little wallaby angled off in another direction, its back smoldering.

The tableland curved in a gentle downward slope. Suddenly it dropped away at an eroded gully, a cut at least six feet deep. Colin barely had time to yell "Hang on!" as the mare gathered her legs beneath her and flung herself across the yawning crack in the earth.

———————

"Where's Edan?" Sloan looked around impatiently. The boy was always wandering off somewhere.

"I don't know." Mary Aileen shrugged. She adjusted the little leather harness on Smoke. Here in the outback they kept the cat tethered, lest she become rapt stalking some small creature and lose her way in the unfamiliar wilderness. Two kittens tumbled over each other, a third snoozed, curled at its mum's feet. The fourth crawled over its littermate seeking lunch. There was no way you could tether four kittens, even if you wanted to.

Sam looked up from her crocheting. "He went off toward the cave again a while ago, I believe."

Disgruntled, Sloan headed up the trail. Here in this pristine wilderness he felt restless. He wanted to be near a phone. He wanted to be abreast of things with letters and telegrams. He had planted seeds of inquiry. Surely some would bear fruit. But he wouldn't see the fruit up here, isolated as they were. Besides, it was uncommonly hot and dry for this time of year, not nearly so comfortable as their pleasantly situated home, its temperatures moderated by the nearby ocean.

Sam's sister Linnet and her husband Chris would be back from Europe soon, if they had not returned already. Perhaps he could use his brother-in-law as a liaison in the south.

Edan came running up the path. "Papa! There's a bushfire somewhere out beyond the knob. You can see the smoke. I'll run tell Mum and 'Leen. You can see it from down at the end of the bluff."

The child sped away. What could Sloan do but go look at the smoke? He walked out to the trail's end on the nethermost brow of their hill. There it was, a curtain of yellow-gray haze, very dense near the rounded hills which hid the fire, ethereal as it trickled away into the blue sky. Not much wind, at least from this vantage point. Unless it crowned out, it would creep slowly until it burned itself out on the lip of some rain-washed gully.

Edan returned presently, huffing and puffing, sweating profusely. Sam came close behind him.

"Where's Mary Aileen?" Cole asked.

"Fiddling with her cats." Sam sighed in resignation. "She says she doesn't want to go look at innocent animals burning up. She seems agitated—upset about it."

What could he say? Under the best of circumstances Cole could scarcely guess the paths women's minds followed. There was less chance he could actually understand them.

Edan watched the yellow curtain. "Papa? Are animals really burning up?"

"Some are, I suppose. Birds escape, of course, as do creatures fleet enough to outrun it. Anything living in a hole in the ground escapes."

Sam pressed in close. Cole slipped an arm around her. She, too, was transfixed by the yellow wall. "I've not seen a bushfire before. Up close, I suspect they're quite noisy and frightening."

"I suspect."

Edan squirmed in close to Cole's other side. It was the lad's first literal attempt to get literally close to his father. He reached out and pulled him in tight. "Papa? The birds escape. But the nests burn up, don't they."

"Sometimes the fire creeps along the ground and everything in the trees remains untouched. If the fire crowns—reaches the trees—the nests would burn up, yes. But then the birds return and build new ones."

"I've read," Sam ventured, "that as soon as it rains, the burnt area sprouts all manner of new growth—grass, flowers. I read, too, that some seeds lie in the ground for years and years awaiting a fire; they can't sprout unless they're burned. Mary Aileen is right. Fire is death. But fire also brings life. 'Tis why our Lord uses fire to symbolize His Holy Spirit."

Edan made no comment. He buried his head in Papa's side, and watched.

———

For moments and moments the mare hung suspended in space. Colin clung to her, panic-stricken. She hit the far rim of the gully and scrambled with all four feet. Colin slipped; Hannah bounced behind him and nearly unhorsed him when her weight shifted. They recovered barely in time. The mare galloped on, out of control. Behind them the wall loomed high, blotting out the sun and most of the sky, plunging them into near-darkness.

Max's Lady staggered suddenly and lurched onto her knees. Hannah shrieked. The mare fought her way up to all fours, stumbled a few yards, and collapsed. Colin fell forward over her neck. He scrambled to his feet.

Hannah struggled, her leg pinned beneath the lathered body. Colin grabbed her under the arms and pulled. She yelped, but she pulled free.

"Colin, what about the mare?"

"No time! C'mon!" He seized her wrist and started running. Where could they go on foot to outrace this hell? He'd heard somewhere that fire travels fastest uphill. He and Hannah had two hundred yards of downhill yet, through increasingly dense forest, before they had to worry about an uphill race. They slammed down the slope.

The smoke and the dense trees together reduced the light to near nighttime down in the forest. Colin stopped. "Listen!"

"Water! A waterfall or something—back that way!"

As one they bolted off in the direction of the welcome sound. They crashed noisily into a dark, pleasant bower. Deep green leaves, bushes, and gentle ferns wrapped protectively around them. An unassuming creek babbled at their feet. "Back there!" they cried in unison.

The creek came tumbling over ragged, fern-studded ledges in a ten-foot waterfall. It paused to fill a quiet pool before hastening on its way. Dragging Hannah along, Colin plunged into the water. They pressed as far back against the ledges as possible. The waterfall beat down, close to their heads. For a moment Colin heard only the crashing water. Then came the roar and crackle of burning forest, closer and closer.

Sloan stowed Sam's larger kitchen box. Edan handed him the smaller one, and he slammed the trunk shut.

Sam placed her crocheting and the lunch basket in the front seat and walked around to the back. "I think we have it all. I gave it a second go-over."

He nodded. "I feel rather guilty, cutting our holiday four days short."

"Don't. It's hot and dusty, and I've so much in the way of Christmas preparations to make yet. The children don't seem particularly disappointed."

Cole watched Edan crawl into the back seat. "Take a last turn around with me, Sam." He took her hand and they walked up to the far end of camp. "What's going on with the kids if they aren't disappointed we're heading home so soon? They act like their last friend just died."

"The bushfire unsettled them, I think."

"It's twenty miles away, at least."

"I know. You and I can accept that sort of thing. They don't understand yet about life and death."

"Who does?" Cole looked into her eyes. Together they made a broad circuit around the camp, ostensibly making a last check for anything left behind.

In reality, Sloan hated having to return to the city, to share Sam again with the real world. He assisted her into the auto and closed her door. A strange feeling crept over him as he climbed behind the wheel. Guilty? It was more than that. A still, small voice kept nagging, *Don't go home.*

Ridiculous! He was hearing things. The pressure and grief of Hannah and Colin was affecting him. That was all. He started up the rumbling engine and kicked the touring car into gear. They were off, headed for home.

———

Colin curled up on his side, doubled up in another painful spate of coughing. Fine gray ash, smoke, the permeating stench, all had a terrible effect on his throat and lungs. The brook by his feet babbled along as if nothing untoward had happened in the last few short hours, but their pleasant bower lay in ruins, smoldering, scorched, and shriveled. The waterfall still fell beneath unbroken sunlight. Heat from the fire made the ground beneath Colin unnaturally hot. It seeped into him and made him sweat.

Down the creek a few yards, a gum tree leaned out across the water, the bank partially washed away from its roots. The tree grew horizontally from its base, then turned sharply upward toward the light. He remembered the jarrah tree a continent away that did the same thing. Apparently it was a common occurrence. Upslope a bit stood a similar gum tree, tall and straight, not the least bent.

Papa stands tall like that tree, Colin thought. Though they got along poorly, Colin readily admitted that Papa stood straight and tall, spiritually as well as physically. A sudden whimsical thought startled him: what if Papa were not that straight tree, but the crooked one? Papa's brothers never straightened up, and he came from the same roots. What caused him to turn upward?

His past maybe. Stubbornness. *Jesus!* Of course! Jesus was the only thing separating Papa from his brothers, when you got to the heart of it. Mum. James Otis.

Hannah. The Slotemakers. They all had this different quality you couldn't quite put your finger on.

Dear Papa.

Quite possibly Colin would not survive this. He felt so very, very drained. Weak. *When I am weak, I am strong.* Hannah was only partly right. Her biggest enemy was the land, but Colin's was God. The land was Colin's antagonist by necessity; he was making God his antagonist by choice. They were total opposites, the mindless land and the all-knowing God. Colin must keep fighting the land. But now was the time to put the battle with God to rest. He was so very tired. It was not hard to pray now.

Lord, I admit my sins—particularly my stubbornness. Thank you for Hannah. Dear Hannah. Forgive me for being so crook when she first showed up in my life in the outback. I'd not have made it without her. You sent her. I see that now. From here on, I'm yours, God. Whether I see home again or not, I'm yours. In Jesus, I'm yours— because of Jesus, because of what He did, dying to pay for my sins. God, uh . . . I don't know how to pray. I don't know how to believe in You. Help me believe.

The pleasant vale had been blasted asunder. Smoke still curled from hot spots around him. Acrid heat radiated from all directions. A pitiless sun blazed. The comfortable and the familiar had vanished. And yet, Colin felt at ease now—a most amazing thing! Peace. He belonged to God now, bought and paid for. Whatever happened to him in this ravaged world, he was safe. He was home at last.

Reality forced its way back into his life. He struggled to a sitting position. He should not have allowed Hannah to go wandering. But then, when did she ever listen to him?

Ah! There she came down the hill, her tattered shoes kicking up ash and dust. She splashed clumsily across the creek and slogged up the bank to Colin.

All the grief in the world seemed to twist her fragile face. "Oh, Colin!" She stumbled down beside him and wrapped her arms around his waist. He enclosed her to his side and pressed her head against his shoulder. She sobbed uncontrollably and Colin resumed his violent cough. What a pair they were.

Finally he managed, "You found the mare?"

Her head nodded in little jerks.

"It was awful! There were balls of ugly froth around her mouth and nostrils. And her eyes—"

"I know. I've seen horses trapped in a barn fire at the racecourse. It took me years to get over the nightmares."

She wiped her streaked face with a soot-blackened hand. "It's so strange up there, Colin. There are patches burned to a crisp and others the fire never touched. Strange how it skipped places and burned others. And there are lots of dead animals about. Possums and wallabies and smaller animals."

"Sorry you went?"

"No. I had to see for myself if Max's Lady was still charmed."

"Well, she sure was. In her last hours she saved our lives."

She nodded and sniffled, wiping her face with her skirt. "You coming?"

"Not yet. Sitting up is as energetic as I can get. Give me a while longer."

She lurched to her feet. "I'm going to go up the hill here and see what's ahead." She scrambled off, an endless fount of energy.

Colin flopped back down on his back. Big mistake. It sent him into paroxysms of coughing. He rolled to his side.

"Colin!" Her voice called in the distance, alive with excitement. "Colin, come quick!"

Now what? He forced himself to standing. He forced his legs into motion. Climbing even this gentle hill caused excruciating bouts of coughing. With two brief rests, he finally topped out on the brow. Eagerly, triumphantly, Hannah was pointing to the east.

Colin stared. "The knob! It can't be!"

"Colin, we've gone camping there before around Christmas time. What if they're there now? They could be there—maybe. The fire completely missed them. You can see how it traced the valley. The smoke still hangs in the air."

Colin nodded. Natural dirtslides and near-vertical bare crags had saved the knob as well as the mountain closest them—had turned the fire aside to the north.

"Across two chasms and a mountain before we even get to the knob, Hannah. I don't think I can get that far."

She pointed in the distance. "We could go down that way and around." She swung her arm in an arc. "It's a bit farther, but there'd be less climbing. You can go as far as you can. I've got to go, Colin. I have to reach the campsite."

"What if they're not camping? Chances are, they aren't there at all."

"They are. I just know it. And I've been praying about it. Come on, please?"

And away she went.

CHAPTER THIRTY

MY FATHER'S HOUSE

Sloan finished the last of a sweet, juicy pear and tossed the core into the bush. Sam, beside him at the picnic table, methodically cut her apple into wedges, her preferred method of eating fruit. Mary Aileen sat in the grass nearby, quietly watching the kittens romp across her legs. She had hardly eaten anything. Edan, who usually put away food quite easily outdoors, wasn't eating much either. What, if anything, should Sloan do about this? He wished Edan had not seen the fire. Mary Aileen, with her vivid imagination, had not even seen it and was morose. But wishing doesn't change things.

Sam glanced at him. "You're as morbid as the children."

"I was thinking there's not going to be much of a Christmas this year."

"That's true." She gazed at him, and tried not to think about what Christmas would be like without Colin and Hannah.

"Mary Aileen, Edan. Time to go." Sloan hauled to his feet and packed up the lunch box. He always enjoyed this picnic area by the main road. He liked to linger in more pleasant times. Today he had other things to do. He had the motor running by the time the children were in the back seat. They rolled out easily onto the main highway.

Edan sat up straighter. "Where are we going, Papa? Is this the way home?"

Mary Aileen looked around. "You aren't going to get us lost trying the back way again?"

"I'll try not to." An isolated incident five years ago, and the children still played it up. Yet give an instruction to clean up their rooms, and they'd forget it by the time they reached the top of the stairs.

Sam looked at Cole curiously. "We've never been this way, have we dear?"

"No. I may be doing some good, or I may be making a disastrous mistake. We'll see."

————

Hannah sat on the hot sun-washed hillside and stared at the knob. So near, and so far. If only she could fly. This hillside, the deep vale, and that whole mountain slope separated her from the path that could lead her to the family's camping ground. Colin was right; Mum and Papa almost surely were not there, fervent prayer notwithstanding. And if they weren't, Hannah and Colin were still essentially nowhere, still miles and miles from any good track or habitation.

She should not have gone back to find the dead mare. It wasn't that she didn't want to make sure, or didn't want to say a last goodbye to the dear old animal. But it had worn her out far more than she realized. Her strength was beginning to flag.

She turned and shielded her eyes to look upslope. Where was Colin? She didn't want to get too far ahead of him. And yet, she must not keep returning to him, putting still more miles on her legs.

Stubborn, stubborn Colin. What could she do to bring him to Jesus? *In my father's house are many mansions.* She'd read that somewhere. She would be home safe one day. Poor Colin was bushed in the worst possible sense, spiritually bushed. And she didn't know how to lead him to safety. The fire and its horror, the loss of the mare, Colin's illness and awful weakness all weighed heavily upon her spirit. She knew it was useless, but she began to weep.

The ragged little bush track they found themselves on did indeed lead where Sloan thought it would. He stopped the car. Just ahead, the track angled away to the north and down through the trees, following the valley beside them. It would end up somewhere around Bathhurst, most likely. Or maybe Katoomba. Its destination was not really important. This particular area was. They were now as deep into the mountains as this track would take them.

As they left the track, the touring car waddled drunkenly up through the trees and out onto a broad downslope.

He stopped again and jumped out, waving for the children to follow.

He walked out the slope farther than the car could have taken them. If his plan worked, it would be well worth it. There in the distance hung the curtain of smoke from the fire. Sloan had taken a fifty-fifty chance and won. The veil could quite as easily have grown, but it had shrunk.

Edan stood beside him.

"Where's your sister?"

"Tying her cat to a shrub. She says the track was too rough for the kittens and she's worried about them. She'll be coming."

"Charming creatures, those kittens. But a royal pain."

To Sloan's delighted surprise, Edan cackled gleefully. "I always thought so, but you daren't tell her that."

"No, we won't tell her that." Cole hugged his son. "Do you see the veil of smoke now?" He pointed out across the valley.

Edan's demeanor chilled. "Yes. It's way out there."

"Is it bigger or smaller than it was?"

"It's smaller. Not so thick, and yellow. Not so scary."

"That's right. The fire is just about out now. I wanted you to see that there comes an end to destruction and bad things. If a fire is not put out by man, it eventually hits open country or treeless slopes and burns itself out. It doesn't just keep on destroying."

Edan left Cole's side to stroll farther out on the slope.

Mary Aileen caught up to them and stood beside her father. "Where are we?"

"That knob beyond camp is to our left and probably a little behind us. We can't see it for the trees."

"Then the fire went beyond that hill." Mary Aileen pointed.

"That's right. I'll inquire around when we get back and find out what I can. The *Bulletin* will probably have some information on it. After the next rain we'll explore out there and see what new greenery is sprouting."

Edan joined them with a question, "You're sure, Papa, that there will be new things growing?"

"Yes, I'm certain of it, son."

"Are there any people out there?"

"No. There aren't any people out there."

They remained awhile longer. Sam had joined them now, and Cole was pleased to see the children pointing out the distant smoke for her, telling about the dwindled fire and the new growth to come.

Thank you, Lord, Cole prayed. *I don't like taking chances like this. Thank you for being with me and making it work.*

"Time to go home." Sloan wrapped an arm around Sam and led the way back to the car. Mary Aileen scooped up her kitten box and released Smoke from her tether, telling them they would soon be safe at home. Edan bounded into the back seat with a good deal more enthusiasm than before.

Sam smiled at her husband, glowing. "Brilliant idea, my dear."

"Praise the Lord!"

"Indeed."

They lumbered down to the rutted track and headed home.

―――――

"Colin, you can't quit now."

He looked terrible. His skin was ghastly white, the contrast made greater by the soot smudges, dust and dirt. He lay with his knees to his chest under the shade of a gum tree. "You have to stop coming back to me, girl. You can't help me by sitting here. Get yourself out. Go."

"I can't go without you, Colin. Don't say that to me."

"You have to. Please, Hannah. I'll come along as I'm able. I won't quit."

He was right. She knew he was right. His only chance was her finding the way out, and a puny chance it was. Why was she so reluctant to leave him? "I'll bring help."

He nodded amid more coughing. She hugged him as best she could and started walking again.

The sun would abandon her in a couple hours. Then what? She dared not continue in the darkness. The knob up there, her landmark and beacon, did not glow in the dark. She would drop down into this valley because it was the easiest way to go, and worry about climbing to the ridgetop later. Right now she barely mustered the strength to go downhill.

She looked back frequently, but she couldn't see Colin anymore. And even now the place where she knew he lay looked just like every other place. She'd never find him again. The enormity of their peril brought another flood of tears.

―――――

Sloan glanced into the back seat. "Mary Aileen, why are you bobbing around all over the place?"

"One of the kittens got out of the box. Papa, can you pull over?"

He pulled to the shoulder and shifted into neutral. He twisted in the seat. Edan exchanged knowing looks with him and rolled his eyes upward. They both grinned.

Sam was out of her seat and stooping at the opened back door, helping Mary Aileen search nooks and crannies. She stood again. "Cole, it's not here."

"Where else would it be? It certainly couldn't climb out of the car."

"She had it when we left the picnic area. It must be back where we stopped last."

"Then a fox has it by now. That's been two hours."

"Paa—paa!" wailed his elder daughter.

Sloan stared at Sam. Sam held his eye firmly. "Please," she said simply.

"Get in," he grumbled. With a glance up and down the track he cranked the wheel tightly. The touring car lurched out into the roadway, back in the direction they'd come. *Of all the miserable, useless things God ever created, kittens must rank at the top,* Sloan thought to himself.

———————

Hannah hadn't intended to actually sit down on this dusty slope. Her knees buckled. Regardless, here she sat in a tangled heap. Her tongue was stuck to the roof of her mouth and she couldn't see well. Her vision seemed to be closing in.

Maybe she would take a little nap, just a rest, and continue on when this torrid sun slipped closer to the hills. She rolled to her side. It felt so very good to close her eyes.

———————

"Mary Aileen, walk ahead of the car and make sure I don't run over the thing." Sloan waited as she leaped out.

"I'll help." Edan jumped out, too. They walked briskly, their eyes searching the slope. Sloan shoved the car into first and eased forward.

He parked it where he'd parked before, and looked over at Sam who was looking straight ahead in silence. He called to the children, "Start back where the box was and work out this way."

Mary Aileen put Smoke down and held her leash expectantly. "Go find your baby!" But the cat didn't seem to have a clear vision of the task. She wandered about at random sniffing the grass.

Sam had gotten out now and was searching the bushes. She straightened and walked over to Cole. "We have about twenty minutes of light left, you think? That kitten could be ten feet away and we wouldn't see it. It *would* be the black one that wandered off."

He nodded grimly. "How good is their sense of smell?"

"I have no idea. Smoke can smell keenly, but I don't know about kittens."

"Let's search the slope again. It possibly followed our scent out that way.

Mary Aileen stared ahead distraught. At the top of her lungs she was calling, "Topsy! Tahhhp-seee!"

"That's silly, 'Leen! Kittens don't come when you call them by name." Edan continued out to the point where they had gathered to observe the fire.

She scowled at him. "You certainly don't care if I try, do you?" She stopped for a bit then called again, "Tahhhp-seee!" She walked farther out. "Tahhhp-seee!"

Sloan glanced at Sam. Tears glistened in the waning light as she shook her head. "Too many things out here in the bush are looking for a meal."

"I'm afraid so." Sloan paused, listening to Mary Aileen's tortured call. "Maybe we shouldn't have come back here."

"Of course we had to come back and look, just to know we did all we could."

Sloan had no idea how to tackle this impossible task. Rather than look for a small black kitten in the gathering dusk, he ought to be looking for a way to let Mary Aileen down gently when night fell and they abandoned the search.

But Mary Aileen was running toward him, sobbing so steadily she could barely breathe. She clutched a black kitten to her breast.

A sweeping wave of relief flowed over him; Cole would never have thought he could generate such strong feelings over a kitten. "Let's go home." He wrapped an arm around his daughter and headed for the car.

"Wait, Papa!" Edan was still out beyond the breast of the slope. "Papa!"

"Now, what?" Sloan left Mary Aileen and walked back out to the open slope. The weariness of the day was catching up to him, or was it all the burdens he carried lately? "Come on, Edan."

"Papa. Someone's out there. I heard them call."

"It's a wonga, Edan. A wonga pigeon way off somewhere, or some other bird. Let's go home."

"No. I'm sure it's a person. Papa, please." There he stood, so very small and fragile. Sloan hesitated. Edan wheeled around and shouted at the top of his lungs. Silence. "There! See?" he cried triumphantly.

"It's probably your echo. I didn't hear anything."

"You didn't hear the baby rock warblers, either."

Sloan had to admit the lad had a point there. Against his better judgment, against reason, he decided to go along with the lad. "Okay. We'll go downhill a little farther. Just a little."

On the open hillside opposite, Sloan saw a movement. A dark little form came down the far slope, slipping and staggering. A very tiny voice rose above the subtle sounds of the summer evening. That voice . . . The very small person stumbled and began to run toward them.

"Papa! I think that's—"

But Sloan wasn't listening. He cast aside thirty years and any other burden that might slow him. With the full strength of youth he raced down into the vale and up the other side.

She was running to him. She was here! She was here!

He seized that forlorn little form and pressed it tightly against his heart as he dropped to his knees. He rocked back and forth while the child sobbed and he sobbed. His heart swelled so much it choked off any power of prayer he once enjoyed. Thanks burgeoned hopelessly beyond words and he could think of nothing adequate to say to God.

She was filthy—dirty, tear-streaked, smudged with soot. *Soot*?! She encountered that bushfire! She survived that fire. While he casually surveyed the smoke from a cold, safe distance, his little Hannah was. . . . He could not cease kissing the filthy cheek. Her dirt soiled his clothes and he could not cease holding her tight against him. Hannah!

Hannah's desperate embrace loosened. "Colin."

"Where?"

She twisted and pointed vaguely uphill.

"There's your mum." With the greatest reluctance he set her free.

Sloan jogged up the slope. He paused for a bit in the gloaming, to catch his breath. He could toss aside thirty years for a few minutes, perhaps, but not forever. Sweat poured from his face and soaked his shirt. "Colin?" He bellowed it to the stars. "Son?"

The sheer, unimaginable size of this miracle absolutely overwhelmed him. *Hannah.* In a place none of them had ever gone before, convening at the same moment. . . . Out of all Australia, after all these bitter months. . . .

"Son! Colin!"

Sloan sucked in air, startled, as a rock-wallaby shot straight up out of a boulder field and zig-zagged away over the rocks. Bats flitted about in the clear sky of evening. Night creatures were replacing those of the day. In its third quarter, the moon would provide no light once the sun was gone. Sloan wouldn't be able to see anything.

Deep in the dusky forest far ahead, a barely discernible tree seemed to move, straight and tall. It stopped. It extended an arm and leaned heavily against another tree. Momentarily rested, it moved again with halting steps.

Sloan ran uphill as far as his tortured lungs would allow. Involuntarily he slowed to a hasty, anxious walk, gulping air. The tree took human form then, coughed long and hard, and stumbled forward.

He was back. He had grown. He wasn't just bigger. Not just older. It was more than that. Much more.

Still rushing forward, Sloan reached out. He stretched his arms as far as they would go, and his son, his son tumbled into them.

"Papa," he whispered hoarsely, "I'm sorry."

His son. His son.

"Welcome home."